SON of THUNDER

"This book is to be neither an accusation nor a confession, and least of all an adventure, for death is not an adventure to those who stand face to face with it. It will try simply to tell of a generation of men who, even though they may have escaped shells, were destroyed by the war."

Introduction to All Quiet on the Western Front, *by Erich Maria Remarque*

SON of THUNDER

J.D. Wetterling

Rivilo Books
Bluffton, South Carolina

Text design by Barbara Lisenby
Jacket design by David O'Malley
Publisher: Felix C. Lowe

Library of Congress Cataloging-in-Publication Data

Wetterling, J. D.   1943-
   Son of Thunder / by J. D. Wetterling
          p.   cm
      ISBN 0-9630731-8-4
         1. Vietnamese Conflict, 1961-1975—Fiction. I. Title
   PS3573.E9266S6 1998
   813' .54—dc21   98-12397 CIP

Author website address: www.jdwetterling.com

First Edition: November 1998   5 4 3 2 1 98 99 00 01

Printed in the United States of America on acid-free paper

DEDICATED TO

Lance at panel 57W, line037,
Lynn at panel 51W, line 032,
Vince at panel 27W, line 103,
on the
Vietnam War Memorial,
Washington D.C.

My friends,
heroes who will be a part of the dust of Southeast Asia
till the end of time.
May their names, indelibly engraved on that wall,
likewise be found in the Book of Life.

Greater love has no one than this,
that he lay down his life for his friends.
John 15:13

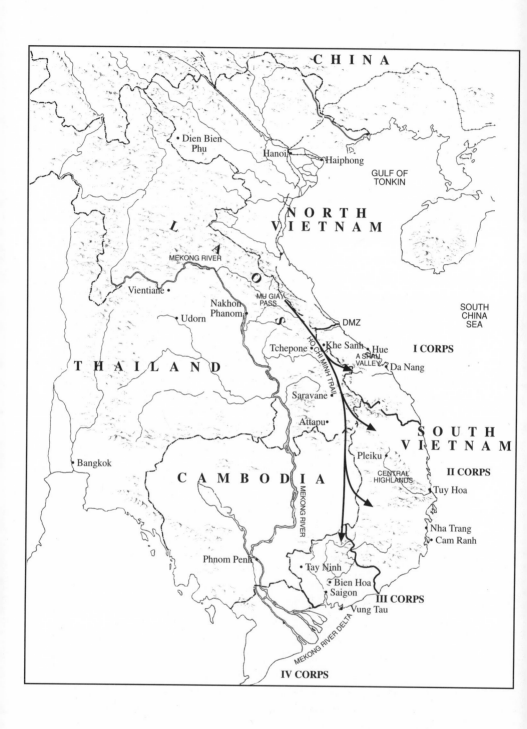

It was a perfect Sunday morning for a baptism by fire. A magnificent clear blue sky covered the azure and emerald stained glass of the South China Sea, and a meandering tan ribbon of sand separated the sea from the lush, ragged green of the tropical jungle. Fire and brimstone were not a part of the spectacular scenery over the eastern shore of South Vietnam, but both were there, loaded and locked in the barrels of ten big anti-aircraft guns just over the horizon to the northwest.

Two F-100 Super Sabre jet fighter-bombers, in jungle camouflage greens and browns, streaked through the heavy air of the tropics at fourteen thousand feet armed to the teeth with the weapons of war. The leader of the two-ship flight, called Dusty Five One Flight, was Lieutenant Colonel Jack English, a crusty eighteen-year Air Force veteran and Operations Officer of the 629th Tactical Fighter Squadron, Tuy Hoa ("TWO-ee-wa"-rhymes with Ma) Airbase, Republic of Vietnam.

His wingman was 25-year-old First Lieutenant John D. Ellsworth, fresh out of fighter pilot school in New Mexico. This was as good as it could get in John's view—son of a poor Midwestern farmer, half a world from home, driving a single-seat, single-engine, supersonic jet fighter in a war to liberate a whole nation of poor farmers from Communist oppression.

"Gung-ho" was the standard term, but as an adjective it was inadequate for John's mind-set. His goal in pilot training had been to finish high enough in his class to draw a fighter assignment to Vietnam. When he graduated first in his class he was disappointed that there were no F-105 assignments offered. He had dreamed of spending the war in a single-seat "Thud" over the Red River Valley of North Vietnam, hammering away at Ho Chi Minh's heartland around Hanoi and Haiphong. That it was the most dangerous mission of the war did not register in a mind that considered living dangerously the pinnacle of fighter pilot cool. He took the next best assignment available, F-100s, then fought his way up to graduate "Top Gun." His greatest concern in fighter pilot school had been that the war would end before he got there. Mortality had not yet registered in a young mind under the influence of that group psychosis the recruiting posters called esprit de corps. The Lieutenants' motto, repeated ad nausea at the bar was, "It's a lousy war, but it's the only one we've got." On that Sunday morning, in the cramped, noisy womb of that swept-wing angel of death, the war suited John perfectly.

At Chu Lai, about 160 miles north, the two F-100's banked left and rolled out headed northwesterly across the rugged, jungle-covered mountains of Vietnam's central highlands, heading for the A Shau Valley on the border between South Vietnam and Laos. There was something different about this day. Like cattle sensing a storm brewing, man and machine sensed death on the horizon, but greenhorn John thought it was just a case of pre-game jitters.

The air war in South Vietnam and Laos was at its peak and the A Shau Valley was one of the primary battlegrounds. As the southern terminus of one of the branches of the Ho Chi Minh Trail, this beautiful wandering valley, just fifty-five miles west of the big coastal city of Da Nang, had been the scene of some of the war's bloodiest battles.

In March of '68, President Johnson halted the bombing of most of North Vietnam. It was a so-called "goodwill" gesture aimed at furthering the peace talks in Paris between North Vietnam's Le Duc Tho and Henry Kissinger. One thing it did accomplish: the flow of North Vietnamese supplies down the Trail through Laos and into South Vietnam increased many-fold. At night the truck traffic was as heavy as the Los Angeles Freeway at rush hour. While Tho and Kissinger grappled for position like two sumo wrestlers on the front pages of the world's newspapers, Uncle Ho was moving his big anti-aircraft guns, no longer needed back home, onto the Trail to protect his supply lines.

The A Shau valley, long and narrow with a steep mountain rim and triple canopy jungle, was currently in the hands of the Army of the Republic of (South) Vietnam—ARVN for short—and the US Army, but Ho Chi Minh wanted it back, and another bloody battle was brewing.

Dusty Five One Flight's mission that morning was called "road interdiction" on the frag order from Seventh Air Force. That meant cratering the roads in the daytime so the big Russian-made two-and-a-half ton trucks, loaded with war supplies, couldn't travel them at night. The strategy was very close to worthless. Countless North Vietnamese with two-dollar shovels could negate millions of dollars worth of air power in a matter of a few hours. That section of the Trail that led over the western ridge into the A Shau was so crucial to Ho's resupply efforts that he had moved in several dozen anti-aircraft artillery pieces to protect the shovelers.

Colonel English, a salty Korean War veteran, had sensed a hot mission. In the pre-flight briefing that morning he had lectured John at length on how to duel anti-aircraft artillery batteries and live to tell about it.

"Lieutenant, keep that plane turning at all times or there won't be a piece of you large enough to ship home. You'll be a part of the Southeast Asian dust till the end of time." He slapped his hand knuckle side down on the table. That meant 'crash and burn' in fighter pilot sign language. His message was crystal clear. "Fly steep dive angles on your bomb runs. That guy on the other end of the gun will be as scared as you are. But he probably can't run and hide. We've been finding them handcuffed to their weapons lately."

John was only two months into a twelve-month tour of duty and had yet to see big anti-aircraft artillery fired at anybody, thanks to some judicious scheduling on the part of Colonel English. But apparently the Colonel figured John was now ready for the real stuff and the young Lieutenant hung on every word of his hero's advice as reverently as if he were listening to the Pope giving the benediction.

Lieutenant Colonel English didn't carry an ounce of fat on his six-foot frame. Two wars and a few thousand hours of jet fighter time had stooped his shoulders a bit, but his blue eyes burned with the intensity of a man who loved his work. He was a young tiger in an aging, graying body, a mentor and role model, and John worshipped him.

When the briefing was over Colonel English concluded with his famous invitation, the one all the lieutenants knew by heart. "Well, there's a couple of supersonic angels all gussied up and waiting out there on the flightline, Lieutenant. Let's go light their fire and dance the wild blue."

They arrived over A Shau just as another flight of two F-100's, Panther Two One Flight, was bombing the target under the direction of the Forward Air Controller. The FAC, whose call sign was Golf One, was flying an O-1, a single-engine "Bird Dog" spotter plane no bigger than a Piper Cub. John and Colonel English switched to Golf One's radio frequency and listened in on the conversation as they watched the F-100's attacking the target. It was shooting back. As Dusty Flight circled high and to the east, John could see the muzzle flashes of 37-millimeter guns, the geyser of tracers which represented every fourth or fifth bullet, and the sickening black puffs of flak bursts as the bullets exploded at preset altitudes.

"Panther Two Two is in from the west," the pilot called as one of the planes dove on the target.

There was a tone and intensity in that voice that John would recognize anywhere—he'd heard it many times before. It was Rock Dillon, his friend from fighter pilot school, the guy he had consumed countless beers with at the Officer's Club, competed against for "Top Gun" honors, and beaten by the slimmest of margins. He was the only guy John knew who might, just might, have a greater passion for this business than he had himself. John wanted to call out to him but knew better than to distract him at a time when the utmost concentration was so critical.

Rock dropped two bombs and started to pull out of his dive. Just as he got the nose of his plane pointed back toward blue sky, one of the North Vietnamese guns found its mark. The plane, without a word from Rock, rolled upside down and split-essed straight into the ground in an enormous fireball.

There was stunned silence on the radio. John could hear his own pulse thumping in his ears. All the butterflies from all the football games he'd ever played were congregating in his gut. The cockpit air conditioner was turned down so low it was blowing flakes of frost, but John was drenched in sweat. His tongue felt like an oversized cud of sawdust in a mouth totally devoid of saliva. He fumbled for the water flask in the lower pocket of his G-suit and released his oxygen mask to take a drink. He was hyper-ventilating so badly he choked on the water. After re-attaching the oxygen mask, he flipped the toggle switch to one hundred percent oxygen and tried to concentrate on taking deep breaths. He had no doubt about what would happen next.

The FAC, from his position west of the target, broke the silence by stating the obvious. "Well, I guess there's no need to call Search-and-Rescue on this one. I'm sorry, Panther Two One. You might as well take it on home. I'll file a report from this end."

"Roger, Golf One," Panther Two One replied. He sounded like a whipped pup.

"Dusty Five One Flight, this is Golf One. Did you see where that ground fire was coming from?"

"That's affirmative, Golf One," Colonel English replied. His voice was calm and confident—just another day at the office. It was a tone John worked hard to emulate.

"Well, that's your target. Use your own tactics and make as few or as many passes as you want. I'm holding two miles west of the ridge at 12,000 feet. I'll be well out of your way. You're cleared to attack." The FAC's voice was sad and weary. His words sounded like a eulogy, as if he were resigned to letting two more fighter pilots bury themselves in the jungle.

"Dusty Flight, set 'em up hot. Arm nose-tail. Bomb pairs," Colonel English ordered. His ominous command produced a rush of adrenaline through John and jolted him out of his shell-shocked state. His right hand felt like it had five thumbs as he fumbled with the armament switches.

At fourteen thousand feet directly over the target, the flak bursts were well below the two F-100's, but they formed a broken deck of black clouds partially obscuring John's view of the ground.

"Lead's in from the north," called Colonel English as he rolled belly up to the morning sun and pointed his nose down toward the target in a 45-degree angle. There was a steely, torqued-jaw tone to his voice as he stared down the barrels of those big guns.

John continued the circular orbit around to the west, laid the stick over against his left knee and rolled in as Colonel English was midway through his first dive bomb run. He made his radio call, but what he heard through his own earphones sounded like a stranger talking—the tone was an octave higher, with just a hint of a quaver.

Colonel English was barely visible among the black clouds of flak. The target, on the other hand, was perfectly clear—two circular gun sites with five guns each next to the snaking dirt road on the ridge. They were so new they had not yet been covered with camouflage netting.

The guns in one of those sites rotated around toward John, the circle of muzzle flashes winked away on the ground, and in the same instant his plane was enveloped by tracers and black flak bursts. He had preset his gun sight for a forty-five-degree dive angle and five hundred knots airspeed, but he had rolled in so close to the target that his dive-angle was almost straight down, the airspeed was already passing 500 knots, and all his parameters were wrong and getting worse. There was no way he could hit the target out of such a messed up dive.

John's face and exploding bullets the size of walnuts were closing on one another at over 1000 miles per hour and he thought he was inhaling his last breath. In total panic, he punched the bomb release button just to get rid of the bombs and pulled back hard on the control stick. Too hard....

His G-suit inflated automatically, squeezing his legs and abdomen like a tourniquet. John grunted like a weight lifter but the centrifugal force of the dive recovery drove him down into his seat so hard that it drained the blood from his eyeballs. He blacked out.

With his vision gone and only his inner ear and seat of the pants to guide him, he held the control stick steady and counted to five to make sure the plane was headed skyward again, then eased up on the back pressure. Ten seconds or so later, with the G-forces off his body, his vision returned and he desperately scanned the instrument panel to reorient himself.

"What's the matter, Two?" Colonel English asked from some far away corner of the cosmos.

It was only then that John realized he had not felt the "thump-thump" of two bombs leaving the plane when he had punched the pickle button atop the control stick.

His eyes rotated instantly to the armament control panel on the side console. The switch settings were wrong. Then another quick glance at the instrument panel sent shivers through his sweat-soaked body. The accelerometer gauge told him he had over-stressed the wings—nine G's of centrifugal force on the wings during that terror-stricken dive recovery. According to the book, seven and one-half G's were the redline—exceed that and the wings fold up around your ears. John could hear the voice of his old instructor at gunnery school: "That was one ham-fisted piece of stick and rudder work, Lieutenant. You got a death wish or something?" He had lived for this day, dreamed about this day, and now that it had finally arrived, he was so scared he was trying to kill himself.

"Dusty Five Two, this is Five One. How do you read?" This time Colonel English's voice had an irate tone. He could be a mean mother when he wanted to be. John had never met a field grade officer who couldn't.

"Five Two, loud and clear. I couldn't pick up the target for all the flak and I didn't want to waste the bombs." It still sounded like a stranger talking and this time the stranger was telling blatant lies. He was much more concerned about wasting his million-dollar hide than about wasting a couple of thousand dollar bombs. The truth was he should be dead and he knew it. The only thing that could have kept the wings from folding up at nine G's was the weight of those accidentally undropped bombs still hanging on the outboard pylons. If he had gotten the switch settings correct, steep as that dive was, his plane would have disintegrated and rained scrap metal and pieces of his hide all over the A Shau.

Then he committed the most outrageously suicidal act of all. Rather than admit to his flight commander he had screwed up and overstressed the airplane, rather than take that badly damaged F-100 straight home and gingerly put it on the ground, he said nothing.

John took a deep breath and dove into that fire hose of tracers again. From somewhere he could feel copious quantities of adrenaline being injected into his system. His mind felt removed from his skull, as if it were residing in a safe place, watching and pulling the strings on the slow motion puppet that was his body. This time the adrenaline seemed to anesthetize the fear, and it was all mechanical.

The tracers weren't quite as heavy, thanks to Colonel English's good shooting, but they were still right in his face. He pickled off two bombs and pulled out of the dive with a smooth six G's and pointed right at the mid-morning sun.

"Bull's-eye, Two," Colonel English called.

Oh sweet redemption, John thought, but answered with a curt, "Roger."

Confidence returned.

The baptism was over and he had not drowned in spite of himself. The gun camera was not mounted inside his head and there was no co-pilot to witness that fiasco on the first bomb run, so he could write his own history.

After they had dropped all their bombs, they strafed the jungle perimeter around the decimated gun sites, probing for the North Vietnamese ammunition supplies with 20-millimeter cannon fire. By this time the North Vietnamese gunners, if there were any left alive, had lost their enthusiasm for shooting at F-100's and John and Colonel English were unopposed as they worked over that ridge like a couple of mad hornets.

On John's second strafing pass, as he was hosing down the area south of one of the gun sites, a large explosion with black smoke erupted out of the triple canopy jungle.

"You found the ammo dump with that one, Two. Good shooting," called Colonel English. John was clearly back in the colonel's good graces.

Again he replied with a curt, "Roger," but this time his calm, cool, fighter pilot tone of voice had returned.

"Bring it on in, Two, and we'll go down and take a closer look." John pulled up into route formation on Colonel English's left wing and they dove for the valley floor. Coming up the A Shau valley right on the deck, they pulled up into a climbing right-hand turn and popped over the ridge just above the treetops.

The devastation was complete. The gun sites were a smoldering junkyard of twisted gun barrels, scrap iron and bloody body parts. They swung around to the scorched earth where Rock's plane had crashed. There was not a single piece of scrap metal visible in that small, steaming crater.

"Dusty Five One Flight, that was one fantastic piece of work. My bomb damage assessment report will show two gun sites with several guns each destroyed, one ammo dump and fifty Killed-By-Air. It was great working with you. I'm going to put you two in for a hero medal. Good job. Good day," Golf One called. He sounded born again.

"Roger, Golf One, copy the BDA and the KBA. The pleasure was all ours. Sorry about Panther Two Two. Good day." Colonel English was calm and collected as ever. The flight back to Tuy Hoa was just plain thrilling. The effects of the adrenaline had not even begun to wear off. John remembered having a kidney stone attack once. The pain was excruciating and multiple shots of morphine had done no good at all. Suddenly the stone passed, the pain stopped, and he floated right up off the bed propelled by all that morphine. That was nothing compared to this high, and in a single-seat fighter no one else could hear the whoops and hollers of ecstasy—or see the mistakes. They had killed his friend but he made them pay the price, and the proud victor promised himself that he would spend the next ten months extracting a bigger price.

As they flew home over the mountainous jungle of the central highlands, the midday cumulus clouds were already well developed. They frolicked in three dimensions like two larks playing follow-the-leader through a forest of towering, puffy white clouds-in and out and up and down and over and around.

Those forever vivid memories of the carnage at A Shau, the terror of imminent doom that had paralyzed him and the realization that Rock was dead and by all odds he should be too, were stuffed down into that black box—the receptacle for all things too horrifying to think about—at the lowest depths of John's soul. He knew he would have to deal with them later, but right now they were overpowered by the sheer exhilaration of having been shot at and missed.

They parked the Super Sabres at the fuel dump, a grid of huge black rubber bladders full of JP-4 surrounded by earthen revetments but exposed to the sky...or incoming rocket and mortar rounds. Lieutenant Colonel English, sporting a big grin and multiple salt rings under each armpit of his wet flight suit sauntered over to John just as he stepped off the boarding ladder.

"That'll get you a Distinguished Flying Cross or I'll kiss your ass," he roared as he slapped John on his wet back. The turbine blades of the jet engines were still winding down with a deepening metallic whine, making conversation difficult.

"Thank you, sir," John replied, but his grin was something less than jaunty, in spite of his efforts. His knees were wobbly—the steadying effect of the adrenaline had worn off—and he felt at least a decade older than the gung-ho kid who flew off to war just a couple of hours ago.

"You did a good job, son, and I'm proud of you." He shook John's hand. Something under the wings of John's plane caught Colonel English's eye. "What the...?" He ducked under the starboard wing for a closer look followed by John.

Dozens of rivets that held the aluminum skin to the underside of the wing spars were popped and hanging down about half an inch. The colonel pulled a panel loose that revealed the big steel I-beam that was the main spar. It had rivers of hairline cracks in it.

With hands on his knees, Colonel English let out a low whistle and turned and stared at John as if he had just seen him walk on water.

John considered lying about it, but the evidence couldn't be hidden. Aside from the overwhelming evidence they were looking at, the extreme readings of the accelerometer were permanently recorded by the instrument and checked by the crew chief at the end of each flight.

"The accelerometer read nine G's, sir."

Colonel English pondered that for a moment and said in low, reverent tones, "Gawd almighty. I don't know why you didn't splatter yourself all over the A Shau, boy. Someone up there must really like you." He rolled his eyes heavenward. "But I can assure you the old man won't. Let's debrief."

"Yes, sir." John was soaked with sweat but shivering in the hot sun. He wondered if Colonel English noticed. A horrible thought ran through his mind: his flying career might be over.

The debriefing was long, intense and agonizing. The thrill of victory was a distant memory. Colonel English had suggested they debrief in the squadron commander's office. A very somber Colonel Redman, Squadron Commander, sat and listened to Colonel English's comments as John did more humble listening than talking. John admitted that perhaps watching his friend die had effected his performance, and, "Yes, sir," he was scared, but there was no acceptable excuse. John suffered a convenient memory loss as to just what he knew about the state of his over-stressed aircraft and when-another fringe benefit of a single seat fighter. The truth would have gotten him reassigned to the base civil engineering squadron, never to fly again. Any pilot stupid enough to continue to fly a severely damaged plane whose wings he had just tried to pull off in a fit of panic was not an asset to the U. S. Air Force.

"Well, Lieutenant, you have screwed the pooch. Do you think you have learned anything from this experience? Do you think you can go back up there and fly that airplane the way you were taught and not kill yourself and break another one of my airplanes?" Colonel Redman's tired eyes bored right into John's soul. The hurt they conveyed made John feel so contrite he wanted to cry.

"Yes, sir. I'm sorry I broke your airplane. I know I don't deserve a second chance but...I want this...more than anything, sir...and I would appreciate the opportunity to redeem myself." As he talked—begged—the thought that disturbed John even more than the possibility of being permanently grounded was that his own voice did not sound very convincing confident. In the quiet of the squadron commander's austere office, the thought of violent death by those big guns in his face less than an hour ago was more frightening than the actual event. If asked the question, he could not answer how he would react the next time…was not even sure he wanted there to be a next time. His mind was totally muddled by the very event he had lived for and trained for over the last two years.

"Well, I want you to take tomorrow off, Lieutenant, and give serious consideration to what you did wrong…." Colonel Redman leaned back in his chair and paused to let that sink in. John quit breathing. "Then I'm going to do something that I hope I don't live to regret…." Now John fought to keep his lower lip from quivering. "We'll try to put you on the flying schedule Tuesday with Major Gillespie. He can give me a second opinion of your capabilities." That emphasis on 'try' told John it was not a foregone conclusion. "Colonel English, if you don't mind I'd like to have a few words with you. Lieutenant Ellsworth, you're dismissed…you are a very lucky young man."

John rose from his chair and saluted. "Yes, sir. Thank you very much, sir." He exited the scene of his inquisition by the shortest route possible. As he slunk back to his hooch, he found himself thinking that dying a hero up at A Shau would have been preferable. The pain would have been considerably briefer, and everyone would assume he was killed by the enemy, not his own hand. Now his sense of invincibility was as fractured as the main spar of his airplane and courage hemorrhaged from the open wound. He wanted in the worst way to go straight back to the flight line and get into an F-100 and take-off and prove to himself he still had the right stuff. It was like falling off the bicycle as a kid—getting right back on was the best antidote for fear.

Dusty's Pub, on the beach of the South China Sea, was the bar that the lieutenants "volunteered" to build for all the squadron pilots. In a land where the enemy could be anywhere and everywhere, the only safe place to relax was inside the perimeter bunkers and concertina wire. That limited the options to the beach and the bar, and the bar won 90% of the time. It was a twenty-five foot square slab of concrete with only one wall and a flat roof that doubled as a sun deck. Dusty's unique decor included a V-shaped bar extending from the brick wall with eight rattan barstools around it. Behind the bar was a 1950's vintage refrigerator for the beer, and above the fridge hung a felt painting of a naked blonde lounging on a tiger. On the wall to the right of the fridge were two rough wooden shelves that held the group's hard liquor supply. The other three sides of Dusty's Pub were bounded by the pilots' living quarters— very basic mobile homes on skids about six feet from the edge of the concrete slab of the pub. They were so basic they looked more like dark green metal boxcars than living accommodations for four people. The only thing that kept them from being ovens in the oppressive heat of the tropics was one small overworked window-type air-conditioner mounted in a square hole in each end wall of the box car. The remaining floor space of Dusty's was occupied by a half-dozen round wicker tables with woven tops, designed more like low coffee tables than bar tables, with four frameless woven wicker wingback chairs around each.

John and Colonel English's mission to A Shau was by far the best bar story of the evening. Colonel English told the first person version, leaving out the less than glorious parts of John's performance, to John's immense relief. It was a debt he would never be able to repay. The colonel's status rose to near sainthood in John's grateful eyes. Hands in motion, the colonel described the action over the target while all the pub-crawlers analyzed and re-analyzed their tactics and what-if-ed it to death. Mercifully, John's mentor chose to disappear after one telling of the story and two shots of scotch— neat.

John had received such a dose of humility that day that it was easy to sit on a barstool and play humble hero. Even the several beers that usually spelled the end of John's country kid modesty were ineffective. The fear was, hopefully, tucked down out of sight, but just barely below the alcoholic fog level of the pub. Numerous verbal jabs by his associates were unsuccessful in getting John to expound upon Colonel English's version of his baptism.

The Army nurses were over from Phu Hep Army Base, which shared Tuy Hoa Valley and its beach with the air base. They were sweet gals, though not exactly homecoming queens, and they were there. So in the best fighter pilot tradition, standards were adjusted accordingly. First Lieutenant Katherine Moffit was an exception to that adjustment, in John's view. She was the short brunette in jungle fatigues sitting at a corner table, and there was something about her that appealed to John. Most of the jocks would probably say it was her D cups, but John liked to think he had a nobler perspective than that. Several men in the squadron had made passes at her—which was not a claim to fame in this environment—and she was friendly enough, but no one had bragged about getting to first base or even knowing where it was with Kate Moffit. The rap on her was something about a soldier in her past and a dislike of warfare and warriors in general, but that could have been sour grapes by those players who couldn't find first base.

Twice her eyes had met John's recently, but with no reaction on her part and he had yet to work up the courage to speak to her. Back at the fraternity house at the University of Illinois, John had always worked hard to cover up his country-boy-with-no-social-graces self-image. At six feet, one hundred eighty pounds, he felt like he had the right physical assets. The addition of a mustache in the war zone, wider than regulation, was, in his opinion, a capital improvement. It hid his crooked grin. But it did nothing to enhance his courage when it came to approaching women. And tonight, of all nights, he was not feeling like courage personified.

Suddenly she was headed his way.

"May I join you, Lieutenant Ellsworth?" she asked with a smile as she climbed aboard the rattan bar stool next to John.

"Uh-h-h, yes ma'am. My name's John." He rotated about 45 degrees on his barstool and leaned toward her to hear over the din of the Pub.

"I'm Kate. I want to hear your version of today's mission."

"Oh, it was a…uh…just a little Sunday morning baptismal service up in the A Shau. The Colonel said it all…." His words sounded awkward to him, his smile didn't feel right and his face was hot.

"Complete with human sacrifices, I understand." She was still smiling and her tone was friendly, but she obviously wasn't going to make it easy for him.

"Oh, one good friend—one of the world's best fighter pilots—and about, uh, fifty gooks in retribution on the altar of freedom," he said.

"I'm sorry about your friend."

"Thanks…." John was his usual brilliant conversationalist self in the presence of women. "Fifty gooks are not enough retribution for his life."

A frown briefly furrowed Kate's brow as she pondered that remark, and then she said, "I hear you two will probably get a Distinguished Flying Cross."

"I'd rather have my friend, Rock, back...." John very nearly lost it there.

"You're not feeling much like a hero, are you?"

Well, to be honest, ma'am...Kate, I've been trying to drown a number of imponderables in this beer, and I don't feel much of anything. How about...would you be available for sober conversation tomorrow afternoon at 1400?" John could hear his words, but they seemed disassociated from his besotted mind. Courage is a wonderful thing, even when it comes out of a beer can, he thought.

Kate hesitated for a frightening heartbeat, then answered with a drop-dead smile, "I think I could arrange that. It's my day off."

"The beach?"

"Sure."

"I'll pick you up," John said with his first big grin of the evening. Even a blind pig finds an ear of corn once in a while, he thought. That wasn't the end of the conversation. That's just all he remembered. The horizon was rotating around his barstool and it was only partly because of the booze.

*　　*　　*

The sedative effect of the beer wore off somewhere after midnight and the lid came open on the black box. This box wasn't the inert kind that held recorded flight data in airplanes. This one stored up John's fear like a jack-in-the-box, where it grew in the dark like a germ culture until the spring-loaded lid, uncontrolled by his conscious mind, popped open. The multiplied fright sprang forth like a raging, starving gargoyle, and John paid his dues for the day's work.

There were tracers everywhere and John couldn't get the Super Sabre out of its dive. He was pulling on the control stick with both hands for all he was worth, but it was frozen. He could hear Rock calling over the radio, "Pull up! Pull up, John!"

"Wake up! Wake up, damn it!" Ron shouted as he shook John with both hands.

John's left leg was doubled up with his knee in his chest. With both hands he was trying to pull it right through his rib cage. He was drenched with sweat and the bed sheets were soaked.

"I think I've been hit." John felt his forehead. "It feels like the top of my skull has been blown away."

"It's all that beer you consumed last night, hog breath. Take some aspirin and calm down." Ron lay back down on the bottom bunk.

John wondered why no one was awake in the other bunk if he had really been putting on such a show, but then he remembered the other two roommates were both on night alert. He rolled out of the top bunk, crash-landed on the floor and stumbled to the bathroom. It felt like the trailer was afloat in a rough sea. Palming three aspirin, he forced down two glasses of water and struggled back into the top bunk and the sweat-soaked sheets.

"Tell me, Ron," John asked as he stared up into the blackness, "did Kate talk to me last night?"

"Yeah. You're taking her to the beach tomorrow. Pick her up at 1400. Now let me get some sleep, asshole."

"Oh, great! I was afraid that was part of the dream. Sorry to wake you."

Ron Johnson was a friend when he wasn't rudely awakened from a sound sleep. He was another classmate from F-100 school, Class 68-FR. He was the only guy John ever met who really went to Slippery Rock State University and played football. He looked like the running back that he had been, stocky and still in good shape with a black flat top. Ron's wife had often invited John over to dinner at their house, probably out of concern for his dietary habits. John's date was usually their basset hound. The dog drank water out of the commode and his ears were always wet when he put his head and paws in John's lap. They had given him the Biblical name of John the Basset.

It was nearly noon before John's body even twitched again. After a shower, shave and a lot more water he felt miraculously fit. He pulled on a freshly washed, un-ironed flying suit and strolled down the sidewalk between two dozen pilots' hooches enroute to the chow hall.

Tuy Hoa Air Base had only one large chow hall for the wing of three fighter squadrons and all the necessary support groups. The big beige metal building faced the South China Sea across a blacktop road and 100 yards of sand beach to the east. It formed a natural barrier of sorts for the base. The Tuy Hoa River formed the northern barrier, with a barren quarter mile stretch of sand serving as the open field of fire between the river bank and the northern perimeter machine gun bunkers. The chow hall and all the buildings on the base were clustered near the beach on the east side of two parallel runways running northeast/southwest, one a two-mile chunk of concrete for fast movers like F-100s and the other 4000 feet of perforated steel planking—PSP—for light planes and cargo planes. There was not a single tree or blade of grass inside the perimeter fence. The only thing that was there the day the USAF civil engineers arrived was coarse brown sand. Even now, five years into the war, the only vegetation was a few flower beds around the pilots' hooches and Dusty's Pub. It was a stark, dismal place by any definition.

It was another torrid day below the Tropic of Cancer and John's fifty-yard walk generated a freshly sweat-soaked uniform, but it felt great to be alive and inhaling the salt air of the South China Sea, in plain view not 100 yards away. But in spite of a hot date on a day off, John felt sadness and anger over the loss of Rock and a gnawing uncertainty about his abilities as a fighter pilot—the kiss of death in this business. He wasn't even certain he had a future as a fighter pilot at this point. Today was really supposed to be a day of punishment, like a kid being sent to his room to think it over after being a bad boy.

After an uninspiring chow hall ration of minute steak, soupy instant mashed potatoes and a wilted salad, John returned to the lieutenants' motor pool next to the squadron lounge—Dusty's Pub. It was the adjacent 25-foot slab of concrete, and it, too, was surrounded by four junior officers' trailers. The field grade officers, majors and above, slept just two to a trailer—one in each end—and were slightly removed from the noise of the lieutenants' motor pool and the squadron lounge.

The motor pool contained three motor scooters variously consumed by rust. They were strictly unofficial transportation, passed along to new lieutenants as old lieutenants completed their one-year tour and rotated back to the real world.

John climbed onto the first one he came to, checked the gas supply, fired it up and headed for Phu Hep Army Base. It was only a mile down a dirt road south of Tuy Hoa Air Base. The road was actually the main drag between the nearest big city—Nha Trang—one hundred winding, rutted miles south, and the thatched roof hamlet of Tuy Hoa, just north across the Tuy Hoa River from the air base. It was full of pedestrian and bicycle traffic. Ninety percent of the humanity on the road wore shiny, black pajamas and pointed straw hats. The Tuy Hoa Valley was a farming community and both sides of the road were lined with rice paddies. Some of the more well-to-do farmers turned the muddy soil with a water buffalo and a sharp stick whose shape looked unchanged from the dawn of the agricultural age. Poorer farmers used something akin to a wooden spade. The air was full of that fetid odor of animal and human excrement—the fertilizer that made the rice grow. Children played in the yards of tiny thatched roof and wall hooches devoid of indoor plumbing, electricity or windows.

Everyone John met returned his smile. They seemed so industrious and happy-aside from the living standard and Oriental looks they were not a bit different than the kind of farm country folks John had grown up with on the other side of the world. It seemed a tragedy to John that these pleasant, unassuming people should have to be involved in such a war. Why couldn't those old communists in Hanoi let these people live in peace? And why wasn't the United States fighting this war on North Vietnam's turf instead of disrupting the lives of so many innocent people who just wanted to be left alone to live their bare subsistence but happy lives? The sledge hammer reaction to the North's guerrilla tactics in South Vietnam was destroying the innocent while trying to save them.

The guard at Phu Hep's main gate waved John through. The Army base was more rudimentary and temporary looking than Tuy Hoa Air Base, with more wooden structures with tin roofs instead of metal buildings, and tents everywhere. Eight hundred yards of black top later he pulled up in front of the nurses' barracks, nondescript square wooden structures with tin gable roofs and window air conditioning units—a sign of officers' living quarters in the tropics.

Dressed in fatigues and combat boots, Kate came out through the door before he could park the motorscooter. It was not an outfit designed for sex appeal, and certainly not a first date, but Kate's smile made up for that. John opened the right saddlebag to stow her beach bag and she climbed aboard behind him.

"How are you feeling today, Hero?" She asked as she put her arms around him from behind.

"Worth at least a million bucks, but don't call me hero."

"Well how about Handsome John, then," she responded. Her mouth was so close to his right ear that her hot breath generated the most delightful chills down his spine.

They motored back out the gate, past the rice paddies, farmers and grinning children and back to Dusty's motor pool.

"You can change in my hooch. All of my associates are at the office," John said. The trailer had one room on both ends with a bathroom in the middle. The floors were covered with an ugly dark brown linoleum and the walls with cheap blond wood paneling. There was an 8-by-16 inch window on each side wall, up near the ceiling, with just enough dark curtain material to keep out the light. With solid metal doorways the whole unit was just a plain box of refrigerated air that kept torrential rains off and shut out the world. John's three roommates and he had decided to put the two bunk beds in one end and make a living room out of the other, instead of the standard floor plan of one bunk bed in each end. That way there was always a quiet place to sleep and a place to read, write or just waste time at any hour of day or night, since this war business was a 24-hour-a-day thing. The living area consisted of a three-cushion sofa of unknown origin and vintage along one wall, a desk and three-foot high refrigerator on the opposite wall with just enough room left over to walk between them. The walls were papered with a collage of every Playboy centerfold from at least the last decade.

John opened the door of the hooch and was wilted by the smell of the little Vietnamese cleaning lady. She was a sweet, ever-smiling little lady about four and a half feet tall wearing the standard black uniform with matching stained teeth. She was very efficient, but her odor was like nothing he'd ever smelled before coming to Vietnam. It must have had something to do with hygiene and diet, because she always looked clean. For the price of a few beers, she kept the hooch and the pilots' clothes clean, but the lieutenants had to vacate the premises when she was around. Luckily, she was on her way out.

"Number one job, Mama-san."

She just nodded her head several times as she smiled a wide smile with one eye closed and said something in Vietnamese. If she knew a word of English, she never used it.

"Kate, sometimes Mama-san brings along her two daughters, about ten and twelve years old. They are the most beautiful little girls. I just love 'em to pieces."

"I think these people are all beautiful, John."

John held the door for Kate and ushered her into the bathroom, apologizing for the smell as Mama-san left the hooch. "I think that perfume is called 'Afternoon in Tuy Hoa City'. It lingers long after the company has gone."

Kate just chuckled. She didn't seem to mind.

He got out of his sweaty flying suit and into a swimsuit while Kate changed in the bathroom, but he left his boots on. The black-top road they had to cross could fry bare feet. He filled a cooler with a six-pack of beer and grabbed an old army blanket to lie on. Kate came out of the bathroom wearing a yellow two-piece swimsuit under an unbuttoned, oversized fatigue jacket stripped of all rank and insignia.

"What do you think?" She said as she winged out the fatigue jacket with both hands.

He stared as long as he dared, swallowed, and said, "It, uh, takes my breath away."

"Thank you," she beamed. "I just got it in Bangkok a couple of weeks ago."

"It's beautiful...like the girl wearing it." An awkward silence followed, as John was taken aback by his own glibness. "Uh, you might want to wear your boots till we get across the beach road, or I can carry you across. That black top is hot enough to grill steaks on."

She tilted her head slightly and stared at John with tongue on upper lip as she pondered her choices and all their implications. "My boots don't match this ensemble," she decided, smiling. She had no comment at all about the wallpaper of their living room.

When they reached the chow hall John scooped up Kate and carried her across the road and onto the beach. She was heavier and more compact than he expected.

The beach was wide. A hundred yards east, the South China Sea lapped placidly at the shore. The tan, coarse sand was difficult to walk on, even at the water's edge, with dunes just high enough to lend privacy to someone sitting near the water. They spread the GI blanket between the dunes and the edge of the wet sand. Aside from a few sandpipers and sea gulls, they had the beach to themselves.

Kate removed her fatigue jacket and dropped it on a corner of the blanket. Her tan skin and short, dark hair accented by the yellow suit and sparkling, emerald-green eyes stood out against the dunes like a mirage. She sat down beside him and began to apply suntan lotion as he unzipped and pulled off his flying boots.

"War is hell. Don't you agree?" She said with a smile.

John froze for a split-second with both hands on one boot and his foot in the air. He couldn't tell if she was trying to make a joke or provoke an argument. He pulled the boot off, dropped it beside the blanket on the sand, and looked at Kate.

"Well, it sure was yesterday, but I'm on…uh…vacation, I guess you call it, today and besides…politics and philosophy are not really my thing. I want to talk about you. Where are you from and what are you doing in a place like this?" She could try if she wanted, but John intended to try his best to avoid an argument with a pacifist, if that's what she was. With what he had just been through—was still going through—he didn't feel like debating that subject.

"Ooh, that's a boring topic. I'm from everywhere and nowhere because I'm an Army brat. But as a kid I spent a lot of time with my grandparents in L. A."

"Los Angeles?" John interrupted. "I would never have guessed you were a California girl."

"No, lower Alabama. Thanks for asking…you're sharp." She paused to smile at him as he chuckled. "It was a little vegetable farm and my idea of heaven after life on army bases." She rolled over on her stomach and laid her head on her forearms. "Would you mind putting some lotion on my backside?"

"I would not mind at all. Thanks for asking…." John reached for the lotion bottle. This time Kate giggled and it had a remedial effect on John's shyness. "I'm from heaven myself—a farm in western Illinois—but I never thought of it that way."

"I thought you had that fresh-from-the-farm air of credibility about you…."

John threw his head backed and laughed. "There was a time in my college days when I would have considered that an insult. My nickname at the Phi Delt fraternity house was "Kicker." That was short for "Shitkicker." I worked so hard to change that image…. I'm already sorry I told you that. If you drop that name at Dusty's Pub I'll rue the day I ever laid eyes on you."

"Oh, I don't want you to rue. I'll stick to 'Handsome John'. You haven't forgotten about that lotion, have you?"

"Oh, no…sorry. I even remember where you wanted it." John squeezed a clear, thin lotion out of the bottle onto her back between her shoulder blades. It ran down the valley of her backbone, under the strap of her suit top, and puddled in two dimples below her waistline. Neither of them talked as he concentrated on covering every square centimeter of her backside. Her skin was smooth as velvet, except for a brief time when goose bumps rose as he diligently rubbed the lotion on the back of her legs. He had some major physical manifestations himself as the world of war was overpowered by more basic considerations. This is some penance for being a bad boy, he thought, but only briefly. This little lady was doing an excellent job of keeping his troubled mind off his worries.

"Hey, thanks...good hands." With just the slightest flush to her face, Kate rolled over and sat up.

"You're welcome. The pleasure was all mine. So tell me, what brings you to a place like this?"

"The U.S. Army, silly boy. It certainly was not choice. My father is a bird colonel on General Abrams' staff at MAC-V Headquarters in Saigon. But don't let that fool you. I am most assuredly not into this war. I don't even step on bugs. Patching up men mutilated by other men just reinforces my conviction about the nature of mankind—and I'm certainly not a career type. I took this Army hitch to make my daddy happy—it worked—and that's the only reason I did it. I'll be a civilian in eight months and I can't wait."

She stared out to sea and the silence got awkward, but John once again fought off her invitation to debate. "Where did you go to nurses' training?"

"Denver General."

"Will you go back there when you get out of the Army?"

"I hope so."

"Could I interest you in a beer?" John asked as he opened the cooler and reached in.

"Is it from the same dog that bit you last night?"

John froze again. The green-eyed lady's mind was quick and the tongue was acidic. "The same.... Kate, you're brutal. Is your answer yes or no?"

"Yes." She laughed again. It was a laugh that neutralized the acid and it was infectious. "You absorb punishment well. It's my way of compensating for my inadequacies. I'm sorry."

"Forgiven," John said as he pulled two Black Labels out of the cooler. There was a comment fraught with hidden meaning, he thought. He grabbed the five-inch, folding Buck knife he carried in a pocket sewed to his right flying boot and stabbed the tops of both cans twice and twisted.

"That's a wicked looking can opener. Is that Air Force issue?"

"No. My dad gave it to me just before I left the States. I had the pocket sewed to the boot in the Philippines. We stopped there on the way over to attend Jungle Survival School. With a little bit of luck, stabbing beer cans is the only use it'll get."

"Deo volente...Shalom." She raised her beer toward his and tapped his can.

"Cheers, Kate." John didn't understand a word of Kate's toast, but the cold beer felt good inside his hot body.

"Did you enjoy Jungle Survival?"

"Yeah, it was a kick. It was even educational. The thing that sticks in my mind was the snake lecture. The instructor said there were one hundred kinds of snakes in Southeast Asia. Ninety-nine are deadly poison and the other one eats you whole." Kate appeared to genuinely enjoy his humor. Her laugh gave him a chance to change the subject back to her.

"Living in Denver I bet you like to ski?"

"Sure do. You?" She asked.

"Yes, but I'm not very good at it. I spent Christmas vacation of '67 at Arapaho but never got off the beginner's slope. I was afraid I'd break a leg and the war would end before I could get here." Oops. As soon as the words came out of his mouth he knew it was a mistake. He'd left himself wide open for the very thing he was trying to avoid—a pacifist haymaker. God almighty, maybe I do have a death wish, he thought to himself.

Kate took the opening and gave it everything she had. "Oh, you fighter pilot types are so weird. I suppose you're going to tell me it's a lousy war but it's the only one we've got," she said.

"Well, that's the sanitized version. Actually it's a shitty...."

Kate reached over and poured her beer in John's lap. Startled, John reached up and grabbed her wrist and they wrestled for the beer can. In their laughing struggle, her bathing suit top worked down a couple of inches below her tan line, revealing a sight John found outrageous. There, on her left breast, was a tattoo. It was a paratrooper insignia. Who, in her right mind, would deface such a thing of beauty? It was like finding permanent graffiti on bosom of the Venus de Milo.

Kate caught John's darkening, open-mouthed stare and looked down over her cheekbones at her bosom. She dropped the beer can in his lap and with both hands she hiked her top up while John quickly relocated the beer can.

"What...?"

"The mark of the devil," she quickly interrupted. Her face clouded, her voice was hoarse and she sat up primly and stared out to sea. This time there was an extended silence that got really uncomfortable and he could not bring himself to look at her. He wanted to hear more explanation than that, but none was forthcoming. He took a long drag on his beer and tried to calm down. In the midwestern Bible belt where John grew up only tramps and circus ladies wore tattoos. He thought he heard a sniffle coming from Kate, and decided the gentlemanly thing to do was try to change the subject.

"Think it'll rain?" He offered.

Kate shattered the silence with laughter and said, "Only on the just, country boy." She sniffed again and the storm cloud passed... but not the impression.

They spent the next hour drinking beer and perspiring and swapping stories about growing up in the country. Then, out of the blue, Kate said, "Tell me, John, what does it feel like to kill fifty people?"

"You don't give up, do you?" The battle was joined. He sat with knees drawn up and arms around his legs, staring at the eastern horizon shimmering in the afternoon heat. He decided on the honest approach. She was far too sharp-witted to play mind games with. "To answer your question, it feels very good if you've just watched them kill one of your friends. But my main concern was...uh ...about trying to do my job without killing myself or being killed by Charlie. All I could see most of the time was the business end of those guns." He considered telling her about the carnage he witnessed when it was over, but thought better of it. "I don't think you're talking to a psycho here, if that's your real question."

She ignored his counter punch. "Did you ever watch a man die? I mean close up...right in his face, holding his hand...half his body blown away?" The passion in her tone of voice just confirmed the conviction of her words. She rotated 180 degrees on her fanny so she could more easily look into his eyes as they talked.

"No." John expected an anti-war diatribe, but she let it drop with another long silence as her eyes locked on his. She had magnetic eyes.

Finally she asked, "Were you scared?"

"You know fighter pilots are fearless...." That sounded like a lie, even to John. His guilty plea was a nervous laugh as he had to look away from her gaze.

"Bullshit, Lieutenant."

John hesitated before he responded. "Drill sergeant language does not become a lady of your class, Kate." But it went with the tattoo, he thought to himself. For the second time in the afternoon the sweetness and light began to fade from the beach party.

"You're evading my question, John?"

John caved in. "I confess I was scared out of my wits, at first. I put that Super Sabre so far outside the envelope I can't even tell you why I'm still here to talk about it." John just blurted it out.

"Envelope?" she asked.

"I over-stressed the airplane. I put nine G's on the wings. They're supposed to fold up around your ears at seven and one-half G's."

"Oh...tell me...I've never really understood G's."

"G is for gravity. The pressure on the wings of an airplane as it turns or pulls out of a dive is measured in G's. One G is your weight as you lie here on the beach. Two G's would be twice your weight. An airplane in level flight has a one-G load on the wings. Pulling out of a dive usually puts four to six G's of pressure on the wings. If I were sitting on a bathroom scale at the time, it would read four times my normal weight."

"Hmm.... Am I making you uncomfortable or do you always squirm like that?"

John tried to choose his words carefully as he stared at an afternoon squall forming far out to sea. She served sarcasm with syrup-what a unique talent. His nervousness about his future must have been showing, but he was certainly not going to share that with Lieutenant Moffit or any other lieutenant. He was glad he had chosen truth, otherwise she would have buried his brains in the sand, but now he was going to have to dance around it. "I squirm a lot when I'm around pretty girls and...uh...your mind is a whole lot quicker than the average girl I've known...and yeah, your questions are making me uncomfortable, but, uh, it's okay, as long as you remember your confidentiality oath, Doctor. I find you...very therapeutic." He forced a smile.

"You say the nicest things, country boy." She leaned over and kissed him on the cheek. "That's pretty good stuff for a bashful war-monger. Somewhat outside the obnoxious fighter pilot parameters."

"I hope I'm not being a traitor to the fraternal order of fighter pilots."

"I think...that as hard as you try to bend your personality into this preconceived image of what you think a macho throttle jockey is supposed to be, you don't really fit."

"I'm crushed..."

"No. I'm serious. I believe that under that effort at a fearless fa-cade there's just the soul of a shy guy trying to stay alive in this crazy killing place." Her smile and the compassion she exuded somehow took the sting out of her sharp words, but it was the words that he responded to.

"You're wrong there, Kate Moffit. I am here because I volunteered to be here. I believe in this cause. Freedom is what it's all about and these poor peasant farmers...I can relate to them because I come from a long line of peasant farmer stock and I love 'em dearly...they are having their freedom and their property taken away by an oppressive regime of old communist bastards...and I'm going to do my best to keep it from happening. And Rock was here for the same reason, and before I'm done there are going to be 50 times 50 dead gooks on the alter of freedom...in honor of him." John's face felt flushed and he knew he was talking too loudly. Kate had an in-tent, analytical look on her face as she stared back at him and ab-sorbed his diatribe.

"Kate, I'm sorry. You have found my weakness. Why do I feel like I'm standing here naked in front of you? I love what I do and I do it very well most of the time. And it's a noble cause, in spite of some very stupid politicians trying to play General and botching it badly. There's no place else I'd rather be than fighting this war." He was aware of the defensiveness of his tone and his words. She had driven to the heart of the matter—laid him open like a book.

"You're a worthy adversary, John."

He looked deep into those smoldering green eyes. Her smile was irresistible, even if it did have a hint of exasperation in it. This time he leaned forward and gave her the briefest kiss on the lips, sending a charge of electricity down his spine. It also bought him a reprieve from Kate Moffit's psychiatric couch.

Drawing back in silence with her eyes fixed on his, she appeared to savor the moment, then answered with a conciliatory tone. "You're different, country boy, and in a nice way...and I hope you prove me wrong, but let's save it for another day. Nurse Moffit's critical care clinic is closed...." Then, a parting shot: "I just think all wars are wrong except in self-defense."

John thought of a really snotty retort. He thought that anyone who tattooed her boobs could use some clinical care, too, but he let it pass after those kind words of positive feedback. "Well, I guess I can understand that view, Kate, but once a nation goes to war, for whatever reason, don't you think it should fight to win? Isn't it a travesty to waste human life for anything less?"

She stared back into his eyes as she pondered her response, then said, "Let's take a recess and go for a swim." She didn't wait for an answer.

He struggled to his feet and followed her into the surf. Like two kids playing hooky from school, they jumped and splashed and dunked one another. Finally they sat down, exhausted, in the shallow surf, their backs to the beach and the afternoon sun.

They lay on their sides on the sand facing one another with heads propped on elbows, oblivious to the world as the surf lapped at their feet and the afternoon cumulus clouds floated by overhead. The war seemed far away inside Kate's aura. All things considered, this sexy mystery lady with a polar opposite worldview was a pretty decent diversion for John's day of punishment.

*　　*　　*

By happy hour, they were back in the squadron lounge. Kate looked prettier than he remembered in jungle fatigues. He made a point of checking it out, and there was no airborne insignia on her uniform. Someday, and soon, he was going to have to know the story behind that trashy, low class, bizarre devil's mark on her breast. Someone, somehow, somewhere had "requisitioned" a frozen quarter of beef and run it through a radial arm saw at the Base Engineering Squadron, cutting it into one-inch thick steaks. Everyone not on duty turned out, including the nurses from Phu Hep. There was no difference between Monday and Saturday at Dusty's Pub. It wasn't a Monday to Friday line of work, so every night was a Saturday night. Those scheduled for dawn patrol just went to bed a little earlier, that's all. Those flying night missions or sitting night alert just moved their happy hour to 0500 instead of 1700, and the drinking lamp was lit twenty-four hours a day.

Ron wandered into the lounge. He enjoyed life drunk or sober. He never got into those funks like John did—couldn't stand those soulful blues records by Nina Simone that John played over and over until the mood passed. John's mother would have called Ron wholesome, that is if she never was exposed to his vocabulary. Spying Kate and John, Ron came over to the table. John was prepared for a wise guy remark.

"You have an 0500 brief in the morning with Major Gillespie. Mission to Three Corps, Ace. I'm briefing at 0530 so I'll go down to the flight line with you. Hi, Kate, how was your afternoon?"

"Fine, thank you," she said sweetly.

"Except for the company?" Ron offered.

"Well, he's the best of a sorry lot," Kate shot back. "Like you guys always say, if your standards are too high…lower your standards."

"Really?" Ron gave them a theatrical look of surprise. "Well let me warn you, John and I go way back and he is rotten to the core." John wasn't listening. He was thrilled with the news that he was scheduled to fly, confirming the fact that he still had a flying career. When his eyes refocused he was staring at Kate. She was intently staring back, wearing an I-wish-I-knew-what-was-on-your-mind smile.

John stuck to soda that night. Natural intoxicants like Kate Moffit were better than booze. And he was on the flying schedule tomorrow. How much better could life get?

By 2200 the nurses were headed toward the olive drab six-pack truck for the trip back to Phu Hep. Since motor scooters were not authorized outside the base after dark, John walked Kate toward the truck. They trailed behind the other nurses. As they walked by the squadron bunker, about fifty feet from the Pub, he took her hand and they ducked into the entrance near the sidewalk. It was just a basic box on the sandy ground about twenty feet by thirty feet by eight high with three-foot thick, sand-filled walls and four layers of sandbags on a flat roof. In the murky darkness of the bunker they embraced. There was such a height mismatch that it was tough to embrace her and kiss her at the same time.

"Kate, I had a great time today. See you at happy hour tomorrow?"

"Well…we have so many social options here in metropolitan Tuy Hoa, you know…but yours is the best offer I have. And like they say at the Pub, 'don't bust your ass' and no show on me." She was looking straight up into his eyes with her chin on his chest. Those green eyes seemed to glow in the dark like cat eyes.

"Lady, you come from all sides at once. I hope I get the chance to figure you out."

"Play your cards right and maybe you will, G.I. Goodnight."

Only Kate Moffit could talk like that and not sound like a hooker, John thought. Her non-verbal communication overpowered her words.

"Goodnight, Kate."

They stepped out of the darkened bunker and she turned right and he left. John floated back to his hooch, undressed and climbed into his bunk, completely on autopilot, his mind overwhelmed by the quick-witted, green-eyed enigma with the endearing insults. He still could not put his finger on what it was about her that appealed to him—it was not her worldview or her strong will, and it sure wasn't the devil's mark. Perhaps it was that infectious laugh and those magnetic eyes. He couldn't imagine a future with a tattooed pacifist, but war is hell and she just might make for a delightfully diversionary present.

*   *   *

"So, Kate, how was your hot date this afternoon," Lieutenant Smith asked as the truck headed back to Phu Hep.

"Well, he passed the Katherine-the-self-righteous-bitch test—he asked to see me again. I just hate it when I do that, but these flyboys are so pretentious I just can't resist shooting them down. He was pretty dodge-y, though—I couldn't bring him down—and he didn't try to show me he was the world's greatest gift to women. I think under that fighter jockey veneer there just might be some redeeming qualities. And his roots are rural—that's a plus. I had fun. We'll see."

"Methinks yon Katherine analyzeth too much," a voice in the back seat said.

Lieutenant Smith responded, "Kate, this is the wrong place to look for Mister Right. You're always going to be outranked by airplanes here, girl. Lighten up."

"Moi? Lighten up? Are you kidding?" she said melodramatically.

An olive drab Army truck filled with six nurses erupted in laughter.

Colonel English fixed a bleary, red-eyed gaze on Ron and John from behind the scheduling counter to the left as they walked through the door of squadron operations at 0445 hours.

"There's been a schedule change, men. The first couple of two-ship, in-country missions have been combined into a four-ship, out-country. Seems there was some heavy truck traffic through Mu Gia Pass last night. You'll be rendezvousing with a tanker for air-to-air refueling over Pleiku. Ordinance is seven-hundred-fifty-pound slick bombs. Major Gillespie will lead. Lieutenant Day is number two, Lieutenant Ellsworth is three, and Lieutenant Johnson, four. Some guys get all the luck."

Then he looked John square in the eye. "Ellsworth, follow me." He rose and walked back down the hall to his office, holding the door for John and closing it behind him. John held his breath when the door latch clicked shut.

"That airplane you flew Sunday is so busted up it's going to be down two weeks for repairs. The old man just damn near changed his mind when he heard that. You defied all the odds, son. I convinced him that we should give you another chance. I saw what you could do once you got your initiation behind you up at A Shau, and I was damned proud of you, boy. You could be one of the best that ever was, but if it happens again...or anything like it...you'll be a supply officer for the rest of your Air Force career. The squadron commander's goodwill has been 100% depleted in your case. I won't be able to save your ass a second time. Copy?"

"Copy, sir. Thank you, sir."

"You must never...ever get rough with that airplane or she'll turn on you and destroy you both." Colonel English was so close to

John's face he could smell last night's scotch. "That Super Sabre was called a widow-maker long before you started flying…for good reason. Smooth hands…. Smooth hands. Remember, you're dancing the wild blue, not wrestling greased hogs down on the farm. Am I communicating with you, Lieutenant?"

"Loud and clear, sir. Thank you, sir."

"Dismissed."

John exhaled, snapped off a salute, did an about face and escaped to the fresh air of the hallway. John tried to ignore the inquisitive looks of the other lieutenants as they sat down to brief for the mission. He knew they were thinking that he had probably left a significant piece of his ass in Colonel English's office—it was the squadron woodshed. But as far as John was concerned the scar tissue would forever commemorate another valuable lesson at the master's knee. The war was far from over and already he owed Colonel English his career. Somehow, somewhere he'd find a way to make the payback, but how do you do that in this business? He had no idea.

If A Shau was the hottest in-country target, Mu Gia Pass was the hottest out-country target. As the southernmost of only two passes through the rugged mountain range separating the western border of North Vietnam from Laos, it marked the beginning of the Ho Chi Minh Trail. Because it was a strategic choke point, U.S. Air Force, Navy and Marine fighters, had, over a period of several months, bombed it until it resembled a giant rock quarry. What started out as a series of narrow, winding mountain roads had been bombed wide enough to construct a superhighway. Since it was so critical to the supply effort of North Vietnam, it was surrounded by numerous anti-aircraft artillery pieces of all sizes. With the halt of US bombing north of the 19th parallel in North Vietnam, the AAA batteries multiplied and the ground fire was murderous.

As the weatherman, Captain Raines, pontificated his way through his portion of the pre-flight briefing, John wondered how someone could be so wrong so often and still be so pompous. John decided he must have been practicing for a TV job on the evening news-clearly not a duty, honor, country guy like the fighter jocks or even other weathermen that he had known—and tuned him out as he daydreamed about other things. He was glad he didn't learn of the schedule change till he arrived for work. Going to sleep with visions of Kate on the beach was infinitely more pleasing than watching a re-run of the previous night's midnight movie or worrying about the next day's mission. He'd slept like a baby.

Major Gillespie, unlit cigar angling out of his mouth, opened the briefing checklist. "Call sign, Dusty Three One, flight of four. Time hack; in ten seconds the time will be o-five-ten hours local.... Ready, hack." Major Gillespie droned on through the checklist. His dull monotone told all assembled that even he wasn't listening to his own briefing. John half-listened-just in case he got asked a question-as he stared at the map of Vietnam that took up one whole wall, floor to ceiling of the 10-foot square briefing room. The map had plastic over the top of it so it could be written on with grease pencil-the all-purpose communication tool of all pilots. Six inch circles on the map identified the TACAN stations located around Vietnam, the navigation aid that all fighter planes used. An instrument in the cockpit received signals from the TACAN station that indicated the direction and distance to the station. The wall adjacent to the wall map contained a large chalkboard, the other necessary ingredient of a fighter squadron's preflight briefing room. Most fighter squadrons had three or four such rooms, each identical, right down to the square table and four chairs. John always tried to get the chair across from the wall map, an aid to daydreaming during boring preflight briefings. Not all of them were so, especially Colonel English's briefings. Those were like sitting at King Arthur's table as he imparted the wisdom of the ages. But Major Gillespie's briefings required a daydream aid to stay awake.

Major G. had thick white hair and too much belly and butt for his flight suit. Ron Johnson, behind his back, called him Major Blivet—twenty pounds of shit in a ten pound bag. He looked old enough to have flown top cover at the crucifixion, thanks to the hospitality of the North Koreans in the early fifties. He'd been their guest for three and a half years after punching out of an F-80 near the Yalu River in the summer of '50.

He was a lovable old toad, but far too cautious for the immortal young hot shots with fire in their bellies. They knew before he even got to that part in the checklist, that if the target was shooting back, they were going to make one pass each, salvo everything, and go home. This was Major Gillespie's last tour of duty before retirement and he fully intended to have a retirement to enjoy.

John wanted a second coffee in the worst way but had learned painfully, early on, that the relief tube on an F-100 had only enough capacity for one cup of used coffee. Finally, the briefing ended and they all walked to the head for one last, nervous bladder-drain, and then on to the equipment room.

The four pilots jockeyed for position at the equipment counter. It was not much different than a coatroom counter, except that behind the 15-foot long counter the rows of racks held items a lot more exotic than hats and coats. Special racks held each pilot's backpack parachute, g-suit, survival vest, shoulder holster, Mae West flotation gear and helmet bag-twenty-five pounds of absolutely critical equipment for a fighter pilot. On the wall to the left behind the counter the helmets and oxygen masks hung on special pegs and the wall to the right contained a workbench where specialists repaired equipment. A safe in the rear held the pilots' .38 revolvers and a one-foot square box at the right end of the counter held the cartridges for pilots to load and unload them before and after missions—spare ammo was carried in the survival vest. John could always sense the seriousness of a mission by the decibel level in the room as men zipped up G-suits, checked survival gear, parachutes and oxygen masks. The hotter the mission, the quieter the room. This morning the place was a funeral parlor. The only sounds were the cylinders of .38 caliber revolvers spinning, the slap of leather as they went into shoulder holsters and the sound of zippers and snaps. Everyone worked hard to avoid looking anyone else in the eye, lest the apprehension show. The butterflies in the gut were starting early. As a group they walked down the center hallway of Dusty Squadron from the equipment room toward the main entrance. Like four scuba divers, they clattered and clumped along corseted from the waist down in g-suits, parachutes slung over one shoulder, survival vests unzipped and Mae Wests unsnapped against the heat, carrying helmets, thick plastic checklist books and kneeboards in padded, olive-drab draw-string bags. There were no wisecracks, no bawdy repartee, no grandiose exits—and no smiles.

Even the ride across the tarmac to the airplanes in the squadron step van was silent. There were padded benches on both sides of the van's interior—it looked like a bread delivery truck, painted blue, without the advertising on the sides. All four pilots sat staring down between their feet, alone with their thoughts. John noticed a faint odor of stale beer. That was probably roommate Mike Day. The kid seemed to do his best flying with a hangover. For such a young guy, he already had a nicely developed beer belly.

The van stopped at Major Gillespie's revetment first. Each revetment held one loaded F-100. They were constructed with common walls like a one-story condominium with three walls and no roof. The three sand-filled steel walls were ten feet high and four feet thick. The walls blocked any movement of air, turning the revetment with its steel planking into an oven at mid-day. Major G. stood up, removed his still unlit but well-chewed cigar and laid it in the van driver's ashtray, then stepped out the side door. "Be standing by on freq at five five past the hour, gentlemen," he said glaring at his watch.

Three forearms went up in unison as the three wingmen all checked the time.

*   *   *

"Tuy Hoa Tower, Dusty Three One, flight of four, ready for take-off. Northwest bound."

"Roger, Dusty Three One Flight, cleared for take-off. Good hunting."

"Good day."

There it was again—that boot in the butt as the afterburner kicked in on take-off roll—and another chapter of life in the fast lane began. Four Super Sabres took off on Runway 21 in five second intervals, pointed inland. They turned right after take-off, fanned out across the rice paddies of that beautiful valley by the sea and began the climbing join-up on the lead plane. The sun was just coming up. It felt great to be alive and airborne.

As John closed on the lead plane, he snuggled in close and looked it over carefully, then dropped down a few feet to check out the underside. Four 750-pound olive drab bombs with yellow circles on the nose, two under each swept wing, hung from individual pylons. Each was mounted on either side of the 12-foot long tapered drop tanks hanging from the center pylon of each wing. The drop tanks were painted just like the airplane, top and sides jungle camouflage colors and the bottom light sky blue. Each bomb, about five feet long and 18 inches in diameter at the fattest part, had a two inch wide yellow circle painted about six inches back from the brass fuse mounted in the bluntly tapered nose and X-shaped fins in the rear. As many times as John had seen these bombs explode from the air, he really had no comprehension of the terror it must strike in the heart of an enemy soldier who sees it falling toward him. It just looked like so much inert cast iron hanging there. He had never stood on the ground in the vicinity of an exploding bomb and had no desire to—that's what the grunts were for. He preferred the view from his skybox.

He slid back up on Major Gillespie's wing and gave him a thumbs up signal, indicating that all was properly attached. Having just returned from the overhaul facility in Taiwan, the plane had a brand new jungle camouflage paint job and the last six feet of the fuselage had not yet blackened from the intense heat of the tailpipe and afterburner, nor had the muzzle blasts from the four internal cannon blackened the underside of the nose five feet aft of the oval intake duct. If there was a prettier piece of machinery in all creation, John had never seen it.

Box Niner One, a KC-135 jet tanker, was already on station at twelve thousand feet over Plieku when Dusty Flight arrived at the rendezvous. Although they had only been flying thirty minutes, they needed a top-off to make it to Mu Gia Pass and back. The three wingmen slid into echelon right formation, everyone on a line angling back forty-five degrees from the lead plane, and moved up near the tanker's right wing tip. The central highlands were socked in, the solid undercast a field of snow five thousand feet below with a clear blue dome above.

One by one, Dusty Three One Flight dropped down and behind the big tanker. It was just a 707 airliner with one big fuel tank inside instead of seats. The refueling boom poked down forty feet from the tail of the tanker in an angle thirty degrees to the fuselage. At the end of the boom was eight feet of four-inch rubber hose and a drogue shaped like a giant badminton birdie. It was about sixteen inches across at the wide end.

It was called the probe and drogue method of air-to-air refueling. With a closure rate of about one knot, the F-100 poked that drogue with its probe. To make it more challenging, the probe was located on the right wing of the F-100. It was just at the edge of the pilot's peripheral vision as he stared straight ahead at the tanker. If the air was smooth, it was do-able with the most precise flying. In rough air or when the tanker's autopilot wasn't working, it was like pinning the tail on a dancing donkey.

Major Gillespie struggled on the hook-up, stabbing at the drogue twice before successfully hooking up on the third try.

The secret was to stay relaxed. Tense up and the smoothness would go out of your flying. John decided Major Gillespie was probably a little tense without his cigar to chew on. When he got his fuel load topped off, he backed away and moved over to the left wing of the tanker. John couldn't help thinking of his friend, Rock, as he flew alongside the big tanker waiting for his turn at refueling. This day would be for him, he told himself, and every day henceforth that he had a chance to kill North Vietnamese. He made a mental note to write Rock's wife a letter.

One by one Dusty Three Two, Three Three, and Three Four hooked up. All three lieutenants made the hook-up on the first try, a point not to be lost on the lieutenants but never to be discussed in Major Gillespie's presence.

"Thank you Box Niner One," Major Gillespie called.

"You're welcome, Dusty Flight. We'll be on station for three more hours if you need us on the way home."

"Roger, Niner One. Good day."

They pulled away from the KC-135 and picked up a heading of three hundred thirty degrees to arc around and approach Mu Gia Pass from the southwest. The tension continued to build. It was another perfect day to be flying but nobody was basking in the joy of flight or enjoying the gorgeous wild scenery of northeastern Laos. John reached for his water flask, having learned over A Shau that it was easier to drink before the adrenaline begins to flow. He checked and double checked all the switch settings that could be set up in advance, set the pipper—the electronic sight—for a forty-five dive angle, dialed in the forecast altimeter setting for the target elevation and set the sight dimmer rheostat to bright setting. This time he was determined to get it right the first time—he would not screw the pooch.

Twenty-five miles south of Mu Gia Major Gillespie called the FAC. "Squid Zero One, this is Dusty Three One, flight of four Fox one hundreds, sixteen seven hundred fifty pound bombs, thirty-two hundred rounds of twenty mike mike."

"Copy your munitions, Dusty Three One Flight. We've got some trucks broke down out in the open in the pass and that will be your target. Triple A this morning has been very heavy. The flight ahead of you has got them some kind of pissed off. There's at least 57-millimeter guns active down there, perhaps bigger. If you can see them, go ahead and try to neutralize them if you want. I strongly recommend just one pass apiece. It's a very long walk to friendly territory from here."

"Roger, Squid Zero One. Dusty Flight, set 'em up hot. Arm nose tail, bomb salvo."

In quick, crisp succession they all responded on the radio.

"Twoop."

"Threep."

"Fourp."

They spaced out equidistant in a left-hand circle over the target at fourteen thousand feet, the maximum altitude an F-100 could lug a load of bombs on a hot summer day in the Orient.

"Lead's in from the north," Major Gillespie called as he dove on the target. As the first one down the chute, he had the best survival odds. By the time three and four dove on the target the gunners had plenty of time to get their proper lead and wind correction worked out-if they survived lead's bombs.

Try as he might to be fighter-pilot-cool about it, Major Gillespie forgot to take his thumb off the mike button, located on the throttle. The microphone itself was located inside the oxygen mask about one inch from his mouth. As Major Gillespie dove on the target, three gun sites opened up. The air in the vicinity of his plane was full of flak bursts—larger and blacker than those over the A Shau Valley. The heavy breathing the flak created in Major Gillespie was broadcast over his radio for all the world to hear as he dove on the target. The closer he got, the heavier the flak, the faster and deeper his breathing, with special emphasis on the exhalation. John could think of only two circumstances in a man's life when he makes a sound like that—when he thinks he's approaching the climax of life...or love.

Major Gillespie got his bombs away, pulled out of his dive and turned right then quick left. Somewhere in there, by accident or design, he got his thumb off the mike button. His salvo of bombs manufactured a pile of little rocks from big rocks, but at one hundred meters from any truck John could see, little else was accomplished.

Mike Day was halfway down the chute on his pass out of the west. As John rolled in from the south, he picked up the muzzle flashes from one of the gun sites.

"Three's in from the south against the guns," John called without even making a conscious decision. And he was surprised at his own voice—calm, cool, even bored. Just right. And he made sure to get his thumb off the microphone button. He had learned a lifetime of lessons in those few intense moments over A Shau, including this: fear of embarrassment or failure was a far greater motivating force than fear of death when flying under the influence of adrenaline. The conversation with Colonel English, less than two hours ago, was permanently copied on his gray matter—smooth hands... smooth hands.

Those big guns drew him like a magnet. Dusty Three One, Three Two and Three Four could have the trucks. He wanted the guns. For reasons he could not understand, he was focused-alive-and in complete control diving into the oncoming leaden traffic. It was not remotely like his baptismal flight just two days ago. If he was going to get blasted into oblivion, it was okay, some things were worth dying for, but he wanted to do it dueling a big gun, not while he was trying to waste a lousy truck.

The Russian-made 57-millimeter tracers, coming straight at his face, floated and wobbled slightly. It was all in slow motion again, but this time, in spite of all the tracers and the physical and mental activity of guiding his turning, twisting, diving F-100, John sat there with his right thumb cocked waiting for things to happen. He was one cool dude, as if it were just another day on the practice range aiming at bull's-eyes on the desert floor of New Mexico. Finally he reached the bomb release altitude precisely as he reached the right airspeed. The pipper moved through the middle of the target, his thumb came uncocked and he mashed the pickle button on the control stick.

The staccato "thump, thump, thump, thump" told him the bombs were away, and he knew it was well done. It had that good, deep-in-the-gut feel to it. Another of Uncle Ho's triple A sites was going to be history. John knew it without looking back at the target. "This one's for Rock," he called to no one in particular over the radio as he pulled out of his dive.

"Shack, Three Three," Squid shouted. "Hot Damn."

Another bullseye. Chills from head to toe! John laid the stick over in a victory roll as he rocketed back up to altitude.

Ron, coming in behind John as Tail End Charlie, flew through clear air. His salvo of bombs dropped right onto the bed of a large truck. When the dust settled there was a huge crater and scrap metal all over the Mu Gia Pass Expressway.

"Great work, Dusty Three One Flight. I can confirm one triple A site destroyed, one truck destroyed and two damaged. Stop in again the next time you're in town."

"Roger, Squid Zero One. Pleasure doing business with you. Good day," Major Gillespie called.

The thrill of victory was short-lived. The big amber Master Caution Light, top dead center on the instrument panel, was glowing brightly two feet in front of John's nose. It felt like it was wired directly to his heart, which was thumping in his ears again. A glance down at the warning light panel isolated the problem. The engine oil overheat light was on and the oil pressure gauge was falling.

He broke off the rejoin on Major G.'s wing and pointed the plane straight west—the nearest friendly territory. After two deep breaths, exhaling hard, he called as calmly as he could. "Dusty Three One, this is Three Three. Emergency. I've got an oil overheat light, falling oil pressure, and I'm heading for Udorn." The big air base at Udorn, Thailand was the closest two miles worth of concrete on which to land, if he could get that far.

"Are you hit? Are you hit? You have the lead. We'll follow you," Major Gillespie shouted.

"Negative hits. Didn't see any and or feel any. Stand clear while I clean the wings, then look me over, sir," John called. He punched the red emergency jettison button just above the gear lever, and explosive charges fired off two empty 375-gallon drop tanks and four pylons that had held the bombs. He wanted minimum drag and maximum glide out of those wings. Under the best of circumstances an F-100 with engine out assumed the gliding characteristics of an early model Buick.

Major Gillespie moved under and slightly behind to look John over. "You're clean. I don't see any damage. Dusty Five Four," he called to Ron, "Go guard frequency and put out a mayday. Come back on the throttle, Five Three. Reduce altitude." John had already read the emergency checklist strapped to his left thigh and was headed toward a lower altitude, but acknowledged with a double click of the mike button. Now they were flying straight and level and well within the range of everything except small arms fire but there were no other options. The live-or-die coin was airborne and spinning, and there was nothing to do but wait for it to land.

John's radio automatically monitored guard channel, the international emergency frequency. He could hear Ron, as Dusty Three Four, transmitting on guard.

"Mayday. Mayday. Mayday. Dusty Three One Flight on guard. Dusty Three Three, a fox one hundred losing oil pressure and headed for Udorn. We're approximately one hundred sixty miles due east."

"Dusty Three One Flight, this is Udorn tower transmitting on guard. Do you want us to launch the Jolly Green?"

"Affirmative. Affirmative," Ron replied.

That was comforting. If the engine stopped and John had to punch out, it would be mighty nice to have that big rescue helicopter overhead as soon as his feet hit the ground. Most of the folks down there would not be friendly.

John leveled out at six thousand feet with the overheat light still on. The oil pressure gauge indicated a slight decrease in the rate at which he was losing pressure. It was only a matter of time before the engine would seize up from a lack of lubrication. The question was, would that be before or after he got that sick machine on the ground. He cleaned up everything loose in the cockpit and re-checked all straps and buckles. There was nothing else to do but sit there and wait.

John mentally made an inventory of everything in his survival vest, felt the thirty-eight revolver in his left side shoulder holster, felt the folding Buck knife in the pocket on his right flying boot and rehearsed a parachute landing fall in his mind. He'd done it 100 times as a member of the University of Illinois Sky Diving Club, but there they had a flat open field to land in with fraternity brothers and girlfriends waiting with the beer cooler.

"How's it looking, Dusty Three Three?" Major G. called.

"It's gonna be close," John responded. Even he knew his voice was cracking like an adolescent's.

At one hundred miles east they crossed the border into Thailand, relieving one worry—the friendliness of John's welcoming party if he did bail out. They overflew Nakhon Phanom, the home of the Jolly Green Squadron. Naked Fanny had only half enough runway necessary to land on, even though it was a U.S. air base. The big Jolly Green helicopter had just become airborne.

"Dusty Three One Flight, this is Jolly Green One. We have you in sight. Want us to follow you on over to Udorn?"

"We'd appreciate that very much, Jolly Green." Ron answered.

"Wilco, Dusty. We can't stay with you but we'll follow," Jolly Green replied.

"Udorn tower, Dusty Three One Flight is fifty miles east. Please have emergency equipment standing by," Ron called.

John had never been to Udorn before, but with the TACAN station located right on the field, he simply put the needle at twelve o'clock on the compass card and homed in. As the runway came into sight he lined up on final and began an idle descent approach.

Three miles out the tower called, "Dusty Three Three, have you in sight. You're cleared to land."

One mile from the end of the runway the oil pressure gauge went to zero, and just as the rubber screeched onto the concrete the fire warning light came on. John reached up with his left hand and pulled the drag chute handle, then brought the throttle back around the horn to Idle-Cutoff.

"I've got a fire light," he called as the Udorn base rescue helicopter, a double-rotored HH-43B, flew overhead with the big red fire suppression kit swinging in a sling under its belly.

At the seven thousand-foot marker John veered off onto the high-speed taxiway and rolled to a stop.

John unhooked the seat belt and shoulder harness, raised the canopy, and climbed over the edge of the canopy rail, hanging onto it like a chinning bar till he was hanging full length, then dropped about four feet to the ground. The jolt of the ground brought him down to his knees. Mother Earth felt mighty fine, even if it was covered with concrete.

When the fire truck arrived he was still on his knees, trying to get his breathing under control and his body to quit shaking. There was no fire. Cutting off the fuel supply to the engine had probably snuffed it. Major Gillespie, Ron, and Mike were just touching down as the Base Safety Officer arrived in a pick-up truck to carry John to base operations. They swung over to the transient parking area to pick up the other three pilots.

Major Gillespie was the first one into the pick-up. "Lieutenant, that was a good piece of flying and one great piece of shooting. Colonel English was right. He said he'd bet his bottom dollar you'd make me look good this morning. You can fly my wing anytime." Major G. extended his hand. That was the ultimate compliment in this racket and John knew it.

"Thank you, sir." John tried to sound modest, which was surprisingly easy to do after spending thirty minutes wondering if his number was up. His legs were still wobbly and he thought his handshake felt cold and clammy.

"I'll get on the horn and see what they want us to do," Major Gillespie said when they arrived in front of Base Operations.

Ron and Mike sprawled out in easy chairs in the lounge area, sucking on Cokes, while John paced the floor, trying to look cool while he worked off the tension. Twice in two consecutive flights now he had felt the hot breath of the Grim Reaper. The three of them relived the excitement of the morning and razzed one another. The same three guys who were so sober and quiet before the flight now couldn't shut up.

"Your voice was about three octaves above middle C when you called that emergency, John," Mike said.

"Yours was squeaking like my kid sister's when you called in on your bomb run," John shot back.

"Seems to me like some little lady is going to get stood up tonight at happy hour, Ellsworth," Ron said.

"Naw, I doubt it. I'm too valuable to leave over here sitting on the ground with a sick airplane. They'll probably decide that you or Mike should stay with it," John replied.

"Oh boy, it's gone to his head. He gets lucky twice in forty-eight hours and he thinks he's God's gift to the war effort," Ron said.

"I think maybe he got lucky Monday afternoon on the beach, too," Mike joined in.

"I don't think you know the difference between luck and skill," John answered.

"Does that mean you got lucky two or three times in the last two days?" Mike asked.

"Eat your heart out," John replied.

"You ate what?" Mike shot back.

"Okay men, here's the scoop," Major Gillespie interjected. Somewhere he had found a cigar. "We're going to refuel and head on back. Ellsworth, you'll stay with the plane. A C-130 will have a new engine and maintenance crew over here by dark. They should have you flying by late tomorrow afternoon or first thing the next morning."

"Yes, sir," John replied, accompanied by snickers from the other two lieutenants.

"We'll be glad to keep your nurse entertained while you're out of town, Lieutenant Ellsworth," Mike said.

"Don't bother," John shot back. "Now that she knows me she'll throw rocks at you. See you guys."

With laughs and handshakes all around, the party broke up. John got walking directions to the Officer's Club and headed that way. The air base had a more permanent look to it than Tuy Hoa, with some large wooden buildings intermingled with steel buildings, and manicured grass and tropical shade trees.

Udorn, three times as big as Tuy Hoa in acreage and airplanes, was populated mostly by F-4 Phantoms, twin-engine, two-place fighter planes of much more recent vintage than the fifteen-year-old F-100. Everyone—that is, all single-seat, single-engine fighter pilots—knew that any plane that had two engines and required two pilots didn't really qualify as a fighter.

Several of John's friends from basic flight training who didn't finish high enough in their class to draw an F-100 assignment chose the back seat of a Phantom. There were no other fighter choices. Some of them were at Udorn. John decided he could get drunk and swap lies with old buddies and have a nice holiday, the second in two days. This one would not have the ominous connotations of the last one, but then he wouldn't have green-eyed Kate to enjoy it with either. Since Thailand was a friendly country, he could get off base and try some of those bathhouses he'd heard so much about.

Udorn's Officers' Club had a cafeteria line. John ordered a beer, cheeseburger and fries and headed for an unoccupied table. It was only 1100 hours but he felt like he had given the taxpayers an honest day's work and it felt good to be alone with his thoughts.

Life in the war zone was definitely looking up. He had been given a second chance and he had redeemed himself. He had taken everything the North Vietnamese gunners could dish out and returned the same in spades. He had exonerated himself under fire and hopefully would be back in Colonel English's good graces. He had collected the scalps of at least a few dozen more gooks in honor of Rock. He had met an intriguing lady, never a part of the dream, to spice up life in the war zone. And, to top it off, he had the rest of the day off to get soaked, steamed, massaged and then probably knee-walking drunk with old friends. Now tell me, he thought, how could it possibly get any better than this?

"What's with the Cheshire cat smile, Lieutenant?"

It jolted John out of his self-satisfied reverie. "Hey, Sam. Great to see ya. Have a seat."

Sam Peterson was a happy-go-lucky guy with a military bearing that left a little bit to be desired, an easy grin and unruly, blond hair. He had his own way of walking—he just threw his feet out and stepped on them. John and Sam had been fraternity brothers at the University of Illinois. They had spent many an afternoon at Kam's after ROTC drills, drinking draft beer and dreaming about flying fighters in combat.

Sam's father ran a small fixed-base flying operation and charter service out of Rockford Airport. As a result, Sam had started flying about the same time John started riding a bicycle. In spite of all his experience, Sam couldn't handle advanced jet training quite well enough to make F-100's. He ended up in the back seat of an F-4 Phantom, an ignominious position for a new pilot—the Navy flew the same plane and they used navigators in the back. What a pity for Sam. He loved flying as much as he loved his wife and two children.

"How's life in the back seat of a two-holer, Sam?"

"The back seat of a Phantom sucks, John, especially when your aircraft commander considers you excess baggage. He's a World War II veteran who thinks he knows it all, can't fly worth a hoot and he's probably going to kill us both or get us locked up in the Hanoi Hilton." Sam shouted at the bartender, about ten feet away behind the bar, "Bring me a draft, Benny. So how's it with you, my friend? You lost? You're a long way from home."

"It was the closest port in a storm, Sam. We were up playing in the Mu Gia Pass sandbox and my airplane got sick. So I'm stuck for a couple of days. But Phantoms still beat flying one of those many-motored trash haulers, don't they?" John asked.

"Ask me next year, if I'm still alive."

"Where were you this morning?"

"The Song Tre Bridge again, just south of Hanoi. I've been there umpteen times and it's still standing."

"I've heard you Phantom jockeys couldn't hit the ground if you fell."

"Well, I sure know one who can't. I don't think there's anything inherently wrong with the flying machine. It's just the guys in the front seat. The younger guys, who volunteered for a second tour over here so they could move up to the front seat faster, seem to do all right. Hey, what are you doing this afternoon?"

"Zip."

"Well, how about we run down to the Sans Souci Bath House? It'll be good for what ails both of us."

"Sounds good to me. Should I find a bed before we go out to play?"

"No sweat. My roommate's pulling night alert. You can use his bed. Sans Souci will scrub all the Vietnamese in-country crud off your body so he won't mind."

The Sans Souci was just a couple miles from the base on the main drag into town. It was a pleasant ride-on a motor scooter again. Two-wheelers made the world go 'round in the Orient, whether hand-drawn carts, rickshaws or bicycles—motorized or peddled.

The mama-san in charge treated Sam like an old valued customer as did her employees. They were such pleasant, pretty girls. They began with the Thai equivalent of a Jacuzzi tub and two lovely, young ladies with washcloths and soap to do the scrubbing, and a never-ending supply of cold beer. That was followed by a steam bath in a box where only their heads stuck out. And then, the grand finale—a full body massage from top to bottom that didn't miss a single sinew and climaxed with the love muscle. Since it was midday and business was slow, the Mama-san let Ron and John remain alone on the massage table after their work was done. They spent an hour catching up on all the news.

"Ah, life is good. So how's Ma and the kids, Sam?"

"They're doing fine. I miss them like crazy. It's really tough being gone when your kids are small. Betty says Sam, Jr. doesn't remember his father, and I've only been gone three months. Jennie starts the first grade this fall. I'm just trying to hang on till I meet Betty for R&R in Hawaii in January. I've kissed off all that career stuff we used to talk about back in college. Betty wants me to go the airline pilot route, and I guess I agree. Dad's charter service was just bought out by a regional carrier and he can get me on with them. Maybe I'd feel different if I were flying F-100's, John. The only thing I enjoy about this tour is the Sans Souci Bath House. So how's your life?"

"Well, aside from watching a good friend crash and burn in the A Shau a few days ago, then trying to kill myself with some really ham-fisted flying when they sent me in against the same target, I'm doing all right...don't ask me why. Had a successful mission this morning at Mu Gia. And get this...I met an Army nurse, stationed just a mile from Tuy Hoa, and spent yesterday afternoon on the beach at Tuy Hoa with her. No future but a fun present...war is hell."

"You always were the luckiest guy I ever met. World class stick-and-rudder man, and now a lady-killer...in the war zone, no less."

"Well, what can I say?" John said with a big grin. He saw no need to disavow that impression.

"Don't try the humble gambit, John. It doesn't fit you. You know, you've had that grin for as long as I've known you. I remember Hell Week at the Phi Delt House, sleeping on that cold concrete floor in the basement. You had that same stupid grin even then."

"Maybe I've changed in my advancing years, Sam."

John dozed off and woke up feeling great. For a moment he wished he was flying out of Thailand, just so he could get worked over regularly by those lovely little girls with the magic hands. They motored back to the O'Club in time for happy hour and grabbed the last empty table in the huge bar.

"Sam, what's a good way to kill tomorrow, aside from the Sans Souci Bath House?"

"There's a Forward Air Controller squadron here flying OV-10A's. They're about nine times safer than the average FAC plane and they've got a reasonably comfortable back seat. Spend four of five hours on the Trail between Mu Gia and Tchepone. You won't be bored."

"Sounds like fun. Who do I see to set it up?"

"He's walking toward us right now. Capt. Wild Bill Clark, meet John Ellsworth, old fraternity brother from Illinois."

Bill Clark was a smoky, thin six-footer with a black walrus mustache just starting to turn gray. He wore his flight suit unzipped half way to his navel, collar turned up and sleeves rolled up two turns. He looked like he'd been in the war zone all his life.

"Bill, John's looking for a way to entertain himself tomorrow. He drives F-100's out of Tuy Hoa and he's here with a sick plane. I told him you might have a back seat available."

"We could probably swing that, if he's crazy enough to want to come along. Business has been awful exciting lately. The southbound truck traffic looks like the Jersey Turnpike. Say, John, you weren't over Mu Gia this morning were you?"

"Yeah. Dusty Three Three working with Squid Zero One."

"Well, it's a small world. I was Squid Zero One. You were number three? Good God, you shot the eyes out of them this morning. I directed three more flights in there after you and they were unopposed. Those gunners you didn't kill you scared into some deep hole, I guess. Sure, I'd enjoy having you ride along with me. I'm scheduled for an 0600 take-off. Living on an F-4 base, I don't get much of a chance to fraternize with real fighter jocks," Bill said with a sideways look at Sam.

"Don't look at me like that. I'm just back seat ballast, building up my time for the airlines," Sam shot back.

"Another round?" Bill asked. "I'm buying. I owe you John. You sure took the heat off my day. Those fifty-sevens give me indigestion."

"You're on. Thanks," John replied.

"I flew F-100's my first tour out of Ben Hoa," Wild Bill continued. "Ma and the kids took a hike in the middle of that tour so I volunteered for a second tour as a FAC. Lucked out with this assignment. The OV-10 is a dream machine and on the Trail you don't have to worry about troops-in-contact or hitting friendlies. Why, you could miss the target by a mile and not hit a friendly troop. Thailand is a fantastic place to go to war from. Got a little Thai girlfriend who thinks the sun sets just below my tailbone, which of course it does. Not too bad for a street kid from Newark. I hope this war never ends." Bill slouched back in his chair, beer bottle resting on his taut belly.

"You'll have your wish if we don't quit fighting it with one hand tied behind our backs," John interjected. "You know, Senator Goldwater had the right idea. Send in the B-52's and bomb Hanoi and mine Haiphong Harbor-stop 'em at the source. I voted for the guy and I'm proud of it. Mark my words, if this war is won, it will be won with Goldwater's strategy. Every general since the beginning of time would agree with him."

"But generals are not a very large voting block, John, and they're not calling the shots in this war anyway," Sam replied, "and when the liberals who dominate the press are against you it's all over. We couldn't win World War II with the attitude in America today...."

"And how about that President Johnson, stopping the bombing of the North?" John interrupted. "My God, the guy's read every book except Patton's. I wish I could have had him along a few days ago. I watched my friend die because Johnson's bombing halt allowed old Ho to move his big guns all the way into South Vietnam."

"I just want to go home," Sam said as he stared into his beer.

"You win wars by busting assets and killing bad guys, not by playing some kind of wimpy, half-hearted defense." John said, ignoring Sam's comment. "I just don't understand. It blows my mind how easily the politicians write off the lives of American soldiers, to say nothing of these poor South Vietnamese people, for no other reason than personal political gain. It's like Johnson and Kissinger really care only about their popularity with the evening news anchors and the editorial writers and the campus protesters."

"Of course you're right. But let's be thankful for what we've got," Bill said. "The three most important things in life are flying, fornication and inebriation, in that order, and except for this empty bottle, I've got the best of all three. 'Nother round?"

"Sure."

"Likewise."

No one seemed to share John's intense feelings about the state of events in which they found themselves, so he dropped it and concentrated on the business at hand. The night got pretty foggy again, and the seas rough. Somebody put him to bed. He vaguely remembered putting one leg over the side of the bed and a bare foot on the floor to keep the bed from spinning.

It was 1100 hours before the pounding inside his skull woke him up. Pity the poor teetotalers, he thought. When they wake up in the morning that's as good as they're going to feel all day. He consumed the usual antidote—vast quantities of water, three aspirin and was fifteen minutes into a long hot shower before he realized he had missed his flight with Wild Bill. He was probably flying home by now.

John climbed into his flying suit, which now reeked of sweat, smoke, and spilled beer. He found the chow hall and then wandered on over to the FAC unit's operations building.

"What time is Captain Clark due back?" He asked a sergeant in jungle fatigues behind the scheduling counter.

"He's an hour overdue, sir."

"Is anybody in contact with him?"

"No, sir. He controlled two air strikes this morning over Mu Gia and when the third flight showed up they couldn't raise him on the radio."

"Search-and-Rescue launched?"

"Yes, sir."

The shiver that ran through John's body was not due to the D.T.'s. He stepped back out into the hot tropical sun and began to walk. He didn't know how far he walked or even where. Funny, when he looked up there was the Officer's Club—he had homed on it like a moth to a candle. Time for a little hair of dog.

The bar was crowded but subdued. Udorn was indeed a big base, but when one of the fraternity didn't come home, the word traveled around at Mach I. A couple of beers later Sam walked in, ashen-faced. He saw John, came straight over to his table, and gave him a big bear hug. Sam wasn't smiling.

"Oh God, am I glad to see you, brother. Did you hear about Wild Bill?"

"I know he's overdue...or he was a few hours ago, anyway."

"John, I didn't have the heart to wake you up in time to fly with Wild Bill this morning. Drunk as you were you had a rough night. Somewhere east of midnight you were thrashing around like a crazy man. I got up and turned the lights on. You were all hunkered down at the foot of the bed. You didn't look at all like the fearless fighter pilot I know."

"Sometimes at night I miss my mom."

"Well, brother, your mom is going to love me for saving your grubby hide. The Jolly Greens just brought in Bill's body."

"Say again?"

"They peeled him like an onion. He was tied to a tree in a clearing. They castrated him and skinned about two-thirds of him."

The rumbling began way down deep. John opened his mouth to say "excuse me" but no words came out. Somehow he found the head and a vacant booth. His knees gave way in front of the stool. Long after his stomach had been violently emptied the spasms continued.

"Come on, brother. Let me put you to bed again." Sam had John by the hair.

Through glassy eyes, John looked up at Sam as he helped him to his feet. They picked their way across the bar. Someone made a remark about how F-100 drivers couldn't hold their booze. It generated no response from John and very little reaction from the subdued crowd.

As they walked slowly toward Sam's quarters, John's gait began to smooth out.

"Thanks, Sam."

"You're welcome, John. But you know that's not the first time I've pulled your face out of a pot."

"No, I mean thanks for not waking me up this morning. You saved my life."

"You're welcome, again, my friend. Like I said before, you're the luckiest guy I know."

"Lucky I've got a friend like you, Sam." The black box got another load of terrifying imponderables dumped into it.

Without a ton-and-a-half of cast-iron slung under the wings, the F-100 rocketed off the runway at Udorn like a homesick angel. The trip back to Tuy Hoa was a one-hour joy ride across never-never land-never-never, if he had to bail out over that territory, were they going to take John alive. If nothing else, the .38 revolver tucked under his left armpit was his ticket out of there. If life in the fast lane had to end, better that way than Wild Bill's way. With six shots in the cylinder, perhaps he could take a few with him, but it was a given he was checking out.

That was the vow Sam and John made after talking late into the night. John agreed to explain it all to Betty if it ever came to pass and Sam agreed he'd run down to the farm, only about ninety miles southwest of Rockford, and explain it to John's mother if he didn't return.

Back at Tuy Hoa, John took a chance and called Phu Hep nurses' quarters from the phone in Dusty Squadron Operations. Someone answered and called Kate to the phone.

"Hello, Lieutenant Moffit. I'm sorry I'm two days late for our date...."

"Well, you're the talk of the town again, flyboy."

"Lies.... Bald-faced lies if you heard them at Dusty's Pub."

"I heard you dueled the guns again."

"Yeah, and the guns lost again."

"You're a sick puppy, Lieutenant."

"You say the nicest things, Nurse Moffit. And how was your day?"

"We turned out one quadriplegic and filled two body bags....

God bless America. See you at five."

John hesitated as he envisioned the picture she had just painted, then thought about Wild Bill being put into a black rubber bag and zipped up and said, "Good-bye." He dropped the phone trying to put it back on the cradle. 'How was your day' was a question he would never ask her again, he decided.

He checked the schedule board as he hung up the phone. "Ellsworth" was just coming out of the end of the grease pencil wielded by Colonel English. A load of "Snakes and nape"—high drag bombs and napalm—to III Corps. He was leading a two-ship with Colonel English on his wing. Leading!?

"Time to see if you're flight leader material, Lieutenant. Major Gillespie briefed me on the Mu Gia Pass mission. He thinks you're one shit-hot fighter pilot. So do I. Time to get you out front so you can show the rest of them how it's done."

"Thank you, sir. I'm ready."

"We'll keep you in-country for a while, too. You've defied the odds and it's still early in your tour. You've got nearly ten months left to survive."

"I appreciate the consideration, sir, but I believe you make your own luck. Send me where I can do the most damage."

Colonel abruptly stopped writing on the scheduling board and turned to face John. "Perhaps I've been remiss in telling you this, Lieutenant, especially after what you tried to do to yourself the other day. I said you are a shit-hot fighter pilot, but you are not nearly as good as you think you are. That ego of yours still has to fit into the cockpit. You keep talking like that and I'll put your ass back in number four and you'll be Tail-end Charlie for the rest of the tour. We brief at 1100."

"Yes, sir." Colonel English had an uncanny way of exploding the oversized balloon that was John's ego. Yet John thought so much of Colonel English, wanted so badly to be like him, that his ass-chewings provoked no resentment—after all, that was the military way of instruction—but rather it engendered disappointment in himself that his actions had once again displeased his mentor and role model.

It was good to be back among friends at Dusty's Pub. In two short months of associating with thirty guys who had more or less similar temperaments, goals, and frustrations, some heavy-duty bonding had occurred. Although the lieutenants bragged a lot and ragged on one another constantly, the camaraderie went deep. They were all college grads and there by choice. They had chosen the cramped, smelly confines of an F-100 cockpit, and the action, over the more spacious but prosaic offices of corporate America, and nobody was updating his resume.

The Mu Gia Pass mission scuttlebutt had been thoroughly distributed the night before in John's absence, most assuredly by Mike and Ron. As usual, the myth exceeded reality.

The nurses from Phu Hep arrived at 1700 sharp. Kate's eye caught John's eye as they entered the Pub and she joined him at the bar. Her green eyes were sparkling.

"Welcome home," she said.

"Pleasure to be here. You look stunning as usual in your jungle ensemble."

"Thanks, Handsome John."

"Let's find a quieter spot," John suggested. Of course that was impossible in the close confines of Dusty's Pub, but they did find a table to themselves in a corner. The rest of the guys politely left them mostly alone, except for congratulatory handshakes from those John hadn't seen since his return from Udorn.

"What's your pleasure, Kate?"

"A soft drink will be fine."

It was strictly a self-service bar. "Be right back." John moved behind the v-shaped bar and opened the door of the refrigerator. As the painting of the naked lady lounging on the tiger caught John's eye, he thought, I bet Kate would look better on that tiger. John grabbed a cola and a beer and a glass, and returned to the table. He poured the cola in the glass for Kate.

"Shalom," she said as she raised her glass.

"Amen," John responded as he tapped her glass with his can, secretly proud of himself for responding in what we guessed was the appropriate manner to Kate's toast. "Pardon my ignorance, Kate, but what does 'Shalom' mean?"

"Peace."

"Well, perhaps I need to take my 'Amen' back until we drive the Commies back to Hanoi."

"So be it, Son of Thunder. Speak to me of your latest signs and wonders before the Philistines. I've never met a legend in his own time before," she said with a smile.

Boy, she was an enigma. He wasn't sure what she meant—and once again the words didn't match the tone or the smile. "You have such an affectionate way of communicating." He paused for effect. "My friend Sam over in Thailand told me humility doesn't become me. What are you saying?"

"I disagree with your friend but I know it's counter-culture here at Fearless Fighter Pilots, Incorporated." At least she was still smiling. "Please don't misunderstand me. I know that self-confidence is a crucial part of survival in your business." Kate leaned across the small wicker table and squeezed John's forearm, her eyes fixed on his as she talked.

"I'd say you're a very astute observer of the Tuy Hoa scene." John put his hand on top of Kate's and they were nearly nose-to-nose across the small table.

"So tell me about Mu Gia Pass."

"Well, they shot at me and I shot back and they missed and I didn't. That's about all there was to it." John knew she didn't want the long answer. She had made it clear enough to him without saying it: she did not approve of his vocation...and he didn't want to think about hers.

"How do those guys aim at you?"

"We had no indications of radar lock-on so I guess it's like aiming a big squirrel rifle, except the gunner sits in a seat. It looks like a 1947 John Deere tractor seat-all steel—and it's very uncomfortable. He's almost on his back when he's shooting at me, because his gun barrel has got to match my dive-angle. And, he may or may not be handcuffed to his gun. So his pucker-factor must be about one hundred percent, don't you imagine?"

"I can't imagine. You seem more full of...vinegar today than a couple days ago," Kate observed.

"Well, I feel a whole lot better about my job performance today. I spent the whole flight to Mu Gia inside the envelope-dancing the wild blue instead of wrestling greased hogs...."

"What?"

"Oh, just a little technique I picked up at my guru's knee."

"Colonel English?"

"No less...my hero."

"But John, why do I still get this image of a little boy whistling as he walks by the cemetery on a dark night?" She had not released her grip on his forearm or taken her eyes off him.

"Well, I guess the jig is up. You know I'm a phony. If you report me they'll probably take my wings away for sure, or worse yet, they'll make me fly sideways in one of those committee-driven airplanes."

"I'm serious, John."

The old humorous lateral arabesque wasn't working this evening. "Maybe it keeps the lid on the black box."

"Tell me more about this black box."

"Would you prefer that I lie on a couch for this session?" He delivered that shot with a sober face.

"I'm sorry. I'm being a bitch again...."

John noticed the cutest bouquet of wrinkles between her eyebrows as she frowned into her drink in self-deprecation. He let her suffer for a few seconds, then responded, "I prefer 'sassy.' Sassy little lady."

Her frown disappeared and her smile returned. "Well, at least you still call me a lady. What was wrong with your airplane?" She leaned back in her chair and sipped her cola.

"Busted oil line, I guess. None of those gunners laid a glove on me." John glanced around the Pub as he squirmed under her gaze.

Kate was quiet for a moment, a wondering look in her eye. "And Udorn?"

"Nice place. Big. Huge bar. Lots of different flying units over there, but mostly Phantoms. I spent most of the time with Sam Peterson, an old fraternity brother from college, and a friend of his who was a FAC. Sam took me to his favorite bathhouse and we had a few beers. Someday you must meet him.... Listen, did you know the moon is full? How about a walk by the sea in the moonlight with the Son of Thunder?"

She said, "I'd love to," and so did her eyes as well as her smile and her tone.

As they walked slowly across the soft sand of the beach, John ventured, "Do I dare ask...what are the implications of 'Son of Thunder'?"

"Oh, it's in the Bible. Jesus called one of his favorite disciples that. It was descriptive of his impetuous personality. His name was John, too."

"Has a nice ring to it. I like it. I don't know about the impetuous part though."

"Well, that's the part I'm most sure of." Kate laughed.

"I see." John nodded his head. He loved to make her laugh, even when it was unintentional. He just couldn't figure out how to react to her concoction of cynicism and sugar.

With Kate's head snuggled in the hollow of John's right shoulder, they walked slowly arm-in-arm to the water's edge. The moon was so bright it overpowered all but a few dozen stars. Their only company was a handful of shadowy Vietnamese fishermen several yards off the beach. Her perfume had a far greater intoxicating effect than the beer John had consumed.

Her eyes were like emeralds in the moonlight. Her warm breath quavered in his ear as he kissed her neck, and the communication was all wonderfully non-verbal.

It ended abruptly, with the honking horn of one U.S. Army six-passenger truck filled with five impatient nurses.

* * *

"So what's the word tonight, Kate." Lieutenant Smith asked as she drove the truck away from Dusty's Pub.

Kate's analysis was considerably briefer this time. "The word is 'incorrigible.'"

* * *

John arrived at Squadron Ops at 1030 hours, thirty minutes prior to briefing time, and two hours prior to take-off. He was pumped. There was never a wingman born who didn't think he'd make a great flight leader. To get the chance to prove it as a first lieutenant with only 10 weeks of combat experience was a real trip, especially after that major mistake at A Shau. Apparently the old man, with the advice of Colonel English and Major Gillespie, had a major change of heart.

But over-stressing the airplane in Colonel English's presence was the first and last gross error John intended to make in front of him or anybody else. In a line of work that was so brutally unforgiving of incompetence, error, or neglect, he had truly defied the odds. There was no rational explanation for having survived that episode. The hairline cracks in the spars could have given way at any time on any later dive recovery during that mission. But right now there was a war to be won...and retribution. He had the rest of his life to think about the why's and wherefore's. He tucked it all into that mental black box and nailed the lid down tight.

Five hundred pound Snake-eye bombs and napalm to III Corps usually meant close air support for troops-in-contact with the enemy, but the flight wouldn't know for sure until it rendezvoused with the FAC. John poured his self-imposed ration of one cup of coffee, checked the weather and then carefully reviewed the pre-flight briefing checklist, mentally rehearsing what he would say. He was determined to make his mentor proud of him.

The scary thing about Snakes and nape was they were designed to be dropped from very close range. Troops-in-contact meant friendlies would be very close to where the bombs were dropping. John was paranoid about missing the target and incinerating an American soldier. Dropping bombs at very low levels and high speeds close to friendly troops required the gutsiest kind of combat flying. F-100's were authorized to drop napalm just fifty meters from friendly troops but the grunts had better be flat on the ground or in foxholes. If they stood up to watch the show at that range, there was a good chance they'd end up being part of it. Dropping bombs from very close range greatly improved the chances of hitting the target, the theory being that if you were standing close enough to the back end of the bull and were swinging a base fiddle, you couldn't miss. With friendlies so close to the bull, not missing was crucial. Then there was the matter, while concentrating on the bull's ass at 400 knots and fifty feet off the ground, of not running into enemy bullets, assorted tall trees or the ground.

John dutifully discussed this at length with Colonel English during the briefing-that and a hundred other mandatory items in the checklist-even though he knew the colonel had heard it all a thousand times before.

They saddled up at 1145, the hottest part of a hot day, and at 1200 sharp John lowered the canopy at the end of Runway 21 and called, "Dusty One One Flight, check in."

"Two." Colonel English had lowered his canopy in unison with John and was ready and waiting on freq.

"Tuy Hoa Tower, Dusty One One, flight of two Fox 100's, southwest bound."

"Dusty One One, cleared for takeoff."

The two F-100's taxied slowly onto the runway and bobbed to a stop astraddle the centerline with Colonel English to the right and slightly behind John. Using the index finger of his right hand pointed straight up and his thumb pointed at the horizon, John waggled the run up signal to his wingman. The J-57 jet engine spooled up to one hundred percent power with a deafening, ground shaking roar.

He checked the engine instruments, looked back at Colonel English, got an affirmative head nod that all was well and lifted his feet off the toe-brakes. Simultaneously he moved the throttle outboard into afterburner and felt that delirious kick in the butt. There's a higher level of existence that simply doesn't commence until the afterburner kicks in on take-off roll, John thought.

After eating up eight thousand feet of runway, John's airplane slipped the surly bonds and they were airborne. Five hundred feet in the air and clawing for altitude, he came back one-half percent on the throttle and trimmed her up for the climb. Five minutes later Colonel English, who had started his take-off roll five seconds after John, caught up. Heading 230 degrees from the Tuy Hoa Valley, it got hazy, really hazy-in fact it was like flying around inside a milk bottle. It had something to do with all that humidity the jungle threw off. It added a challenging little wrinkle to John's first mission as a flight leader-just being able to rendezvous with an O-1, a little plane about the size of a Piper Cub, who was also flying around inside that milk bottle somewhere.

Fifty miles north of Saigon, still headed 230 degrees, they switched over to the forward air controller's radio frequency.

"Hooter Three One, this is Dusty One One Flight, over," John called.

"Dusty One One Flight, this is Hooter Three One. Glad you're here. Hustle on over to the 330 degree radial at fifty miles off the Bien Hoa TACAN. We've got a column of armored personnel carriers that just got ambushed on the road ten miles north of Tay Ninh. Heavy casualties. Whatcha carrying today?" Hooter asked.

"Dusty One One Flight is carrying four Snake-eyes, four cans of napalm and sixteen hundred rounds of twenty mike mike," John responded.

"Perfect load. You're going to have to get down amongst them. The APC's have bad guys within fifty meters of them on both sides of the road, and the visibility is less than a mile."

That was worth a few chills-zero margin for error.

Another bothersome thing about Tay Ninh was that huge mountain just east of town. It rose up out of a perfectly flat plain, like Stone Mountain east of Atlanta. The two hornets and a mosquito were flying around inside the milk bottle, trying to find one another and now they discover there's a big rock taking up a significant part of the bottle.

John took them down to two thousand feet and picked up the mountain, Tay Ninh, and the road leading north out of town. So far so good, he thought. They bent it around to the right and headed up the road.

Ten APC's were stopped dead in the road. The lead one and the rear one were both burning and there was nowhere for the middle eight to go—a perfect ambush. It must have been North Vietnamese Regulars, and lots of them.

"Dusty One One, this is Hooter Three One. I have you in sight. I'm directly over the APC's at twenty-five hundred feet and I need to stay right here to keep everybody in sight. You'll have to make your passes under me. I'm in contact with the ground commander and he's really getting creamed, so go ahead and hop right to it." He gave Dusty Flight the necessary target info—temperature, winds and barometric pressure.

"Roger, Hooter, Dusty One One Flight, set 'em up hot, arm nose-tail, bomb single. Dusty One Two, you take the east side of the road and I'll take the west.

"Two Copy," Colonel English replied.

"Dusty, this is Hooter again. Put your napalm right on the tree line on each side of the road next to the APC's. That's exactly fifty meters off the road."

"Roger, Hooter. Tell the ground commander to get everyone's head down. They're going to feel some heat."

"Roger, Dusty. They're already down and feeling heat. Those poor bastards are digging holes in the road with their teeth and fingernails."

"Roger. Dusty One One's in from the north." John lined up right on the road and dove down to fifty feet off the deck. At four hundred knots his exhaust was blowing rooster tails in the dusty road. He was expecting a wall of invisible small arms fire and a lucky shot could be just as deadly as the big stuff. He gauged fifty feet by feel-he didn't dare look inside the cockpit going that fast that close to the ground. Fifty feet to him was when the seat of his pants felt so close to dragging in the dirt that it provoked an involuntary pucker reaction.

The tops of the trees on both sides of the road were higher than he was, so he eased back up a bit and slid over to the right to get over the tree line. Abeam the APC's he scraped the first can of napalm off on the treetops. The jungle was full of fireflies as every AK-47 rifle down there was pointed right at him firing on full automatic.

He bent her around hard to the right and climbed back up to two thousand feet as he watched Colonel English fly the eastern tree line in exactly the same way. Two shiny aluminum-colored canisters, six feet long and tapered at both ends, tumbled end-over-end from the underside of the wings, hit the trees and exploded. Five hundred pounds of gelatinous napalm burned with ferocious intensity as great globs of it splattered through the trees, incinerating an area the size of a football field.

"Bullseye, Dusty. Oh God, we love ya. I can hear the grunts cheering on the ground over the commander's radio." His voice was loud and cracking with emotion. "Put your next nape just south of where you put the first one," Hooter directed.

"Roger. Lead's in from the north." They used the same approach and got the same results.

"Dusty Flight, put your Snake-eyes about one hundred meters farther into the trees. Any gooks still alive should be moving back into the jungle. Maybe we can intercept them."

"Roger. Lead's in. Have you in sight, Hooter," John dropped both Snakes.

"Two's in."

"Great work again, Dusty. Now if you'd just put your 20-millimeter into the tree line just ahead of the APC's. Let's make sure there's no other surprises in store for the grunts on up the road."

Dusty Flight hosed down the tree line with all the 20-millimeter rounds they had on board. Coming off his final strafing pass, John pulled the nose up and laid her over into a quick victory roll. Colonel English did the same. The grunts expected it and of course they ate it up. So did John. It reminded him of Chief Illiniwek doing his touchdown dance at the Illinois football games.

John gave Colonel English a big wing rock signal to join up and the colonel snuggled up close on his left wing.

"Dusty One One Flight, I'll forward your BDA after the grunts get a body count. Gonna be tough to count most of those bodies. I'm guessing at least a couple of hundred and you've earned the eternal gratitude of those guys in the APC's. It was sure a pleasure working with you. Come back and see us again real soon, ya hear. Good day," Hooter signed off.

"Good day, Hooter Three One. Pleasure here, too. Dusty One One Flight let's go Winchester." John dialed in the squadron's confidential radio frequency, 303.0, and checked in. "Dusty One One Flight."

"Twoop."

"Dusty One Two, look me over carefully. I think we took a lot of small arms fire on the first pass," John called.

"Roger, lead," Colonel English replied as he dropped down and moved under John's plane. A long silence ensued. Finally he said, "I count about a dozen holes, some in the flaps, a couple in your left leading edge wing slat and three or four right behind the cockpit about two feet from your head. Keep an eye on your slats on final approach for landing. You may have some control problems. How are your gauges?"

"Everything looks okay here. Take the lead while I check you over."

"Roger. I have the lead," Colonel English said and moved ahead. He was pretty peppered with holes himself but there were no hits in anything vital. John reported the battle damage to Colonel English and retook the lead.

They climbed on up to twenty thousand feet and headed straight back to Tuy Hoa. That got them up out of the haze and gave them maximum gliding distance, should one of those AK-47 slugs be stuck in something vital and about to make its presence known. With that much battle damage, it also didn't make any sense to play around on the way home, especially with the number two man in the squadron on the wing. So it was straight and level from point A to point B. There was nothing to do but work at flying very smoothly.

"Pretend it's an airliner and you don't want to spill a drop of a single martini in the back," John's old instructor at advanced jet training used to say. That was no easy task in an F-100. It had no autopilot and was impossible to trim up "hands-off." It was like flying on top of a rubber ball, first one wing would drop, correct it and then the other wing would drop, then the nose. Flying it was a constant series of tiny corrections, but John thought that was a mighty small price to pay for such sheer ecstasy.

The adrenaline high lasted longer when there was no chance to play or work it off but that did not detract from the intensity of it. In fact, the thought that John's actions directly saved the lives of Americans added to his high, somehow lending more legitimacy to all that killing.

They circled Tuy Hoa to the south for the over-water approach to Runway 21.

"Tuy Hoa Tower, Dusty One One Flight, ten south for landing, requesting precautionary straight-in approach. Both aircraft have battle damage with potential control problems. Request crash vehicles be standing by," John called.

"Roger, Dusty One One Flight, cleared for straight-in approach to Runway 21. Dusty One Two, make a three hundred sixty degree turn for spacing. Crash crews are being alerted."

John looked back and got a thumbs up from Colonel English as he peeled away to the right. Five miles out over the sea on final approach, the left wing felt heavy. A quick glance over the canopy rail revealed the left leading edge slat stuck in the up position. He wasn't getting as much lift out of the wing at normal approach speed. He added twenty knots, cross-controlled with a little left rudder and right aileron, and his wounded angel got earthbound in reasonably good shape. He met the runway only a little more violently than usual because of the extra speed.

As he turned off at the end of the runway, John looked back just in time to see Colonel English touch down with two swirling puffs of blue smoke as his main wheels met the runway at a hundred forty knots. He parked in the de-arming area at the end of the runway, raised the canopy and gave the crash crews a thumbs-up. Colonel English joined him and they swapped thumbs-up signals and smiles. Enroute to the Squadron Ops building in the step van, Colonel English was most complimentary. His post-flight grin said it all. "Lieutenant, you're a natural born flight leader, and you can put a bomb on a target as well as I can. Action just seems to follow you around doesn't it? The most lively two missions I've had in six months have been the last two I've had with you. I'll brief the old man on our mission and recommend he make you a flight leader. He'll want to fly with you before he signs off on your status." Congratulations, Lieutenant."

This time John's grin matched Colonel English's. "Thank you, sir." He couldn't think of anything else that needed saying or that he dared say.

*   *   *

"Sir, Lieutenant Ellsworth is the best thing I've seen in a long time. He reminds me of me." Colonel English reported to the Squadron Commander.

"But is he safe?" Colonel Redman asked in his ever-tired voice.

"Well, sir, he's got an ego as big as the airplane, but then so did I when I was that age. But he's safe. The A Shau mission has been a good lesson for him, I believe, and he's a born leader," Colonel English replied.

"I sure hope you're right, Jack. The vibes I get are a little more unsettling. Schedule me to fly with him tomorrow and let's keep him in-country for awhile."

"Yes, sir."

"One more thing, Jack. I'm going to give him a two-day pass after I fly with him. He's had some red hot missions lately. I think he could use a little decompression."

"Yes sir."

Lieutenant Matt Jordan played a mean guitar, and he knew the tune to every raunchy drinking song that had ever been written. When he wasn't flying he was composing crude ditties to old melodies. Matt was the life of the party, whether it was stag or mixed. He was a little squirt, with black hair and a stereotype little-guy syndrome, and as a result he fit right in with the rest of the inflated young egos of the 629th TAC Fighter Squadron.

With Matt leading, a pub full of mostly inebriated lieutenants sang loudly and horribly. In the midst of their singing, Colonel English walked into the lounge with a coffee cup in his hand and a slightly pickled look on his face. He came over to John and turned the coffee cup upside down on the bar in a sweeping motion, as if it were a dice cup.

The singing stopped in mid-tune as a dozen mangled AK-47 slugs hit the plywood bar. The sound of the rolling metal dice was followed by "oohs" and "aahs" and swear words spoken in the most reverential tones.

With his best post-flight grin, old mentor English said, "Here's some souvenirs for your kids, Lieutenant, if you should live long enough to have any."

"You've taught me all I know, sir. I'm going to live forever," John answered. "These all mine?"

"Yep. The maintenance officer just brought yours and mine around to my hooch. He said he'd have both planes fixed by daylight, but an inch or two either way and we'd both have been walking. You lead a charmed life, son, and it must have rubbed off on me," Colonel English said as he slapped John on the back.

"Here's to charm," some slurred voice said, probably Matt, and every hand was raised with a container of the liquor of choice. "To charm." That was followed by, "To Colonel English" and "To Ellsworth." From there it degenerated into toasts to various parts of the female anatomy, complete with vulgar adjectives.

"I'll arm wrestle any puke in the pub for a ration of scotch." Colonel English announced.

There were no takers, even though John thought there were several lieutenants who could probably whip him if they had the nerve to try.

"Sir, I'd be honored to share mine," John said as he slid his scotch bottle down the bar toward the colonel. "It's not senior officer caliber, though."

"That's mighty kind of you, son. Thanks." Someone slid a glass down the bar and Colonel English poured himself a shooter and raised it for a toast. "Here's to bad wars, bad women, and good airplanes."

Everyone joined in with "Here, here," and the colonel threw the shooter down with one gulp.

"Now if you will excuse me, gentlemen, I have an early date with an angel...and we are going to dance"—he drug the word out with a rising inflection—"the wild blue."

The bar was silent as the eyes of every young fighter puke in the pub stared at the departing figure of the man they all wanted to be. The lieutenants exhausted their repertoire of songs that night. The gals from Phu Hep were partying elsewhere, and Kate was pulling the evening shift at the hospital. Of course it was too much to expect to spend all his waking hours with either his airborne angel or his two-legged earthbound version, but John was disappointed anyway.

John capped his scotch bottle early and put it on the shelf on the wall next to the naked lady and the tiger. As he rounded the bar he saw Colonels English's coffee cup still sitting there. It had a Hounds of Heaven insignia painted on one side, the emblem of the 524th Tactical Fighter Training Squadron that John himself had been a part of as a student fighter pilot, though long after Colonel English had been there as an instructor. He picked it up, thinking he would drop it off at the colonel's hooch enroute to his own. It wasn't really on the way, but he owed Colonel English a lifetime of favors and besides, he could always use the points. As he approached the colonel's hooch he saw a crack of light around the door, which should have meant that his mentor was still up. He rapped on the metal door of a green box that differed from his own only by the name in the F-100 silhouette on the door.

"Come in," a tired sounding voice responded.

John opened the door. "Sir, you left your coffee cup on the bar."

"Hey, thanks...Ellsworth. Come on in, Lieutenant." Colonel English seemed to light up at the sight of John. He sat in an overstuffed chair in the far corner from the door in a room exactly the same size as the one John shared with three other guys. A floor lamp next to the chair, a single bed, a desk, a dresser and a small refrigerator made up the rest of the furniture in the room. It was depressingly baren, with no pictures anywhere. An expensive looking stereo with a speaker at each end of the bed was the only non-US government owned piece of equipment visible. Classical music floated out of the speakers—an interesting kind of music for a rough, tough, hell-for-leather fighter pilot to be listening to. It occurred to John that some prison cells might be more opulent than a senior officer's quarters in the war zone. He stepped up the two steps and over the threshold of the door with trepidation, like an outdoor dog on the farm being invited into the house for the first time. Socializing with senior officers was not really proper military protocol, but it was not some kind of hard and fast rule.

The colonel was still in his flight suit, which was now dried with multiple salt rings all the way to the belt line, but that was the beauty of a flight suit—it was all-purpose wear. The regulations did not require that they be ironed so they were as low maintenance as clothes could get, and with eight zippered pockets-two on each leg, two on the chest, and one on each upper arm—they held all the essentials a man could ever need and then some. His high-topped, canvas and leather jungle flying boots stood unzipped beside his chair and his feet, clad in a double pair of white wool socks were perched on a well-worn footstool. His flight suit was unzipped half way to his navel, revealing a matted chest-full of curly, salt and pepper hair.

"How about a drink, Lieutenant, in celebration of your milestone and our success this afternoon? In fact, I'll break out the really good stuff. This has been a memorable day for you. Here, have a seat." He stood up and pulled out the desk chair and slid it toward John.

It wasn't an easy decision but John said, "Yes, thank you, sir." John sat down stiffly in the straight back, uncomfortable wooden chair.

"Damn, I'll never forget the day I got flight leader qualified in Korea in an F-86." As he talked the colonel got on his knees and reached under his bed, sliding out a wooden box labeled "Single Malt Scotch Whiskey" with some unpronounceable name in fancy script above that. "It was wintertime and colder'n a well digger's ass in the Klondike." He chuckled at the memory as he pulled a bottle out of the box, blew the dust off the top and broke the seal with a twist. "And those F-86's started h-a-a-r-r-r-d-d when they were cold." He reached for two glasses borrowed from the chow hall on the refrigerator top and poured two fingers in both.

"Now there's only one way to appreciate the quality of this finest of all fermentation, son, and that's neat. You don't want to bruise it with ice or taint it with water." He took a glass in each hand and handed one to John. "It's just a damn shame we've both already polluted our taste buds with that junior officer stuff we had at the Pub." He held his glass up for a toast and John imitated him. "Here's to duty, honor, country…and faster airplanes." The colonel was a different man off-duty with a few belts in him—friendlier and more relaxed.

Colonel English threw back a third of the glass, held it in his mouth briefly, swallowed and smacked his lips with great pleasure. John took a modest sip and swallowed. He appreciated the velvet fire all the way down his esophagus and into his stomach, where it flamed up and made his earlobes tingle. It was indeed the finest firewater he had ever consumed.

"Wow. That's the finest scotch I've ever tasted, sir. I'll remember this part of this day, too."

"Well, keep flying like you did today and keep your ass out of trouble and someday you'll be able to afford this libation yourself, son." The colonel returned to his Korean War story and numerous others as John sat sipping and listening and congratulating himself on his good fortune. To his knowledge no other lieutenant had ever been invited into the inner sanctum of Lieutenant Colonel Jack English, therein to sip the nectar of the gods.

John was still sober enough to know this was the last place in the world to get knee-walking, no matter how good the scotch, and he rationed his nectar like an old lady, refusing an offer to freshen his glass when the colonel recharged his. But it did enhance his courage enough to ask Colonel English a question that he and Sam had talked about two days ago in Udorn.

"Sir, I've been wondering, and if I'm out of line, send me home, but why on earth are we fighting this war with one hand tied behind our back? Why have we unilaterally quit taking this war to the North Vietnamese heartland? Why are we down here in the south killing our friends in the process of trying to kill our enemies?"

Colonel English looked at the ceiling as he pondered his reply. "Good question...and I'll give you an answer that'll someday be in the history books, if one of five top generals ever writes a truthful biography. Otherwise, you'll be one of a very small group that will ever know this story...and it needs to stay that way. Are we communicating?"

"Yes, sir."

"I thought so. Well, you may know I did a Pentagon tour before coming to Tuy Hoa. Worked the command post there. You've probably heard that lieutenant colonels at the Pentagon are lower than second lieutenants at the fighter squadron level. That is true. The Chairman and all four Joint Chiefs of Staff had a date with old LBJ at the Oval Office and I got to play flunky, carrying their maps and charts and stuff up there for their presentation to the President. Well, when we got there, the easel that was supposed to be waiting for us wasn't—sounds like a military operation, right?—so I got to be a human easel in the Oval Office when the President chewed the asses of FIVE four-star generals like they were some kind of raw recruits at Parris Island or something. This would have been...oh...fall of '65 I think it was." The colonel paused to sip and savor his scotch as he stared at the ceiling.

"Anyway, General Wheeler and the boys were there to convince the President that we could bring old Ho Chi Minh to his knees in three weeks if we would just launch a major non-stop bombing attack on Hanoi and Haiphong with fighters and bombers—they had hardly any air defenses back then. I held the maps like an easel with ears as the generals drew their lines and poked their pointers and made their case, each one of them. They sure had me convinced. Anyway, when they were done the Prez lit into them, calling them every nasty name I'd ever heard and a few I hadn't. Oh, man, could that south Texas politician chew ass. He said there was no way he was going to be responsible for World War III. He said Secretary of Defense MacNamara was right—it would bring China and the USSR into the war and they would launch their ICBM's and the world would come to an end and it would all be the fault of those no good stupid SOB generals over at the Pentagon who didn't know shit from shinola. And, well, as they say, you know the rest of the story. We've been watching American boys die ever since with no end in sight."

"That's a sad story, sir."

"And getting sadder every day...but our job, Lieutenant, is to be good soldiers and follow our orders and do or die. It's been that way since big Julius...Caesar pissed off every mother in Rome when he marched off to Gaul with their sons and it'll be that way till the second comin'. Now I know this probably busts your bubble about duty and patriotism, son. When you're young and idealistic you want to think that the folks that are in charge are smart and know what's going on and have the purist of motives. It ain't that way, ain't ever been that way, ain't ever gonna be that way. Now I need to go to bed while I can still find it, son. Nice chattin' with ya."

"Same here, sir, and thanks for the fine scotch and thanks again for the second chance and I'll do my best...."

"Git outta here 'n quit groveling, boy. It ain't necessary and it ain't becomin' a fighter pilot of your caliber. G'night."

"Good night, sir."

John walked the few yards to his hooch with his head in the clouds. He thought of a dozen questions that he wished he had asked the colonel. He realized that for all that conversation John knew no more about the colonel as a man than he did before he walked in. Did he have a family? Had he ever been married? Where was he from? There was no hint in his room. But John sure knew this much. He was the man, professionally at least, that John wanted to be and the man that he could never adequately repay for all he had done for him—the man who considered "Thank you" a form of groveling.

*   *   *

John didn't know what time he packed it in that night, but the midnight movie was an Academy Award horror flick. The demons got out of the black box and he was swinging from a parachute coming down on top of a crowd of Viet Cong soldiers. Everyone of them had a knife in his hand and they were jumping up and down and cheering like crazy...and his .38 was missing from his shoulder holster. He was hyperventilating so hard he thought his heart would explode.

Suddenly a gust of wind blew his parachute toward a rice paddy. Just as his face splashed into the muddy water, he heard Ron shouting, "Damnit John, this has got to stop! Next time I'm going to throw a whole bucket of water in your face. I've got an 0500 briefing time."

This time even Mike Day and Brian Hanson in the other bunk were awakened by his performance.

"Oh, man, I'm sorry. I'll go sleep out on the sofa," He mumbled. John grabbed his pillow and stopped for aspirin and water on his way through the bathroom. The sofa was about four inches too short for his frame, but his mind was functioning just well enough that he knew he had to give his roommates a break.

He knew he should see a doctor, but he was afraid he'd get grounded for "manifestation of apprehension," an official medical term that covered, among other things, airsickness when guys couldn't get over it and washed out of pilot training. The lieutenants at Dusty's Pub derisively called it chicken-shit-itis, and it was as far removed from John Ellsworth's conscious self-image as the edge of the solar system. He was even afraid that his roommates would report him to the shrink. On top of that he thought maybe Kate's compassionate, clinical look, when her eyes put a hammer lock on his, was due to some telegraphed signal from his tormented soul.

Sleep did not return, so John got up and went for a run, throbbing head and all-fine scotch apparently produced the same aftereffects as the junior grade stuff. Since the age of twelve, running was his antidote for insanity and fear-in-the-night demons. In Vietnam it had the added benefit of helping sweat off a hangover—an antidote for the antidote, he thought.

It was one of those inky nights with at least a billion stars visible. With only shorts and sneakers, he legged it out around the perimeter road just inside the concertina wire. There were just enough low streetlights that looked like taxiway lights to see to run by. Every hundred yards he came upon the mound of a perimeter bunker. He always waved even though they were dark. Those guys were sitting in there with Starlight Scopes that allowed them to see in the dark and he knew they could see him. Talk was they were going to put those things in airplanes soon.

The guards had learned to expect anything from those crazy fighter pilots. He was sure they gave no thought to the one who ran in the middle of the night because it was less painful than the midnight movie.

By the time he returned to the hooch he had covered around three miles. He wandered into the lounge to check the clipboard with tomorrow's flying schedule. It hung on a nail behind the bar. Someone always brought it over from Ops at the end of the day.

He was up for a mission with the old man. "Check ride for Flt. Lead," it said. Snakes and nape to III Corps again. Brief at 1200 hours. Plenty of time left to get some sleep before work.

*   *   *

Lieutenant Colonel Daniel Redman was a unique soul in the world of fighter pilots. In the two months or so that John had known him, he never heard a swear word come out of the colonel's mouth. Although they'd catch him with a Jack Daniels in his hand once in a rare while, no one ever saw him drunk. Everyone genuinely liked him. He stood up for his men. After John's A Shau escapade with the over-stressed wings, the Wing Commander, a bantam rooster of a bird colonel, had suggested to Colonel Redman that the young lieutenant perhaps ought to stand down for a couple weeks and think about it. Colonel Redman, after discussing it with Colonel English, let the Wing Commander know in quiet, polite terms, that it was the lieutenant's first run-in with AAA and he had just watched it kill his friend. His flight leader, Lieutenant Colonel English, had said it was the heaviest he had seen in two wars, and after his initial, frightened reaction the kid was calm and cool, dead on target with his bombs.

"Now do me a favor, son, and don't make a liar out of me with the Wing Commander," Lieutenant Colonel Redman said quietly after he had related that story to John.

"You can count on it, sir, and I really do appreciate your going to bat for me," John responded with all seriousness.

During the pre-flight briefing John went through the checklist items in the greatest detail. Then they saddled up and went out and made toothpicks out of a bunch of trees. They dropped their bombs as the FAC directed. He said there were bunkers down there, but they couldn't see a thing in the dense jungle. They put all their bombs within twenty meters of the FAC's smoking marker rocket. That was another thing about the old man—for a field grade officer he was still a good stick-and-rudder man. Of course they didn't play around on the way home either. War is serious business and fighter pilots are all mature, sane adults...and the earth is flat.

The colonel loved it. He thought John was the best young flight leader he'd seen in a long time and was proud to have such a fine professional on his team. The old man had probably given that speech a few dozen times before, but to John it felt like it was all original thought, inspired by his own brilliant flight leadership. Lieutenant Colonel Redman was six feet tall, clean-shaven-another rarity in the war zone-and stood ramrod straight, but you knew he was a weary, unhappy man. He'd do his job by the book and run the best squadron in the wing, but he'd rather be home with his wife, children and grandchildren. In a lunatic war in a deranged part of a psychotic world, he was an immovable pillar of sanity. John loved him like his own father. He made John a flight leader and if the colonel had asked John to fly a load of napalm to hell for him, he'd have done it.

Instead, Lieutenant Colonel Redman suggested he take a couple of days off and celebrate. "You haven't been off the base since you got here have you?"

"Not on leave, sir."

"Well, why don't you take the courier down to Saigon or hop over to Bangkok and take a bath?"

"That sounds like a great idea, sir. Thank you."

"Just let me know when and where you're going...and congratu-lations, Flight Leader." Lieutenant Colonel Redman stuck out his hand. His handshake was tired. John realized that his own was a real dead fish, too.

The thought occurred to John that his roomie, Ron, might have been talking to the old man about his midnight movies. God knows where that could lead, but he was in too good of spirits to worry about it right now.

John walked out of the briefing room and straight to the phone on the coffee counter next to the equipment room. After an intermi-nable wait, Kate answered the phone.

"Is this Flight Leader Ellsworth?" she asked.

"How did you know?"

"Everyone knew you were scheduled for a check ride with the old man and no one expected you to fail, least of all me," Kate replied.

"Well, thank you. How would you like to celebrate with me?"

"Sure. When and where?" she asked.

"Let me know how soon you can get two days off, starting ASAP, and we'll work around that. I'd like to see Saigon…"

"Two days!" she laughed.

"Am I being too forward? Is that asking too much? Am I crazy?"

"No, no, and probably," she said, still laughing. "I don't know if the Army can move as fast as tomorrow, but let me work on it."

"In the meantime, can you make it over to Dusty's Pub for Happy Hour today?"

"I was planning on it."

"Great. See you in an hour."

John walked back to his quarters from Squadron Ops. It was only half a mile. He took a long, leisurely shower and lay down for awhile, but sleep was impossible. He was wound too tightly. This was some kind of special day, even though the mission was a boring old toothpick maker.

Kate and the team from Phu Hep showed up on time, as usual. Women in the military don't play those make-them-wait games, John decided.

John had staked out their table in the corner. He rose as Kate approached. She walked right up to him, gave him a quick kiss on the lips, flashed that smile that got prettier every time he saw it and said, "Congratulations, John."

"Thanks…. What's your pleasure?"

"Straight cola on the rocks will be fine, and hurry back. Have I got a story for you."

"Hmm." He walked toward the bar in a daze and returned with two colas on ice.

"Tell me your story."

"Well, right after I hung up from talking with you I called MAC-V Headquarters and talked to Daddy. He says a courier flight is coming through here at 1200 tomorrow and he can get us two seats on it. It'll put us at Tan Son Nhut in Saigon at 1400 hours, and he'll be waiting for us."

"Wow. Talk about pulling rank. Does he know about me?"

"He does now. I told him you were an F-100 pilot and a friend. He said a couple of F-100's had just saved one of the companies of the 101st Airborne Division from annihilation in an ambush north of Tay Ninh. When I told him that was you he just went crazy...."

"How did you know? We haven't talked about that," John asked.

"John, stories like that one travel at the speed of sound."

She just sat there, smiling in silence, as he tried to absorb it all. Finally he said, "Friend...hmm...I like the sound of that. I'm also impressed with the way you get things done. Aggressive ladies, especially petite, green-eyed sassy lassies, turn me on."

Her smile turned mischievous. "You're so easy."

Ron came over just as John was fighting an urge to take Kate's hand and lead her to the bunker.

"Hi, Kate. Still wasting your time with this guy, I see," Ron said.

"Hope springs eternal," she responded.

"Ron, you'll be happy to know I'm taking off for two days." He watched Ron closely as he told him but got no visible reaction one way or another as to his role in John's good fortune.

"Good for you...good for me." Good old Ron. He could have spilled the beans about the midnight movies right there in front of Kate, but he didn't. John made a mental note to have a long talk with the friend who tolerated a nightmarish roommate.

"What shall we do about accommodations?" John asked.

"I've taken care of that, too. Daddy says they have this building they use as a Visiting Officers Quarters at MAC-V. Ever since the Tet Offensive it's been too chancy staying downtown. General Abrams has moved all his staff inside the perimeter fence. Daddy used to share this beautiful French colonial house with a couple of other men, complete with domestic staff of Vietnamese. He really hated to give that up. Anyway, he says we can use his car and driver to see the sights. Staff Sergeant Billy Ray Fosbury from Waycross, Georgia, is Daddy's aide and driver. You'll like him. Also, we're on for dinner tomorrow night at the Officer's Open Mess with Daddy. He wants to introduce you to General Abrams, so pack a pair of Class B's and trim your mustache back to regulation."

"You are amazing, Kate, but what am I going to do with my hands without a mustache to twirl?" John asked.

"I'm going to miss those little curls too, Handsome John, but I'm afraid that's the price we're just going to have to pay," she said.

"Well, guess I'll pay. I've never been even close to a four-star general before."

"Daddy thinks the world of General Abrams. He's a sweet man…"

"I've never heard a general described as sweet before. I thought the Army was like a septic tank, only the really big chunks floated to the top," he said.

Kate laughed, but only for an instant. "Don't toss that one out at the dinner table tomorrow night, Lieutenant."

"Course not. I told you I don't have a death wish." Kate cringed at his reaction, and John immediately regretted his words. "Wow, two days and two nights in the Paris of the Orient with the prettiest lady I know. Now I'm going to have to have a scotch on the rocks or I won't sleep a wink tonight." He rose to go to the bar.

Somehow John got through the night peacefully. Perhaps it had something to do with the anticipation of a flight the next day and since he was off the next day the killer midnight butterflies took a pass. He decided to try to keep a mental record of that. Maybe he could self-diagnose this malady and cure it himself.

*   *   *

At high noon they stood in the shade of the Tuy Hoa Base Operations building on the parking ramp side. It wasn't air conditioned inside and the shade outside was only a fraction of a degree cooler. The perforated steel planking was sizzling in the intense mid-day sun. John wore his flying suit. Kate was in an olive drab skirt and blouse.

"Your Class B's become you more than fatigues," John observed.

"Thank you, but anything is more becoming on anybody than jungle fatigues," she answered.

Their conversation was interrupted by the sound of a flight of four F-100's overhead in echelon right formation on initial approach. Everyone was sucked in tight—about four-foot spacing. Over the noise John explained to Kate how it was important to put on a good show for those unfortunate souls who were condemned to spending the war with both feet on the ground, especially the maintenance crew chiefs. They spent all day in the oven of those parking revetments where there wasn't a breath of air. Seeing their plane looking good on initial approach was the closest thing to a thrill they ever got on the job.

One thousand feet above the runway and half way down it, the lead plane snapped smartly into a sixty-degree banked turn to the left for his downwind landing leg. He was followed in three-second intervals by number two, three and four.

John concluded, "As many times as I've watched that scene, it still gives me chills."

"I think that's a sign of true love," she said wistfully, unsmiling. "And apparently your flying reflects it."

A T-39 slanted across the ramp pointed right toward them. It came to a stop not thirty feet away as the tail-mounted jet engine on the left side was winding down. The door hinged downward on the left side of the fuselage just forward of the wing and a sergeant came down the steps built into the back of the cabin door. He swapped canvass courier pouches with another sergeant from Base Ops and walked over to Kate and John.

"Lieutenants Ellsworth and Moffit?" he asked as he saluted. They both nodded and returned the salute. "Come aboard sir, ma'am, and we'll be on our way."

They got airborne in half the distance of a fully loaded F-100 and climbed twice as fast, curving around to the south. They shared the small cabin with the crew chief, several courier pouches and a half dozen cardboard boxes in the luggage racks aft. Kate and John sat facing one another across a small table. John rode backwards. It was not easy to talk over the whine of two jet engines, so Kate gazed intently out the window at the Vietnamese countryside. John fixed his gaze on Kate's profile. Her short, dark hair curved behind her ears, a single small, golden globe was attached to each pierced ear-lobe, and her nose turned up slightly. Maybe this furlough would be a time of enlightenment, when this enigmatic tattooed lady would reveal who she really was. Saigon did not strike John as intriguing, in anticipation, as the green-eyed little lady with her cheek against the porthole.

Colonel Oswald "Ozzie" Moffit was a short, fire-plug of a man with square jaw, bushy black eyebrows and regulation U.S. Army issue blood in his veins. His chest was so broad that his hairy arms swung at nearly 45-degree angles to his torso. He walked across the apron of Tan Son Nhut Air Base like a man with a lot of important things to do and not much time to do them.

John followed Kate off the T-39, clunked his flying boots together and gave the colonel his saltiest fighter pilot salute. Colonel Moffit returned the salute with barely a glance and enveloped Kate in a bear hug.

"Hello, sweetheart. You look lovelier every time I see you. God, I've missed you."

"Oh, Daddy, I've missed you, too." Kate talked like she was having trouble breathing inside that bear hug. "I want you to meet my friend, John Ellsworth."

With that Colonel Moffit allowed Kate her freedom and stuck out a beefy hand. "I'm honored to meet you, John Ellsworth."

John saw it coming but he was beaten anyway and his hand was crushed in the colonel's death grip.

"I briefed General Abrams myself this morning on your rescue mission in III Corps. He's anxious to meet you, too. He's entertaining some Pentagon pukes for dinner tonight, but he asked if he could meet you afterwards."

"I'd be most honored, sir."

"Great. Now here's the plan." He was a no-nonsense talker. "I've got to get over to Long Binh. I'm catching a helicopter up the ramp aways here. Those asinine politicians back in Washington have got us jumping through hoops. Sergeant Fosbury will drop me off and then take you over to the MAC-V visiting officer's quarters. They're expecting you. There's a swimming pool on the roof. Enjoy yourselves. Cocktails at 1800, dinner at 1900. Any questions?"

"No, sir." John wouldn't have had the nerve to ask if there had been.

"Then let's move 'em out."

The T-39 crew chief had carried their bags to the Ford sedan and Sergeant Fosbury put them in the trunk.

Colonel Ozzie rode in front for that short trip, allowing Kate and John to sit together in the rear seat. She smiled and put her hand on his on the car seat between them.

"See you kids tonight. Have fun." And the colonel was gone.
It took an hour to thread through the humanity-choked road from Tan Son Nhut, northwest of the city, to the MAC-V Visiting Officers Quarters. Billy Ray played the polite tour guide. Kate apparently didn't think it appropriate to have any serious discussions in the presence of Daddy's batman, so John was content to hold her hand. Saigon had obviously been a lovely place a few decades ago, when the French were in charge. The influence showed in the architecture and the elegant dress of the higher-class Vietnamese ladies. They were almost a different race from their pajama-clad country cousins. But the city was clearly long in the tooth now-rundown and seriously over populated.

Billy Ray parked in front of the VOQ, in the slot marked "General Officers Only" and nearest to the door, of course. It was just a three-story, square box with an exterior of tired tan stucco that had probably begun life 30 or 40 years ago as a French hotel. He jumped out and opened the door for Kate, then John and proceeded to open the trunk.

They were assigned adjacent rooms on the second floor by an enlisted man behind the counter of the tiny, threadbare lobby, either in spite of or because of the colonel's planning. It wasn't the Ritz-closer to a 1950's Route 66 motel—but it was certainly adequate. They bid Sergeant Fosbury adieu and John carried Kate's luggage into her room. It contained only the basics-four tan walls, one each double bed, window, table and chair and bath. He put her suitcase down and she was waiting for him. She embraced him enthusiastically and they kissed, standing in the middle of her room.

"How about a dip in the pool before dinner?" she asked.

"Sounds great to me."

"Give me thirty minutes to unpack and then knock on my door."

"Roger that." John did an about-face and headed out the door, down the hall and into his room. It was a mirror image of Kate's. He took three minutes to unpack, hang out his class B's and get into some civilian slacks and shirt. He went down to the check-in counter and got directions to the liquor store. Twenty minutes later he returned with two cold six-packs of beer and a fifth of expensive scotch.

He heard the shower running in Kate's room on the other side of the wall, so he did the same. One minute early, attired in swim trunks and barefoot, with a six-pack of beer wrapped in a towel, he knocked on Kate's door. She opened the door wearing her famous yellow two-piece and beach cover-up. On tiptoe, she gave him a quick peck and then scurried around for slippers, towel and suntan lotion.

"All set," she said with a smile.

They took the stairway up to the rooftop pool, with Kate in the lead and John in close trail. The pool and deck areas were deserted. The pool felt like an over-sized hot tub in the late afternoon sun but was refreshing and salt-free. The trip had been about three hours, door-to-door, with a half-dozen intermediate stops by the courier plane. After a couple of leisurely laps to remove the kinks of travel, John rested with his feet on the bottom and his back against the wall at the five-foot depth. Kate snuggled up backside to John and he encircled her waist with one hand from behind. It was just deep enough that she needed his arm to hold her head out of the water.

"What shall we see this weekend?" John asked.

"Well, there's the Cercle Sportif, an elegant old French estate that's now an athletic club and restaurant. The press and embassy people hang out there. Then we'll have to run down to the big Army PX in Cholon and check out the stereo gear and cameras and stuff. They have those new Japanese watches—Seiko, I think they're called. Then perhaps a drive down Tu Do Street, just to view the scenery."

"Kate, you talk like you've been here before."

"No, I haven't. Those were just some suggestions Daddy had. Sound okay? Sergeant Fosbury will be at our beck and call."

"Sounds great! Let's lay on the deck and bake awhile."

"Okay." Kate came up out of the water on to the sun deck as gracefully as a swan.

John grabbed the suntan lotion as she spread the towel.

"May I?" he asked holding up the bottle of lotion.

"Sure," Kate said with a grin.

Back side. Front side. John covered every delicious nook and cranny of her trim, compact little body that wasn't covered by yellow material.

"Mmmmmmmm, good hands. You do great work, John."

"Thanks. My F-100 likes good hands too when we dance the wild blue."

"You know there's a psychiatric term for people who love inanimate objects."

"Don't tell me. I don't want to know, Nurse Moffit." John knew he had asked for that one, so he decided to get off the shoptalk. The half-wall of the rooftop pool deck shut out the skyline of Saigon as they lay on the deck. It was just sun, clouds and water, and Kate and John.

"It feels like another world here doesn't it? Wouldn't this be a good place for time to stand still—no yesterday, no tomorrow, only now forever and ever?"

"You can be a poet when you want to be. When you talk like that I know there's hope for you." Kate rolled over and used her cover-up for a pillow.

"Well, I confess I just made that stuff up."

"Do you ever think about why you are here...what life is all about?"

Kate was winding up again and John didn't mind. Her presence alone on a rooftop in Saigon was worth that price.

"Yes, I have pondered the great questions of existence on this crazy planet, Kate, but I'm not pumping from a very deep well on the subject of metaphysics. I was a business major in college and recently my priorities have been more in the realm of just staying alive."

"Then why do you look for trouble?"

"Kate, I do not 'look' for trouble." In spite of his best intentions he was already exasperated. "Why do you assume that I do?" He didn't wait for an answer. "My job is to be the best fighter pilot I can be. I do that by busting assets, making the enemy die for his country and saving American lives. Isn't that how wars are won? Isn't that the reason my country sent me here? Don't these people and our soldiers deserve this?" His anger was showing now.

She stared intently into John's eyes without speaking and he felt his vulnerability welling up again.

"Kate, I love the South Vietnamese people. I want to help them. They don't want to harm anybody. They just want to be left alone to raise their families. They ask for less than any humans I know- just an acre or two to grow their rice and feed their families. I have absolutely no guilt feelings about killing the people who are trying to take away their land and their freedom and their lives and killing my friends in the process."

"Then what do you think is causing your nightmares, John?"

"How did..."

"Never mind."

"Well...uh...fear, I guess, Doctor. It doesn't seem to be a problem when the adrenaline is flowing...and I don't have time to think about it."

Kate sat up and scooted around to John's side. She put her arm around his shoulders. "John...that's a brave thing for you to admit. If you were not afraid...I would not be sitting here with you. Fear is healthy...and very conducive to longevity in your endeavors. It is a sick mind that knows no fear. I know...."

"Does that mean that you look at me as just some kind of medical project? Am I just your lab rat?" He wanted to look her in the eye but he was afraid he would not like what he saw.

Kate laughed and the tension was broken. She tweaked his nose. "Can you wiggle your nose like a little white mouse?" She leaned over and kissed him on the cheek. "I would never be caught kissing a rat," she said and she kissed him again. "John, I'm just trying to understand you."

A flood of relief washed through John. He turned and kissed her on the lips and his whole body chilled. A long soulful kiss later, he moved his head away just far enough for his eyes to focus on hers. "Are you making any progress?"

"I think so, country boy."

* * *

John dropped Kate off at her door at 1645. "Be ready at 1750. I believe the O'Club is about a five minute walk from here and we certainly don't want to keep the Colonel waiting, do we?" John said.

With a big smile, Kate said, "Did you like my Daddy?"

"Yes, I did. And I was very impressed."

"He liked you, too. I have never heard him address a junior officer without his rank before. That's a very good sign." She gave him a quick kiss and pirouetted into her room.

John figured he had time for a ten-minute catnap, and he fell spread-eagled onto the bed. He heard the shower come on in Kate's bathroom and he thought he could hear singing.

Exactly ten minutes later his eyes came open—he never needed an alarm clock, except for mornings after heavy drinking occasions. The shower had stopped next door. He grabbed the four remaining bottles of beer and opened the tiny refrigerator, which doubled as a nightstand. It wasn't working. He checked the thermostat and the electric outlet—nothing amiss there. Without thinking, he grabbed the beer and headed out the door, still in his swimsuit.

He knocked gently on Kate's door.

"Who's there?" a cheerful voice said.

"Housekeeping," he answered.

Kate opened the door, a small towel wrapped around her hair and a bath towel wrapped around her torso, tucked under her arms and hanging to mid-thigh.

"Ooh, what a handsome housekeeper."

"May I borrow a cup of cold air? My fridge isn't working."

"Sure, neighbor." She led him to her refrigerator and opened the door.

He deposited the beer on the shelf and stood up.

"I'm glad you're here. I need your help. Have a seat." She pushed him playfully back onto the bed. "I can't decide which dress to wear to dinner."

"How about the olive drab one?"

"No, no, silly boy. No uniforms. This is Paris East and I must wear an evening dress." She pulled two dresses from the closet, one black and apparently off-the-shoulder, with two very thin straps holding it on the hanger. The other was emerald green and matched her eyes perfectly. The bodice was more demure. It gathered at the waist, with a full skirt out of something that looked like chiffon.

She held them up by their hangers, one on each side with her hands just above shoulder height, one leg bent at the knee and crossed in front of the other like a Parisian model. The white towel on her head and around her torso funneled his attention to those magnetic green eyes.

"Which one do you like best?"

Without hesitation he answered, "The one that matches your eyes."

"I like a man who know what he wants." She brought the dress down and in front of her. "Now kiss me quick and go get ready."

He rose from his seat on the bed, stooped to kiss her lightly on the lips then headed for the door.

*   *   *

Standing under the pitiful dribble of water coming from the corroded shower head, John pondered the events of the afternoon. Katherine Moffit was more relaxed, more open, but still an utter mystery to him. His soul baring on the rooftop seemed to do no damage, and he felt he was getting better at handling her probing questions. He thought briefly about who must have told her about his nightmares. It had to be one of his roommates, but his response to her comment seemed to have a positive effect on her disposition. Her non-verbal communication seemed genuinely affectionate, and he was attracted to her, but the tattooed lady who probed the depths of his soul still had not revealed who she was.

*   *   *

Colonel Moffit was waiting at the bar as the doorman ushered them in. Security had gotten a lot tighter since the Tet Offensive in the spring. They had flashed their I.D. cards twice to get that far, even though John wore a pair of khakis. Colonel Moffit hopped off the barstool, and once again, Kate came first. He held her by the shoulders at arm's length, beaming as he looked her over and kissed her cheek.

"You look lovely in that dress, Kate. Green is your color."

"Thanks, Daddy. John thinks so, too." Kate was positively giddy. She was a different person in her father's presence—a sweet, lovable little girl.

With that Ozzie turned to John and stuck out his hand. This time John came a little closer to holding his own.

"How are the accommodations, John?"

"They're fine, sir, and the roof-top pool is delightful."

"How about a drink?"

"Please. I'll have a scotch and soda, tall glass." He intended to make it last the entire cocktail hour.

"I'll have the same, Daddy."

The bartender had been patiently waiting and moved to fix the drinks without Colonel Moffit having to repeat the order. The Colonel was half way through a bourbon on the rocks, judging from his breath and his glass.

Kate mounted the barstool on the Colonel's right and John sat on Kate's right. "Daddy, I filled John in on some of your suggestions for doing the town. Do we need reservations at the Cercle Sportif for lunch?"

"I'll have Sergeant Fosbury check it out and make them if necessary. I'm going to be traveling all day tomorrow, from before sun up till after dark, so Sergeant Fosbury will be at your disposal. Things have been pretty quiet downtown lately, but you need to keep the windows rolled up when you're in the car—the air conditioner works fine. Sergeant Fosbury keeps an M-16 in front on the passenger seat and there's one on the back seat for me, or you in this case. You checked out on that piece, John?"

"Yes, sir, but I'm more comfortable with something considerably bigger."

"I'm sure. And quite a bit faster than a Ford Sedan, too. I tell you, young man, if I were your age I'd be doing the same thing. The Army just can't offer anything comparable to a jet fighter. I don't know how you do it, going that fast that close to the ground and bombing with such pin-point accuracy. The Army would be out of business without you guys in this war. There's about a hundred men up north of Tay Ninh that think the sun rises and sets on your backside, boy. You'll be hearing from them. They're talking Silver Star. Got one of those?"

"No, sir. Supposedly there's a DFC in the mill somewhere, for some work we did up around the A Shau."

"Well, it'll come across my desk. That's higher than a Distinguished Flying Cross, you know."

John didn't know why, but this conversation was making him very uncomfortable. He tried to get off the subject.

"Yes, sir, I know. I'd be very honored. The F-100 is a fine piece of machinery and flies like an angel. There are newer, more advanced planes here—F-4's, A-6's, A-7's, and F-105's—but when it comes to visual bombing, nothing with a jet engine can touch it, if it's flown by a good pilot. It's the last of the seat-of-the-pants fighters and you just can't beat the T.L.A.R. method in the hands of an experienced pilot."

"T.L.A.R.?" Kate asked.

"That-looks-about-right," John said, closing one eye and holding his right hand in front of him, his thumb punching an imaginary pickle button on an imaginary control stick.

"Isn't that amazing," Colonel Moffit marveled. "All that technology and it still comes down to Kentucky windage."

Kate was in heaven, a perpetual smile on her face and her hands in constant motion. She hugged Daddy's big arm, squeezed John's triceps, leaned her head against his shoulder, then Daddy's shoulder. Her head swiveled like a front-row-center spectator at a tennis match. It was clear that John had made Kate's short list of most important men in the universe, at least for this night.

By dinnertime Colonel Moffit had polished off his third bourbon on the rocks and was mellowing quite nicely. Three abreast with arms locked, Kate in the middle, they paraded into the dining room. It was a subdued, dimly lit place. Really pretty elegant for a war zone-table cloths, wine glasses, water glasses, five piece silver place settings and a Caucasian piano player. Not a bad place to unwind after a hard day at the office, juggling intractable military problems with preposterous political solutions, John thought. Then, right at dinnertime, all of America gets to second-guess you through the biased eyes of the evening TV newsman. He wouldn't swap his cramped airborne office with any general in the place—not even old Abe himself-for all the rice in the Mekong Delta.

General Abrams was sitting at a large circular table across the room, with three distinguished looking diplomatic types and two other military men with multiple stars on their collars. His shoulders were a little stooped. John wondered if the war had done that already—he'd only replaced General Westmoreland a month ago. He had a wide, friendly face. John could understand why Kate had called him "sweet"—not at all like a large chunk floating atop the septic tank.

"Would you care to see a wine list, sir?" a very proper waiter asked Colonel Moffit. John guessed he was an enlisted man waiting tables in his off-duty time, judging from his white-sidewalled haircut.

"Yes, please, and what's the special tonight?"

"Our special tonight is Chicken Kiev, with white wine sauce, rice pilaf and mixed vegetables or roast prime beef au jus, sir."

Kate and John chose the Chicken Kiev while the colonel perused the wine list.

"I'll have the roast prime, rare, and bring us a bottle of Chateauneuf du Pape and a bottle of Pouilly Fuisse, please."

The conversation took a decidedly lighter tone. The colonel regaled John and embarrassed Kate with stories of her youth in Ft. Benning, Georgia, Ft. Leonard Wood, Missouri, and all the other garden spots the U.S. Army sends its families. Kate was an only child and Daddy was clearly a doting father. John forced himself to go long on the water and short on the white wine, nodding in agreement, laughing at all the proper places and enjoying every minute of dinner with the Moffit family, sans Mother.

As they were polishing off a dessert of fresh strawberries and cream, the pow-wow at the big circular table broke up. General Abrams ambled over to the table. Four stars on one khaki shirt collar were an impressive sight but he was as comfortable as an old shoe. He absolutely shattered John's stereotype of generals. They all rose as he approached.

"Colonel Moffit, you have a lovely daughter. Ma'am it's a pleasure to meet you. Such beauty is a rare thing around this place."

"Thank you, General. I'd like you to meet my friend, Lieutenant John Ellsworth," Kate said with an awed but friendly tone.

He had big hands, but a gentle handshake, perhaps because he shook Kate's hand ahead of John's.

"Lieutenant Ellsworth, it's my pleasure to meet you. I've heard some very good things about you."

"Thank you, sir. I'm honored to meet you."

"General, you'll be getting a Silver Star citation request across your desk in a few weeks on Lieutenant Ellsworth," Ozzie interjected.

"It will be an honor, Ozzie. Lieutenant, when the paperwork has gone through all the channels, come on back down here and I'll pin it on you myself. Can you arrange that Colonel Moffit?"

"Yes, sir."

wn away. John was pretty impressed himself. He
was what it felt like to a tennis star when he read
the sports pages.

ids enjoy yourselves. Colonel Moffit, you must be
proud."

"Yes, sir, I am. Goodnight, sir," Ozzie said.

Their table was silent in the afterglow of meeting history up
close and personal. General Creighton W. Abrams was a famous
World War II tank commander—they even named the Army's new
tank after him. John knew it was a moment he'd someday relate to
his grandchildren. Yes, sir, kids, he even pinned on my Silver Star.

Colonel Moffit was holding his wineglass up in the air in front of
him and his lips were moving.

"...a toast to Silver Stars."

Clink, clink, clink. John recovered and got with the program.

"To the Moffit family." A triple clink.

"To a great evening in Paris East." Triple clink.

"Well, kids, it's taps for me. I've got a long day tomorrow. Stay
here as long as you like. I instructed the bartender not to let you pay
for anything. There'll be a small dance band cranking up in a few
minutes. What time shall I send Sergeant Fosbury around in the
morning?"

"We're on vacation, Daddy. Can we call him when we get
squared away?"

"Sure, Precious." He gave her a bear hug and a kiss. "Goodnight.
Goodnight, John."

"Goodnight, sir, and thanks very much for an unforgettable
evening."

"Oh, you're welcome. My God, you earned it, boy. Take good
care of my daughter. She's all Ethel and I have. I don't know what
we'd do if something happened to her."

"You can count on it, sir." John did not want to contemplate what
the Colonel would do if he failed to take care of Ozzie's only daughter.

Kate and John sat back down as Colonel Moffit walked across the
dining room.

John put his hand on Kate's hand on the table and smiled at her
wordlessly. She tilted her head back, closed her eyes and inhaled
deeply.

"Oh, John, is this night for real? Am I dreaming?"

"Near as I can tell this is the real McCoy. Would you care to dance?"

"Oh, be still my heart." She raised her hand like a proper Southern debutante who'd just been asked to dance by the man of her dreams. John had never seen her so happy. He liked her this way. He liked her a lot.

The band played old folks' music—the kind they could dance cheek-to-cheek to and the only kind John cared to hear. They floated around the deserted dance floor in a world of their own, Kate very deftly managing to stay out of the way of both of John's left feet.

Halfway through the third consecutive slow dance, Kate reached up and pulled his head down to whisper in his ear.

"Let's call it a day, Handsome John."

*   *   *

Kate and John walked hand in hand down the dimly lit sidewalk to the VOQ. Although it was only 2200, it was a pretty quiet place-not at all like Tuy Hoa Air Base.

As they approached Kate's room, she turned to him and said, "Would you like to go for a quick swim in the moonlight?"

"Sure. Let me hang up this uniform. It's the only one I brought."

"I want to change, too. Knock on my door as soon as you're ready." She was half way through the door when she stopped, turned around and came to him. Squeezing him with all her might she inhaled deeply through clenched teeth and said, "John, I can't remember when I've had a more enjoyable evening."

Sixty seconds later John was standing in front of her door again in swim trunks and bare feet. He knocked gently on the door.

"It's open," he heard Kate say.

She was just buttoning her cover-up when he came through the door.

"Shall we take some beer?"

"Who needs it?" he said.

It had been months since John had gone through an evening with such a minuscule ration of alcohol.

There was only one dim yellow patio light to illuminate the pool deck but that and a quarter moon were just enough. Saigon was a sea of deep yellow lights with patches of blackness where no electricity existed. The dark seemed darker in that part of the world. Periodically the skyline would be broken by the white phosphorus light of a flare floating to earth under a small parachute. Out of the west there was the rhythmic pounding of heavy artillery, probably 155-millimeter howitzers, as the Army probed for the illusive VC.

They sat down at poolside and slowly slid into the water. Once again the rest of the world disappeared behind the half-wall of the pool deck. The water was as warm as the womb. John wrapped his arms around Kate from behind and leaned back against the pool wall. Her buoyancy put her nearly at his height as he leaned down to kiss her neck. She crossed her arms and held his hands in hers. They said nothing for a long time. No words could enhance the magic of that moment.

Kate loosened her hairy bandoleer and rotated in John's arms. She wrapped her arms around his neck and their lips met. She felt so fine. They kissed and caressed and snuggled and laughed in the moonlight.

It seemed they'd only been there a few minutes when John heard the chimes of a distant church steeple in the muggy night. He counted to twelve.

"Bedtime, don't you think?"

"Yeah." He had no idea what was coming next.

John lifted Kate out of the water and sat her on the deck. As he pulled himself out of the water she dried off and put on her cover-up.

They went down the stairs and stopped at the door to Kate's room.

"Good night, John." Kate stood on tiptoe as they embraced. "It really was a delightful day."

"And our holiday has only begun," John answered without, he hoped, betraying the disappointment he felt. "Good night, Kate."

John walked down the hall and turned into his room. He told himself, as he undressed, that he really didn't expect this evening to end any other way. Most of life might be accelerated in the war zone, but that didn't include the mating dance with Katherine Moffit.

At 1100 John called Sergeant Billy Ray Fosbury from Kate's room. "Sergeant Fosbury, we're getting a late start this morning. Were you able to find out if Cercle Sportif requires reservations for lunch?"

"Yes, sir. I called them earlier and they said reservations are not required. Lunch is served from 1100 to 1400 hours. What time would you like to go?"

"Could you come by in thirty minutes?"

"Yes, sir. I'll be there in thirty minutes, sir."

"Thanks, Sergeant. Good-bye."

John hung up the phone and watched Kate, dressed in a full blue skirt and white blouse, brushing her hair in front of the bathroom mirror.

It suddenly occurred to John that Kate did not wear makeup. When her hair was brushed she was ready to go. Most female boudoir scenes are a three-act play, but with Kate it was a short, sexy skit.

She came out of the bathroom smiling.

"Penny for your thoughts."

"I just now realized you don't wear makeup."

"Would you prefer that I did?"

"Heavens, no. It would be a waste of time and money."

John had on civvies—gray slacks, yellow knit shirt and loafers. Billy had told them it was better to look like reporters or writers than military people in this town.

Sergeant Fosbury was waiting in the general officers' parking spot with the car running and windows up. It was only about a dozen steps through the steam bath of mid-day Saigon from the air-conditioned comfort of the VOQ to the car.

He saw them coming and jumped to open the door. "Good morning, sir, ma'am," he said as they both went in the same rear door.

"Good morning, Sergeant. We really appreciate your escorting us around."

"My pleasure, sir." He had slid behind the wheel and turned to face them. "I would like to give you all a short emergency preparedness briefing before we begin. If we should run into any trouble both of you get down on the floor in the back. The M-16 is on the floor back there. You can put it on the seat beside you if you like, sir. There is a clip in it, safety on, but no shell in the chamber. It's set for full automatic. Colonel Moffit said you're checked out on it." John nodded.

"There are two more clips under the seat. There are more ammo clips in the glove compartment along with two hand grenades. I would also suggest you sort of keep an eye on where we go so you could find your way back alone if anything happened to me. The radio here is tied into headquarters security and you can call for help if needed, but you need to be able to tell them where you are. I'm not trying to scare ya'll, ma'am, sir, we've never had to use these weapons, but we believe in being prepared.

"Understood, Sergeant. Such are the hazards of vacationing in the war zone, I guess."

"What time did Daddy get off this morning, Billy?" Kate asked.

"I put him on the helicopter at sun-up, ma'am. I'm sure you didn't see it but the sunrise was spectacular this morning." Billy Ray was immaculate in his olive-drab uniform. It looked like his shiny black hair was tamed with Wildroot.

Two turns later John was lost and completely turned around. He had always had a terrible sense of direction. Some guys could point to North no matter where they were, but not John. If airplanes didn't have compasses he'd never find his way home.

Black pedicabs were everywhere. They looked like a rickshaw cab, one wheel on either side, but the driver pedaled from behind, where there was one wheel—sort of like a tricycle pedaled backwards. The cab held one paying passenger comfortably and two if they were Vietnamese. The back, sidewalls and top provided sun protection and privacy from every angle except dead ahead—which is exactly what the passenger would be in a head-on collision.

They rode pretty much in silence as they took in all the sights-the pedicabs, motorscooters, a few small French Renaults and Citroens. Street vendors, squatting in Oriental fashion, were cooking something Kate and John were spared from smelling inside the car. There were human-drawn, two-wheeled carts with bags of what was probably rice. The Mekong Delta, which was everything south of Saigon, was one of the best and largest rice growing regions in the world. Men and women were carrying two big buckets on carry poles across their shoulders. Dozens and dozens of street vendors were selling U.S. made cigarettes, watches, small radios and jewelry-all black market stuff. John wondered where they got it all.

The thoroughfares were wide and cobblestoned. There were no lane markers, so the various forms of traffic moved more in the nature of a cattle drive than the thin orderly ribbons of vehicles on the Eisenhower Expressway.

It occurred to John that if Sergeant Billy Ray Fosbury ever had to run from trouble, that Ford sedan was going to leave a lot of dead pedestrians, street vendors, pedicab clients and drivers in its wake. It also struck him that Billy Ray, for all his southern charm and genteel manner, would not hesitate to do so if that's what it took to save the colonel's precious daughter. He found that observation comforting.

They came to a large traffic circle with a statue of some unknown Caucasian, covered with bird droppings, in the center. A huge Catholic church with a tall steeple dominated the landscape. John wondered if it was the church bell he had heard at midnight. The herd milled right and spit them out the other side of the traffic circle. Shortly thereafter, they were in front of the Cercle Sportif. They were waved through the gate in a high, masonry wall into a magnificent French colonial setting. It wasn't Versailles and needed a little paint in places, but in the middle of a troubled city it was an oasis of beauty and tranquillity. Were it not for the asphalt parking area, it would have felt like they had stepped through a time warp into circa 1897.

"Sergeant Fosbury, would you care to eat with us?" John was hoping he'd say no.

"No, sir, I must stay with the vehicle when it's off base."

"Can I bring you something?"

"That's very kind, sir, but I packed a sandwich. Enjoy your lunch."

"Thanks, Billy Ray," Kate said as she stepped out of the car and squeezed the sergeant's arm.

Cercle Sportif obviously began life as some very wealthy person's mansion. It had probably been one of the rubber plantation owners around the turn of the century. They were escorted to a huge verandah on the back side of the house. The twenty-five or so circular tables all had views of a manicured garden, centered on a reflecting pool about twenty feet wide and seventy-five feet long. Gravel walkways led through the garden with low, neatly trimmed hedges separating beds of roses from beds of bird-of-paradise and other beautiful flowers that John had never seen before. Huge bougainvillea cascaded over the back wall, seventy-five yards behind the house, in fluorescent pink brilliance. Off to the left he saw several tennis courts. It was truly a world of its own, an island of staid affluence in a sea of poverty and chaos.

John and Kate were ushered to a table near the verandah railing with a fabulous view of the gardens through white diagonal latticework. The place was filling up steadily with the noonday crowd. A handful of people looked self-important and familiar. Maybe he had seen them on TV.

"John, are you going to make the Air Force a career?" Kate arranged a white cloth napkin in her lap.

"They'll need dynamite to blast me out of the cockpit at 65, Kate."

Kate smiled and shook her head as if she were looking at a lovable pup who had just soiled the living room carpet. "Dumb question," she said.

"I know, you think I'm nuts." He really didn't want every conversation to begin with a confrontation, but this lady obviously loathed small talk as much as he did, so he tossed her a reconciliation lead. "I really don't care for the military Mickey Mouse. It's just the price you pay to fly fighters."

Now that had the desired results. She sat back in her chair and loosened up a bit. "Ever think about the airlines?"

"Yeah...bo-o-r-r-ing. All that right-side-up stuff from point A to B."

A waitress showed up and interrupted what was shaping up to be an emotional yo-yo of a conversation.

"Would you care for a cocktail before lunch?" a pretty Vietnamese lady in a white ao dai asked in perfect English.

"I would prefer a cup of coffee," Kate said.

"Make it two," John added. Before Kate could wind up on the same subject again John asked, " What do you hope to do at Denver General?"

"I'm interested in this new open heart surgery. You know, they're starting to do some amazing things with by-pass surgery—prolonging life in heart patients. That interests me a great deal. I may have to go back to school for awhile."

"You'd be great at that, Kate. That kind of work is sort of like flying fighters. Minimal margin for error, keen senses, split-second decisions and all that...."

"Well, perhaps, but it's not life-threatening. No one is shooting at me. And we're trying to save lives, not take them."

They spent nearly two hours at Cercle Sportif. Leaving the verandah they decided to drive down to Cholon and do some shopping at the big PX. Actually Kate decided, but John would have agreed to anything.

Billy Ray eased the Ford back out into the river of Oriental humanity and they headed for Cholon.

Cholon was the Chinatown of Saigon, but it all looked the same to John. It had borne the brunt of the Tet Offensive five months earlier. Several city blocks were nothing but piles of rubble and charred, burned-out shells of buildings. The Army Post Exchange, though not very heavily fortified, stood untouched amid this rubble. It was a bastion of American capitalism in the middle of a city teetering at the subsistence level. John wondered if perhaps the PX survived Tet unscathed because it was the main supplier of all those street vendors peddling black market cigarettes, watches, jewelry, and portable radios—stuff an enlisted man could get out in his lunch box if he was trying to feed a family on Army pay.

The traffic was a lot lighter in Cholon. Not many people could live in that rubble. Another olive drab Ford sedan passed them as they moved slowly along listening to Sergeant Fosbury's travelogue. Its back seat contained an Army colonel and a Vietnamese military officer. Billy Ray waved as he recognized the driver. The car turned left at the next intersection and Billy Ray followed.

As Billy Ray turned the corner, they could see there was some kind of accident blocking the street ahead. The car that had just passed them was about fifty yards in front. They watched as the brake lights came on and it came to a complete stop, horn honking. Billy slowed down and they were no more than thirty yards behind the car when a small figure clad in black darted out of the crowd, threw some kind of package under the car and sprinted in John and Kate's direction.

Even as Billy Ray was hitting the brakes John was yelling, "Stop, stop, Billy. Get down, Kate!" John jammed her down hard onto the floor and covered her body with his. In the next instant a deafening explosion rang in their ears and the concussion pushed their car backwards. Without thinking, John raised up to see if the sprinting figure in black had a similar present for them. The blast had knocked the man down but he was getting to his feet. He ran right on by their car—escape appeared to be the only thought on his mind. John caught a fleeting glimpse of jet-black hair, dark glasses and elbows and knees as he came right by his side of the car. If he'd been thinking quickly enough, he could have thrown open the car door and stopped him in his tracks, but there was still a chance he could get him.

John reached for the M-16, yelling like a maniac. "Billy, get on that radio. Stay down, Kate." He jumped out of the car and ran through a hail of falling debris. The guy had about a twenty-yard lead on John. He flipped off the safety and jacked a round into the chamber without looking as he ran. Billy Ray had said it was set on full automatic and John took his word for it. The figure darted off down the deserted alley to the right and between two piles of rubble. As John rounded the pile, the black-clad figure was only about fifteen yards ahead of him going straight away. John stopped, and from a crouch, M-16 at the waist, walked 5.62-millimeter slugs diagonally up his back. His body cartwheeled—his head didn't even hit the ground on the first revolution—and rolled like a rabbit on the dead run hit by a shotgun blast.

He lay in a mangled heap more or less face down as John approached cautiously. John kicked the man gingerly like he'd kick a wounded rattlesnake, fearing it might have enough life left to bite him. The man wasn't dead but he was close. John dropped to his knees and rolled him over. He looked young, maybe fourteen, which meant he was probably twenty-four. He was a bloody mess, with lower jaw broken and hanging at an odd angle. He sounded like he was choking on his own blood. His eyes were open but John didn't think he was seeing anything and he no longer hated the guy. John considered putting him out of his misery, even put the M-16 up to his bloody head, but he couldn't pull the trigger.

John left him there to die a slow death and stumbled back to the street. When he saw the blood and gore in the street, the hate came back. He turned around and looked at the dying man. He was making hideous, pitiful, gurgling sounds as he slowly choked to death, but John still couldn't pull the trigger.

John jogged up to the car. Kate wasn't there. Neither was Billy. He grabbed a second ammo clip out of the glove compartment and trotted anxiously up to the crowd at the scene of the explosion.

The car was blasted beyond recognition. Kate was on her knees over a little Vietnamese girl, working out of a miserable little first aid kit that Sergeant Fosbury probably kept in the car. Billy Ray was hovering over her, M-16 at port arms, glancing nervously around the growing crowd. He noticed John as he approached.

"Sir, she insisted on tending to the wounded. No one survived in the car. Help's on the way."

"It's okay, Billy," John said as he knelt and put an arm around Kate. "Are you okay?"

"I think so. You?" she said as she glanced up from her work.

"I'm okay. The guy who did it is down the street aways, dying...."

"Let's go!" she said, jumping up.

"Go where?"

"To the man who's dying down the street."

"Well...okay."

Kate sprinted down the street with John following. I tried to waste the murderer and Kate wants to save him, John thought. Boy, do we ever live in two different worlds.

Kate sped up when they rounded the pile of rubble and she saw the man in his death throes.

"Oh, God, John, he looks so young. How 'bout a knife? Do you have a pocketknife? He needs a tracheotomy, right now!"

John handed his penknife to Kate.

She wiped the blood off his throat, located his Adam's apple, made an incision and twisted the knife—the same motion John used to open a beer can with his Buck knife. The sound of pressure release was even similar. She left the knife in to hold the wound open. John could handle all the death and killing. He couldn't handle Kate calmly and deliberately cutting a hole in a dying man's throat with a dull penknife that he'd been using to clean his fingernails for the last five years.

"I'll be back." John didn't wait for an answer. He staggered behind a blackened pile of concrete, stucco and timbers, and violently tossed the Cercle Sportif luncheon special. As he stood there hunkered over, hands on shaky knees trying to refocus his eyes, he wondered what was happening to him. Twice in two weeks now he had barfed his guts out and he wasn't ill either time. He had thought his head was into this war. It was obvious to him his stomach wasn't. With glassy eyes and rubbery legs he rejoined Kate. She was astride the man, both hands on his breastbone, rhythmically pumping hard and shouting, "Come on, baby. Don't give up. Don't die."

Sirens were approaching. Kate, covered with blood, slumped over the dead man, head hanging down. Her face had a look of abject failure. "Oh, John, I hate this war," she screamed. He helped her up and embraced her as she sobbed.

The stench of death, when the anal sphincter lets go, combined with the vomit that had strained through John's mustache was more than he could handle. Cholon was becoming a very wobbly place. The horizon began to rock back and forth as the gyros in his middle ear wound down.

John became Kate's next battlefield patient.

He slumped over, Kate's shoulder dug into his gut and her arms wrapped around the back of his thighs. The next thing he remembered was sitting at the curb with his head between his knees. It smelled like someone had jammed his nose into an ammonia bottle. A medic sat beside him, steadying him.

There were ambulances and military police everywhere. Kate was moving around among the wounded, helping the corpsmen. When she saw John looking at her she came over and sat down on the curb beside him.

"I'll keep an eye on him, corpsman. There's nothing more I can do for anyone else." She put her arm around his shoulders and gave him a weak, weary smile. "How're you feeling, John?"

"A little woozy and horribly embarrassed. I'd make a lousy foot soldier, wouldn't I?"

"You clearly don't have the stomach for it...and learning that is the only good thing to come out of this afternoon in hell."

* * *

Dinner was one somber affair that night. John and Kate spent an interminable time in the intelligence debrief after they'd let them go back to the VOQ to get cleaned up. Everyone was very complimentary about their action under fire. Everyone commented on how lucky they were. If the other car hadn't passed them before the ambush.... If they had been closer at the time of the explosion... if...if.... Six Vietnamese were killed besides the three men in the car, and another half dozen Vietnamese were wounded.

Sergeant Fosbury had gotten in touch with Colonel Moffit and he had cut his day short to be with them for dinner. They chose to take their cocktails in the dining room rather than the bar. John decided to join Colonel Moffit on the hard stuff and ordered a double Johnny Walker, neat. Kate asked for water with hers.

"Colonel Moffit, your daughter was magnificent this afternoon...calm and cool and courageous. She is one very special lady."

"Yes, she is, John. I'm proud of both you kids and Sergeant Fosbury. Colonel Carnes was a good friend of mine. Harry was on the J-6 staff for General Abrams. That was his Vietnamese counterpart with him in the car, Colonel Tran Van Ho. Intelligence has identified the assassin as a known Viet Cong soldier."

"I may be out of line, sir, but why aren't we taking this war to the source? Why do we let them come down here and kill innocent people?" It was the same question John had asked Colonel English and he wanted to take it right on up the chain of command. He held his breath till Colonel Moffit responded.

"There's never been a war like this one, John. This measured response business is the latest thing from the "think tanks" and it's all wrong and every one from General Abrams on down knows it...but don't get me started. I'm a career soldier and I know how to follow orders, even ones I don't agree with."

John realized he had touched a very sore subject with the Colonel and he wanted to ask him why someone in the upper echelons of the command structure did not try the General Wheeler approach again-stand up and state the obvious: The President has no clothes and his staff is stark naked, too. But he bit his tongue and just nodded his head sagely.

"We're mighty happy you got the guy, John. The V.C. love to show the people they can strike anywhere with impunity." The Colonel gave John an admiring smile and it told John that it was time to end this line of conversation.

"Listen, would you kids like to go out to Vung Tau, the in-country R&R base? I could have someone run you out there in a chopper. It's only twenty-five miles."

Kate and John looked at one another. "Could we sleep on it, sir. I've certainly lost my taste for the sights of Saigon." Kate nodded her head slowly in agreement. "On the other hand we have a nice beach of our own up in the Tuy Hoa Valley."

"I'd prefer you stay away from downtown," Colonel Moffit said. "Kate, dear, I don't think we ought to tell your mother about this day."

"I agree, Daddy, and I'm going to have to call it a day. Lugging 180-pound fighter pilots around is hard work." Kate flashed a tired but sweet smile John's way. He put his hand on Kate's as the Colonel watched. They hadn't told the colonel about that part of the afternoon.

"Sir, I proved to myself I'm not cut out for the infantry this afternoon."

"Well, you also proved you're as accurate with an M-16 as you are with an F-100, John."

"I guess it's the same concentration, but it's too up close and intimate for my stomach, sir," John said as he rose.

Kate gave her father a big hug and Ozzie gave John a handshake and a firm pat on the back.

"Good night, kids, just let me know what I can do."

"Good night, sir."

"Good night, Daddy."

*   *   *

As they approached Kate's door, she said, "Would you like to... come in?" She kissed John before he could respond, as if it were needed to influence his decision.

"I'd love to."

Kate took John by the hand and led him into the room and over to the edge of the double bed.

"Please sit right here."

John obliged her.

Kate took the only chair in the room, a straight-back wooden chair at a well-worn writing table in front of the only window. She placed it in front of John and sat on it with her knees touching his. He felt her trembling.

"What...?"

"Shhhh." Kate reached out with both hands and took John's hands, staring intently into his eyes. "John, there is something I must tell you."

John leaned forward and kissed her. Kate allowed that for a few brief seconds, and then drew back, her eyes filled to overflowing, tears running down both cheeks.

"This afternoon...the look on your face when you reached for the M-16 to chase that guy. It reminded me of an awful time in my life. It frightened me...more than anything else that happened today. Phillip was a Green Beret...my fiancé...he volunteered for a second tour and was killed...."

"I'm sorry."

Kate freed her right hand and tried to cover John's mouth.

"There's more..."

"I don't want to know any more."

"You must." Now the tears increased and her breathing became shaky. "Phillip was...crazy...an animal. He loved killing. He loved ...hurting people...even people he said he loved. It was the war that made him that way ...."

"Are you saying that I remind you of that...of him?" John was incredulous.

Kate's head bobbed slowly up and down as she stared at her lap, and a small squeaky voice said, "Sometimes."

There was long period of silence as Kate wept softly and a stunned John tried to sort out what he had just heard. He had truly believed this relationship was progressing nicely and suddenly he had just stepped on a land mine.

"What must I do to convince you I am not a psycho, Kate?"

"I don't know, but keep trying, okay?"

"Uh...."

"John." She raised her head and stared at him through glassy eyes. "Would you…could you…just for tonight, would you just hold me…and sleep here beside me? If I'm asking the impossible you can go on back to your room. I'll understand. It's been an awful day and I'm afraid…I need…you to stay with me."

"I want to stay."

"Oh, thank you." She rose and hugged him as he sat there, smothering him in her bosom. Then she rose and went into the bathroom. In a daze John threw back the bedspread, undressed to his underwear, laid his uniform over the chair and slid under the sheet.

Kate came out in what looked like a size XL T-shirt that reached to her knees, padded around the bed and turned off the light. She snuggled up to John, put her arm over his chest, gave him one soulful kiss and then lay on her back next to him. Neither spoke.

John lay wide-eyed. He couldn't believe this day or this night, what had happened or what was happening. She had asked him to do the near impossible and he had agreed. Katherine Moffit was one amazing woman and still a mystery, but the true self was starting to reveal itself. Beneath that pit bull will of her's, that in-charge facade was a frightened—damaged, maybe—insecure little girl. And she got that way not because she was a tramp or a circus lady, but because of her choice of men. It explained a lot of her inquisitive manner toward him. Well, he would show her he was in her beloved daddy's mold, not the Army wacko. Maybe it was the trauma of the day. Maybe this was a test, this bizarre, adolescent but trusting request, whether or not she would admit that to herself. But John took comfort in his new knowledge that the seemingly self-assured lady also had trouble getting through the night. And it felt very good to be snuggled up in bed with Kate in an old French hotel in Saigon, even if the requirements were platonic.

The stubby, glowing hands on John's Air Force issue aviator's hack watch said 0530. The room was cold as the air conditioning unit rattled and vibrated its way through the night. It looked like one of those window units but a special hole had been cut in the wall, near the window, to mount it. John got up and felt for the bedspread at the foot of the bed. He put it on the bed and slid back under the covers. Kate was half on her side, half on her stomach, with her back to John and one knee drawn up near her elbow.

He snuggled up to her, put an arm over her back and side and lay very still. She didn't move. He wanted to make love to her so badly he ached.

His mind was still reeling from Kate's actions and revelations. Her regard for life, of any kind, was incredible. That miserable little gook had just killed her Daddy's good friend, but she didn't know that and it wouldn't have made any difference if she had. She knew that John had tried to kill him but that didn't make any difference either. He was a living human being on the brink and she tried her best to save him.

When he added yesterday's experiences to Kate's revelation about Phillip, it all started to add up—why she hated the war so much. And something in John convinced her to give him a chance, even though he probably epitomized everything she loathed about man's inhumanity. It was a trust he would not, could not violate. To his utter amazement he had just done it. But what if that brainless grunt Phillip has permanently damaged her, physically or psychically or both...? For a brief moment a sick feeling ran through him—maybe Kate is irreparably damaged goods.

"M-m-m-m. Good morning, John. How are you this morning?"

"I feel great, and you?"

"I feel like one very lucky lady."

John propped his head on his elbow and kissed her nose and then her lips. He studied those busy, green eyes in the minutest detail, from as close as his eyes would focus, and her eyelashes as they fanned the air in perfect unison—one blink every second heartbeat. Kate's eyebrows were as expressive as her eyes as they ranged over the lower third of her forehead.

"Would you like to go up to the roof-top and watch the dawn of a new day, Katherine the Greatest?"

"Okay."

*   *   *

The eastern horizon was a row of towering, ragged black cumulous clouds standing at close ranks in front of a fluorescent crimson stage curtain. John sat astraddle one of the pool deck chaise lounges with Kate, beach cover-up hanging loosely over her nightshirt, sitting right in front of him at the foot of the lounge. His chin rested on the top of her head as they both watched the dawn. Slowly the crimson curtain rose to reveal a yellow curtain, which then turned light blue from the top down. Out of the west came a rumble like a wooden-wheeled wagon rolling down a cobblestone street.

"What's that rumble?" Kate asked.

"It's the son of thunder rising with dawn."

"You're a piece of work. What's it really?

"It's a B-52 bombing raid. They're flying so high you can't see or hear the planes."

"What a terrifying thing that would be to live through."

"You should see it. I watched the bombs hit from the air once. We were scheduled for work in III Corps when the Bongos, the B-52's, were due in, and we had to hold off to the side of the target area until they made their pass—hundreds of bombs. We couldn't see the actual bombs falling—just the havoc they wreaked. It looked like a giant invisible roto-tiller plowing through the jungle, turning it into a freshly plowed garden."

"That sounds hideous. How many people must die in one of those things?"

"Well, they don't do it in populated areas, at least not yet. Supposedly the targets are troop concentrations and base camps. Senator Goldwater wanted to do it up north in Hanoi. It probably would end the war about as quickly as anything I can think of ... short of nuking the place. And it would keep us from destroying the very people we are trying to help."

"I don't even want to think about it. Isn't the sunrise beautiful?"

"It's fabulous and the company is even better." John tightened his bear hug around her middle. "Sunrise has always been my favorite time of day. Growing up on the farm I can remember heading for the barn in the dark of early morning, half-asleep, to milk the cows by hand. My brother and I took one apiece while my father milked two. I can still see those sunrises through the barn door as I sat on a one-legged stool with my head buried in the flank of a Holstein cow."

"How old were you then?" Kate asked.

"I think I started my milking career at age eight. That's where these fat knuckles came from." John held both hands in front of her face. "When I first got interested in girls I used to worry about my hands smelling like a cow. There was no soap then that could re-move the aroma of being intimate with a cow twice a day."

"Growing up on your parents' farm sounds like so much fun. Would you take me there sometime when we've both survived this awful place?"

"I'd love to. But the cows are gone now, as is most of the live-stock. Most folks in Henderson County specialize in grain farming, with just a few dairy farms with fancy machinery—no one milks by hand anymore. It's considered unsanitary."

"Oh, too bad. I was looking forward to that. What can we do for fun then?"

"We could skinny dip in the pond by the light of the moon, lis-ten to the frogs croak and the cicadas chirp and make love till the cows come home."

"And what time would they come home?"

"Oh, about sun-up, when it's time for them to be milked."

"Sounds like a fairy tale, John. I can't wait."

John kissed her on the earlobe from behind, and there in front of his eyes, down the front of the size XL T-shirt, was the paratrooper tattoo. His breath caught, right in her ear.

Kate leaned her head to one side and turned toward him with a questioning look.

"Tell me about your tattoo, Kate."

She glanced down at her bosom and knew that he had seen it again. She was silent for a few seconds...and then the sniffles began. "I was eighteen years old and Phillip had just gotten out of Ft. Benning. He had just graduated from paratrooper school and was so gung-ho. He demanded...and got...my virginity...." Her whole body convulsed and she sobbed and sobbed. After several minutes of sobbing while John silently held her she said, "And then he...convinced me to get this brand that marked me as his...the mark of the devil. Oh, John, I am so sorry...." She was a mess. "I let him talk me into it—it was a stupid thing to do and I am so sorry. And I will pay for it forever...it's like...the Scarlet Letter." Kate cried again and John's heart bled for her.

John didn't know how to respond. She had answered the very question that had bothered him the most and he was sorry he had asked. He was embarrassed and disgusted with himself, again. Would he ever be able to look at that tattoo without getting mad at the airborne psycho that did it—perhaps scarred her for life and branded her to boot? He kissed her neck as he held her tightly.

"John...I am not the girl you would want...to bring home to mother. If...you don't want to see me again...I'll understand."

Well, there was a thought that had not crossed his mind—any of it—but it spoke volumes for where Kate's mind was. After another long silence John had an idea. He said, "Kate, would you go on R&R with me to Hawaii...in December?"

The tears began again, but this time motivated by joy and combined with that trademark smile that he loved so much. "Oh, yes. I'd love to." She stood up, turned around and climbed astride John's lap and hugged him hard and long, and he got so instantly, intensely excited he thought he would burst a blood vessel, a fact that could not have gone unnoticed by the little lady in his lap. In the process he also realized that their noses were at exactly the same altitude with her on his lap, making kissing her much less of a contortion—a wonderful discovery on a couple of levels.

John held her tightly for several minutes and kissed her intermittently until her breathing gradually changed from heavy laden to turned on. Hesitantly she backed away and John reluctantly broke the clinch as she stood and repositioned herself sideways on his lap.

"Do you think we could both arrange to get R&R at the same time, John?"

"You seem to know how to get results when you set your mind to it. You set this trip up in about sixty minutes. Hawaii might take you a little longer but I'll bet you can do it. Let's both put in our leave requests as soon as we get back to Tuy Hoa."

"Okay…. John, thank you for putting up with me. Thank you for tolerating all my insults. Thank you…for not telling…the 'sassy lady'…where she could get off. Thank you for holding me through the night…."

John stopped her with a kiss. "You're welcome. You're worth it."

"I am so glad you think so…. Hey, are you hungry, John? I'm famished. I hardly ate anything for dinner."

"Well, let's go get some breakfast."

An hour later, after a shower and shave, John walked Kate over to the white metal building that was the General Officer's Open Mess. It was 0800 and they had the place to themselves. Over a leisurely breakfast of eggs Benedict, juice and coffee, they planned their Hawaiian R&R.

Then, abruptly, she changed the subject. "John, I want you to know that nothing you could say—and you are a poet—would mean more to me than what you did last night. I know how hard that is for a man, and I promise I won't do that to you again. I just… didn't think I could make it through the night without you."

John was stuck for words. He just stared back at her, hoping those magnetic eyes could see through his right down into the depths of his heart, where feelings too powerful to verbalize smoldered like hot lava.

"We'll get a two room suite in Hawaii…or two beds…okay?" Her voice was soft and pleading.

"Sure. After last night I can do anything in your presence."

"You can do anything you set your mind to, John Ellsworth. I am convinced." She was ecstatic.

Finally Kate excused herself and called Colonel Moffit's office from the O'Club while John polished off a final cup of coffee. She returned, smiling.

"Daddy would like to have lunch with us and then see us off at 1330 on the courier. That'll put us in Tuy Hoa in time to get some beach time. What do you think?"

"Sounds fine. I'm ready for the tranquillity of the Tuy Hoa Beach."

*   *   *

They called it mobile control, but that was a misnomer. It seldom moved. It was a glass box about six feet by eight feet by seven feet high and sat near the edge of the runway about five hundred feet down from the approach end. A light wind was blowing out to sea, so the active runway was 21. John sat in the glass box on the southeast side of the runway, with a view of the planes touching down right in front of him. Beyond the runway about a hundred yards were the machine gun bunkers covering the field of fire on the northern perimeter of the base. They were mounds of sand about fifty yards apart and ten feet high with a four-walled sandbagged six-by-six foot parapet on top that held a 50-caliber machine gun. A flat tin roof protected the gun crew from the sun and rain. Beyond the bunkers was the river with the thatched roofs of Tuy Hoa village in the distance. Dominating the horizon, just north of the village, was a nearly perfectly hemispherical shaped hill about 500 feet high that poked up incongruously out of the valley floor near the mouth of the river. It had a commanding view of the entire valley, a rough half circle about five miles in diameter from the hill at the center to the rugged foothills of the Central Highlands at the perimeter. As such it was the perfect location for a U.S. Army artillery battery atop the hill. The guys worked only the night shift, it seemed to John, and it had taken a few weeks for him to get used to those 155 artillery pieces booming their way through the night. The noisy little overworked air conditioner in his hooch did not drown them out.

In all it was a beautiful oriental panorama set against a blue sky. Take away the weapons of war and it was a view that probably hadn't changed for centuries. John was filled with sadness as he thought about how this ugly war must have traumatized this idyllic little river valley, how the farmers must resent both the war and the constant roar of warplanes day and night and the artillery fire all night long. What a shame. What a commentary on the disease of communism and the depravity of mankind in general. And then he remembered Colonel English's story, about how it could all be settled in two weeks and it made him angry.

The sole purpose of the mobile control officer was to make sure no Super Sabre tried to land without lowering his landing gear. There were visual and audio warning systems in the cockpit, but in an F-100 it was not automatic. A hand had to physically reach up on the upper left hand side of the instrument panel and move the lever straight down about three inches. Once every few thousand landings somebody forgot.

Landing gear-up shortened the landing roll considerably. It also shortened two careers—that of the pilot and that of the mobile control officer. The glass box had a radio tuned to the tower frequency and a flare gun mounted to shoot across the nose of the landing plane in case the radio didn't work. God forbid a pilot should ever get a flare fired across his nose just prior to touchdown.

Tuy Hoa was not O'Hare Airport-F-100's only landed about every thirty minutes with a few assorted multi-engine planes in between. A small air-conditioner just barely held its own in that solar oven in the brutal tropical sun. There was plenty of time to sit in the glass box and ponder the weekend and the revelations of Kate.

He and Kate had only been away about fifty hours. It felt like fifty days. Colonel Redman could not have prescribed a better medicine and John loved him and Colonel English all the more for it. Such love and respect for commanding officers was a rare thing in a military unit, and John knew he was a very lucky lieutenant. The leave certainly could have been more restful and more satisfying, but it was an unforgettable experience. The sassy part of the green-eyed lass had disappeared completely by the end of the weekend-he hoped for good. It was a major accomplishment that stoked a growing yearning in John. Whether it would ever be fulfilled was another matter, but common looks were growing more beautiful with each experience together, and amid the psychic scar tissue there was truly inner beauty. The mark of the devil, though, however sad the story, was still a stumbling block for John. It would always be a scarlet letter for him too—a surprising self-revelation that in this day and age he was such a prude. It precluded any consideration along the lines of Kate's comment that she was not bring-home-to-mother material. The tattooed lady was right.

In the meantime his other lover, the inanimate one that made no demands and had no hang-ups, sat patiently, armed and ready, waiting to mate on schedule at 1300. In her embrace they would soar to the heavens, climb and dive and turn and roll, and climax with awesome explosive force. And all she required was a smooth hand. John thought of Kate's comment about there being a clinical name for such a passion, and he was mildly curious about what it was, but it certainly did not effect the relationship, however psychotic it might be.

John was scheduled to carry daisy cutters to IV Corps, the northern-most zone, beginning at the DMZ between North and South Vietnam and extending down to an east-west line about a hundred miles south of Da Nang. Briefing time was 1200, following his three-hour stint in mobile control. The flight's call sign would be Dusty Four One and Four Two, with Mike Day on his wing.

Daisy cutters did just what their name implied. They were 750-pound bombs with a thirty-six-inch fuse extension on its nose. It was really just a three-foot piece of three-inch diameter pipe attached to the nose of a standard bomb, with an impact fuse mounted out at the end of the pipe. This would make the bomb explode three feet above the ground rather than right at ground level. It mowed a much wider swath through the jungle that way. A soldier lying flat on the ground fifty feet from a regular bomb that exploded on the surface just might survive—the ground tended to deflect the force of the explosion upward in a funnel shaped pattern. His ears would ring and his eyes would probably water, but he might live to fight another day. If a daisy cutter exploded fifty feet away from him, they'd have to pick the meat off the shrapnel.

Daisy cutters had another purpose. They made instant LZ's—landing zones—in the dense jungle for Army helicopters. Two daisy cutters could create a circular fort about thirty meters in diameter, complete with log walls—the logs lying more or less horizontally, rather than the vertical way of General Custer's day.

During the pre-flight briefing, Mike was determined as ever to get John to admit he'd scored with Lieutenant Moffit. As soon as they sat down to brief he asked John, "Well, how was it?"

John played it straight-faced.

"Saigon's a lovely place. I'd particularly recommend the National Museum."

"Yeah, right, but did you get lucky?" Two years out of college and Lieutenant Mike Day still acted like an underclassman. But he was a good stick-and-rudder man—not as good as he thought he was, but good enough. In addition to his immature mind he had an immature body. About ten pounds of baby fat hung at the waistline, upper arms, cheeks and chin. He sported a sparse blond mustache with a large gap in the middle. It made him the butt of all the "real men don't..." jokes.

John ignored the question. "In ten seconds the time will be 1202 hours local...."

They strapped on the Super Sabres at 1245 hours and were airborne at 1300 sharp, "feet wet north," which meant over the water just a half-mile off the beach. The old cockpit felt good. The smell of hot hydraulic fluid, the chill of the air conditioner and the muffled whine of spinning turbine blades told him he was home again. It was right where he belonged, he thought as he fondled the control stick with the feather light touch of his right hand.

John decided that whoever designed that control stick grip must have had a Ph.D. in "feel good." There was a smooth curve, ledge or notch for all four fingers and the thumb. The pickle button was right next to the thumb rest and the gun trigger just above the index finger. If Linus, that kid in the comic strips, ever got his hands on a control stick grip, he'd throw away his blanket, John thought. Even the newer, more advanced planes had the same control stick grip-they just couldn't improve on perfection.

Dusty Four One Flight leveled at fourteen thousand feet and John waggled the rudder to signal Mike to loosen up the formation and enjoy the scenery. He felt a whole lot more relaxed with a fellow lieutenant on his wing.

There was a destroyer below them, steaming in a slow circle. John made a mental note to drop down and say hello, if they had a chance, on the way home.

Half way between Chu Lai and Da Nang they switched over to the FAC frequency.

"Lobo Zero One, this is Dusty Four One Flight, over."

"Dusty Four One, this is Lobo. Good afternoon to you. The First Cav has a vertical assault going this afternoon and we need an LZ prep for about a dozen helicopters. Meet me over at the 190 radial at 60 DME off the Big D TACAN, and I'm ready to copy your munitions."

John played the little geometry game with his thumb and index finger on the heading indicator compass card to figure out how to find the rendezvous, sixty miles south southwest of the Da Nang navigational aid. When he had picked up the proper heading he passed along their munitions.

"Lobo, Dusty Flight is carrying eight MK-82 daisy cutters and

1600 rounds of twenty mike mike and we're about one minute east of you."

"Copy, Dusty. I'm going to go ahead and put down a smoke rocket where I want you to make the LZ." He gave them target barometric pressure, altitude and estimated winds—all the external things that could effect the accuracy of their bombing. "I'd appreciate a salvo on a single pass so we can make the LZ as big as possible—we've got a passel of grunts coming in here. Nearest friendlies will be one klick to the east. Make your run north to south and we'll be okay."

"Dusty, copy. Set 'em up hot, Dusty Flight." John was glad the good guys were a kilometer away. He felt a little rusty after his short vacation.

"Twoop," was all John heard, all he needed to hear, from Mike Day.

Since the grunts were making an assault, it was a reasonable assumption there was something down that was worth assaulting. It was also reasonable to assume that they might get a kick out of shooting down an F-100 Super Sabre. So John came in at a thirty-degree dive in a big curve, and put the pipper on the base of the white phosphorous smoke on the ground. Keeping the wings level over any target for more than five seconds was a sure sign a pilot was tired of living. He wasn't so rusty he had forgotten that.

"Bombs away," he called as he pulled out of the dive.

"Good work, lead. Now, Two, if you could make that circle into an oval we'll be in good shape," Lobo instructed.

"Roger. Two's in from the north."

John watched Mike's bombs come off his plane and impact at the edge of the Indian fort that he had created.

"You men do good work, Dusty Flight. Now, if you've got some loiter time, hang around and we may be able to use your guns, depending on what the First Cav runs into. Did ya'll see any ground fire?"

"Negative on the ground fire, Lobo. We're good for about twenty minutes. We'll run on up to ten thou and orbit."

"Roger that, Dusty. I'm going to be talking to the chopper pilots for awhile but I'll also be monitoring this frequency."

Out of the southeast, probably from Chu Lai, came twelve UH-1 Huey slicks. The troop carrying helicopters were escorted by four

Huey Cobra gunships, spinning their way across the jungle just above the treetops. John and Mike had made the LZ big enough to accommodate two Hueys at a time. Six men jumped out of each chopper and ran for the western perimeter of the LZ. The four Huey Cobras flew top cover just above them. From ten thousand feet the men on the ground looked like ants scurrying around. The empty Huey slicks departed the LZ to the southwest, to avoid the helicopters inbound from the southeast, and then headed back to Chu Lai.

It was a well-oiled operation—until some gook found one of those big fat Hueys just too tempting a target. It was one of the empty Hueys headed back to Chu Lai. The first thing John noticed was black smoke boiling out of the thing and somebody was screaming, "Mayday, mayday, mayday," over the emergency frequency.

"We're going in. We're going in." And then a blood curdling scream as some trauma—probably a bullet—caused the chopper pilot's hand to freeze on the mike button.

"Oh, my God...." Mike said reverently over the radio.

"Be ready, Two. We're going down there and kick some ass. There's a ton of air traffic around here, so keep that head swiveling," John called.

"Roger."

"Dusty Four One, this is Lobo. Did you see the Huey go in?"

"Affirmative, Lobo."

"Okay, the choppers are going to continue the vertical assault but they'll come out of the LZ to the northeast after they unload. The Cobras will hold east of the downed Huey until you've softened up the area. Walk your twenty mike mike in a north-south line fifty meters left and right of the downed chopper. One of the pilots and the door gunner have survived and we're in contact with them. One of the other Hueys will attempt the pick up if you can discourage the ground fire.

"Roger, Lobo. Four Two, you take the west side and I'll take the east. Take your spacing and follow me down."

A double click on the mike button told John that Lieutenant Day had copied the message.

John rolled upside down, pulled the nose through the horizon and pointed it straight down.

"Speed brakes...now," he called to Mike, and then he thumbed the slide switch on top the throttle. They had a long way down to go, and 34,000 pounds of F-100 accelerated in a hurry pointed straight down. At 6000 feet John shallowed the dive out to thirty degrees, raised the speed brake, flipped on the gun switch and caged the gun sight in preparation for his strafing run. He didn't really expect the gooks to shoot at him with all those slow, low helicopters buzzing around. They'd probably lay low and keep their powder dry till he and Mike were gone.

His 20-millimeter high explosive incendiary rounds had a charge that exploded on impact and started a fire if it hit something burnable. Those explosions clearly marked the path of the bullets through the jungle. John aimed fifty meters east and fifty meters short of the downed helicopter and sprayed bullets in a line a hundred meters long. Mike did the same on the west side of the helicopter.

They came around for one more pass. The vibration of four cannons firing seventeen hundred rounds a minute caused the pipper to jitter as John held the trigger down and walked the bullets through the trees.

There were no victory rolls on this mission—the battle was still in process. The Huey Cobra gunships then moved in to keep the heat on the bad guys as Mike and John headed back toward home on a southeasterly heading. The scream of the helicopter pilot dying was still ringing in John's ears. It reminded him that the little guy that he had wasted in Cholon never uttered a cry of anguish-perhaps he couldn't, or perhaps he was a very brave, well-disciplined soldier. At any rate this wasn't one of those thrill-of-victory flights home through the long, delirious burning blue the poet talked about.

He didn't even feel like going down and saying hello to the destroyer they passed on the way up. Mike kept double clicking his mike button. They both knew what he was communicating, but he just didn't want to blurt it out over the radio. "Come on, lead, let's go down and show off in front of those poor unfortunate Navy guys." But maybe they weren't so unfortunate. They killed from such long distance they never got to see the fruits of their labors.

John also thought about Kate on one of those Hueys. She was on flight status with the Army and she got to fly out to Special Forces camps regularly. She was laying it on the line a whole lot more than she realized, he thought, or else she just chose not to talk about it.

Well, they were a hundred miles from home and John hadn't rolled his angel one single time. Knowing Mike Day, John's reputation could suffer irreparable damage if he didn't get with it. He'd be accused of falling in love and going soft....

He motioned Mike into close trail, rolled over and split-essed down to five thousand feet. He sucked on a good solid five G's coming out of the dive just to make Mike sweat a little back there, ten feet behind and five feet below his tail. He was smooth as glass on the control stick. If Lieutenant Day couldn't hack it back there, John didn't want him to blame it on a ham-fisted flight lead. They came back up into a thirty-degree climb and John pulled it over into a big sweeping barrel roll. Then he dropped the nose below the horizon, picked up five hundred knots and pulled up into a four-G loop, coasting across the top inverted at 140 knots-just barely flying speed. He was giving young Lieutenant Day a workout he wouldn't soon forget, and since he couldn't see Mike back there, Mike could tell the world he was doing just great-whether he was or not.

Coming down the back side of the loop at 500 knots, John smoothly fed in four G's and called, "How ya doing back there, Mike?"

A straining, grunting voice replied, "I've gotta...hard-on that a...cat couldn't scratch."

Atta boy, Mike, he thought, but settled for a double click of his mike button.

Lieutenant Vic Wilson walked through the door of the 629th TAC Fighter Squadron for the first time on Halloween Day, 1968. He was another country boy—from a wheat farm in Kansas. Maybe that's why they hit if off so well right from the beginning. While John had worked hard to outgrow that farmer image, Vic wore it with pride and comfort. He was a tall, sandy-haired kid with broad but slightly stooped shoulders and a wide smile. No one would ever have mistaken him for an Academy grad. John thought Vic was considerably more laid back than he, but beneath Vic's breastbone lay the soul of a tiger. No one asked for, let alone qualified for or graduated from fighter pilot school without it.

Vic went through the standard ration of three missions in the two-seater F-100F model. The first ride was really as a passenger in the back seat and the next two were in the front seat with an instructor pilot in the back. Then he was on his own in the F-100D model.

John got to lead Vic on his first mission in the D model. Of course it was a boring bummer of a mission. New guys always got scheduled for the toothpick missions. They would go out and bomb supposed "strategic truck parks, supply depots, and enemy bunkers," as the battle damage assessment report would say, but from John's view all they did was make toothpicks out of trees. John felt as protective as a big brother. Vic managed to put his bombs within twenty meters of where the FAC wanted, which was good for a new guy. Sometimes it took rookies awhile to get adjusted to the fact there wasn't a big bull's-eye painted on the ground, and no familiar landmarks to tell him when he was perfectly offset from the target for the proper dive angle.

Coming home, John put Vic in close on his right wing and they did some easy acrobatics. This was more than just fun, hard work, it was vital to longevity in the business. There was no survivable alternative to staying on lead's wing, no matter what. No matter how rough the weather, how heavy the rain, how dark the night; no matter if the pucker-factor was so great the wingman was inhaling his seat cushion, he hung in there.

After a fifteen-minute workout—Vic hacked it just fine—John motioned him back out to route formation and they spent the rest of the flight home sightseeing and playing around. As toys for big boys go, it just couldn't get any better than this, John thought.

*　　*　　*

The Veterans' Day party commenced at 1700 with the arrival of the girls from Phu Hep. It really wasn't any different than any other party, except that it was an excuse for the pilots to wear their party suits.

The size of the crowd at Dusty's Pub had doubled with the arrival in late summer of the New Mexico Air National Guard. The capture of the U.S.S. Pueblo by the North Koreans in January of '68 and the ensuing saber rattling stretched the U.S. Air Force's resources, coming as it did at the peak of the air war in Southeast Asia. Four air guard units were called to active duty and sent to Vietnam to spring loose some regular Air Force pilots for Korean duty. Several of the junior executives at Fearless Fighter Pilots, Inc. held their breath as names had been called for Korean duty. John wasn't called—but it was close. One of his roommates, Brian Hanson, got called, and he was upset, to say the least. Vic Wilson got assigned the empty bunk.

The Air Guard guys had it made, flying an earlier model of the same plane—the F-100C—with a fraction of the military Mickey Mouse. They were basically civilian fighter pilots—holding down regular jobs, often airline pilot jobs and flying fighters on weekends. When the good stuff came along, they got in on the action with government guaranteed seniority in their civilian jobs. John decided that was a better deal. He had been such a gung-ho ROTC jock in college he never even considered anything but regular Air Force-didn't know such an alternative even existed.

The 629th party suits were brand new, short-sleeved, cotton coveralls roughly approximating a flying suit but without the tapered sleeves and legs and only one zipper instead of thirteen. They were powder blue, with wings and names stitched on the chest in white and squadron patches on the right shoulders. Some of the lieutenants had a couple of extra patches as well. One was a white skull and cross-bones on a black, flag-shaped background with the words "Yankee Air Pirate" stitched on it. Hanoi Hannah, on Radio Hanoi, had coined that phrase early on and in typical fashion the fraternity had turned a derogatory phrase into a prideful, high fashion one. John also wore another patch that was made up to look like a ski patch which said, "Ski Mu Gia Pass, 100 Exciting Trails".

When the squadron had ordered them from a tailor in Hong Kong, most of the guys had party suits made for their wives and girlfriends, too. John had one made for Kate and it was tailor-made to accentuate her figure. She wore it with a white ascot, and in John's view, it was a killer.

The New Mexico Guard on the other hand, wore bib overalls-the Osh Kosh B'gosh kind—for party suits. It was their way of "pimping the pompous peacocks" who called themselves regular Air Force. But John thought it was all in good humor, and great fun.

"Kate, I would like you to meet Vic Wilson, my new roommate and my wingman this afternoon." Vic had no party suit yet, so he was stuck with his regular issue flight suit.

"Hello, Vic. It's nice meeting you." Kate offered her hand.

"My pleasure, Kate." Vic held her hand as if it were fine crystal.

"Vic's a good pilot, Kate. You just can't beat those country boys. When I'm through showing him the ropes he'll be one of the greatest."

"Oh, give me a break, John. Vic, I want you to pay particular attention to John's humility lessons. But I warn you, they are very short lessons." Kate was smiling. She had learned the rules of social intercourse well at Dusty's Pub—thrust and parry, bob and weave.

"And I'll warn you, Vic, that Kate has eyes like Superman. She sees through everything and I'm crazy about her. What's everyone drinking?"

"Beer will be fine."

"Cola."

"Be right back." It took a while to wade across the sea of bib overalls and powder blue flying suits. The guys in the bibs were making a big play for Kate's associates from Phu Hep. They, too, had a lot of new arrivals and they were really great gals, but the same rules applied as far as the fighter pilots were concerned, with one genuine exception—a tall blonde Lieutenant named Sue Allen. But John was not on the playing field in that regard. Kate occupied his free time in mostly delightful fashion.

As John headed back to the table with a beer for Vic, cola for Kate, and a Johnny Walker on the rocks for himself, he could see Kate and Vic talking. She was doing her interviewer thing. He knew from first hand experience how good she was at that.

"John, Vic tells me he's a chess player. You should get him to teach you," Kate said.

"Well, I'm game. It might help my image, huh? Vic, Kate's determined to make a civilized gentleman out of me."

"Well, why not? You can't be a gunslinger forever," Vic said.

It was time to change the subject. Vic was venturing into that area where relations between Kate and John got a little tense. After almost six months of F-100 combat flying and four months of Kate, there was not the slightest indication in John's psyche that the new was beginning to wear off the gunslinger business.

The midnight movies were getting worse, whether or not he'd spent the evening with Kate. John's antidote was consuming nothing but straight scotch, with or without ice, after 1700. Beer just wasn't doing the job anymore.

Kate seemed to be trying her best to be supportive without being an irritant, hoping perhaps that patience and consideration would win out.

In the meantime, for John it was just one day at a time. He had busted his butt to get here. All his life he had worked for tomorrow. Well, tomorrow had arrived, and he intended to live it to the max.

"John, my leave orders for R&R came through today," Kate announced.

"Fantastic. I should get our room reservations any day now—high room, ocean view, Ilikai Hotel, Waikiki Beach. You know that's only thirty days from today?"

"It's going to be so much fun, John."

Vic was gone. John sensed he knew it had become a two-person conversation.

"How about a walk on the beach?" John asked. As they departed the lounge, Matt Jordan was on the umpteenth verse of an obnox-

ious song that was only funny if you were drunk. Everyone was join-
ing in on the chorus and life was grand. John retrieved a blanket out
of the hooch and they headed out across the soft sand of the beach.

It was a pitch-black night and all the stars in the universe were
shining. It was so clear and dark that the Milky Way was not just a
vaporous swath across the sky. There were two distinct, parallel
bands, like a superhighway with smaller single lane roads shooting
off in odd directions. The South China Sea was so flat that the
brightest stars cast a reflection like a full moon on a millpond. The
lights of the chow hall entrance door, a hundred yards across the
sand from the water's edge, provided the only available light.

They spread the blanket between the water and the dunes and sat
down.

"Kate, you were the belle of the ball again tonight. You look just
ravishing in that outfit."

"I think you're a very biased observer."

Wordlessly, Kate lay back on the blanket. John moved to her and
their lips met and it felt so good. All his problems seemed to evaporate in Kate's arms. He kissed and snuggled all those delightful
nooks and crannies of her face and neck and ears. She had become
so familiar, so comfortable and yet still so new and exciting. That
tattoo continued to bug him, but that night in the dark it was invisible. It was just Kate and John in their own little world, or so they
both thought. Then....

Kate stiffened with a jolt, as if 220 volts had just gone through
her body. It wasn't fifteen feet away and closing in a dead run-a
black figure emerging from a black sea. The faintest glint of the
chow hall light on the shiny steel of a bayonet fixed his position.

They met at the edge of the blanket. Coming up off the ground
John exploded upward and forward like an offensive tackle coming
out of a three-point stance. Something as hot as hell itself creased
the back of his scalp and then his shoulder was buried in the guy's
gut. He kept driving upward and the man flipped on over his head.
John heard a small squeal of anguish from Kate. The black figure
landed on his back on the other side of Kate, near her feet, and was
rolling over and struggling to get up. John reached down and
grabbed the knife from his boot, flicked it open and dived on him.

He smelled awful. John's body smothered the small figure, who
struggled like he had the wind knocked out of him. The knife was

still in John's hand. He spun 180 degrees while staying on top of him. He grabbed the face from behind with his left hand and pulled the knife hard across what should have been his throat. The figure went instantly limp with a gurgling sound. John released his grip on the face and the head fell at an odd angle.

Kate, in a weak voice, was calling hoarsely, "Help me...help me."

A short rifle with bayonet was standing nearly straight up from the left side of her chest. In a rage John buried the knife to the hilt between the shoulder blades of the black clad figure and left it there. He scrambled over to Kate without getting off his knees.

"Help me...." Kate grunted in agony, her voice now a whisper.

He moved his hands down the rifle to the bayonet and gingerly felt down the blade. The bayonet felt like it was stuck through the flesh of her upper arm, between her arm and her chest, but there was so much blood he wasn't sure. It felt like his hands were in a bowl of warm, thick soup. He pulled the bayonet out and flung it behind him. It was as small as a child's toy rifle. He guessed it was an AK-47.

The blackness of the night was shattered by an enormous fiery explosion in the vicinity of the flight line, a quarter-mile to the west, then another and another. The split-second of light that accompanied the fiery explosions revealed at least a dozen shadowy figures moving up the beach fifty yards to the north. The base was obviously under attack and all or some of the attackers were coming up the beach.

"Kate, we've got to get out of here." No answer.

He scooped her up and ran. It was one of those nightmare runs. He was moving his legs as fast as he could but he felt like he was going nowhere in the soft sand. He could hear Huey Cobra gunships rising from Phu Hep a mile away. There was sporadic machine gun fire on the flight line followed by more explosions. The night sky was filling up with flares and he knew he had to be a big, slow-moving target for somebody. John headed toward the chow hall, 100 yards away, and then decided the squadron bunker near Dusty's Pub would be safer. As he veered to his right he expected to feel bullets in his back with each step. Carrying Kate as fast as he could go prevented John from looking back to see if anyone was gaining on them. Kate was limp in his arms and he didn't know if she was alive or dead.

He ran forever. His lungs were on fire and his legs felt like lead. Finally he reached the road and fifty yards later he was at the door of the squadron bunker. Vic was standing in the door and shined a flashlight in John's face as he approached the bunker.

"Oh, my God," Vic said. John and Kate looked like something out of a horror film.

John was so out of breath he could hardly talk. "Nurses...here? Doc?"

"Yes, yes. Get in here. Make way. Make way. Wounded! Doc! Doc!"

John turned sideways to carry Kate through the door. It was ghostly inside and nearly a full house in mass confusion. Someone tried to take Kate out of his arms but he was having none of that. Wading through the crowd in the semi-darkness, lit only by a few flashlights, he dropped to his knees on the sandy floor near the back wall, still clutching Kate. Someone shined a flashlight down on both of them from behind.

"Oh wow, somebody tried to scalp you, man."

Suddenly John realized that the back of his party suit was soaked and something was running down his neck. A blanket materialized in front of them and he laid Kate on it as gently as he could. Her eyes were closed.

"Kate?" he whispered in her ear and held his breath.

Slowly her good arm came up and wrapped around his neck.

"Oh, Kate...."

Someone had him by the shoulders. The nurses from Phu Hep swung into action. "Stand back, guys, please. Turn your backs and give us some privacy. Come on, John, let's have a look at that head wound."

"Work on it right here. I'm not movin'!"

Doc and one of the nurses knelt on the other side of Kate. Doc lowered the zipper of her party suit and attacked the material with a pair of scissors. He cut off the sleeve and then cut more material horizontally at the base of her rib cage.

A husky female voice behind John asked for the scissors and attacked the back side of his suit while Doc and the nurse examined Kate's chest. In the dim wavering light of the flashlight John could see a gash beginning at Kate's breastbone and running horizontally through the middle of her tattoo and down the side of her rib cage.

The triceps muscle of her left arm looked partially severed.

The voice behind him said, "No back wounds. All the blood must be from the head wound." The bunker was quiet as a tomb, as everyone strained to listen to the diagnosis of the two squadron lovers.

Someone ran up to the bunker door and asked for Colonel Redman.

"Sir, it's a sapper squad attack. They apparently made a beach assault and headed for the airplanes. We have this area secured, but please stay in the bunker till further notice."

"What's a sapper squad?" a voice asked.

"It's a demolition squad, sir. They tossed satchel charges under the airplanes. Some of them aren't even carrying guns—just explosives."

"Sergeant, we got a couple of wounded in here. Let me know when we can get them over to the infirmary. Doc's here and we're trying to determine the extent of the wounds," Colonel Redman told him.

"Wounded, sir? Where were they when they were wounded?" The question was relayed to John.

"The beach...water's edge...abeam the chow hall...dead gook." John's head was bowed and his voice was barely audible.

"Say again?" The husky voice shouted in his ear and he repeated it.

"Sir, we'll get a squad down there right away."

Then Doc was talking. "No broken bones. The chest wound is just a flesh wound. Partially severed left triceps. She could use a unit of blood, but she'll be all right. A very lucky lady." A cheer went up from every soul in the place, except John. Hot tears ran down his cheeks.

"How's John?" Doc asked.

The husky voice replied, "Just a scalp wound, Doc, but he bled like a stuck pig."

"Then don't light any matches near him, it'll be straight alcohol," Ron said.

Another cheer and a roar of laughter, and the party reconvened in the bunker. Kate managed a weak smile. John's whole body trembled as he crashed from the adrenaline. "Could anybody spare something to drink?" John asked weakly. A cold can of Black Label was thrust in his face. He had trouble getting it to his lips, so he just went ahead and drank it all while he had it there.

It wasn't his bunk. It was a hospital bed and he had one block-buster of a headache. It's time to quit drinking, he thought for the umpteenth time in the last few months. He reached up and put his hand on his head, as if that would help any. There were bandages up there. He began to tremble as the events on the beach came back to him.

If he'd had one ounce less of scotch to drink before the beach, his reaction time would have been a split second faster, and he would have taken that bayonet right in the lips. If some sixth sense hadn't jolted Kate, the same bayonet would have skewered them both with one thrust. If he could have hung on to the little gook he wouldn't have flipped over his head and Kate wouldn't have been touched. If he hadn't taken Kate to the beach at all…. The list of "if's" and "just happened's" in this war was reaching paranoia length. Vic walked through the door wearing a sweat-soaked flight suit and his ever-present smile.

"How you feeling, roommate?"

"Well, aside from the worst hangover I've ever felt, I'll probably make it."

"Doc says you got a couple dozen stitches and you're missing a two-by-four swath of hair."

"How's Kate?"

"She's going to be okay. Doc says she'll have some scars–right where you hang the Purple Heart."

"Is she here?"

"Yeah, next room in fact."

John sat up and swung his feet over the edge of the bed. The throbbing in his head was perfectly synchronized with his heartbeat.

"Easy, John. I don't think they want you out of bed and Kate's not awake anyway."

Slowly he lay back down. His skull felt like it would shatter if it hit the pillow too hard.

"Vic, I really appreciate your coming by."

"Hey man, us rednecks gotta stick together," he drawled and made a spitting motion toward the foot of the bed.

A chuckle came out of John's mouth, but was choked off by a meat cleaver in the back of his skull.

"What time is it, Vic?"

"Ten hundred."

"What was happening last night? How many planes did we lose? Anybody dead?"

"Apparently there were about twenty gooks, made a beach landing and headed straight for the flight line. No Americans killed. You know the oriental mind. Machinery is worth more than manpower. In fact only one F-100 was destroyed, but three C-130's were wiped out. I suppose they figured the bigger the plane, the more valuable."

"Amazing. You know one satchel charge in Dusty's Pub last night would have paralyzed two squadrons for months. As it is, they haven't slowed down our war effort one iota," John said.

"Most of them didn't even have guns. You ran into one of the only guys carrying an AK-47."

"Vic, it was a really stupid thing to do. We could have both been killed. It honestly never occurred to me that the beach was unsafe."

"Well, John, it didn't occur to anybody it was unsafe. That's why all the pilots' hooches are located along the beach."

"How many of them did we snuff?"

"There's twenty dead, and they think that's all of them. The Cobras were airborne all night. The show from the squadron sun deck was spectacular."

"Basically it was a kamikaze mission, wasn't it?"

"Sure, no doubt about it."

"Vic, tell me something...am I in trouble?"

"For what? Are you kidding me? You're the only fighter pilot on the base to decapitate a gook with your bare hands and a pocket knife while your flight suit was down around your ankles."

"My suit wasn't down around my ankles. I'd be dead if it had been."

"Well, you know what they say, John. Don't let the facts stand between you and the legend."

"Vic, I don't feel like any legend...."

"I'm kidding, John. This may be a blow to your wounded ego, but there isn't a jock in the Pub who thinks you're intimate with that gal, least of all me. She's a class act and you and I both know it."

"Appreciate your telling me that, John, and for your ears only it's the gospel truth. Listen, Vic, I'd sure like to have that Buck knife back. That was a present from Dad. I left it between the guy's shoulder blades."

Vic unzipped the lower leg pocket of his flight suit, reached in and drew out John's knife. He handed it to him.

Someone had cleaned it up. It was a lock-blade, five-inch, wooden-handled knife. An oval brass plate in the center of the wooden handle bore the inscription, "To John from Dad, 5-5-68." Someone had carved a small V-shaped notch in the wooden handle. "They brought it to the bunker last night after you told them where to find the guy. There's an AK-47 you could probably have, too, if you want it."

"No thanks. I don't want any reminders like that."

"Well, I've got to brief in thirty minutes with Lieutenant Colonel English."

"Listen, if I write a note to Kate could you see that it gets into her room so she sees it when she wakes up?"

"Sure."

There was no writing paper in the room, so John disassembled a miniature Kleenex box and wrote on the white side of it with Vic's ball-point.

> Dear Kate,
> Colonel Moffit is going to have what's left of my scalp.
> I'm sorry. Please forgive me.
> John.

He folded it over and handed it to Vic. "Thanks for waiting, Vic, and thanks again for coming."

"No sweat, pal. Get some rest and let that hair grow back in so we can go flying again. I'm anxious for the next lesson." He shook John's hand, did an exaggerated about-face and marched out the door.

When John awoke a second time, a corpsman was fiddling with his bandages. His head had settled down to a dull ache and he was famished.

"Sir, a message from the patient next door." He handed John a piece of paper.

Dear John,
You saved my life and you're sorry?? You're my hero,
Son Of Thunder!!
Kate.

"Corpsman, am I authorized to walk around?"

"Yes, sir, if you feel up to it."

"I'm up to it. What time is it? I'm really hungry."

"It's 1130, sir. Lunch will be served in thirty minutes. The lady is in the room to your right."

John had on one of those tied-in-the-back hospital gowns that left nothing on his backside to the imagination, but he could care less. He padded out the door on less than steady legs and hung a right.

Kate's eyes were closed. Her hospital bed was elevated and her right arm was bandaged and immobilized against her torso. John leaned over and kissed her on the lips. Her eyes opened and a weak smile creased her face.

"Oh, John," she cried, but he wouldn't let her say any more. He kissed her again. He had to grab the bed rail to keep from falling over from dizziness with his eyes closed. Finally he raised up and took her hand.

"How're you feeling?" Kate asked weakly.

"Bit of a headache. How 'bout you?"

"I hurt a lot, but I'll be fit as a fiddle by Hawaii. Daddy's coming in this afternoon."

"Should I hide? He told me to take good care of you and I feel like I've failed miserably."

"Please get off that guilt trip...countr ...boy. You keep...trying to walk...on water."

"Kate, I really don't deserve you."

"I'm thrilled...that you think that."

*   *   *

Kate's eyes were closed but she wasn't sleeping. A dull ache in her chest and arm prevented that and it was another hour yet before she could have any more pain killer. She heard the brisk, short steps of a heavy man in a hurry coming down the hall-it had to be Daddy.

"Hi, Daddy."

"Hi, Princess. I love you." Ozzie leaned over the bed and kissed her cheek. "How're you feeling?"

"A little sore, but I'll be all right. Guess we better not tell Mother about this one either, huh?"

"You're right, dear. I talked to the doctor out front. He said you'll be good as new in a couple of weeks."

"Yes, I know, Daddy. John is next door. Would you stop in and cheer him up? Sir Galahad is feeling guilty about what happened. It's not his fault. He saved my life."

"Sure, Precious."

Fifteen minutes later Colonel Moffit gave her another peck on the cheek, squeezed her good arm, and was gone as quickly as he came.

* * *

It was a week of mobile control officer and squadron duty officer before the stitches came out and John was allowed to fly again. Kate was released from the infirmary after a week but was confined to quarters for a further two-week period of convalescence. Colonel Ozzie was happy that Kate was going to be all right, and if he had a grudge against John, he sure didn't show it. He indicated that the Silver Star paperwork was progressing and that he expected to see John back in Saigon in a few months to accept it.

* * *

John was number three on a four-ship, Steel Tiger mission-pre-flight briefing at 1400. Steel Tiger was just another name for the same old game of road interdiction and truck patrol on the Ho Chi Minh Trail in Laos. Lieutenant Colonel English was leading, Vic was flying number two and Mike Day, number four.

Their scheduled rendezvous point with the FAC was one hundred miles northwest of the Pleiku TACAN, which put them over the Bolovens Plateau in southern Laos. The weather was crummy and John was nervous. Hangovers usually didn't last past noon. To top it off, he didn't feel in perfect sync with his metallic angel after a one-week layoff. And then the pipper quit working thirty minutes after take-off. It had checked out perfectly in the pre-flight. He had gotten the orange dot of light, surrounded by a circle of eight diamonds, projected off the double panes of see-through reflector glass right behind the windshield and directly in front of his face. He had moved it through the full range of sight settings and it had been right on the money.

All circuit breakers and switches checked okay. He reached for a black grease pencil in the pocket of his upper left sleeve. He drew a black dot on the reflector glass where he thought the piper would be for bombs and one above it to use with the guns. Now we'll see what kind of fighter pilot you really are, Ellsworth, he thought. Besides, he didn't want to report his problem to Colonel English and risk missing out on a combat mission on the wing of his hero. If he ended up shooting bulls eyes without a gunsight, then his mentor would be proud of him. And since they were going to be dropping bombs at least fifty miles from friendlies, a less than perfect accuracy wasn't going to cost any lives that he cared about.

"Decoy Two Two, this is Dusty Six One Flight, over," Colonel English called to the FAC.

"Dusty Six One Flight, this is Decoy. Good afternoon to ya. I'm directly over Attapu at six thousand feet in an O-2. Are you familiar with the river ford just west of town?"

"Affirmative, Decoy."

"I'd like you to crater the approaches and the crossing itself. Say your munitions, please."

"Roger, Decoy. We're a flight of four Fox 100's, carrying sixteen seven hundred fifty pound bombs with delayed fuses and 3200 rounds of twenty mike mike."

"Copy, Dusty. The weather is lousy and getting worse. Broken deck at 8000 feet and visibility less than three miles. I'll be holding directly over the river crossing just under 8000. I'll have to be able to see you on each pass or I will not clear you to drop. Expect triple A fire all quadrants."

This was not going to be a walk in the park. The river ford at Attapu was a choke point and well defended. Dusty Flight had two choices: dive through the clouds and hope they could pick up the target in time to hit it, or stay below the cloud deck and well within the range of the anti-aircraft guns. Of course there was a third option that never got exercised—forget it and go home. John was glad that he didn't have to make the decision.

Colonel English chose to go below. They got into extended

trail—500 feet apart—dived down through a hole in follow-the-leader fashion. The lousy visibility meant that Charlie would have trouble seeing them, but it also meant they'd have trouble seeing each other and the FAC.

"Dusty Flight, set 'em up hot, bomb salvo-one pass apiece," Colonel English called. John thought that was smart. He shared his mentor's feeling that a lousy river ford was not worth more than one pass, especially with somebody shooting at them. John's head was throbbing. He flipped the switch to 100 percent oxygen and turned the air-conditioner up till it was blowing frost particles out the port. They moved into a left-handed daisy wheel over the river ford. It was clearly a well-used river crossing. The dirt approaches were heavily rutted and wide. John varied his altitude up and down by a thousand feet in the turn. Surely Charlie knew the height of those clouds. All he'd have to do is set the altitude fuses to explode at 8000 feet and barrage fire in their direction.

John was more than nervous. Here were four of the world's greatest fighter pilots hanging their asses on the line to crater a lousy road and river ford. The North Vietnamese would have the craters filled and the trucks would be rolling again before midnight, even though the delayed fuses would make extra-deep craters. At least they had to hang it out for only one pass, he thought.

"One's in from the west. FAC in sight," Colonel English called.

"You're cleared. I have you in sight," Decoy replied.

Ten seconds later Ron called, "Two's in from the south. FAC in sight."

"Cleared, Two," Decoy called.

For some reason nobody on the ground took a swing at Colonel English, but they threw everything they had at Ron.

The colonel's bombs walked across the river as Ron was half way down the chute. John had no time to worry about him. It was his turn in the barrel. "Three's in from the east. FAC in sight," he called.

"In sight. Cleared, Three," Decoy replied. The air was so thick the bullets left vapor trails as they homed in on him. It was like diving into a water hose. He heard Mike call, "Four's in from the north. FAC not in sight."

"I have you in sight, Four. You're cleared hot."

The cloud deck kept John's dive angle to thirty degrees and he felt like a sitting duck. As the grease pencil mark moved across the river he mashed the pickle button and sucked on six G's, changing heading with ever other breath. Once he got the nose above the horizon he looked back to see where his bombs landed. Mike was just coming off the target. He watched as Mike broke hard left...and inhaled the FAC!

"Mid-air. Mid-air," John shouted.

Mike's F-100 sheered the twin booms off the little push-pull Cessna O-2.

It appeared to come to a stop in mid-air-like Wiley Coyote off a cliff—then flipped over onto its back and began to fall.

Mike was on guard frequency screaming, "May day. May day." His voice was at least two octaves higher than normal. Black smoke was coming out his tail pipe. He was headed southeast, which was the best direction to be going, but there was no way he was going to make Pleiku, ninety miles away, in that airplane.

John looked back at the O-2 as it fluttered like a leaf to the ground. He saw the left door blow off the plane and the pilot come out the opening. An orange and white parachute inflated. It swung twice like a pendulum before he hit the ground on the riverbank. He was immediately surrounded by a swarm of ants-gooks.

Colonel English was calling, "Dusty Six Two, go up top and raise Search-and-Rescue on guard. Six Three, you and I'll stay with Six Four. Dusty Six Four, how do you read?"

"Loud and clear. I've got a master caution light and a fire warning light. This bird's not going to make it."

"Roger, Four. Hold that heading and keep climbing. Stay with it as long as you can or until I tell you to get out. We're behind and to both sides of you."

"Roger." It was a whimper. Mike Day was scared. The ego was nowhere to be seen. Mike was about to find out if he really had the right stuff.

Flames broke through the belly of Mike's plane. A wise old fighter pilot once told John, "Don't believe that bar talk about JP-4 being less flammable than gasoline." Maybe Colonel English had told him, because he was the one calling "Bail out. Bail out. Bail out." It was the moment of truth for Lieutenant Mike Day. A pilot practiced everything there was to do in an F-100, except one thing. He knew that, sure enough, everything worked just like the operator's manual said it would. But, for the ejection procedure, he had to accept it on blind faith and at a time when there were no alternatives.

The canopy blew off Mike's plane and disappeared quickly behind them. One half second later the seat, with Mike in it, fired straight up. As he cleared the tail both Colonel English and John came to idle and hit the speed brakes, buying a few seconds of time before they flew on by him.

Mike and the seat parted company as the butt-slapper strap pushed him out of the seat. It fell away, and the orange and white striped parachute opened while Mike still had the forward momentum of the plane. John could see his helmeted head slump forward on his chest as the parachute jerked him to a stop with his feet above his head and began its descent.

Just above the stall speed, Colonel English called, "Speed brakes and throttle now." They both accelerated back to flying speed and made a right-hand U-turn to keep an eye on Mike's parachute. John caught a glimpse of the pilotless F-100, doing slow rolls, leaving a black smoke corkscrew contrail behind. It crashed into a jungle-covered hillside in a fiery explosion.

Mike's emergency locator beacon, mounted on one of the parachute straps, had performed as advertised and was putting out an ear-splitting wail on the guard frequency. It over-powered Vic's transmission five thousand feet above them as he talked to Search-and-Rescue at Pleiku. They watched Mike's parachute come down in the dense jungle and hang up in a tree. A perfect landmark for the Jolly Green helicopter, John thought.

The wailing on guard frequency stopped. That was a good sign. It meant Mike was at least in good enough shape and presence of mind to shut off the automatic beacon. Now he could talk to them on the portable radio in his survival vest. God bless him, the kid was thinking, and if this didn't put some maturity on him, nothing would.

Vic checked back in on frequency to tell them Jolly Green would need forty-five minutes. Their fighter escorts, the A-1 Skyraiders, the World War II propeller driven fighters that everyone called Spads, would be there in twenty minutes.

"Dusty Flight, fuel check. Lead is Texaco plus six hundred pounds."

"Two's Texaco plus five hundred."

"Three's Texaco plus five hundred."

"Roger. Dusty Flight, we should have enough fuel to stay here till the Spads arrive," Colonel English called. The weather was closing in and darkness was an hour away. If everything didn't click just right, Mike Day was going to be in for a long night.

"Dusty Six One, this is Six Four." Mike was calling on guard frequency on his portable radio, the only frequency it had.

"Roger, Dusty Six Four. Say your status," Colonel English replied.

"I'm hung up in a tree. I can't see the ground." He sounded like a very frightened little boy. He could easily be swinging two hundred feet off the ground in the tall, dense, triple-canopy jungle.

"Don't even try to get down, Four. If you can't see the ground that means they can't see you. We've got a good mark on your chute. Spads will be here in fifteen minutes and Jolly Green in forty. We'll be able to stay with you until the Spads arrive. Don't use your radio more than once every ten minutes unless we call you."

"Roger, standing by."

"Anybody see Decoy get out?"

"Affirmative," John called. "And he was surrounded as soon as he hit the ground."

"Damn," Colonel English replied. "Dusty Flight, let's keep our orbit moving around so we don't pinpoint Six Four for the gooks, but stay away from the river crossing." John had never heard the Colonel swear over the radio-a major breach of regulations.

The weather was really closing in. It was not looking good for a successful pickup.

"Dusty Six One Flight, this is Fishbait One One, the Jolly Green escort, over."

"Roger, Fishbait, this is Dusty Six One."

"Dusty, Fishbait here. Give me a long count for an ADF steer, please."

"Roger, Fishbait. This is Dusty Six One Flight. One...two... three...four...five...six...seven...eight...nine...ten...nine...eight... seven...six...five...four...three...two...one. Dusty out."

"We got a fix. We'll be there in two or three minutes. Are you in contact with the pilot? If so, say his status."

"Affirmative, Fishbait. He is still in the parachute in the trees.

Doesn't know how far off the ground he is. Reports he's otherwise okay. Chute is clearly visible from our position," Colonel English reported.

Fishbait materialized out of the murk to the southeast.

"Tally ho, Fishbait. Eleven o'clock low at a mile," John called as he spotted a flight of two Skyraiders, closing in on them from nearly dead ahead and low.

"Dusty has a tally on you, Fishbait. We're going to have to pack it in as soon as you pick up the chute. It's at our three o'clock position, one mile."

"I have the chute in sight, Dusty Flight," Fishbait called.

"Roger. I'd like to talk to the downed pilot before we leave," Colonel English asked.

"Go ahead, Dusty."

"Dusty Six Four, this is Six One on guard, over," Colonel English called.

"Go ahead," a meek voice replied.

"The Spads are here and we're Texaco fuel. Keep the faith, son, and keep your wits and we'll see you soon."

"Roger."

"Fishbait, appreciate your prompt response. Take care of our boy."

"Roger, Dusty. We'll get him out of there. Good day."

Vic and John moved in on Colonel English's left and right wings and headed for twenty thousand feet. They poked their noses into the clouds and didn't break out until just short of Tuy Hoa. Vic and John were forced to fly tight formation in the dark, rain-filled clouds. That was always good for a headache all by itself. John's helmet felt a couple of sizes too small. The oxygen mask dug into his cheekbones and he had to urinate in the worst way. If the weather had been nice he could manage the relief tube, but there was no way in that klag. The corset effect of the G-suit on a full bladder made it worse. He had to concentrate one hundred percent on staying on lead's wing, so he couldn't unzip the suit. He decided if worse came to worse he'd just wet his pants. If Astronaut Gordon Cooper could fill up his pressure suit prior to blast-off in a brand new Mercury capsule, John thought he could urinate all over the floor of a fourteen-year-old airplane cockpit.

It was so dark in the clouds that the only things visible on Colonel English's plane were his wing tip light, vertical stabilizer light and dorsal faring light on top of the fuselage right behind his cockpit. John was sucked in so close to Colonel English that the colonel's red wing tip light was right outside the Plexiglas of his cockpit. The turbulence gave him vertigo, a feeling that he was anything but right side up and straight and level. He kept sneaking glances at the attitude indicator without moving his head, which was aimed unflinchingly at that red light like an Irish setter at point.

The body can lie to a pilot big time. He knew Colonel English had to be straight and level, and he knew the attitude indicator was correct, yet his seat of the pants senses said he was in a sixty-degree right bank. It became a game of sheer, brute force will power. Believe it, believe it, believe it, he repeated to himself. He was on the ragged edge of the human performance envelope.

In the back of his mind, gnawing away, was that really rotten feeling of coming home a man short. He knew Colonel English was feeling the same way, asking himself what he could have done to prevent it. That's what the accident review board was going to be asking him, too.

They knew before the debrief was over that Mike Day was going to spend the night swinging in the trees above the Ho Chi Minh Trail. The weather and approaching nightfall just made rescue impossible. When the phone rang John knew it was the command post with the message. They said Search-and-Rescue would commence at first light in the morning. It still gave him chills. By the next morning, under the best of circumstances, the leg straps of Mike's parachute, supporting all his weight, would have numbed his legs. He'd probably have drunk all his water, carried in two whisky flasks, one in each lower leg pocket of his G-suit. He wouldn't have slept a wink all night. At least he'd be alive. The best poor old Decoy Two Two, the FAC, could hope for was to spend the war in the living hell of the Hanoi Hilton. In the worst case, he'd already be done hoping and breathing.

After taking care of his immediate need at the urinal, John joined the de-briefing and the pilots talked at length about "See and be seen," and what lessons could be learned from this tragedy. The squadron commander, the wing commander and a slew of staff officers sat in on the debriefing. Like so many things about air combat, with maximum human performance and minimal margin for error an everyday requirement, midair's were difficult to avoid yet impossible to forgive if pilot error was the cause. John could not fathom his hero, Colonel English, taking the rap for this, but the military mentality often required the sacrifice of some supervisor's career in such cases. If any rules of engagement were broken, it would have been by Decoy. He was not where he said he was. In the heat of battle he'd drifted off the top of the target and that got Colonel English off the hook with this committee. But there would be a higher review of their report and the colonel would have to sweat out those results before he knew for sure that he still had a flying career. John wanted to console Colonel English, tell him how much he meant to him, but that was not the military way. Besides, the colonel was as cool in the midst of all of this as when he was dancing through flak with his supersonic angel, and he did not appear to need any help whatsoever. Cool dude…John's hero.

Dusty's Pub was like a heart surgeon's waiting room. Just as much booze got consumed but it wasn't accompanied by dirty songs and bawdy repartee.

To make matters worse, a lieutenant from one of the other squadrons had just been grounded permanently for flying through the trees. The story was he just got too busy shooting and forgot to fly the airplane. The guy was incredibly lucky to be alive, but his flying career was over. The disease of target fixation was a part of every preflight briefing because it was easier to catch than a cold, with low dive angles above a ragged jungle canopy that varied in height by a hundred feet. The far-away glassy-eyed looks of the lieutenants around the bar as the story was told indicated to John there were multiple near misses in Dusty's Pub.

John decided to call Kate. He reached her in her quarters.

"Hello, Kate, how are you feeling?"

"Getting better every day. I forgot how grand life was when you don't have to work with mutilated bodies all day. I'll be in great shape by Hawaii. How was your day?"

"We left Mike swinging in his parachute from the top of a tree up on the Trail."

"Oh, no."

"He was all right when we left him. Search-and-Rescue will be there at dawn."

"The guns get him?"

"No, he had a mid-air with the FAC. The visibility was lousy. We're not sure."

"Did the FAC survive?"

"He was alive when his parachute hit the ground. That's all we know for sure." John didn't think any good could come from telling her the rest of that story.

"And how are you doing?"

"I'm a little whipped, physically and mentally, but I'll survive."

"I know you will. Why don't you hang up the phone and go straight to bed?"

"I think that's great advice, Kate. I'll take it. Goodnight."

"Goodnight, John."

Vic and John both hit the rack early. Ron was still at the Pub and Mike...well, he was surely facing the worst night of his life. Vic had a kind of inner tranquillity about him, like it was all just some kind of dream and soon he'd wake up back on that wheat farm in Kansas and everything would be fine. John was envious of his peace of mind.

Sleep was not in the cards for John. Vic was snoring lightly sixty seconds after his head hit the pillow.

John slipped out of bed and went into the living room/den/play-room. He pulled Nina Simone out of her well-worn album cover and put her on the turntable.

Nina and John were on the same wavelength. When he was down, he didn't want anybody in the dumps with him except Nina, with her deep mournful voice and haunting piano playing. John's mind skipped back and forth between poor young Mikey, the FAC and Colonel Jack English. No one among the lieutenants knew a thing about Colonel English's personal life, or even if he had one outside the cockpit. He never talked about anything but his first love-jet fighters. John couldn't imagine him doing anything else but flying.

Vic found John draped over the sofa the next morning. He didn't feel too bad. His head was nearly back to its normal hat size and Nina had worked where booze had failed.

"Was I snoring too loud for you, John?"

"Not at all. I just couldn't sleep. Some day you'll have to tell me how you go to sleep so easily."

*   *   *

Ron Johnson and John were scheduled for day alert—twelve hours of sitting around, from 0600 to 1800, in G-suits and survival vests waiting for the phone to ring. John carried his parachute to the airplane, parked in the revetment closest to the alert shack—about a fifty-yard sprint. He put the parachute in the back of the seat, in the hollow designed for it, being careful to lay the leg straps and shoulder straps just right for a quick hook-up. On a normal mission, he'd don the parachute on the ground, snap the two leg straps and the chest strap and climb into the cockpit. That was the slow way.

After the parachute was set, he checked the flags attached to the ground safety pins on the ejection seat. The flags were made of heavy red cloth about four inches by twenty inches, the idea being a pilot couldn't miss seeing them and the safety pins they were attached to. He laid the checklist with Velcro thigh strap on the left console and propped his flying helmet on the right canopy rail, with oxygen hose and radio cord plugged in. John walked around the plane with its maintenance crew chief, Sergeant Larry Adams. The plane was loaded with four seven hundred fifty-pound bombs. He finished the pre-flight by reaching up with both hands and chinning himself on the oval air intake duct to make a visual check for foreign objects in the duct. Now the airplane was properly cocked for alert. "You've got her in great shape this morning, Sarge. Let's hope we get a live one," he said as they walked across the steel planking of the apron. The crew chiefs' alert shack was adjacent to the pilots' shack. They were both dull places, until the phone rang.

John walked in, partially unzipped his G-suit and sat down to breakfast. The best thing about alert, short of the phone ringing, was the food. It was the same menu as the chow hall—the same cooks rotated through there—but somehow it tasted better. That was all relative, of course. It was light-years away from Mom's cooking.

He polished off a plate of two over-easy, half a pound of bacon, several pieces of toast, and coffee. There was only one thing on his mind-Mike Day. John picked up the phone to the command post, the same one that delivered the scramble messages, and asked for a progress report on the Search-and-Rescue effort.

"No word yet, sir."

"Would you give us a holler if you hear anything, Sarge? Ask for Lieutenant Ellsworth."

"Sure will, sir."

"Thanks." John grabbed a dog-eared Zane Gray western and lay down on the couch. Flights scrambled off the alert pad used a different call sign—Litter instead of Dusty. There were four other guys sharing alert with them. The rest were all carrying high drag bombs and napalm. That was usually a better mission off the alert pad. Generally scrambles were rescue missions of some sort, like troops-in-contact needing close air support.

Two of the alert pilots were New Mexico Air Guard guys. John had been looking for a chance for a sober talk with them about job opportunities, but his mind wasn't really on the long-term future. He was as antsy as a caged animal and nothing short of good news about Mike, or getting airborne, was going to solve his problem.

He tried talking with Ron. They did a lot of what-if-ing about yesterday's mission. It was good to talk to a friend who had not been along but knew the situation. He could be a bit more objective. They debated who was to blame, FAC or fighter pilot, both or neither. There was no question what the rules of engagement said. While it was every pilot's job to practice "See and be seen," if a FAC said, "You're cleared to drop," and he had the fighter in sight, the fighter pilot's ass was covered. There were folks who made a career out of keeping their asses covered.

"But you can be just as dead as if you weren't cleared," John said. "That's right, but if you go around high and dry, then you've doubled the amount of time that Charlie has to hammer away at you, especially when you're working under a ceiling like that. It's a tough call, John." It was one of those situations that required a personal policy decision in advance, because when the situation arose the pilot would have to react instantly. John's mind was made up. If the FAC said he was in front of John somewhere and John couldn't see him, he wasn't going down the chute. Period.

"Here's the bottom line, Ron. Stay out of occupied airspace, whether it's occupied by another plane or by flak or by trees. Violate that rule and you are dead meat, career-wise, life-wise, or both."

"Roger that, brother."

The scramble phone rang at 0700 sharp. It jolted John, as it always did, even though he was expecting it to ring any minute. He was closest to the phone and grabbed it.

"Scramble Litter One One Flight to Steel Tiger-Search-and-Rescue. Further instructions from the command post after you're airborne."

"Copy." John slammed the phone back on the hook.

"Come on, Ron, let's go rescue Mikey," John shouted.

John's G-suit was fully zipped before he got out the door. He sprinted across the apron. Sergeant Adams had a head start on him and widened the lead as he ran, shirtless, for their spring-loaded Super Sabre.

John caught the bottom rung of the boarding ladder on the dead run-Sergeant Adams was standing there bracing it, panting and smiling. The sergeant went up the ladder right behind John. John jumped down into the seat, flipped on the battery switch, stand-by inverter and punched the red starter button. The starter cartridge fired with a muffled explosion, black smoke billowed out from under the belly of the beast and the turbine blades began to rotate. Sergeant Adams helped him with his parachute buckles, lap belt and shoulder straps and at the same time John kept his eyes on the gauges while the engine began to wind up. The tachometer came off the peg, the oil pressure began to rise and John brought the throttle around the horn from cut-off to idle. The "Ignition On" light told him they were starting to cook. John lifted his helmet off the canopy rail as Sergeant Adams removed the ladder from the side of the airplane. He put the helmet on, snapped the chinstrap and clicked the mike button twice to see if the radio was on line. It was, and he got a double click back from Ron – he was right with John. One last quick glance at the gauges and he raised both fists together, with thumbs pointed out and moved them smartly apart to signal Sergeant Adams to pull the wheel chocks. With his left hand, he ran the throttle up, and with his right he held the oxygen mask temporarily to his face.

"Tuy Hoa Tower, Litter One One, scramble two Fox-100's."

"Roger, Litter One One. Scramble Runway 21."

Just as that big lead sled began to roll, John tapped the toe brakes atop the rudder pedals to make sure they were working. Two minutes after putting his foot on the bottom rung of the ladder, they were moving. He held his left fist out to Larry Adams and gave him a snappy thumbs up. Sergeant Adams returned the signal, followed it with a big grin and saluted. His thrills were over and Litter Flight's were just beginning.

As they taxied the mile and a quarter to the runway, John strapped the checklist to his left thigh and clipboard to his right thigh and re-checked all the pre-flight items in the checklist.

They pulled into the arming area, just short of the end of the runway, and the arming crew raced around the airplane. The crew pulled red-flagged ground safety pins out of the bomb pylons, nose wheel, and main gear and checked for oil and hydraulic leaks. They watched as John cycled the speed brakes, flaps and all control surfaces. On a thumbs up from the crew chief, John set the flaps to the intermediate position, set the trim for take-off, turned the pitot heat on and the transponder from stand-by to normal. The crew chief held up seven red flags, indicating all the safety pins had been pulled. John answered by showing him his ejection seat red flag and trigger safety red flag, and they were ready.

Ron and John lowered their canopies in unison and taxied onto the runway. John waggled the run-up signal to Ron, stood on the toe brakes and slowly ran the throttle up to "Military Thrust"—the forward throttle stop. The plane shuddered and shook in a thunderous roar as it strained against the brakes. The oil pressure gauge read 45 PSI, the exhaust temperature gage showed 550 degrees Centigrade, and the exhaust pressure ratio gauge was pointing to 1.9. All set. He glanced back at Ron.

Ron's black-visored helmet was bobbing up and down—he was ready. John came off the toe brakes and began to roll. He moved the throttle outboard into afterburner, the eyelids on the tail pipe opened, and there it was again—that orgasmic boot in the butt-and like sex, it was new every time.

John felt back in sync with the airplane. Man and metal were one again and they were flying to the rescue of one of God's chosen from the clutches of the infidels. When Ron had joined up on his right wing, they looked each other over carefully and John called the command post at Tuy Hoa.

"Litter One One Flight, this is Surfside," the command post replied. "Jolly Green needs some flak suppression just east of Attapu. One of the Spads has had to return home with battle damage. There is a tanker on station over Pleiku if you need his services." He gave John all the tanker rendezvous and Jolly Green data, and he wrote it down with a grease pencil on the clipboard strapped to his right thigh. "It's one of our boys down there." The command post ended with a hopeful, "Good luck."

"Roger, Surfside. I was with him yesterday when he went down and I know right where he's at," John answered. He was sorry he had not thought ahead to the possibility that they might be scrambled to help on Mike's rescue. There was a range of subjects he would have discussed with Ron if he'd thought they'd be doing this. But it was too late now and Ron was a good fighter pilot. They'd flown together many times in the last few months.

There were a lot of possibilities. The fact that the North Vietnamese Army probably had Decoy's emergency radio, carried in his survival vest, was ominous. If they understood English, and they probably did, monitoring the conversations with Search-and-Rescue would help them locate Mike. They may have already found him and killed him or captured him. They would leave the parachute in the tree as bait for their flak trap. There would be a limit to how many guns they could move in overnight, and it probably would be the smaller, more portable stuff. That was not much of a consoling thought. The fifty-caliber up through the 23-millimeter guns could make a pilot just as dead.

The HH-3 Jolly Green helicopter was one giant, immobile whale hanging from a huge five-bladed rotor just above the treetops in the midst of a pick-up. Those helicopter pilots were known as the gutsiest guys in the war zone. Ron and John were going to have to silence those guns if Jolly Green was to have a prayer of rescuing Mike.

They checked in with Jolly Green. He and the single remaining Spad were holding high and well to the east of Mike's location.

"Good morning, Jolly Green, this is Litter One One Flight," John called.

"Good morning, Litter One One. Spad Zero One will be directing your activities. It's too hot for us down there. I hope you can do us some good." Jolly Green pilot's voice sounded tired.

"I hope so, too. Spad Zero One, this is Litter One One. I was with Dusty Six Four yesterday and I think I can still find him. We're carrying eight seven-hundred-fifty-pound bombs and 1600 rounds of twenty mike mike. We've got thirty minutes of time on target, with a tanker back-up if we need it."

"Copy, Litter. We've talked to the downed pilot this morning. He's okay, but he's having trouble talking and is very dehydrated. Says he hears children below him, but he may be hallucinating. He also thinks the ground fire that we've been getting is west of his position, but he's not sure of his directions. I have been unable to locate it. We think the gooks are monitoring our conversation on guard channel, so let's stay on this freq and Jolly Green and I will talk to the pilot on guard only when necessary."

"Roger, Spad. I'd like to do a little scouting around down there before we start to throw bombs into the trees," John called. He knew that in the daytime it was possible to get right down on top of the trees and, going that fast, the gunners would only see an F-100 that split second it was directly overhead.

"Well, you know the objective, Litter. Keep your Mach up." John didn't have to be told to go fast.

"Roger. Litter One One Flight, set 'em up hot. Bomb single. Two, follow me through but stay up high. Keep your eye peeled for those guns."

"Two, copy."

"Spad, Litter One One again. If you get a chance, tell the downed pilot his friends are here, never fear." John called.

"Roger, Litter."

John made a turn over the target, picked up Mike's parachute and circled around to the east to dive out of the sun. He dove for the deck a half-mile short and two hundred meters south of Mike's chute. He didn't want to give Mike's position away, or have his jet blast shake his parachute loose. John intended to be smoking.

He leveled at one hundred feet above the treetops doing five hundred knots. Lower would have been better, but the jungle canopy was of such irregular height that he didn't want to take the top out of a tree while looking for a gun site.

John surprised them. There was a small clearing two hundred meters southwest of Mike's chute. There were five irregularly located mobile guns of a caliber that he couldn't identify, under a hastily hung camouflage net. A handful of men were standing around each gun, scanning the sky. John was by them before they saw him. He bent it around hard to the left and stayed on the deck until he was a good mile away, and began to climb.

"No joy on the guns, lead," Ron called.

"I got a tally on them, Two, about two hundred meters southwest of Mike. Stay high and hold off to the north and keep an eye out for other guns. I'll see if I can surprise them a second time."

John turned the bomb switch from single to pairs—he wanted to be sure he got them all—and came out of the sun, again, in a thirty-degree dive angle. He was half way down the chute before he picked up the gun site. It was right on the nose, and so were orange tracers crossing right to the left and just over his head—23-millimeter. He ducked reflexively. The pipper moved through the target. He let two bombs go and hauled back on the pole. As soon as the nose was above the horizon, he banked hard left and looked back over his left shoulder to view the damages. Missed long....

He roared like a wounded lion-his bombs had hit a good fifty meters beyond the target. Of all the times and all the places.... It was the World Series of air combat, the count was full in the bottom of the ninth and Dizzy D. Ellsworth threw a wild pitch. Those tracers had surprised him and he had flinched and it broke his concentration.

"Lead, I've got the other gun site located. It's half a klick north of the first one. You all right?" Ron asked.

John hesitated before he answered. No, he wasn't all right. He was mad and embarrassed, but this was no time for explanations.

"No excuse, sir. He who flinches loses. Listen, this one isn't in the book. You attack the north guns, right-hand turns. I'll try again on the south ones, left-hand turns—simultaneously. Keep your eye on your target and I'll stay out of your way. We'll both come out of the sun. A thirty-degree dive angle will put the sun right behind you. Set 'em on bomb pairs." This wasn't a dance step John wanted to try with a new partner, but he knew Ron and he could do it. His target was clear now-fifty meters short of his first two bomb craters, and they'd be four hundred meters apart as they dove on their respective targets.

John watched Ron roll his light blue belly up to the sun and point his nose down toward the target, and he went in for another try. This time John was ready for anything, and so were the North Vietnamese. The air was full of orange tracers.

The bombs hit their targets just a split-second apart, all in the strike zone.

"Great work, Stan," Ron called.

"Likewise, Ollie." The anguish of the boondocked bombs was forgotten. "I'll go down for another look. Stay high and if anything else opens up, stuff 'em with your last two bombs."

"Roger."

John made a north-south run that took him over both gun sites and just west of Mike's parachute at tree top height. He saw nothing but blood and guts and scrap metal. There was no sign of life in either place.

"See anything else, Two?" John asked.

"Negative, lead," Ron answered.

"Spad Zero One, Litter One One, here. Come over and have a look. I think we've taken the fight out of them."

"Wilco, Litter. Dusty says he still hears children below him and small caliber slugs whining through the trees." John had turned off the guard channel monitor so it wouldn't interrupt Ron and him while they were working over the target. He turned it back on.

"Roger Spad, and we're good for another fifteen minutes." John was glad the tanker was on station. The fifteen minutes was stretching it by at least ten.

A minute later Spad called the Jolly Green. "Come on over and see what you think, Jolly Green." Another A-1 showed up from the southeast as Jolly Green approached Mike's parachute. Ron and John continued to make dry passes while Jolly Green went to work, just to keep the gooks' heads down and distracted as much as possible.

"Spad and Litter, this is Jolly Green. We're going to attempt the pick-up. We're sending the crew chief down on the forest penetrator to help the pilot."

Jolly Green hovered right over Mike, its enormous rotor blowing the tops of the trees around and re-arranging Mike's parachute. Ron and John watched the crew chief come out the wide door on the right side of the helicopter, just behind the two pilots. He sat down on the forest penetrator and was lowered down out of sight into the trees. The forest penetrator was a yellow cylinder about three feet long and eight inches in diameter, with the bottom end pointed. It had three fold-up seats about four inches by ten inches long at its base, just above the point. The crew chief was out of sight for an eternity. On the guard channel they heard him report small arms fire coming from the west.

"Litter, give us a strafing run north-south on the west side, will ya?" Spad asked.

"Roger, Spad." John flipped the guarded gun switch on, caged the pipper and sprayed the general area west of the Jolly Green with twenty mike mike. Ron gave them a second dose.

"Bring us up, Jolly Green. I've got him aboard, and we're taking ground fire from right below us," the crew chief called.

"Jolly Green is taking hits! We're moving out!" In the radio background, as the chopper pilot talked to John, he could hear the sounds of bullets hitting Jolly Green. It sounded to John like he was talking from inside a metal garbage can and someone was throwing rocks at the can.

The Jolly Green rose above the treetops and began to move to the east as he continued to climb with Mike and the crew chief dangling at the bottom of the cable.

"Spad, we've got two more bombs, if you like," John volunteered.

"By all means, Litter. Put it on top of the parachute. No need to give the gooks bait for another flack trap," Spad replied.

Ron rolled in, aimed for the parachute still hanging in the treetops, and created a new clearing in the jungle. It revealed a number of hooches around the edge of the clearing. Maybe Mike did hear children's voices…and maybe Ron just killed them….

Litter Flight watched the Jolly Green climbing away to the east as it slowly hoisted its precious load up into the cabin. Under normal circumstances that had to be a scary ride. To Mike Day it was probably the happiest ride he'd ever taken.

John was so happy his eyes were stinging. "Jolly Green, we need to move along here. Anything more we can do for ya?"

"Negative, Litter Flight. Sure appreciate the help. Our battle damage is minimal. We'll drop your boy off at Pleiku and have a doctor look at him. He should be home by happy hour. I see him back in the cabin here hugging the crew chief. He's got a grin that goes around his face twice."

John suddenly understood, better than ever before, why there wasn't a Jolly Green crew member in any bar in Southeast Asia that ever paid for a drink if there was a fighter pilot in the place.

"Copy, Jolly Green. Spad Zero One, it was a pleasure. Sorry I wasted the taxpayers' money on the first pass," John called.

"Don't worry about it, Litter. The F-4 pukes consider fifty meters long a bull's-eye. Good day."

"Good day. Litter One One Flight, say fuel," John called.

"Two is Texaco minus five hundred pounds."

"Roger, Two, let's run over and get a dollar's worth from the tanker."

"Copy."

*   *   *

Litter Flight poked the tanker's drogue and took on two thousand pounds apiece. It was twice what they needed—the extra was for the victory dance and John was sure the taxpayers wouldn't mind. They headed due east over the central highlands. Vietnam was such a pretty place from ten thousand feet, sitting in air-conditioned comfort and basking in victory, John thought. He motioned Ron into extended trail and they played follow-the-leader around the cumulus build-ups. They hit the coastline and headed for the deck.

John spied a U.S. Navy freighter. "Two, take the stern and roll left. I'll take the bow and roll right." They came at it broadside. John came by the bow level with the eyeballs of a seaman waving wildly. He pulled her up and laid her over in a right-hand victory roll, and then another. Lieutenant Mike Day would have approved. They approached Tuy Hoa from the north, feet wet, and called the tower.

"Tuy Hoa Tower, Litter One One, flight of two, five north for landing. Requesting a pitch-up pattern," John called.

The tower would know what that meant. Every soul on Tuy Hoa Air Base knew the wing was one man short the previous night. Their request told the tower, if word hadn't reached them yet, that the mission was a winner.

"Roger, Litter Flight. Welcome home. You're cleared for a pitch-up pattern." Instead of flying down the runway at a thousand feet off the ground and making an oval pattern, John headed for the deck again.

He put Ron on his left wing and Ron sucked it in as close as his courage and capability would allow. They came across the beach on the initial approach to Runway 21 at one hundred feet off the ground. They flew the length of the runway at that height, and at the end John pulled it up hard in a right-hand Immelmann turn, ending up at 1000 feet, 250 knots, and headed in the opposite direction on the down wind leg to landing. Three seconds later Ron did the same thing. Every man and woman at Tuy Hoa and Phu Hep, whether or not he or she knew the first thing about airplanes or flying, knew the news was good.

* * *

John came down the ladder after parking back at the alert revetment.

"We won, Sarge." He slapped Sergeant Adams on the back. The crew chief was staring open mouthed at the left drop tank. John followed his eyes.

Wedged between the top of the drop tank and the pylon that attached it to the bottom of the left wing, was a handful of tree leaves. "Holy cow, sir. Looks like you were down in the weeds."

John's face felt like it was on fire. He glanced around to see if anyone was watching. He pulled the leaves out, studied them for a while, and then stuck them in his helmet bag. "How about this be our little secret, Sarge?" He hoped his panic wasn't showing.

"Oh, for sure, Lieutenant. After all, you were hanging it out to save Lieutenant Day, sir, and there ain't no damage I cain't hide."

"Thanks, pal. I'm going to have to sit down here in the shade for just a minute. What's your favorite kind of booze?" John could hear his heart thumping in his ears as he sat down unceremoniously under the wing and stared at the horizon. It had been a long time since he'd heard that bass drum beat. It accompanied Colonel English's words of warning after his baptism by fire in A Shau: "If it happens again...or anything like it...you'll be a supply officer for the rest of your Air Force career. Copy?" Another bullet had missed his heart by a millimeter, and like the one over A Shau, it was self-inflicted. Only one thing was certain in his stunned brain. If the word of this got back to Colonel English or the old man, life as he knew it would be over—it would have been better to have died in the jungle.

This one wasn't an ordinary party. The C-130 from Pleiku taxied up in front of Base Operations and was met by every fighter pilot in the 629th who wasn't working. They stood in front of the fire truck awaiting Mike's arrival. The C-130 stopped, shut down its four big fat propellers and lowered the rear-loading ramp.

Mike Day slid off the top of a cargo bay full of new F-100 tires onto the loading ramp. When he reached solid ground, he dropped to his hands and knees, kissed the filthy steel planking and rose with a big smile and both arms raised above his head in a victory salute. A roar went up from the assembled group and the firemen took that opportunity to open up on Mike with the fire hose. The force of the water had to hurt but it was surely the best hurting he'd done in a while.

Colonel Redman levered the cork off a champagne bottle and poured it on Mike's head. Everyone drank the second magnum straight from the bottle, Mike first.

Then they all piled into the step van for the ride to Dusty's Pub. It was standing room only and raucous and happy.

A lot of grown men hugged one another back at the lounge and the toasts were never-ending. The prodigal son had nothing on Mike Day. No one killed the fatted calf but somebody had stolen the hindquarter of one and sawed it into steaks again.

The boys in bibs from the New Mexico Guard and the nurses from Phu Hep were there. Even Kate had violated her doctor's orders to be there. She had not been at Dusty's Pub since that fateful night on the beach and was as big a celebrity that night as Mike. To everyone's chagrin, especially John's, she was too sore to be hugged by anybody and her arm was in a sling. She looked beatific—like the

Mona Lisa.

Matt Jordon had written a song especially for the occasion that began, "Rock-a-bye Mikey, in the treetop," and that was the only clean line in the whole tune.

Everyone wanted to hear Mike's story and he must have told it at least twenty times.

"Swear to God, I slept like a baby...cried every fifteen minutes. And swear to God, I was scared to death," Mike said, and everybody cheered. It took a big man to admit that in front of such a crowd, but Mike had come of age. "I want to especially thank my room-mates, Ron and John, without whom the women of America would have been deprived of a national treasure." More cheers, and the gals from Phu Hep lined up and kissed and hugged him one at a time. He even walked over to Kate so she could peck him on the cheek.

John tried to paste on his best smile as he sat beside Kate and left the celebration to the others. He felt mighty happy about Mike, but that massive dose of self-doubt that he'd pulled out of his wing py-lon had destroyed what should have been one of the greatest nights in his life. He had no idea how those leaves got there, could not recall seeing a treetop even near him as he played that rescue scene over and over in his head. That was the scariest part of all, even scarier than the thought that, once again, he'd tried to kill himself by his own sheer incompetence, and lived to be haunted by it.

He knew that if Colonel English found out his flying career was over. Could he trust the sergeant? It would make a mighty juicy story at the NCO Club bar. Should he bribe him or would the bottle of Jack Daniels do it? He drained his Johnny W. neat in a single swallow.

"How are you feeling, John?" Kate asked.

"Tired. Dead tired. Don't think I slept a wink last night. But I'll be rested up for Hawaii. It's been so long, I'm not sure I remember what the real world is like."

Kate's smile was accompanied by a furrowed brow and the bou-quet of wrinkles.

*   *   *

The World Airway's 707 touched down at Hickam Air Force Base, Hawaii, just as the sun peeked over the back side of Diamondhead. The dawn of day one in an American paradise had arrived and John was ready. The prospect of no flying for a week had loosened a tension spring within him the minute that airliner had put the wheels in the well and he slept like the dead for the entire flight.

John gently nudged Kate, dozing fitfully on his shoulder. The view of the eastern sky through their window was a view he wanted to remember forever, and he wanted Kate to remember it, too.

Six military buses took the contents of their plane fifteen miles east to Ft. DeRussey on Waikiki Beach. It was surely one of the prettiest and most expensive pieces of real estate the U.S. Army owned. In the base auditorium, husbands met wives and boyfriends met girlfriends for the first time in many months. It was a passionate scene. John and Kate sat through a mercifully and uncharacteristically short briefing about how to conduct themselves on R&R, and they were free for a week. The Ilikai Hotel was less than a block up Ala Moana Street, so Kate and John walked and carried their bags. A young, suntanned bellhop with jet-black hair took the bags at the front entrance. His blue nametag identified him as Lonnie. They followed him into an elegant airy lobby and found the check-in desk.

"Ellsworth, party of two. Reservation," John announced.

"Ah, yes, Mr. and Mrs. Ellsworth. Enjoy your stay."

Kate giggled. John had not explained to Kate how he had handled the logistics, or that he had reserved a room with two double beds. As they followed the bellhop across the lobby toward the bank of elevators, she whispered to John, "I think this is another one of those days we won't tell Mother about."

John didn't respond. He just grinned from ear-to-ear.

Their room was magnificent—twenty-second floor, balcony, ocean and marina views. The Ilikai was shaped like an irregular "Y" with the longest leg pointed at the ocean. They were in one of the shorter legs, with a southwesterly view. The price was $34.00 a night, but it was worth it. Kate had insisted on going Dutch treat, so it was an even better deal. It was a big room, dominated by the two large beds with brocade-covered headboards and blue-aqua spreads. John drew the curtains to reveal a sliding glass door and they stepped onto the balcony with its white aluminum railing and chairs. They just stood there silently, arms entwined, absorbing it all. Directly below was the courtyard and fountain and tables with sun umbrellas beyond the fountain. The yacht harbor was full of boats of all sizes and shapes. Beyond was a million square miles of Pacific Ocean just welcoming the sun. To the left of the marina was the beach. It consisted of a blue-green lagoon, as well as ocean front and swaying palm trees.

"This is another world, isn't it, Kate?"

"It's beautiful."

John turned to kiss her and noticed Lonnie was still in the room, patiently waiting. Only slightly embarrassed, John reached into his pocket and handed him a tip.

"Thank you very much, sir. Enjoy your stay." He departed with a friendly smile.

"I need a shower, John. May I go first?"

"Sure." John helped her open her suitcase on the luggage stand. She grabbed a cosmetic bag, gave him a quick peck and a sweet smile, and said, "Happy holiday." Then she stepped into the bathroom and closed the door behind her.

John lay down on the bed nearest the balcony, propped two pillows under his head. He had no idea what would happen this hour, this day or this week. He was just content to be alive in a magic place with a lady with magnetic eyes and a winning smile all for him.

It had been a long trip from Tuy Hoa to Cam Ranh Bay to Guam to Honolulu. They had received the cattle treatment the whole way. Government air charter work was designed for profit, not comfort. The taxpayers, who bought the tickets, didn't have to ride in the seats. He was still dead tired, but sleep could wait till after R&R.

John got out of his shoes, socks and uniform, put on his swimsuit and lay down again.

The bathroom door opened and Kate stepped out, wrapped in a plush white towel, tucked up under her arms and hanging to her knees. It reminded him of their time in Saigon. John saw the scar on the inside of her arm, and just the beginning of the scar on her bosom above the towel. He feasted his eyes.

"Next," she said with a smile.

Then, as if in slow motion, the bathroom door swung shut behind her and caught her towel. She froze in her tracks, but it was too late and there was nothing she could do with a hairbrush in one hand and a cosmetics bag in the other.

There before his eyes, with her towel at her feet, stood the Venus de Milo with arms—a magnificent work of art. Time stood still and John felt welded to the bed.

In the second millennium he saw it. The tan statue was blemished by a bright pink and scarlet zippered scar that began near her breastbone and disappeared around her left side...and the graffiti was gone! He felt like laughing and crying at the same time.

"Kate, it's gone. The devil's mark is gone." He blurted as he bolted out of bed. "It's beautiful. You're beautiful." He hugged her. He kissed her. He laughed. He picked her up, cradled her in his arms and danced and spun around the room.

"I love you, Kate."

Kate was all smiles as she wrapped her arms around his neck and kissed him. John's eyes clanked shut when their lips met—it was an involuntary reaction. He lost his balance and they crashed onto the bed. John barely noticed and Kate offered no resistance. A slow, tender passion gradually built to a frenzy and they soared to the mountaintop and together they celebrated the summit...and it was wonderful beyond his wildest dreams.

*　　*　　*

When he awoke it took a second to figure out where he was. Lying on his side, he was able to read his watch without moving—0900 hours. He'd only been here a couple of hours. He rolled onto his back and saw Kate wearing her XL T-shirt asleep beside him.

He turned to her, only vaguely conscious of and totally uncaring that he was naked. He raised her chin with his hand and kissed her lips.

"Sorry I conked out on you, but it was the sleep of the totally satisfied. Please consider it a compliment."

"Now I know why that Super Sabre responds so well in your hands. You are a super...lover."

John was left speechless by her praise. He stared deep into her emerald eyes. In what seemed like no time at all, total satisfaction turned into raging hunger, but Kate broke the spell.

"Could you please feed me? I'm famished."

"Sure. How about we order room service?" John tried not to sound disappointed.

They checked the menu, John ordered, and headed for the bathroom. Showers always were one of John's favorite thinking places. He turned the water up as hot as he could stand it, and as it cascaded down on the top of his head he basked in the glory of the trip to the mountaintop.

John was sure he would never meet her peer as a lover, but it would be tougher from here on. Sex was like food. He would be hungry again by lunchtime, would crave a snack at mid-afternoon and would be famished by dinnertime—and it would be that way tomorrow and the day after.

Phillip apparently had left no other physical marks aside from the ill-fated tattoo, whose removal he was sure had been a conscious decision on Kate's part. That was such overwhelming good news to him that he shivered under the hot water when he thought of it. In fact, if that tattoo hadn't been gone he was sure he would not have come unglued from the bed when the towel came off. And if there were any other psychological scars, John couldn't see them.

When John came out of the bathroom Kate appeared in great spirits and someone was knocking at the door. It was the waiter with the breakfast cart. He positioned it so they could sit on the edge of the bed with the Pacific Ocean in front of them. A single freighter blowing black smoke broke the horizon. Closer in, a sparkling white passenger liner steamed into port. All levels in the bow were full of passengers watching the arrival. The sounds of the fountain, twenty-two stories below, drifted through the open balcony door. A light, on-shore breeze held the temperature at just the right level.

They toasted Hawaii with orange juice. They toasted each other with Hawaiian coffee. They laughed. They kissed. John fed Kate. She fed him.

After breakfast John took a look at the HONOLULU STAR-JOURNAL that had arrived on the breakfast cart. Kate busied herself unpacking her suitcase and hanging her clothes in the closet.

The front page headline read, "Anti-war Fever Grows on Campus." John read the article and was immediately angry.

"Kate, I get so upset at these college kids demonstrating against the war. They don't have a clue about how those poor South Vietnamese people are suffering. What do you suppose they think they can accomplish?"

"Perhaps they are just exercising their rights of free speech. Perhaps they think America should not go to war unless its own security is directly threatened." Kate was positively chirpy as she worked and talked.

"Kate, when you say, 'Perhaps' is that just a polite way of saying, 'I believe?' "

"Perhaps...yes. Killing is always wrong. War is absolutely wrong unless in self defense."

"How about the draft dodgers? Should we pardon them for their treason because they have so-called philosophical differences with their duly elected government?"

"That's a tough question, John. I think the right thing to do is to serve in a non-combat position as a conscientious objector...like me."

"Hey, I agree with you on that point. Hurrah! Common ground! But I think the dodgers should be treated just like any other law-breaker in our country. Try 'em and convict 'em and put 'em in jail. It's not a matter of principle with them like I think it is with you... they're just self-centered cowards, that's all."

Kate just smiled and shrugged her shoulders and John was thrilled to end their first civilized political discussion on such a positive note. He wondered if her lack of the usual challenging discussion was due to their newfound intimacy.

It was past midday before they decided to rejoin the rest of the world of Waikiki. Dressed in shorts and tennis shoes, they took the elevator down to the main lobby to get the lay of the land. It was a busy place.

They wandered past the check-in counter and along the little shops just off the lobby. As they passed a newstand, Kate said, "I didn't know you were a newspaper reader, John."

"Well, since I don't talk about anything but you, me, and air-planes, I can understand that. I got hooked on newspapers when I was ten years old. The Korean War was on and the CHICAGO DAILY NEWS back page was always full of pictures, generally about the war...and airplanes. I was always hoping I'd see a picture of my uncle, but I never did."

"Some day I want to hear about your uncle. Oh, look at that!" Kate had spied a swimsuit in the window of the next shop. "Would I look good in that, John?" It was an elegant black one-piece, but rather demure.

"I'm sure you would."

"Really? Do you think so? Would my scar show?"

"I don't think so, Kate. But I like your scar. It accentuates your beauty." He gave her a hug.

"Thank you, country boy. Anyway, sometime while we're here, I'd like to try it on. Would you come with me?"

"Sounds like fun."

They wandered out into the sunny courtyard. A huge reflecting pool was elevated about three feet above the ground level with a circular fountain at one end and a square fountain at the other. An Hawaiian band entertained midday alfresco diners at the tables clustered just beyond the fountains. They walked past the diners and around the ocean end of the hotel to the beach.

The shoes came off at the edge of the sand and John and Kate walked around the large placid lagoon to the surf's edge. They splashed along toward Hawaii's most well known sight, the old extinct volcano, Diamondhead. They walked all the way to Kaipiolani Park—it must have been a mile—before they turned around. The temperature was just right, the air was fragrant with the intoxicating aroma of flowers and the ocean lapped placidly at their feet. There were long periods when neither of them spoke but the silence was far from uncomfortable with Kate.

After the beach they crossed Hobron Lane to check out the boats at the docks in the yacht harbor, diagonally in front of the Ilikai.

"Kate, I have always wanted to ride in a sail boat. Have you ever sailed?"

"No, but it looks like fun. Maybe we should see about renting one."

"All right. Keep your eyes open."

There must be a lot of rich folks in Hawaii, based on the number and size of all the toys in the yacht harbor, John thought. Unlike his toy, Uncle Sam wasn't picking up the tab for these. They headed for the part of the docks that had the largest collection of sailboat masts.

In the next-to-last slip at the end of a long dock sat a white, wooden-hulled boat, about fifty feet long with two wooden masts. It looked like a very old boat that was well taken care of. Sitting in the cockpit, concentrating on a disassembled fishing reel, sat a grizzled man with salt and pepper beard and a badly faded, blue denim, Greek fisherman's cap. He looked like he'd spent all of his forty or fifty years on the high seas.

A sign, hanging from the cockpit safety rail, read:

NI SA BULA
Sunlite, Moonlite
Half Day (Nite) $15.00
Whole Day (Nite) $25.00
Capt. Henry Hyde
Inquire Within

"Kate," John whispered, "this is it."

"Let's talk to him."

John cleared his throat and said, "Are you Captain Hyde?"

"Aye, mate. At your service."

"What do you call this boat?"

"I call it home, mate. You could call it a ketch."

"Any chance you could take us out in the next few days?"

"Ever' chance. Tomorrow'd be the best day. Got a high pressure ridge moving in day after and it'll stir up the sea a bit. Ever sail before?"

They both shook their heads no.

"Then I recommend tomorrow."

"John, why don't we take half a day and half a night? Go out at noon and come back at midnight?"

"Perfect." John repeated Kate's request.

"Jolly good, old chap. Bring your own food and a sandwich for the captain. I'm a single-hander on this vessel."

"Single-hander?"

"No crew, mate."

"Oh, of course. I'm a single-hander myself. Noon tomorrow?"

"Noon it is. Cheerio." His concentration went back to his fishing gear.

Kate held John's arm with both hands as they walked back up the dock. She was as excited as a little kid.

They returned to the hotel lobby, checked the posted menus on the hotel restaurants, and decided on one before returning to their room.

After a short nap, they caught happy hour at the courtyard fountain restaurant and drank some fantastic concoction through a straw out of green coconut half-shells. Each was festooned with a bright red hibiscus flower and tiny paper umbrella. The hotel was doing a booming business but all the other people there were just outlines in the background—shadows moving about on a stage. Kate was the only person visible to John's eyes.

John ordered a second round of coconuts and they carried them up to their balcony to watch the sunset. They were potent, but then it had been a long time since breakfast.

The deep orange sun sank into the Pacific from a cloudless blue sky. It was half a circle on the horizon when Kate said, "John, when I see a sunset like this, the sun looks like it's a round, orange doorway in a blue wall, like the door of an igloo. It looks like I could walk through it and see a whole new world on the other side."

John stared at the sun. "Yeah. Maybe if we like sailing tomorrow we can have Captain Hyde sail through it and we'll never come back."

"Maybe that's what 'sailing into the sunset' really means."

"You may be onto something, or perhaps the contents of that coconut are getting to you. I think it's time for dinner."

"Would that black dress that you saw in Paris East be appropriate for this evening?"

"Yes."

Kate and John watched the last piece of hot orange drop into the water. They could almost hear the sizzle.

Kate went inside and opened the wooden bi-fold doors into the closet on the wall opposite the balcony. She took the black dress off the hanger and laid it on the bed.

I'm the luckiest guy in the world, he thought.

They dined by candlelight on Chateaubriand for two with Bernaise sauce and some fancy red wine that the guy with a taster's cup on a chain around his neck had recommended.

They turned in early, made love to ecstatic exhaustion and fell asleep in one another's arms.

At 1145 Kate and John were in shorts and shirts walking down the dock, arms loaded with picnic goodies—beer, wine, bread and lunch meat in a grocery bag and beach things in a tote bag. The day had dawned clear and bright with a light breeze. It appeared to be perfect sailing weather.

"Good morning, Captain. Lovely day for a sail."

"Decidedly so, old chap...milady. Welcome aboard." Henry Hyde had on the same battered denim pants, soiled T-shirt and cap that he wore the day before. His hands were all knuckles, calluses and dirty fingernails, but he had a warm handshake.

"Watch your step there. Lots of things to trip over till you get used to the place. There's an icebox below, starboard side, for your food and drinks."

They stepped onto the well-worn teak deck and into the cockpit at the rear of the boat. The cockpit was dominated by a well-varnished wooden wheel with a large compass in a binnacle right in front of it. John went down the steps into the cabin from the cockpit and deposited a package of bologna and a six-pack of beer in the icebox on top of the block of ice.

The cabin was not as neat as the deck. In fact, it looked and smelled like a football locker room after the game. John hustled back up to the deck just as Captain Hyde touched a button that fired up a diesel engine deep in the bowels of the boat. It idled with a deep-throated purr as he moved about the boat casting off the ropes that fastened Ni Sa Bula to her berth. Captain Hyde was surprisingly agile, with a spring in his step that belied his grizzled countenance.

Kate was seated on the left side of the cockpit forward of the wheel, a look of excited anticipation on her face. She wore a white blouse, buttoned in front and tied in a knot three inches above her white shorts—the whiteness of the material accentuating her tan body. John slid her tote bag over and sat beside her as the boat moved out of its berth. He couldn't imagine, as they pulled out, how Captain Hyde could have backed that boat into such a small place. He made a mental note to pay attention to that when they returned at midnight—he wanted to learn all he could about this sailing business.

Once they had cleared the constricted dock area Kate asked the first question. "Captain Hyde, what does Ni Sa Bula mean?"

"It's pronounced 'NEE-saa-BOOLA' and in the Fiji Islands it means, 'Welcome to paradise'."

"Great name. Did you build it?"

"No, ma'am. I found her aground off the Cayman Islands and salvaged her. Refitted her and brought her through the Panama Canal in '59, and she's been home ever since."

"Captain, we want to learn all there is to know about sailing. Do you charge extra for lessons?" John asked.

"Not unless you put her on a reef or dismast her, matey, and I don't intend to let you do either," he said with a twinkle in his eyes. He seemed more alive with the ship underway. John could relate to that.

They cleared the harbor and headed due south.

"Okay, mate, if you'll take the wheel and hold this heading I'll run some sail up."

Kate came around behind the wheel with John as Captain Hyde went forward. The light southwesterly breeze ruffled her hair as she stood smiling beside John. They played with the big wooden wheel and watched the compass react to slight movements of the wheel. It really was just a giant version of the whisky compass that hung from the top of the canopy in the F-100-a compass card floating in alcohol.

Captain Hyde raised the sail in front of the tallest mast—the one in front—then raised the one behind it. Then he raised a sail right over their heads on a mast at the front of the cockpit.

"Lesson number one, kids. The front sail is a jib, the middle one is the main and the one over our heads is the mizzen."

"Jib, main and mizzen. Now all these ropes around here have

names, too, right?" John asked.

"Right-o, mate, but 'ropes' ain't one of 'em. The ropes to the sails are called sheets—jib sheet, main sheet and so forth. The ropes that tied us up to the dock are called lines. And the rope towing that dingy behind us is a painter. There's more but that'll do for now."

Captain Hyde turned the wheel and the boat turned 45 degrees to the left, putting the wind directly across the boat from the right. The Ni Sa Bula heeled to the left and its speed picked up noticeably. It was a little uncomfortable to the two rookies sitting on the low side of the slanting cockpit. Captain Hyde noticed and suggested Kate and John sit on the high side.

"This is called a beam reach when we're going 90 degrees to the wind, and this is the way you get the most speed out of the vessel. We're probably doing about 6 knots here with 12 degrees of heel. Heel is the slant of the vessel."

"That would be...Mach point zero one...about one one-hundredth times the speed of sound."

"You're talking Greek to me, matey. What's 'Mach'?"

Kate and John laughed. Captain Hyde had been talking Greek to them since the lesson began. "Mach is one way of measuring speed in a jet plane. Mach one point zero is the speed of sound, and at six knots we're doing about one one-hundredth of that," John explained.

"So you're a flyboy are ya? And I suppose when you told me you were a singlehander, too, that meant you fly those jets with one seat."

"Right-o, old chap," John said in his best imitation British.

"Jolly good. Then you probably know more about this sailing business than you realize. They tell me airplane wings work on the same principle as these sails. I use the lift to propel the boat forward."

They looked up at the sails and studied them in silence for a while. Sure enough, they were shaped like a wing.

"This must seem slower'n buggery after what you've been used to."

"I reckon it is, Captain, but it fits my mood perfectly and your fuel is considerably cheaper than mine. Would it be all right if we went up front for awhile?"

"By all means. I'll come into the wind a little more and take some of that slant out of the decks for you."

"Kate, I'll get a couple of beers. Captain, can I offer you a beer?"

"Thank you kindly, but I never drink on the job."

John stepped below and dug two beers out of the icebox and a church key out of the grocery bag. He could hear the rush of water as it slid by the hull of the boat. As he came up out of the cabin Kate was talking to Captain Hyde.

"Lovey, make yourself comfortable up there. I'm a very discreet captain. Get starkers if you like. I always do when I'm alone. Hate to do laundry, and it's just plain more comfortable."

Kate smiled politely, but didn't seem to know how to react to the captain's suggestion. Slowly they made their way forward, stepping over and around sheets and lines and ducking under stays that braced the mast. The boat sat very low in the water amidships, but rose gracefully toward each end.

They arrived at the bow and seated themselves on the roof of the cabin with feet on the deck—at least John's feet were. It was just chair-height for him, but Kate's feet dangled above the deck. All of the cabin area above deck level was square and flat and made of wood, not tapered and streamlined and made of fiberglass like most of the newer sailboats in the harbor.

John handed Kate a can of beer and they toasted jibs and mizzens and sheets and the Ni Sa Bula.

"What do you think, John?"

"I think I could take a lot of this. How 'bout you?"

"Yes. It's delightful."

"Are you going to get 'starkers'?"

"Like in stark naked?"

"I believe so, yes."

"N-O." She was smiling but her sunglasses hid her eyes.

They were about a mile off the beach heading in the general direction of the point of land that held Diamondhead. The seas were a little choppy, but the big ketch sliced smoothly through the water with only the slightest fore and aft rocking. There were a surprisingly small number of boats in sight, given the number they saw in the harbor.

"This is the life, Kate. Maybe there's a career in this."

"Are you serious?"

Small talk never lasted long with Kate, John thought. "I'd be open-minded about it."

"Well, you never cease to amaze me, country boy. I'd have to change your name from son of thunder, though."

"How 'bout son of sea breeze?"

"Nice. Tell you what I'd like to do. Tomorrow, whenever we rent a car to tour the island, let's stop at a hospital. I really would like to look into the employment opportunities." As Kate talked, they watched a large canoe with one wooden outrigger, a large square sail and six men paddling, fly across their bow, running with the wind.

"I'll tell you something else I've been thinking about, Kate. Those air guard pilots have it made. They get all the fun part of the job with hardly any of the military Mickey Mouse. Some of them are full-time and some are weekend warriors who fly airlines full-time. Maybe there's an air guard unit here I could get into."

"It's fun dreaming dreams with you, John. One of the guard pilots at Tuy Hoa is a flight engineer with TWA. He thinks it's the greatest. He says the way he looks at it he has two pilots to fly him around from one party to the next, and he gets paid to do it."

"Sounds like he's still a twisted fighter pilot at heart, doesn't it?" John leaned over and kissed her behind the ear.

"Tell me more about your childhood, John. Something else besides getting intimate with cows twice a day."

"My youth is a pretty boring subject. In fact that word explains my whole life. My threshold of boredom is so low it's barely off the floor. I went to a one-room, country grade school for eight years-the only kid in my class and never more than a dozen in the whole school. It was so boring and I hated it so much that it's affected everything I've done since. It feels like my life has been one long battle against boredom and depression, until F-100's ... and you came along."

"Do you think you could ever get bored with me?"

"That's very hard to imagine."

"With F-100's?"

"Never say never." John was not in a confrontational mood.

"Well, I can live with that for now, my dear. I don't want to compound your problems by giving you ultimatums, but your job makes me very uncomfortable."

"Oh, really?" John couldn't resist that sarcastic shot but Kate was in a magnanimous mood and chose to ignore it. He considered her comment an ultimatum nonetheless. "What would make you comfortable?"

"Doctor, lawyer, merchant, airline pilot…almost anything that didn't involve guns and killing. With your determination and intensity you could be anything you wanted, John."

"How about a sailor?"

"Could you live like this? This is not exactly life in the fast lane." Long pause. "Just might…with the right crew. How about another beer?"

"Would you please bring the towels when you come? And my tote bag?"

John made his way back to the cockpit. He thought Kate had made it about as clear as she could without saying it in so many words. At some point in his future he was going to have to make some choices—concerning both his loves. But life is mighty uncertain, he thought, particularly at this juncture. He had used up far more than his share of luck and his war was far from over. Then there was the very real prospect that Colonel English would make one of those decisions for him, if Sergeant Adams ever told their secret. And who is to say that a woman, especially one in love, can't change her mind. Isn't that one of the feminine prerogatives? It was a strange feeling-like having finally arrived at the summit, only to be standing on the edge of a huge cliff. But he was determined to put it all out of his mind, to enjoy the moment and put his tormented brain in neutral.

"Cheers, mate. We'll be coming about in a few minutes. That means we're going to make a U-turn. When you hear me call, just duck so that jib don't smack you in the face."

"Aye, aye, Captain."

"We'll run on over Pearl Harbor way. Anything special you'd like to see?"

"Negative, Captain. I've got my eyes full up front."

"You bloody well do, old chap. She's a rare bird. You're one lucky bloke."

John returned to the bow with two towels, two beers and the tote bag. "The captain says you're a rare bird and I'm a lucky bloke. I agree with him." He handed her a beer.

"Cheers, soul-matey," Kate said with a big smile. She took a long swig. "Let's spread the towels on the deck and lie on them."

"Right-o, lovey. Need some suntan lotion?" John was so taken with the Captain's language and accent that he couldn't help imitating him.

"Please."

They sat down on the towel and John removed his T-shirt. He spent a silent eternity applying the suntan lotion to the most magnificent body he had ever known. The forward cabin afforded them complete privacy from Captain Hyde when they were lying down.

From the rear of the boat Captain Hyde called, "Ready, about."

"Kate, that means we're going to turn around. Stick your foot up in the air for just a second to let him know we heard him."

Kate, lying on her back, stuck both legs up in the air, feet together, toes pointed. The captain responded with, "Hard alee," Kate giggled, and the boat made a U-turn to the right. The jib swung from left to right and they were headed back the way they had come.

They spent the rest of the afternoon on the deck of the bow, talking, laughing, touching and kissing. The dolphins joined them, blowing their hello's as they did S-turns in front of the bow. They appeared so friendly and happy.

"Kate, besides sailboats, what would be your idea of heaven on earth?"

She didn't hesitate a second. "A job in a small health clinic just off Main Street, Aspen, Colorado. Life in one of those hundred year old houses, two outrageously brilliant, beautiful kids, a husband who loves me, the kids, life and comes home laughing every night at 5:30. Long hikes in the summer, skiing in the winter…." She had a faraway look in her eye.

"You've obviously given it a lot of thought. When I come visit you in Denver could we spend a weekend in Aspen?"

"I'd love to John, but a weekend is far too short. You need to stay at least a week. We'll do it in the summer the first time and those mountains will capture your heart.

"You paint a vivid picture, Kate. I can't wait to do that. You know you and Vic have something…an inner peace…a sense of just what you want out of life and how to get it. I wish I felt that way. It's depressing."

"Look at it this way, John. You set a very high goal for yourself and achieved it early. Now you just have to decide which mountain you want to conquer next."

"You make it sound so simple. Maybe I could conquer that mountain at Aspen...but I get dizzy in high places.

"Kiss me, wacko."

The sun began to set as the Ni Sa Bula was abeam the mouth of Pearl Harbor, about three miles out to sea.

Thin, wispy cirrus clouds, like horses' tails, curled at one end only, stretched from the lower left to the upper right of the painting. It looked too beautiful to be real. The wind and the sea had settled, and the sails hung slack at times awaiting a fresh puff of air. Only the occasional groan of the old, wooden boat and the flapping of the sails broke the silence. It was a spiritual experience lived in Kate's presence.

"There's that orange doorway to forever again, Kate," John said as the sun was half submerged in the Pacific. The white, wispy clouds turned to orange and their tails disappeared. Kate just smiled and stared at the disappearing doorway.

"Shall we go fix dinner? I'm starved," Kate asked.

"Me, too."

John put on his shirt, gathered their stuff and they walked the obstacle course back to the cockpit.

John stepped down below and passed up the grocery bag and the stuff in the ice box.

"Whatcha drinking, Captain?"

"There's a plastic jug of water in that ice box, if you please."

"Coming up." He brought the wine bottle and the water jug. Kate made up the sandwiches while John popped the cork on the wine bottle and broke open a bag of chips. The western sky was in its post-sunset kaleidoscope scene, shifting in infinite variations from orange to crimson to purple to blue to black. The eastern horizon was filled with towering cumulus clouds over the mountains behind Honolulu. Their tops stayed snow white long after their bases had turned dark blue above the sparkling, city lights. John couldn't decide which was the prettiest sight, the show in the west or the one in the east.

As they were about finished with the dinner preparations, Captain Hyde brought the Ni Sa Bula about one more time and headed toward Waikiki Beach. He danced around the cockpit as he loosened lines—sheets—on the right-hand side of the boat. The mizzen boom overhead swung from right to left in unison with the boom on the main sail and the jib flopped across to the left side. He ran lines around winches on the left, brought them taut and cleated them off, and straightened up.

"You kids married?"

"No, Captain," John answered.

"Well, if you ever want to be, come on back. A ship's captain can perform marriages, you know."

"Captain Hyde, if I ever get married, you're the man I want to perform the service and Ni Sa Bula will be the ship," Kate replied.

"A brightish idea, what, milady?"

John let it lay.

Kate and John took turns swigging on the wine bottle, and all three of them rotated with a hand in the chips bag.

"Captain, how long you been sailing?"

"Full-time, since right after the big war ended. I took me separation pay from the forces and bought an old wooden sloop and fixed 'er up and sailed into the sunset. Me dear old mother thinks I'm off me onion—a blot on the old escutcheon and all. But I've got no money to speak of, no responsibilities and no regrets. I'm happy as a clam."

"Happiness is all that counts, Captain," Kate said.

"You're wise beyond your years, lovey."

The darkness settled in and millions of lesser stars joined the bright evening star in the night sky. The clouds over the mountains dissipated in the darkness and a full moon rose and overpowered two-thirds of the stars.

The captain put the moon right on the nose, at 12 o'clock high and rising, its reflection a yellow corkscrew on the glassy swells. The wind died completely and the sails hung like wet rags. Captain Hyde allowed John the wheel again and, in the dim light cast by one small bulb half way up the main mast, he dropped all the sails. He returned to the cockpit and fired up the motor and they purred back across Mamala Bay toward Waikiki.

John picked up the wine bottle again and he and Kate wandered forward to their perch in the bow. It was almost chilly in the still night. A breeze would probably have made it uncomfortable. They picked out the flashing control tower light of Honolulu International Airport, which shared its main runway with Hickam Air Force

Base on the west side of the field. The roar of airplanes taking off was an annoying intrusion into their dream world. Funny, John thought, that's always been music to my ears before.

"Kate, never have bologna sandwiches and wine tasted so good."

"You know, I was thinking the same thing. This may be the most fun thing we'll do with our clothes on the whole trip."

"I think you've been around Dusty's Pub too long." If there were other insinuations in that statement, John felt too mellow to stew over them. He put his arm around Kate and she snuggled up as they watched the lights of Waikiki get closer and closer. The breeze began to blow lightly from offshore, bringing with it the fragrance of jasmine.

They motored into the yacht harbor and watched in awe as Captain Hyde backed the big old boat into that narrow slip without touching either side in the process.

When the boat was secured, they stepped ashore. Kate gave Captain Hyde a big hug and John shook his hand and handed him twenty-eight dollars.

"Captain, I've enjoyed this day immensely. You've shown us a new way of life."

"Glad I could be of service, matey. Cheerio."

The first fifty yards they walked felt like they were still on the swaying deck of Ni Sa Bula.

"John, I'm glad you thought of this. I've found a new love."

"So have I. We'll have to do it again. Someday I'll own a boat."

"Will you invite me on it?"

"For sure."

By the time they reached the room, both were so tired they could hardly stand up.

"Kate, there's something about sea air and sunshine. I'm going to sleep like a baby."

"Me, too."

They both undressed and left their clothes where they lay. John didn't remember feeling his head hitting the pillow.

John decided Kate was a morning person. She awoke smiling and happy, and so affectionate.

"Good morning, man I love. How did you sleep?" she asked.

"Best night's sleep on the least amount of booze in months."

"No bad dreams?"

"Only of sugar plums and Katherine the Greatest."

"You were asleep before your head hit the pillow last night, John."

"Yeah, I know. I squandered a night in paradise and I'm just sick about it. Could I make it up to you now?"

"You could try, Super Lover," she replied with a drop-dead smile. And together they slipped the surly bonds and joined the tumbling mirth and danced the skies and accelerated up the long delirious burning blue and topped the windswept heights with ecstatic grace then floated light as a blissful feather back to a satin runway.

Later they had breakfast in bed again and planned their day.

"Shall we rent a car and go for a drive today?" Kate asked.

"Sure. Let me run down to the lobby and buy a paper. We can check the classified job ads while we're at it. You can have the first shift in the bathroom while I'm gone."

*   *   *

John strode across the busy lobby in a euphoric mood. The air was full of laughter and the fragrance of Christmas—a holiday atmosphere. During the night the hotel staff had decorated the lobby with hundreds of potted poinsettias. Christmas carols were playing over the sound system. He couldn't think of a single way that life could be any better. The newsstand was on the right....

He stared at the STAR-BULLETIN in the newspaper rack in

disbelief.... It can't be.... There must be some mistake. The top-center, front-page picture showed a man wearing pajamas with broad vertical stripes. He was bowing like an oriental, and he looked like a zombie—it was Sam Peterson. The large print under the picture said, "Air Force Pilot Confesses to War Crimes." John checked out another newspaper, called THE ADVERTISER, and it had the same picture and it said, "Lt. Sam Peterson of Rockford, Illinois..."

Numb, he bought a copy of each. He stopped in the liquor store and bought a fifth of Johnny Walker Black and in a daze returned to the room.

The shower was still running and the breakfast cart was still by the bed. He poured the water out of a drinking glass on the break-fast cart and poured three fingers of Black into it. He walked to the balcony with bottle, glass and papers in hand.

"...shot down December first over Hanoi. The Aircraft Com-mander is missing in action and not believed to have survived the crash. Before a group of international press, Lt. Peterson recited a confession that he was a 'Yankee Air Pirate' who had 'killed many innocent women and children.' He condemned the imperialist poli-cies of the United States government and begged his fellow airmen to refuse to fly their bombing missions against the peace-loving people of Vietnam."

John tilted the glass to his lips and drained it. Johnny Walker neat fired down his throat like a blowtorch. He clenched his teeth, squeezed tears out of both eyes and inhaled deeply through his nose.

"John, what are you doing?" Kate's shout startled him, but he couldn't face her. Without looking at her he sat down, held out the newspaper and buried his face in his hands, elbows on knees.

After a brief silence he heard, "Isn't this your friend...in Thailand ...you saw last summer at Udorn?"

He nodded his head.

"Oh, John."

She stood in front of him, trying to look at his face through his fingers. He put up no resistance as she held his head and tried to kiss him. He opened his eyes and her face was so close to his it was out of focus.

All the fearless fighter pilot was slowly, quietly draining out through his eyeballs and running down his cheeks. Kate hugged his head, smothering him in terry cloth and bosom.

"Kate, he saved my life when I was there," John said in a muffled voice.

She moved the bottle and glass and sat down on the small balcony table, her knees touching his.

"Do you want to talk about it?"

"I need some more medicine."

Kate poured about half as much into his glass as he had. "Take it easy on that stuff, John. Alcohol isn't the answer."

He sipped it this time. Having seared all the sensors on the first shooter, this one slid down painlessly.

"How did Sam save your life?"

Talking through hands and sniffles, John said, "I met a friend of his when we were in the bar at Udorn. Nice guy. I agreed to go with him the next day in his little plane—he was a FAC—just for kicks, there was nothing else to do. Then I got very drunk. That night I had awful nightmares. Woke up Sam. Next morning Sam felt so sorry for me he didn't wake me up to go fly. My new friend, Bill Clark, went out and got shot down and killed." Kate's eyes puddled as he told the story.

"John, you lead such a charmed life, it just has to be Providence...."

"Kate, Sam should be dead. We agreed after Bill Clark died that neither one of us would be taken alive...."

"YOU WHAT?"

"We agreed..."

"A SUICIDE PACT?" She was screaming.

"Some things are worse than death."

"John, SUICIDE IS MURDER!" Kate was really worked up. She straightened up, turned her back to him and stepped over to the balcony railing, staring off at the horizon with chest heaving.

John's breakfast had not slowed up the alcohol. It had gone straight to his head. He took another shot of scotch and muddled over what to say next. His brain seemed to be moving in slow motion.

"Kate, can you imagine what they must have done to Sam to get him to talk like that? If he survives he may be a vegetable for the rest of his life."

"John, I hate this war. I hate the way it destroys people, physically...mentally...." She whirled around, hands on the railing. "I can't stand this. You go out there and tempt fate. You take chances you don't have to take. You were going to ride with that FAC just...just for the hell of it. The only reason you're alive is because you drank too much. You drink too much a lot. And now this insane suicide pact with Sam...."

She was shouting and sobbing, but John was in no shape to console her or himself. He couldn't even look her in the eye.

"Don't you care at all about my feelings? Am I just another oak leaf cluster on your hero medals?"

"Kate, I..."

"Well, you just go ahead and sit there and...get yourself dog-faced drunk. You...you've got a deathwish!"

Without another word, she went inside, dressed in silence and left.

John watched her go out the door and poured more scotch in his glass. How could it all come unraveled so fast, he wondered. Thirty minutes ago life was perfect.... He drained the glass. Well, I still have my supersonic angel and I'm still the best stick-and-rudder man.... But then he remembered those tree leaves stuck in his airplane, now in an envelope in his dresser drawer back at Tuy Hoa. Are the leaves a sign of the beginning of the end of that affair? He took another long swig of scotch. If this was the pinnacle, what was the point?

John stared at the yacht harbor and thought he could see Captain Hyde walking around the Ni Sa Bula, its masts rocking gently. He gulped down the dregs of his glass, put the scotch bottle back in the paper bag, along with the glass and one of the newspapers and headed for the docks.

"What ho, bucko?" Captain Hyde called as he spied John walking down the dock toward his boat. "Welcome aboard."

"You on duty today, Captain?" His voice sounded slurred and alien to him.

"No, mate. We're expecting a pretty good blow this afternoon. The tourists don't like lumpy seas."

"Can I buy you a drink?" John asked as he pulled the bottle out of the bag.

"You may, ole chap, but not of that stuff. That blended scotch is bloody awful grog, strictly for export. I've got the real thing down below."

He returned with a fifth of a single malt scotch whisky, of all things. "Where's that wee green-eyed lass?" He pitched half a cup of old coffee over the side, wiped the scum line out of his cup with his T-shirt tail and poured it half-full of scotch.

"She went shopping."

"Got a glass, mate?"

John held his out and the captain filled it about one-third full.

"Mud in your eye, blighter," he toasted, and John tapped the captain's cup with his glass.

It tasted even better than Colonel English prime fermentation, even through taste buds numbed by the bloody export stuff.

"Something's troubling you, laddie."

John pulled the folded-up newspaper out of the bag and handed it to Captain Hyde without saying anything. The captain took a long time to read it. Then he gazed at the horizon for awhile, sipping on his cup of velvet grog, before he spoke.

"Your mate?"

"Best mate, back in college."

Another long pause before he spoke again. "I was a P.O.W. for three years in the big one."

"I'm sorry."

"Made me realize what life was really all about. But it was a bleedin' miserable place to learn. Your mate will make it."

"He will?"

"Sure. They broke him early on and he's still alive. The worst is over. Now that he's been on the front page of every newspaper on the planet, they won't dare let him die."

John wanted to believe him. It had a logical ring to it in his scotch-shrouded brain. It wasn't exactly the official Geneva Convention rules, though. John spilled his guts to Captain Hyde. He told him everything about Wild Bill, Sam, their agreement, Kate's hatred of the war, his love of flying, his conversation with Kate on the balcony and the choices he thought he faced—everything except tree leaves and over-stressed airplanes. It took a couple of refills from the captain's bottle to get through it all. Mostly, Captain Hyde just listened.

Finally, after another extended silence, he spoke. "Three pieces of advice about choices, matey. Number one, always choose life. As long as there's life, there's hope. Number two, always choose happiness. If life is happiest living on a sailboat, barely gettin' by, then do it—you only get one bloody go 'round. And number three, never, never turn your back on love. Without love, number one and two don't count."

"Captain, if I wake up in the morning and can't remember your advice, I'll have to come back and ask you to repeat it."

"I'll do it, matey. And let me add, I love the Ni Sa Bula but I'd scuttle her tomorrow for the right woman. Sleeping with sailboats and aeroplanes is a sorry excuse for the real thing."

He'd have a lot more trouble saying that if he'd ever mated with a Super Sabre at Mach I, John thought. But in his besotted mind even he had to admit that making love to someone he loved as much as Kate was like a day in heaven. Then he had another thought as he noticed the Captain's scotch bottle.

"Say, Captain…." John could hardly understand his own slurred words. Could you tell me where I could purchase a bottle of that fine nectar of the gods we just consumed? My boss loves that stuff too and I owe him big time."

"Matey, you can't buy this anywhere south of Glasgow and west of the Prime Meridian, but I'll make you a deal. If you'll go tell that little lassie how much you love her, if you'll tell her it's all your fault, even if me and you think otherwise, and if you'll pass these here callin' cards out to your mates in the squadron, then I'll give you a fresh fraction of a firkin for your bossman. Deal??"

"Deal. Thanks for everything Captain Hyde. I think I'd better get back to my room while I can still find it. Keep this export scotch for your passengers who can't appreciate the real stuff. And…and thanks again. You've been very helpful."

"Cheers, mate."

*   *   *

It was just past noon when she put her key in their hotel room door. The room was deserted, the scotch bottle was gone. There was no note, no message anywhere. Impulsively she ran to the balcony railing and looked down. The courtyard was still full of people and poinsettias. She checked the bathroom and behind the shower curtain.

"I will not give in to this insanity," she said aloud as she went back out through the door.

*   *   *

John walked a long time before he found his room, fighting vertigo every step of the way. He managed to find his door and struggled with the key. Finally he got down on his knees so he could see to get the key into the lock, squinting at it from so close he could have swallowed the doorknob. The door opened and he fell face first on the floor. Blood ran out his nose and puddled on the carpet, but he was too numb to free any pain. The room was rotating around all three axes like a gyroscope. He struggled to his feet, teetered, and fell over backwards in the doorway. This time he just rolled over to his hands and knees and clawed his way over topsy-turvy terrain toward the bright light that was the bathroom. He pulled himself high enough up on the stool to get his head over the edge and vomited enough poison to kill a horse. It spewed out both nostrils and blocked all the air passages. He could not get his breath and he thought his misery was just about over. His mind willed it all to end but the body continued to react on its own like a chicken who'd lost its head to Mom's ax in the backyard. Then another violent spasm in the solar plexus brought up fluid with enough velocity to clear his throat and he sucked in great gulps of air with a foghorn sound. But the porcelain was now coated with so much oily bile that he lost his grip and fell face first on his nose on the ceramic tile. The white tile turned crimson. Then the lights went out.

*   *   *

The concrete was cold on his bare butt as John sat naked on the floor. The place had a vile smell. The vertical bars were about six inches apart and joined to a horizontal bar two inches off the concrete. His legs stuck through the bars to mid-thigh and dangled down. His arms also poked through the bars and rested on his knees. The cell was on an upper floor of the Hanoi Hilton. He felt a splitting pain in his skull, probably from a rifle butt from his last interrogation session, the one where an evil little North Vietnamese officer broke his nose with a vicious backhand. He pressed his face against the cold bars, the only ounce of relief that existed in this hell on earth. If only he had listened to Kate.

His stomach had been empty for hours, maybe days. He heard the surf of the South China Sea against the wharves in Haiphong Harbor. An onshore breeze blew in his face in the pitch black of the night. One of the bars felt loose. With all his strength he tried to widen the space. He only needed two or three more inches. In another month of rice, cockroaches and rat soup he'd be able to get through the spacing the way it was. He strained on the bars until sweat ran down his face.

A blood-curdling scream jolted him. It was James in the next cell. He was so weak from nonstop torture he was screaming like a little girl. They were pulling his fingernails out one at a time. He'd be next. They were trying to pull him away from the bars, but he had a death grip on them.

*   *   *

It was dark when Kate returned to her room and she was sick with worry. She recited all her "comfort" Bible references for her own edification as she walked, but she was not edified. Her old self had come back with a vengeance again and she had turned her temper against the most important human relationship in her life. She had deserted the man she wanted to one day marry...if he could ever find it in his heart to live as one flesh with damaged goods.

She had looked all over for him with zero success. She opened the door to her room and the first thing she saw was the puddle of blood on the carpet at her feet. In two steps she was at the bathroom door. It looked like a Hitchcock movie scene and reeked of sour stomach fluids, urine and alcohol. Then she looked toward the balcony and froze. Twenty feet away, a rabid looking sub-human sat, naked, on the concrete, with a bloodied chest and face and his legs sticking through the railings. With his elbows winged out on each side he was trying to pull the vertical pickets of the railing apart with his hands. He was grunting and straining and frothing at the mouth. It was John. She heard her own blood curdling scream. At the same instant the bars of the railing came out in his hands and he poked his head and shoulders through the hole.

She raced across the room, onto the balcony and tugged on John by his armpits. Her screams now were right in his ear, and balconies on that side of the building were filling up with curious hotel guests. "John! John! Stop! Stop!" Kate was sobbing as she tugged with all her strength. She got him away from the edge and dragged him back into the room. He lay back on the floor, his glassy, unseeing eyes staring straight up at the ceiling. Kate ran to the bathroom sink, wet every cloth and towel she could find and ran back to John, tracking his bodily fluids and stomach contents across the carpet.

He was trying to talk but it was all incoherent gibberish. Kate struggled to clean him up and drag him into bed.

I t was nearly noon the next day before John rejoined the world of the coherent living. There was a large gap in his memory and his head felt like it would shatter if he moved it a millimeter. Kate was at his bedside absorbed in her Bible.

"Kate, I love you. I'm sorry. What am I...going to do about these nightmares? The booze...isn't helping even a little bit anymore." He had a king-size case of the shakes.

"John, your nightmares are caused by what you're doing to yourself in the day time. You need to see a doctor."

"You mean a shrink...and ruin my career?"

"You're not going to have a career. You're not even going to have a life if you don't do something." She held his face with both hands and looked through her teary eyes into his bloodshot ones.

"I can't do that...but I want to quit drinking, right now, forever. Would...you help me?"

"Sure. I'll help you. That would be a great start. What do you want me to do?"

"Don't drink in my presence?"

"That's all? That's easy. I don't even like that stuff. There's a full bottle in there. Do you want me to pour it down the sink."

"No, no, that's...that's...that's for uh...uh...Colonel English. A present."

"Are you going to still feel this way tomorrow at happy hour when the hangover is gone?"

"Sure. Piece of...cake." He smiled weakly. "And Kate, please ... be patient with me...while I duel my demons."

"I will try, John. I will try. Just one day ago you were the man of my dreams. Please, please make my dreams come true. You can do anything you set your mind to...."

"Oh, Kate, I have to close my eyes again. I feel really awful."

"Okay, baby, and when you wake up next time, you're going to be a born again teetotaler."

The Pacific was really lumpy when they awoke, and every lump had a frothy head on it. The sky was a grimy galvanized tub turned upside down over Hawaii—a good day to do land-lubberly things.

Kate and John decided to go out for breakfast. Yesterday had been a lost day for John. It had been a hangover to end all hangovers, accompanied by abject depression. Kate had given him some more of whatever medicine she had in her cosmetic bag and then decided to explore the job market on her own during John's convalescence. He was glad to have the time alone, and he spent almost all of it horizontal and woozy.

"Would you like to do the driving tour today?" John asked over bacon and eggs in a restaurant off the lobby.

"I'd rather do it on a sunny day, but this'll do," Kate said with a perfunctory smile.

The mood was subdued—politely cordial—and certainly not as cozy as the first two days of R&R. The turn of events had taken them over that cliff at the mountaintop they had so recently ecstatically enjoyed. John wondered if he would ever see the top again. There were wounds on both sides, he decided, and they'd take a while to heal. John noted that Kate never apologized for her outburst on the balcony, just before she walked out, even though he had apologized repeatedly for his performance. He assumed from that she felt none was in order—she meant every word she said.

They rented a Ford Fairmont and did the things that tourists do. They walked the white sand beach of Bellows Air Force Station, on the other side of Diamondhead from Honolulu. Then they drove on around the island to the north, past Kaneohe Bay and Kahana Bay, and had lunch at the Polynesian Cultural Center on the north side of Oahu. Hardly a minute passed that John didn't think of Sam, and it made him feel guilty that he was more or less having fun while Sam was suffering in ways he could only imagine.

They drove slowly and stopped often to admire views of the ocean, mountains and waterfalls. There were long periods of silence—and now they were awkward. John decided that Kate probably felt the ball was on his side of the net. Certainly she had made her views plain enough. An alarming thought kept nagging at him. Maybe now she considered him a patient rather than a true love, or worse yet, just pitied him, like that dying gook in Cholon.

By the time they rounded Kaena Point on the western side of Oahu, the weather began to break and jagged patches of blue sky appeared. The frontal passage had brought with it huge waves.

They spent an hour at Makaha Beach, marveling at the skill of the surfers as they shot down the big rolling tubes of water. The sand was covered with beach bunnies but Kate's presence overpowered them all.

"John, could you really shoot yourself if you thought you were about to be captured?" It was the first heavy comment Kate had made all day.

"I don't think so now. I have to admit, in hindsight it sounds so stupid I'm embarrassed. But Wild Bill had been brutally tortured before they killed him and...for the umpteenth time I can't explain, it could easily have been me but wasn't. I was pretty shook up...I guess you had to have been there, Kate. I'm certainly not sorry Sam didn't keep his part of the bargain. What I'm most sorry about is that I brought it up to you."

"Well, John, I don't think you would do it. I think it was just another one of those macho games you play. Son of thunder is far too intense, too strong-willed to give up on life without a fight. And I'll bet Sam felt the same way."

John began to shiver and couldn't stop. "Excuse me, but I'm chilled. Can we go back to the car?"

As they walked to the parking lot Kate continued. "Suicide is murder, John, and it won't solve your problems. Am I making any sense to you?"

"Kate, you make more sense than any one I've ever met. I think I'd already be dead if it weren't for you. I probably would have splattered myself all over the Ilakai courtyard if it weren't for you. Don't give up on me. Please don't quit talking to me."

"I don't intend to—you old lump of coal. I am going to press on you till you shine like a diamond."

"So that's why I burn so intensely for you." It was a poor joke, but it put a light touch on another chapter of very heavy conversation.

Kate laughed anyway. "I still love you, John."

"I love you, too. Suicide really isn't painless...it's off my list of things to do...promise."

"I will hold you to that. What did Captain Hyde have to say?"

"I think he said, 'Choose life, choose happiness, choose love'."

"Well, bless Captain Hyde. I side with your guru."

They got in the car, Kate slid over next to John and they eased on down Highway 90 like a couple of teenagers. Just short of Makakilo City and north of Barbers Point, they picked up the H-1 expressway back to Honolulu. The sky had cleared completely and another spectacular sunset was in the offing. They decided to stop and watch the show. John pulled off the highway at the northeast corner of Pearl Harbor, abeam the memorial to the U.S.S. Arizona-a monument to an earlier period of lunacy, he thought.

After a silent movie that lasted fifteen minutes, they headed on down the road. Just past Pearl Harbor, in the growing darkness, they passed Tripler Army Hospital.

"I was out here yesterday," Kate said. "It was a madhouse-more maimed soldiers than beds. All the worst cases from Vietnam come here." She stared straight ahead as she talked.

"Kate, I think if I spent my tour of duty the way you have, I'd feel the same way you do. Please believe me when I say I don't kill for fun and I don't want to be a dead hero. I just want to fly my Super Sabre and help these dear peasant farmers of South Vietnam and protect our guys on the ground...and love you. And please don't ask me to choose just yet."

"If you really loved me you'd change."

"If you loved me you'd accept me the way I am."

"John the irresistible force versus Katherine the immovable object." There was the slightest smirk on her face.

"Maybe the other way around."

"Whatever." She kissed him on the cheek. "At least we know where we stand."

*　　*　　*

Just after dark John walked into Dusty's Pub, duffel bag in hand. "Let's say hello to John Ellsworth," Matt Jordan called to the drunks congregated there.

About twenty voices in unison, at the top of their lungs, shouted, "Hello-o-o-o As-s-s-s-ho-o-o-o-o-le."

It was the standard greeting, delivered with the customary gusto, but it was probably shouted with even more fervor because everyone knew he'd just spent a week in paradise with his lady.

John's grin was an involuntary reaction. He bowed low, then raised up and gave a Tricky Dick victory sign. Once again, it felt good to be back. But those words, the profanity that was so commonplace it wasn't even noticed by the denizens of Dusty's, now sounded surprisingly gross. He dropped his duffel bag in the hooch, returned to the bar and popped a can of coke.

"Oh, what's this?" Ron Johnson asked.

"Gotta give my liver a break." John knew that story would only get him through a night or two. It would take a better story than that to survive the unmerciful grief that was in store for him. "A tee-totaler!" Maybe he could switch to vodka and coke—buy a fifth of vodka and refill it with water. Would he really live longer or would it just seem longer? Was it worth it? Well, John felt the votes weren't in yet.

Mike Day came over and slapped him on the back. "Get your sperm count back down below the red line?"

"What would you know about sperm counts?" John asked.

Vic wandered in from a late flight, still sweat-soaked. His hair stood up at odd angles. That happened on windy days when the flying helmet was put on over windblown hair. He shook John's hand and smiled.

"Welcome back, brother."

"Thank you. Pleasure to be back. Hair-raising flight?" John asked.

Vic put his hand on his head. "Well, it wasn't Mu Gia Pass but it wasn't bad. Down near the Parrot's Beak area and Duc Lap. Major Gillespie and I. Think we kicked some butt, but it was dark when we left. How was Hawaii?"

"Great. Loved it."

"Didn't get married, did ya?"

"Oh, God, no. Kate's too smart to marry a pagan throttle-jockey with a death wish...assuming he'd ever have the audacity to invite himself into her world for the rest of her life."

"Don't give me that."

"Tell me something, Vic. Do you think I have a death wish?"

Vic chugged half his beer while he thought about that one. "Well, you certainly go about your work with more zest than most, and that's saying quite a lot in this crowd. But you're a lot better than most, too, probably as a result."

"Vic, someone has to care about this war and these people. I could not believe what I read in the papers in Honolulu and saw on TV newscasts. They make it sound like we're some kind of berserk renegades over here and the North Vietnamese Communists are the angels. This is a crazy war-it's a noble cause, even though the execution sucks—but the USA has gotten to be an even crazier place. The people who are calling the shots seem to be taking their advice from college campuses and liberal editorial writers and virtually no one has the true picture of this war. We couldn't win World War II if this mood had prevailed back then, and the biggest problem is I think Kate shares their view."

"I don't think women can comprehend this experience. I don't write about my missions at all in letters to Nancy. That reminds me, Nancy and I've been thinking about getting married in Hawaii. I've signed up for R&R in late March."

"Well, that's great Vic. Sorry I can't be there." It was like Vic had not heard a word John had said about anything but Kate. No one else seemed to get as worked up about the bigger picture of this war as he did. Maybe he was just out of step. Maybe he should just do his job to the minimum standards. Maybe good soldiers weren't supposed to think—just shut up and say "Sir," and survive. Well, not John Ellsworth, he decided.

"How was the Ilikai?"

"Fabulous. I'd recommend it. By the way, you ever sail?"

"In Kansas? Are you kidding?"

"Well, we did. Both for the first time. Great fun. Sorta like flying but in a much slower plane. You should try it."

"I'd be game for that."

"What made me think of it was, the captain of our boat said he could marry folks. I have his business cards back in the hooch.

That'd be different, don't you think? 'Kansas wheat farmer gets married on a sail boat in the Pacific.' You and Nancy'd probably be the talk of the monthly grange meetings for years to come."

"That does sound kinda fun. I'll have to write Nancy and see what she thinks."

"Vic, what does Nancy think about your flying?"

"Well, she doesn't seem to have any problems with it, but we don't talk about it much. I just kinda low key it."

"I guess that's my problem. I'm not a low key person."

Vic chuckled. "John, you have an incredible grasp of the obvious. There's another thing. Nancy isn't here to see it close up like Kate is. In fact, Kate spends her day up to her elbows in the price of war. Speaking of which, you and I are up for a mission to I Corps tomorrow, 1000 brief."

"Hey, great. I feel like I've been gone forever. You may have to retrain me."

"I doubt that, Ace."

"What else is happening?"

"Steel Tiger is still the best thing going. They've started using F-100F's, the two seaters, for FAC work over the Trail in Laos. They call themselves Misty FAC's. It's just getting too hot for O-1's and O-2's. Since our lame brain...I mean lame duck President Johnson called a halt to all bombing of the North last month, even below the 19th parallel, Uncle Ho has moved a lot more guns into Laos...."

"Sounds like peace at any price, doesn't it? And my ass is priceless and even yours is pretty close."

"Yeah." Vic chuckled. "It's hard to believe that anyone in his right mind would think such a strategy would advance the war effort. But anyway, Lieutenant Colonel English is leaving for Phu Cat tonight for ninety days to fly the F-100F FAC planes. Their call sign is 'Misty.' We'll probably be working with them a fair amount."

"Hey, that sounds like fun, Vic, and if Colonel English is doing it then it must be the thing to do. But they don't get to drop bombs do they—just control other fighters over the target?"

"Well, they do load the guns and smoke rockets to mark targets, but that's all. And they go out single-ship. Alternate missions flying front seat and back seat. The guy in the back seat does all the controlling of the strike while the guy in the front does the flying. And they spend all their time in the danger zone—no toothpick missions for them."

"Well, something to think about if my hero's doing it. That reminds me, I have a...I need to go see him before he gets away. See ya later." Presents for senior officers were not authorized military protocol, but John wanted to do this for Colonel English, and he was willing to take his chances.

John hustled to his hooch and dug the scotch bottle out of his duffel bag. It was wrapped in a brown paper bag that had originally held a one-piece black lady's swimsuit from the Ilikai Hotel women's shop. As he approached the colonel's door he heard the classical music playing again. He knocked on the door and the colonel opened it a crack. "Hey, Lieutenant Ellsworth, come in. Kind of a mess here. I'm TDY to Phu Cat for some Misty FAC work. Leaving in a couple hours." The colonel's duffel bag was on the bed and every drawer in the dresser was open.

"Just heard the news at Dusty's when I got back, sir. Is that a volunteer assignment?"

"Sure is. You interested?"

"If you are, I am, sir."

"I will be in touch, Lieutenant. You qualify for any flying outfit I'm running." Words like that from the fighter pilot he respected the most just took John's breath away. This wasn't a thought he'd ever verbalize at Dusty's Pub, but John loved this guy like he loved his father.

"How was R&R? Did you marry that little Army nurse while you were there?" Colonel English continued to toss clothes into the duffel bag as he talked.

John found it really curious that even the colonel would ask such a question. "Nah, I've got vocational disabilities in her view...knew better than to ask. Great time though."

Colonel English paused with a pair of socks in his hand. He cleaned off a spot on the bed and sat down and studied the sock roll as he rotated it in his hand. He had something on his mind but seemed hesitant to talk about it.

John tried to help him out. "You ever been married, sir?"

"Funny you should ask, Lieutenant. Answer's no, but score me a near miss. I was engaged once and she gave me a choice between F-86's and her. I told her I was sure going to miss her...and I still do."

"That's...uh...the point I'm approaching, sir."

"Well, give it a lot of careful thought, son. Like I was telling you before, when you're young and immortal and idealistic you always think there'll be another streetcar come along. But damnit, next thing you know time gets away from you and the streetcars get fewer and farther between and they all seem to have more wear and tear on 'em. And...uh...the older I get the more I realize airplanes aren't all that cuddly in the middle of the night...in spite of how much I like to dance the wild blue with them in the daytime...say, what's in the bag?"

John was so engrossed with the colonel's words he didn't realize he'd been twisting the bag so tightly around the bottle that anyone could tell it was a booze bottle. "Oh, yeah, this is really something. I ran into an old Scottish sailor in Honolulu who shared your taste in fine scotch and he offered me some of his. He said you can't buy this stuff south of Glasgow and west of the Prime Meridian and he just gave it to me. I'd like you to have it, sir. I don't really want to get hooked on anything this expensive and I'm giving my liver a break here and...."

"I'd be pleased to purchase that from you, son. You've probably noticed my off-duty pleasure all comes in fifths—Beethoven and booze. Isn't that pathetic? But I don't want any gifts from lieutenants. It would look like they were sucking up or something. What's it worth to ya?" The colonel fondled the bottle as he read the label. John learned fast at the master's knee. "Sir, I'd take a buck and call it ten."

"We have a deal, Lieutenant. Pleasure doing business with ya." He handed John a ratty, torn one-dollar piece of military script. "I need to get moving. You keep up the good work, ya hear, and some day my claim to fame will be that I taught you all you know. You did one helluva fine job rescuing Lieutenant Day and I've been meaning to tell you that. But don't...don't...uh...kiss off your love life for a piece of machinery...or you'll end up like me—Brahms and a bottle and a lonesome bed. Life is difficult...but I think you can hack it. Look for me up on the Trail, Lieutenant. Most likely we'll kick some ass together. And I'll call down here next opening we get." The colonel rose and sucked the drawstring tight on his duffel bag.

"I'll look forward to it, sir. Goodnight."

John felt like he had the weight of the world on his shoulders as he walked back to his hooch. He was moved—shocked—to discover what a sad, lonesome man his mentor was, the one guy in the whole world John wanted most to emulate. In the period of one week a woman he loved, a salty, lovable old Scottish war veteran and a hero and role model, all with lives bearing the scars of war, had told him that perhaps his priorities were wrong. One of them was not at all subtle about it.

*   *   *

It felt good to be back home in his Sabre's embrace—smelly, cramped, noisy and cold, climbing upstairs with wall-to-wall napalm. Vic and John were scheduled for close air support, which was the usual application for napalm. John would have preferred his first mission after a one-week vacation not be one with friendly troops nearby, where accuracy was so critical. But it was such a pretty day in the tropics and the view of a magnificent lush green earth made it hard to worry about anything as long as he was airborne. There was a kind of reach-out-and touch-the-face-of-God serenity about flying all alone in the vast wild blue in the non-killing moments, an escape from all the dilemmas of life with both feet on the ground. A week of eating anything but chow hall food made his G-suit fit a little too snugly. John decided he'd have to up the roadwork mileage for a few days, and certainly all those calories he would not be consuming in booze would help the cause. Oh, man, he thought, I feel so good I can hardly stand it...and yet he knew he was not the same person who went on vacation ago, by at least a few degrees.

Vic and John met the FAC, Gravel Zero Seven, fifteen miles due west of Hue, the old provincial capital of Vietnam. The North Vietnamese Army had done the greatest damage at Hue during the Tet offensive. It had taken the first Cavalry division a month of house-to-house fighting to retake the city. Several thousand NVA and VC were killed and three times as many civilians had lost their lives. But the NVA never backed off much, and much of the jungle west of the city was a free-fire zone, which meant, "If it moves, shoot."

"Dusty Niner One Flight, this is Gravel Zero One. We've got a patrol below us taking fire from a village. We'd like you to torch it. Friendlies have pulled back to the riverbank one hundred meters due south of the village. You can expect small arms fire. I'll mark the center of the target area with a smoke rocket, just to be sure we're all looking at the same village, and I'm ready anytime you are."

"Let 'er rip, Gravel." John was delighted to have a target he could see. Two out of every three missions he had to take somebody's word about what was under the jungle canopy.

The easiest way to torch the most thatched hooches was from a low-level delivery. Dropped from fifty feet level, a can of napalm could incinerate an area the size of a football field. The steeper the dive angle, the smaller the area that napalm would splatter over.

John rolled in from the west and picked out the largest hooch on the western edge of town.

"Dusty Niner One is in. FAC in sight."

"You're cleared One. I have you in sight."

As John bored in on the hooch, he saw four black-clad figures run in the front door. They're breathing their last, he thought, then proceeded to toss the first can of napalm clear over the roof. A rolling fireball splashed through the center of the village. Pulling off the target he got a boot in the tail that felt just like the afterburner kicking in. Startled, he pulled back harder on the stick, banked left and looked behind to see what had happened. A huge black mushroom cloud rose over the center of town.

"You got a good secondary explosion there, Dusty Niner One. Must have got a munitions storehouse."

"Roger." John was shaking. Where was the adrenaline rush? Must have been the week of easy living, he thought. It made him sloppy and careless. He flipped the toggle switch to one hundred percent oxygen and breathed deeply.

"Dusty Niner Two, this is Niner One. Come look me over. I felt the concussion from that secondary explosion," John called.

"Roger." Vic cut inside John's left-hand turn to catch up with him, as John checked the instrument panel and visually checked what he could of the wings and the tail through his rear-view mirror. He held the turn as Vic slid under him over him, and behind him.

"You look clean."

"Okay, thanks. Let's go back to work, but let's keep a little higher for the rest of the afternoon. I must be getting conservative in my old age."

"Yeah, right, Dad."

Vic rolled in on the village. "Two's in."

"Cleared, Two." Vic laid a fiery swath through the village adjacent to John's blackened swath. They went through that village like two fire-breathing combines going through a Kansas wheat field.

John rolled in again and delivered the next can of napalm from a 10 degree dive and let it go at 250 feet above the ground. It tumbled right through the front door of the big hooch that he'd aimed at on the first pass. They left that village a scorched spot in the dirt.

"Don't believe I'll need your twenty mike mike today, Dusty. The grunts are anxious to sweep that village before nightfall. There's nothing left to sweep but ashes. Appreciate your help and good work. Good day."

When Vic rejoined John on his left wing, John called, "Take the lead and take us home, Two. I need some wing work."

"Roger, I have the lead." Vic moved out and forward. John snuggled in on his right wing, and lined up the wing tip light with the center of the star of the Air Force insignia painted on the side of the fuselage. Nothing rubs the tarnish off the talents like putting the light in the star and getting in close, John thought.

Over the guard frequency John heard someone calling faintly, "Misty One One, this is Spad Zero Two on guard, how do you read?" There was a pause and the transmission was repeated. No answer. A Misty FAC had gone in, bailed out or was missing.

"Sure hope that isn't Colonel English they're looking for."

"Roger that," John replied.

They headed due east for the South China Sea. Once over the water Vic put John through a mild workout of steep turns, lazy eights and a couple of big barrel rolls. The G-forces were just enough to drive the sweat off the top of his head and down into his eyeball sockets, but by the time they were done John felt as honed as a freshly stropped razor.

"Thanks for taking it easy on me, Vic," John called.

"Easy? It's all easy to you, Ace. You looked like you were welded to my wing out there."

The shakes were gone. They'd only lasted a minute of so, but the memory haunted him and it made him very uncomfortable. He wondered if baring his soul to Kate and Captain Hyde in Hawaii had cost him his nerve. Sometimes it worked like that—verbalizing fear made it more real.

The rest of the flight home was a sightseeing trip, but the call for Misty One One on guard frequency was still echoing in John's ear. It couldn't be Colonel English. John knew his mentor was just too good to ever get shot down.

Vic motioned to John to get back into extended trail—about one hundred feet behind him. They headed for sea level in the direction of a Navy destroyer a mile off the beach.

"You take the stern. I'll take the bow," Vic called.

John double clicked the mike button. After the obligatory victory roll passing the ship, they stayed on the deck and said hello to a fisherman and his family in a junk, a gaff-rigged, single-masted sailing vessel that doubled as home for the whole family. Two naked little kids jumped up and down on the deck waving both hands, as they roared by a hundred feet above them. Ma and Pa didn't seem nearly as friendly or amused. The junk looked like it was about the same vintage as Noah's ark, with numerous patches in the sail.

Ten miles north of Tuy Hoa, John retook the lead and called the tower for landing instructions. He gave Vic a thumbs-up signal-he was a good pilot.

They taxied into the refueling pits and shut down. The crew chief, Sergeant White, came up the ladder to greet John.

"You got her in great shape, Sarge. Flew like an angel. Check her over closely, though. I felt the shock wave from a secondary explosion." Briefly John sat in the cockpit and filled Sergeant White in on the mission. Those poor guys busted butt on the planes. It was a real morale boost for them to know their birds performed well and to listen to war stories, and John always tried to oblige.

"Sir, did you hear Colonel English is missing?"

John had just stuffed his flying helmet into its carry bag. He froze.

"Say again."

"Sir, Colonel English was flying a Misty FAC mission today out of Phu Cat. He went out and never came back—just disappeared—nobody knows."

John was soaking wet with sweat and the tropical sun bore down upon him as he sat there, but he chilled from his hair to the soles of his feet. He just sat there, staring down at his lap. The first word that came to his mind was NO. A couple of possibilities went through his mind. Maybe he'd diverted into Thailand without a radio and the word hadn't gotten back yet. Maybe he was alive and hiding out in the jungle. One thought he refused to accept: The world's greatest fighter pilot was NOT dead. Unless somebody saw him go in in broad daylight, unless someone clearly saw his plane

explode without a parachute, unless someone could positively identify the contents of the body bag, Jack English would return. He
could not explain why he felt that way, but he was just sure that Jack
English's heart was somewhere, somehow still beating.

There was an informal, spontaneous wake at Dusty's Pub. John refused to grieve but he was all alone. No one else held out much hope. Lieutenant Colonel Jack English and his back-seater had last been seen hitting the tanker for the second time that day over Pleiku. All was well at that time, apparently. The weather was lousy, and there were rocks in the clouds in Southern Laos. The terrain was rugged, with peaks to 6,000 feet near the border with South Vietnam. They would have been patrolling at low-level, looking for truck parks—the camouflaged parking area where the trucks hid during the day and barrels of fuel were stored. They might have flown up a box-canyon or something, but John just knew that was something the world's greatest fighter pilot would never do. Some thought maybe they knocked him out of the sky so fast neither pilot got out of the airplane, thus no locator beacon wailed away on guard frequency. But that, too, did not satisfy John.

The girls from Phu Hep were over, but happy hour was not happy. Colonel English was mentor to all lieutenants, not just John. Kate gave him a weak, apologetic, funeral parlor smile. He hugged her in return and they found their corner table.

John spoke softly. "Oh Kate, this is tough. Colonel English was at the top of my hero list. I owe him...my whole career...everything. He was as good as they get. I just cannot accept the possibility that he's...gone."

Kate said nothing and put her hand on John's as he talked. He was on the edge of his chair and really leaning into his conversation. She seemed to know that letting him unload on her was the best thing she could do for him. John was grateful for that.

"Kate, can I get you something to drink?"

"No, thanks. You go ahead."

"I don't need anything either. Soft drinks are not very satisfying as a steady diet for a recovering alcoholic."

John had also confided in Vic that he was on the wagon. Vic had just smiled. Now Kate and Vic both knew, and that made it easier for John to keep his vow. John had read somewhere that Charles DeGaulle used that approach to self-discipline. He would tell a few friends about his proposed self-disciplinary feat, then his ego wouldn't let him do otherwise. It was working for John too-if he hadn't told Kate and Vic, this would have been the time he'd be doing a one-and-a-half gainer off the wagon into a jar of Johnny Walker. He really didn't want to have to think. It would be terrific if he could just take his brain's gearshift lever and put it in neutral. He knew of no way of doing that short of pickling it with booze.

The girls decided to leave early.

As John walked Kate to the six-pack, arm around her shoulders and trailing the group, he said, "Kate, I'm not sure how you feel, but Hawaii was a dream come true for me. I think...I hope I will remember it as the lowest point of my life as an alcoholic...and the highest...in terms of...what life can be like...with you. But to come back to something like this on top of Rock and Sam is...uh a load. Thanks for letting me unload on you tonight."

"You're welcome, John. And listen ... I want you to be sure about how I feel. I love you. When your heart aches mine bleeds for you. And when you're out there flying, I pray non-stop that God will bring you safely back to me." She gave him a brief kiss.

John's eyes were stinging. "Say some prayers for Colonel English, will you please? And one more thing...uh...would you happen to have one of those little pills you gave me in Hawaii? I just know tonight is going to be a rough night."

"Well...yes, but I shouldn't be doing this, John. They are very addictive," she whispered. "Do not, repeat, do not take within twelve hours of flying, okay?" She rummaged around in her purse in the dim glow of the sidewalk light. "And don't get hooked on these things, promise?" She put a single pill in his palm.

"Twelve hours, and I promise. Thanks. Goodnight."

After the girls left, John went to his hooch, put on shorts and sneakers and hit the road. Ever since the sapper attack on the base he stayed away from the perimeter road. He jogged down every interior street in the area, past the 628th Squadron Ops, Dusty Ops and 630th Ops, then swung by the Base Exchange, chapel and post office. In all he figured he must have covered three or four miles, and he made it hurt-lungs on fire, muscles screaming for oxygen.

When he returned to the hooch he had the living room end to himself. He dug out Nina Simone and joined her. He knew the words to every soulful song on the album. She sounded better to John when she wasn't filtered through an alcoholic haze. When she sang he could almost smell the sweet oleander of Memphis in the summer, and he'd never even been to Tennessee.

John took Kate's pill and went to bed and slept all night.

* * *

The Christmas season was a dreary, dismal and depressing time for John—no snow, no Christmas tree, no family, among other things. Not a word, not a clue was found of Colonel English or his plane. John had spent hours at intelligence reading combat and rescue reports and MIA reports. He had studied topographical maps of Laos and western Vietnam. It had been almost a month now since he had disappeared and search-and-rescue operations had long since been called off. John refused to give up looking for him, however. He spent every spare moment of every combat mission on the Ho Chi Minh Trail searching the ground, looking for a reflection from a signal mirror, a flare gun, or an orange signal panel laid out on the ground, things all pilots carried in their survival kit. When he was leading the flight, his pre-flight briefing always included a mention of Colonel English and a plea to all flight members to keep that head turning, keep searching and never give up.

Kate had to work Christmas day, so John volunteered for alert. He was in such a foul mood, he was glad Kate couldn't see him in that shape. They had agreed not to exchange presents. It didn't seem right so soon after Colonel English's disappearance. It was really John's idea and Kate didn't put up an argument.

No one got scrambled. Everyone just vegetated for twelve hours.

The foul mood was made worse by a long dry spell of hot missions, but John decided that was having a positive effect on Kate's mood. He had promised her he wouldn't look for trouble, and from her point of view he was doing a great job of keeping his promise. But there had just been no big trouble to get into. It also had another positive effect—the quality of his sleep.

He was learning to live with his little secret with Sergeant Adams. He bought him pints of expensive bourbon tucked in his helmet bag when he came to fly. "Just a little thank you, Sarge, for keeping this plane in such great shape," and the kid had never again brought up the subject of flying through a tree. But John also knew that whiskey could loosen any tongue, and without Colonel English here to plead his case, if he would plead his case, John's love affair with airplanes could still end tomorrow.

*   *   *

It was the first all-lieutenant, four-ship mission anywhere, at least from Tuy Hoa. John was leading it and Vic, Ron, and Mike were flying in the numbers two, three and four positions.

Seventh Air Force had another name for the road interdiction operation in Laos—"Commando Hunt." From John's perspective it looked pretty much like Steel Tiger, except they were using more "fast-mover" FACs-jets—and fewer small plane FACs. Steel Tiger seemed like a more appropriate name. The Air Force had managed to hang several bells on the big cat. There were a lot of long range patrols on the ground along the Trail reporting truck traffic. There was a new sensor system that the Phantoms dropped like a bomb. It split open half way down its trajectory, spewing hundreds of minia-ture microphones with radio transmitters all along the Trail. These little microphones could then transmit the sounds of truck traffic to an airborne command post tuned into their frequency. There were also C-130's carrying Starlight Scopes—they looked like short, very fat telescopes that could see in the dark-directing night fighter strikes on the Trail. A lot more missions were flown and a lot more roads cratered and trucks destroyed, but nothing in South Vietnam indicated it had much impact on the North's ability to wage war. The Steel Tiger, bells and all, was still one mean cat and he was getting better at swatting down airplanes.

Since all four of the lieutenants lived in the same hooch, they walked to squadron operations together. John would never say so to their faces, but he loved these guys, even though any third party lis-tener would swear the opposite from listening to their conversations.

They all knew where they were going, knew they'd be working with a Misty FAC, and knew it would be a hot target. John was mighty proud to be leading the flight but it wasn't a burden he was carrying lightly. This mission was ominous, and he was as nervous and antsy as a thoroughbred in the starting gate.

They sat down to brief at 0800. It was the first working day of a new year—January 2, 1969—and this was serious work. It was combat mission number 182 for John. The weatherman told them to expect scattered-to-broken clouds and haze-visibility three miles in the target area.

John gave his usual briefing about looking for Colonel English. "Remember to keep an eye out for signal mirrors, flare guns, orange signal panels, wreckage, a burnt spot in the ground, blackened holes...or anything out of the ordinary. We're going to be in the general area where Colonel English was patrolling." John's associates just rolled their eyes at one another when John wasn't looking. They were all starting to talk about his inability to accept reality.

John closed the briefing with Colonel English's advice to him back in July. "'Keep the plane turning at all times. Fly steep dive angles and remember that gunner is as scared as you are. His objective is to kill you before you kill him.' Now here's the bet. A six-pack to the guy who does the best job refueling on the tanker, and a six-pack to the one who puts his bombs closest to the target. Let's have a four-way tie on both. One more thing....Don't...screw...the...pooch. Copy?"

"Copy," three lieutenants said in unison.

"Okay, let's go step on that Steel Tiger's tail."

A chorus of, "Yeahs."

They bailed out of the tiny briefing room like the Chicago Bears coming out of the locker room. Colonel Redman was just coming out of his office and intercepted John in the hallway. The other three headed for the latrine, then the equipment room.

"Bring 'em all back alive, Lieutenant Ellsworth. I've got the base photographer standing by to take a picture of the first four-ship, out-country mission made up of all lieutenants. Fly safe."

"Yes, sir, I'll do my best." John knew he'd risk it all to do his best for that man.

Telling four lieutenants on a Steel Tiger mission to "fly safe" was like telling four little boys on their way to school to stay out of the mud puddles. It was inherently impossible—but he knew what the colonel meant.

Not another word was spoken until John stepped off the van in front of his airplane and said, "Be standing by on frequency at forty-five past the hour."

Four canopies came down in unison at the end of Runway 03 and four lieutenants hurled their hot bodies off the concrete, across the beach and into leaden sky.

After Mu Gia Pass, Tchepone was the most popular choke point on the Trail. It was 20 miles southwest of the DMZ and 66 miles nearly due west of Quang Tri, South Vietnam's northernmost city. Route Nine of the Ho Chi Minh Trail crossed the Se Bang Hieng River just a mile and a half west of the town. It was only a dirt road, but a critical route during three major conflicts. The Vietnamese used it during the Japanese occupation and against the French in the Indochina war of '54. Laos was supposedly an independent country and officially neutral, according to the Declaration of Neutrality signed in '67 by the U.S., China, Russia, the U.K. and France. However, Prince Souvanna Phouma, the Prime Minister, was a paper tiger and nothing John saw over the Trail looked very neutral. What a joke, John thought.

The bridge at Tchepone was a flak trap. It had been initially destroyed in '64 but the North Vietnamese kept rebuilding it. Even when the bridge was down they could ford the river after the monsoon season. The by-pass road around the bridge and across the river was so well worn it was plain to see, even on a hazy day. The ridges on both sides of the river were known to contain numerous anti-aircraft gun emplacements.

"Good morning, Dusty Seven One Flight, this is Misty Zero Three. Numerous targets for you this morning at Tchepone. We've got a truck stalled in the river at the ford—looks like he dropped into one of yesterday's bomb craters and flooded the engine. Also we'd like you to work on those three big concrete pilings. If successful at that, they'll never be able to rebuild that thing. We've been receiving heavy ground fire all quadrants."

"Roger, Misty. Dusty Flight, let's go bomb pairs, arm nose tail, sight set." Hitting those pilings would take pinpoint accuracy, and the problem was compounded by the distraction from a lot of flak. Bomb pairs would require only two passes. If any one of the lieutenants questioned John's decision to make only two passes afterwards, he would say he didn't want the base photographer to photograph the return of the four-ship and have only two or three guys in the picture. Kate would be proud of him, he thought.

"Lead's in from the east. I'll take care of the truck." John could see it plainly enough, about half-submerged. The sun was high, approaching midday, and he was his usual steep and fast and turning. Fortunately the haze that impaired his vision would do the same for the gunners. Both ridges came to life and tracers arced in front of him from both sides. But it wasn't that close, and that truck was his. When the smoke cleared and the mud and rocks and mangled truck parts settled back to earth, the Se Bang Hieng rolled on unimpeded by Russian machinery. John felt good about avoiding that flak, after having not seen it for so long.

Vic rolled in against the bridge pilings. John watched him go down the chute and saw the tracers arcing from both ridges-it looked like 37-millimeter. Then, from just a quarter mile east of the bridge, toward the town, a geyser of orange tracers came up right on Vic's nose. It looked to John like those new Russian-made ZPU-23's, because it was spitting a lot of lead. God, it looked close.

Vic got two seven-hundred-fifty-pound bombs away and they hit right smack at the base of the middle bridge piling. I knew that guy was going to be good, John thought. And in the face of all that flak, no less.

"Hold high and dry, Three and Four," John called. He could see exactly where that orange stuff was coming from. "Misty, looks like they moved a 23-millimeter gun up near the bridge, about a quarter mile east."

"Roger, Dusty Seven One. If you can locate it you can have at it," Misty FAC answered.

It was Seven Three's turn in the barrel so John called, "Seven Three, did you see where the orange tracers were coming from?"

"Negative," Ron replied.

"Seven Four, did you see it?"

There was a pause before Mike Day answered. "Negative." He'd been a little tentative since his night in the trees last fall. John thought he was lying, but that was all right. Everyone had to choose his own method of survival.

"I'll take it then. And everybody come in from the east. They seemed to be having some trouble seeing me come in the sun," John called.

"Two, Copy. They didn't have any trouble seeing me coming in from the north. I was bracketed." Good old Vic. He sounded pretty relaxed about it all.

"Three, Copy."

"Four."

"Lead's in." John tried to make it look like he was going for the bridge, but they weren't fooled. The orange tracers came up right away. He figured they had set up near the bridge under the theory that it would be easier to hit a duck flying right at them, or nearly so, than one passing left to right in front of them. Of course the flaw in that logic was, if they didn't get the duck, the duck might get them. The other piece of misfortune for these gunners was that they were up against one dead-eyed duck, John thought. He came down the chute in a modified barrel roll from nearly straight above them. The gunners never solved their tracking solution—there wasn't a tracer within fifty feet of John. His bombs were dead on target.

"That one was for Colonel English, Misty," John called as soon as he quit grunting from the six-G dive recovery.

"Well, that was one helluva tribute, Dusty Seven One. Looks like Two did good work on the middle bridge piling, also. Three and Four, if you can do as well, we'll drop that mother into the river."

John held high and dry while Vic made one more pass and Ron and Mike made two more. He watched the ridges on either side of the river, trying to pinpoint other gun sites for future reference. And he looked for any light reflections that might be a signal mirror. John just could not shake the feeling that somewhere down there Colonel English was holed up. The tropical jungle was such a fruit-ful place, and with the training they had gotten in survival school it would be possible to survive almost indefinitely, John thought. Cer-tainly the natives spent their lifetimes living there with next to no earthly possessions.

They didn't drop the piling into the river. It was a huge concrete thing about twenty-five feet high by ten feet across by four feet thick. They left it heeled over at about a 25-degree angle, like the mast of Ni Sa Bula in a beam reach in a hard blow. It could never be used again.

"Fine work, Dusty Seven One Flight. Colonel English told us you guys were the best."

"Of course, Misty, he taught us all." John replied.

"Amen, brother. We'll see you Dusty guys another day."

Everyone joined up. Vic on John's left wing, Ron and Mike on his right. "Nice work, guys. Let's spread out and get a battle damage check." John was pretty sure he was clean, but he thought he saw damage on Vic's plane. They spread out into two two-ship formations, swapped leads and checked each other over.

"Two, your left wing tip light is missing and I could throw a basketball through your vertical stabilizer. There's a jagged hole a foot in diameter half way up your tail, just in front of the rudder hinge, but they missed your heart by at least ten feet," John called to Vic. The hole was right where the second of two white 12-inch high yellow S's were painted on the tail, identifying the fighter squadron. "Any control problems?" John asked.

Vic slid away from John and exercised the stick and both rudder pedals. "Little mushy around the longitudinal axis...and my heart seems stuck in overdrive."

"Roger, Two. You and I will make a straight-in approach. I'll follow you down. Your heart will be all right as soon as you burn off the excess adrenaline. Seven Three and Four, any problems?"

"Negative, we're clean and horny as ever."

John headed due east for Quang Tri on the coast. The South China Sea was always the safest place to bail out and that was the shortest distance to the water-just in case Vic's bird chose to quit flying.

It was a 320-mile flight down the coastline. Abeam Da Nang John checked with Vic again. If necessary the flight could land at Da Nang amidst the Air Force and Marine F-4's. He gave John a thumbs up, so all four pressed on for home.

Of course, playing around was out of the question with Vic's damage. There was still a rush from the thrill of victory and it felt mighty sweet, and while his courage was renewed, the edge was definitely off the exhilaration of being shot at and missed.

He hadn't admitted it to anybody, but riding the wagon was extremely difficult. There were times it felt like the wagon had square wheels. Jokes weren't nearly as funny when he was the only sober one in the crowd. And it took as much self-discipline as flying the wing in the weather while fighting a case of vertigo. The most disappointing part was it did nothing to decrease the frequency and intensity of the midnight movies. In fact, the absence of an alcoholic haze improved the clarity of the movie screen.

John knew this mission would set relations back again with Kate.

With three other lieutenants involved, there was no way to suppress the bar talk on a strike this hot. He hadn't looked for trouble, but he hadn't run from it either. But he couldn't change anything about it now. In the heat of battle he had reacted instinctively in the manner he had been trained—Colonel English would have been proud—and he had survived. That was the name of this game.

Ten miles from Tuy Hoa, Ron and Mike peeled off to make a normal, two-ship traffic pattern. Vic and John squared away for a straight-in approach over the water, just like a United airliner would do it on a rainy day. That kept the control surface movements to a minimum.

Vic took the lead and John dropped back on his wing, but loose, so he could keep an eye on his tail section. Vic lined up with the runway, dropped the gear, flaps and speed brake and eased her onto the concrete. At fifty feet off the ground John fire-walled the throttle, cleaned up the gear, flaps and brakes and went around for a landing of his own.

They shut all four planes down at the refueling pit and climbed out with big grins all around. Colonel Redman was waiting there with the base photographer. They gathered around the tail of Vic's plane. Vic hopped up on the horizontal stabilizer and put his face in the hole in the tail. The rest of the lieutenants walked around to the other side of the tail.

They posed with Ron and Mike sitting on the leading edge of the horizontal stabilizer. John stood between them and Vic smiled at the camera through the hole in the tail just above them.

"Vic, this ought to make the front page of the KANSAS CITY STAR," John offered as the photographer snapped away.

Colonel Redman appeared to have mixed feelings about it, so they posed in front of the airplane, where the battle damage wouldn't show in the picture...and four mothers and one wife wouldn't get upset.

They headed back to operations and thoroughly debriefed with the intelligence folks and Colonel Redman present. They were all pleased and Colonel Redman was proud of his boys. By voice vote the refueling six-pack of beer was split four ways. Everybody poked the tanker's drogue on the first try. John forfeited his interest to Mike Day. The bombs on target six-pack went to Vic and John, and John deferred to Vic. They all felt pretty proud of themselves.   .

Back at Dusty's Pub they commissioned Matt Jordan to immortalize them with a song. Matt said it would take him a week and indicated that his musical artistry would most assuredly make reference to that second hole in the tail of Vic's plane.

The nurses from Phu Hep heard three versions of the story, each one an embellished interpretation of the facts. Kate was not smiling. She had just returned from a week at Camp Omega, a Special Forces camp in the central highlands, near Pleiku, treating Vietnamese children. John tried to work the interview process on her.

"How was your week?"

"It sure beat patching up dismembered GI's. The Vietnamese are really a beautiful race, especially their children. They have absolutely nothing but they are so happy, and so appreciative. John, you're losing weight. You okay?"

"Yeah, little tired but I'm all right. No one gets fat on chow hall food and I probably cut my caloric intake in half when I quit drinking. What was the matter with the kids?"

"Some kind of flu epidemic." Kate looked a little down herself. There was an uncomfortable silence before she spoke again. "So how are things with you and your other lover?" It came across like she'd been rehearsing it.

John stared back in silence as he struggled for a snotty response worthy of the occasion.

Finally Kate broke the deafening quiet. "John, would you please give me the unadulterated facts of your day?"

"You always ask, and you always hate the answer.... It's my job, Kate...and I do it very well. I would appreciate it if you would write your congressman and vent your righteous indignation on him. Explain to him how American boys are dying because of the outrageous execution of this war by a bunch of self-serving politicians. Tell him that Ho Chi Minh watches the evening news too and even he can tell he's winning the war even though we're kicking his ass every day on the battlefield and tell him to quit taking advice from campus protesters and TV personalities who haven't a clue as to what is going on over here and ask him how he could be so damn stupid and...." Suddenly John realized he was talking loudly and the whole Pub was quiet as they watched and listened to his ranting. Fortunately the patrons were all junior officers that night. Kate dropped the subject with a silent stare.

John changed the subject. "First chance I get I'm going to ask Major Gillespie for permission to take you for a spin in the F-100F, the two-seater model." As the words came out of his mouth he realized his timing couldn't be worse.

"That will be nice." The tone was chilly. She flashed a prim smile but it looked more polite than genuine.

"Think I'm catching the flu. Don't kiss me tonight, please. There are varieties of disease over here we don't even have names for yet."

"Would you like me to round up the girls so you can go home and go to bed?"

"Would you please?"

After they left, John returned to his hooch. He was all alone. Everyone else was busy getting pickled at the bar.

Why? She was an angel, perfect in nearly all respects. So why couldn't she love him like an angel-unconditionally? So his job was dangerous. There were a lot of dangerous jobs in the world and they weren't held by celibates. Comments like she made tonight hurt, yet when he struck back he hated himself for it.

He felt like he was going crazy with love for her, but he could not pay her unspoken price. The time he now had on his hands for sober reflection was painful, the options all depressing. Drunk had been better. They had not been intimate since Hawaii. Their relationship was no longer on that idyllic plain, and even if it were there was no privacy...and Kate was not a bang-in-the-bushes kind of woman.

He donned running shorts and sneakers and hit the road, the physical torment of straining muscle his only refuge from the mental and emotional kind.

*   *   *

"Kate, John's looking a little emaciated. You wearing that boy out?" Sue Allen asked as the six-pack bounced along the rice paddies back to Phu Hep.

Sue was the opposite from Kate in nearly all respects—tall, slender, and blond, with a laid-back, take-the-world-as-it-comes personality.

"The war is wearing him out, Sue. I think the stress is cumulative, in spite of that fearless facade they all try to wear."

"How are you bearing up? I mean, aside from the flu?"

"Sue, if worry could kill, I'd be dead. I can't understand why I always fall for war heroes. Are there no pacifist heroes?"

"They're all in Canada, Kate."

Kate didn't answer.

John knocked on Major Gillespie's office door, adjacent to the Colonel Redman, the squadron commander's office at the end of the central hallway at Squadron Ops. Major

Gillespie had become the squadron operations officer when Lieutenant Colonel English left to go to Misty FAC, so he was the logical person to ask first.

"Sir, are we authorized to carry Army-types in the back seat of the F models if they're on flight status?" John had hauled the flight surgeon on a couple of missions and he really didn't see the difference.

"Why do you ask, Lieutenant Ellsworth?" Major Gillespie had both feet crossed and propped on the corner of his desk. His cigar was lit, creating a solid overcast in the room just above John's head. An oversized ashtray held at least a dozen mangled butts smelling to high heaven.

"Well, sir, Lieutenant Moffit at the 3240th Army hospital at Phu Hep is on flight status, flies in Huey Medivac choppers. I'd...uh... sorta...like to take her up on one of our toothpick missions. You know her father, Colonel Moffit, is on General Abrams' staff at MAC-V." John figured he might as well bring out the big guns early and give it his best shot.

"I think my Jewish brother-in-law would call that 'chutzpah.'"

"Sir?"

"Never mind. Does it mean that much to you? You two have been awful thick."

"Yes, sir. It means everything to me. In spite of her military heritage she's very anti-war and thinks fighter pilots are a lower species. I thought if she could experience firsthand what this kind of flying is like it...it might help my cause."

"So why is she interested in you, Lieutenant?" The major sat up, propped his elbows on his desk and studied his cigar intently.

"God only knows, sir. Her tour is up in March and she'll become a civilian. So I...uh...don't have much time."

"Is she anxious to do this, too?"

"Yes, sir." The room was cool when John entered, but he could feel sweat rolling down his ribcage.

"Well, Lieutenant, I'll see what I can do. You're a good pilot and your services have certainly been appreciated by the old man and me. And that reminds me of something. Seventh Air Force wants us to recommend junior officers for Fighter Weapons School. Interested?"

"Fighter Weapons School? As a lieutenant? That's something new, isn't it."

"You'll be a captain this summer, right? And it'll be great for your career. The guys who make it to the top all cycle through there."

"Right. Yes, sir. Where do I sign? Any fighter pilot worth his salt would fly through hell in a hand basket to get to Fighter Weapons School. When would I go?"

"After your tour here. Play your cards right, do well, and you might be able to stay on as an instructor. Spend three of four years in Vegas. I'll put your name down. You'll be competing with the top junior officers in the other two squadrons for this wing's recommendation. Good luck."

"Thank you, sir. Thank you very much." John saluted, did an about-face and went out the door, his head spinning with the possibilities. Nellis A.F.B. in Las Vegas, Nevada, was a short hop from Denver. He'd schedule a cross-country flight every weekend, if they'd let him. Kate could teach him how to ski, they could spend Saturday nights in the Jacuzzi, she could see what peacetime fighter piloting would be like. Wait till Kate hears this, he thought.

* * *

It took Major G. and the old man a couple of weeks, but they did it. John could hardly wait till happy hour.

"Kate, it's all set. We're scheduled to fly escort tomorrow for the Ranchhand guys. They're the ones in the C-123's who fly over the jungle and spray it with brush killer-'Agent Orange' they call it. We'll just kind of circle around them while they're spraying to keep the bad guys from shooting at them. They're big two-engine cargo jobs with spraying rigs on them, and they fly low and slow. Probably won't see a thing but trees. Vic will be on our wing. It's a perfect time to bring you along. You're going to love it."

"Terrific." Kate's excitement actually seemed genuine this time.

"By the way, I've been meaning to tell you. I've been recommended by the squadron to go to Fighter Weapons School after this tour. Major Gillespie chose me to compete against the best company grade pilots in the other two squadrons, and some committee in Wing Headquarters will make the final decision. That's like graduate school for fighter pilots. And it's in Las Vegas, Nevada, which is a short hop from Denver."

"If it's what you want, then I'm really happy for you, John." She wasn't exactly overwhelmed with the news.

Stunned, John dropped the subject and headed for Matt Jordan's hooch to get a size small flying suit. Maybe she'll get excited about it after this ride, John thought. With the sleeves and pant legs rolled up a couple of turns, it fit her reasonably well. The G-suit and flying helmet were more of a challenge, but Sergeant Owens, the personal equipment technician, was up to it and fixed her up the next morning.

*   *   *

As they approached the airplane John said, "Kate, meet the only other love of my life."

"Awesome. I don't think I can compete," Kate replied with a polite smile.

"Please don't ever quit trying." John followed Kate up the ladder into the rear cockpit of the F-100F. Sergeant Owens had brought her out earlier and briefed her on emergency procedures, but John wanted to go over it with her himself. He helped her with the seat belt and shoulder straps.

"These two yellow handgrips on either side of your seat are the ejection handles. If we have to eject, I'll call 'Bail out' three times. Pull these handles up. When that happens the canopy flies off the airplane and it'll get real breezy in here. Your shoulder harness will pull you back tightly into the seat. Now you must do three very important things before you squeeze the triggers inside those two handgrips. Number one, be sure your head is back hard against this headrest. This notch here fits your helmet and will keep your head from banging around. Number two, hook your heels in those foot-rests just below your seat. Number three, brace your arms inside these armrests...or the canopy rail will cut them both off when you fire out. Copy?"

"Copy. Head, heels, arms. Handgrips, raise. Triggers, squeeze." She was all business, just the way John could picture her in the operating room.

"Right. Now if you have trouble with anything, you just sit tight and be ready, and I'll blow you out from the front seat. The back seat must eject ahead of the front seat. It will go automatically, if it hasn't left already, one half second ahead of my seat when I squeeze my trigger."

"Okay, now after that everything is automatic. When you come down in the parachute, put your feet together, bend your knees slightly, and look straight ahead when you get close to the ground. If you're coming down in the trees, which is highly likely, put one foot on top of the other so you don't come down astraddle something. Also put your arms across your face like this to keep from getting tree branches in your face. Piece of cake, hey?"

"John, let's just fly safe."

"You can count on it. Now your intercom is set up so you and I can talk without you having to press a mike button. If you like, you can rest your hand lightly on the control stick, just to see what it feels like."

"Like this?" She rested her gloved right hand on the control stick grip.

"Right. Doesn't that have a good feel to it? Try to stay away from the gun trigger, here on the front of the grip, and this little red button here near the top. That's the pickle button that releases the bombs. Nothing will happen if you touch them, but just to be safe...."

"John, how come you have the end of the thumb and first two fingers cut out of your gloves?"

"That's so I can tell switches by feel and I don't have to look for them. You'll notice all the switches and knobs have different shapes and sizes."

"Do you really know where all the switches are without looking? There are so many. Here in front and down both sides."

"I can find every single one with my eyes closed, Kate. Now, one more thing…if you'll lean your head to the right here once the canopy is closed, you'll be able to see my face in my rear-view mirror up there. I usually fly with my visor down because it's tinted like sunglasses. You can do whatever is comfortable, but it would be fun if I could look in the rear mirror and see your green eyes back here. Any questions?"

"Will you get mad at me if I get sick all over your other love?" She was smiling.

"No, but you won't get sick. You've got a stomach that matches your will…cast-iron." Cheap shot, he thought regretfully as soon as it had come out of his mouth, but Kate seemed too preoccupied to react, if she heard it at all.

"Sergeant Owens gave me a bag, just in case." She pointed to the lower pocket on her G-suit.

John leaned down and kissed her, then went down the ladder, put on his parachute and climbed into the front cockpit.

They got airborne off Runway 03 at 1000. Out over the water John made a twenty-degree banked turn to the right and looked back to see how Vic was doing on the join-up. It was a crystal-clear day and the Tuy Hoa Valley never looked prettier.

"Oh, John, it's beautiful. And this thing is so fast. How do you keep up with it?"

"Practice and a quick mind, I guess. The secret is to keep the brain ahead of the airplane. First time I flew a jet, the plane landed and my mind was still at twenty thousand feet, but I got better."

"I can see Phu Hep, and our hospital, and here comes Vic."

Vic closed on their right wing, then dropped down to look the belly of John's plane over and popped up on their left wing.

"He's so close, John. He could almost reach out and touch our wing tip. This is amazing."

"Glad you like it, Kate. This is the only way to see the sights, don't you think?"

"You certainly can't beat the view out of this thing."

"It's not a 'thing,' Kate, it's a living, breathing angel with a soul of titanium and steel."

"Oh, yes. I forgot." It was not delivered with warm tones. He ignored it.

"And you ain't seen nothin' yet, baby."

They rendezvoused with the Ranchhands—three C-123's—near

the coast just above Phan Thiet and 110 miles east-northeast of Saigon. They were in the process of defoliating the whole jungle covered coastal plain in that area. The results of earlier spraying were readily apparent—the stuff was very effective. There were miles and miles of bare trees, like the north woods in the winter-time.

They checked in with the Ranchhands and a FAC in an O-1 who would direct their air strike after the escort mission was over. The three C-123's were staggered about a quarter mile behind one another and offset to the side so the swath of their spraying would overlap slightly.

"Kate, Vic and I are going to make a big race track pattern here. He'll be on the other side of the racetrack so that one of us will be in a position to zap anyone who tries to take a shot at the C-123's. They hardly ever do when we're present. They know we can shoot back."

John dove on the Ranchhands and leveled off at their altitude—just above the treetops—and passed them on the right, doing gentle S-turns all the while.

"John, how can you see anything on the ground going this fast?"

"You have to look straight ahead, but you can't do that from the back seat. My perspective is quite a bit different up here. Focus on things further away and it'll be easier."

About a mile in front of the Ranchhands, John pulled up to two thousand feet in a left-hand, climbing turn and headed back toward them on the back side of the race track pattern.

"Okay, see Vic coming up behind them and on their right?"

"Yes. He must be moving three times as fast as they are."

"That's about right. How you doing back there?" John raised his visor and looked in the rear view mirror. He watched as she leaned her head to the right, reached up on her helmet, loosened the knob and raised her tinted visor. She flashed those fabulous green eyes and they were sparkling.

"John, this is positively thrilling."

"Stick around. It gets better."

When the Ranchhands were through, Gobbler One One, the FAC, fired a rocket into a group of three thatched hooches that had been exposed by the defoliation.

"Dusty, I'd like you destroy those structures. Earlier I saw V.C.

packing a lot of stuff out of there. I suspect they're munitions store-houses, so be prepared for secondary explosions."

"Roger, Gobbler. We've only got time for one pass apiece, but that should be enough." John lied about the time part. This was going to be unpleasant for Kate. This was when she would learn firsthand that John's other lover was also an angel of death and destruction. Besides, he wanted to have enough fuel left to show Kate some aerobatics on the way home.

John was carrying napalm, and Vic Snake-eyes.

"Dusty Flight, set 'em up hot. Arm nose tail. Bomb salvo."

"Two."

"Kate, I'm just calling out switch settings to Vic—sort of a re-minder. It's a required call in combat."

"I see."

"Now the idea here is to put the airplane at a predetermined spot in the sky with the right airspeed, dive angle and altitude above the ground. At precisely that point my pipper—the gunsight—should also be right on the target. If all those things happen at the same split second, I hit the pickle button and those hooches are history. Now I'm going to be too busy to talk here for a few seconds."

"Okay."

"Lead's in."

"Cleared, lead," Gobbler called.

John rolled in and made no violent moves on the run-in-this wasn't Steel Tiger—but he kept it in a smooth turn.

At 1000 feet off the ground, he hit the pickle button and pulled out of the shallow dive. As he banked 60 degrees to the left, he said, "Kate, if you'll crank your head around and look over your left shoulder you'll see napalm in action."

Four cans of napalm made a big fireball. It was about two seconds into its fiery act when they first saw it. John could hear Kate's shuddering gasp over the intercom as she viewed the fires of hell in a small place in the jungle.

They continued their turn and watched Vic dive on the remaining hooch that was still standing.

"Kate, if you watch Vic carefully you'll see the bombs come off his plane. Can you see him?"

There was no answer, and then the sound of Kate getting sick.

Vic was in a 20-degree dive angle. John watched as the four

Snakes-eyes came off the plane. The clamshell fins opened; the bombs decelerated and were pointed straight down when they hit the ground on all sides of the hooch. The Snake-eyes exploded with a visible shock wave emanating in three dimensions. Another gasp from Kate.

Vic proceeded to join up with John while John checked out with Gobbler on the radio. The FAC was appreciative. Kate was silent. Finally a weak voice said, "War really is hell, isn't it, John?"

"I'm afraid it is for anyone on the receiving end of that stuff. How's your stomach? Feel up to some aerobatics?"

"Yes. I am not airsick, and I want to do it all."

"You're a brave lady, and I love you." There was no answer as John motioned Vic into extended trail. "First we'll do a nice, easy roll." He pulled the nose up to 10 degrees above the horizon and smoothly laid the stick over about an inch to left. They made the sweetest, smoothest roll John could manage.

"How was that?"

"Smooth. It was like we stood still and the world rolled over."

"Stomach okay?"

"Fine."

"Did the G's bother you when we pulled out of our bombing dive?"

"No, but that was a weird feeling when the G-suit inflated. I could feel it squeezing my calves and thighs and stomach."

"You can help it by grunting, too. What you're trying to do is keep the blood from leaving your upper body, particularly your eyeballs. If it does you won't be able to see till we let up on the G's and the blood has a few seconds to get back into your eyes."

"I see."

"We'll try a loop now. Keep your head on top your shoulders. If I put three or four G's on this bird while you've got your head down, it'll put your chin down around your belly button."

"Roger."

John dropped the nose and they accelerated till the airspeed indicator read five hundred knots. He lined up on a straight section of the road from Phan Thiet northeast to Phan Rang. Smoothly he fed in four G's. As they headed up John could hear Kate grunting in the back seat.

"You have a very sexy grunt, my dear."

Kate didn't, probably couldn't respond. When he had the nose pointed straight up and the airspeed bleeding off rapidly, he eased off the back-pressure on the stick and said, "Kate, if you look straight up over your head at this point you'll see that long, straight highway behind us. That's what I'm lining up on."

Both F-100's coasted over the top of the loop inverted at one hundred fifty knots. John kept a smooth one-G pressure on the stick so Kate stayed firmly in her seat and was never hanging upside down by her shoulder harness. If she'd been holding a martini she wouldn't have spilled a drop, he thought with satisfaction.

"How ya doing, tiger?"

"I'm with you."

"Okay, get ready to grunt. We're going to have to honk on the G's again coming down the back side of this loop."

John pulled the nose right down the highway. Pointed straight down, with the altimeter unwinding at a great rate and the airspeed approaching five hundred knots, he fed in four G's of back pressure and Kate began to grunt again.

When they had leveled out he asked, "How's your stomach?"

"I think I left it inverted on the top side of that loop…no, I'm fine, John. This is really wild."

"I knew you were an aviator at heart, Kate. Want to get upside down again?"

"Uh, okay."

"All right, this time we're going to put Vic on our right wing and do a cloverleaf turn. That's a loop except we're going to begin a 90-degree left turn when we're pointed straight up. We'll hold that new heading till we come out the bottom of the loop. We'll start lined up on the road, and at the top we'll be crossways to the road. At the bottom we'll still be crossways to the road but headed in the opposite direction. Follow?"

"No."

"Well, just watch. I'll take you through it. Then, when the Thunderbirds put on an air show in Denver and the announcer says, 'And now, ladies and gentlemen, the Thunderbirds will perform a cloverleaf turn,' you can say, 'I've been there. It's a piece of cake.'"

"I doubt that."

John signaled Vic onto his right wing, and announced over the radio, "Cloverleaf turn to the left."

Vic responded with a long, "A-a-a-re-e-e-ba-a-a-a-a," like Speedy Gonzales.

"You guys are crazy...." At least she wasn't gasping anymore.

"Best kept secret in the universe. Okay, here we go." John lined up on the same road again and had the airspeed pegged at five hundred knots. This time when the nose was pointed straight up he froze the stick, stepped smoothly on the left rudder pedal, and the nose arced around 90 degrees to the left so that, as they coasted over the top inverted, they were crossways to the road.

"This is a neat trick in this plane, Kate, because the F-100 at high speeds is controlled almost entirely with the stick, but at low speeds it's crucial that you hold the stick still and use the rudder pedals to guide the plane."

"Whatever you say, John."

John glanced at Vic and he was stationary on his right wing. "See Vic out there? He's got the hard part in this maneuver."

"I don't know how you guys do it."

"It's all skill and cunning, Kate. And lots of practice." They screamed down the backside of the cloverleaf turn and four G's later were leveled out at the bottom, still crossways to the road but going in the opposite direction.

"Time to head home, Kate." John waggled the rudder to motion Vic to slip out into route formation and enjoy the scenery, and they headed for the deck.

At a thousand feet, they cruised up the coastline, past the big base at Cam Ranh Bay. Abeam Nha Trang they finally spotted a Navy destroyer to salute. John looked over at Vic and his head nod told him Vic had spied it, too.

"Kate, we're going to drop down and say hello to the Navy over there. I'll warn you, right after we pass the ship I'll pull the nose up and we'll do a victory roll. Okay?"

"Okay."

John pointed the plane toward the bow of the ship and dropped down to fifty feet. He could hear Kate breathing heavily in the back seat. Just past the bow he pulled up and laid it over into a quick roll. "John, that was scary. I thought my fanny was going to touch the water."

"I know the feeling. You can use that feeling to help you gauge altitude. Now you know what flying by-the-seat-of-the-pants means." John didn't bother to tell her how often he played around at fifty feet over a target.

Ten minutes later, they were 1000 feet over Runway 03 prepared to pitchout and land. Vic was tucked in close on John's right wing.

"Be ready for the pitchout, Kate. We're going to crank it into a quick, 60-degree bank turn, here, and if your head isn't ready for it, your helmet is going to bang the side of the canopy. Best bet is to put your head back against that notch in the headrest."

"Okay, I'm ready."

Halfway down the length of the runway, John snapped into a 60-degree bank turn, sucked on two G's, and they made a 180-degree turn onto the downwind leg for landing. Three seconds later Vic followed. On the downwind leg, abeam the end of the runway, John dropped the speed brake, landing gear, and flaps and 30 seconds later, they met the runway.

*   *   *

The planes taxied into the fuel pit and shut down. John hustled out of his harness and climbed out to help Kate. She removed her flying gloves and helmet. The helmet had rearranged her sweaty hair. Her face was flushed but she was smiling. John discretely ignored the full barf bag in her lap.

"Positively thrilling, John, but...."

John didn't let her finish before he leaned down and kissed her.

"I think I have a better understanding of your love for flying... and what I'm up against." It was delivered with a tone of resignation.

It wasn't what John wanted to hear. It crossed his mind that perhaps his plan had backfired, perhaps he really had screwed the pooch this time. Prospective wives and present lovers should never meet, he decided.

John was making progress as a chess player and Vic was a good teacher, but Vic still won with regularity. Part of the problem was John couldn't talk and play the game. Vic seemed entirely capable of carrying on a heavy-duty conversation and playing chess.

They were on night alert, sitting on a full load of napalm, and it had been two days since they had taken Kate along on the Ranchhand escort mission. John looked at Vic over the chessboard, set up on one end of the narrow rectangular dining table in the small L-shaped living/dining room of the alert shack.

"You going to get married in Hawaii on R&R next month?"

"Yeah. Nancy wants to look up your friend on the sailboat."

"Wish I could be there. Where's Nancy from?"

"My home town. She grew up on a farm about two miles from where I did. She's an only child like Kate, and her father raises wheat on a thousand acres. He's offered to take me on as a partner whenever I'm ready."

"Does that appeal to you?"

"Yeah, it does, John. I love this business and the F-100 is some kind of toy to play with, but I just can't fit it in with a wife and a family. And I have to admit that even after this, sitting on a tractor and watching the dawn come up in the middle of a Kansas wheat field is still my definition of the good life."

"More power to you, brother. I've always been envious of how you have your life so together. You know exactly what you want, where you're going and how you're going to get there."

"How do you think Kate liked the plane ride?"

"Well, we must have talked an hour on the phone last night. Said she had a greater appreciation of what she was up against, but basically I think I made a mistake taking her to work with me."

"What did she say about the bombing?"

"Nothin', and I sure didn't bring up the subject. Over the intercom I could hear her gasping and barfing, but I never said a word about it. Oh, wait. She did say something. She said, 'War really is hell isn't it?' And I've heard that come out of her mouth before." Vic pondered that in silence.

"She seemed to really enjoy the aerobatics, but that run on the deck past the destroyer scared her. I could hear her hyperventilating in the back seat."

"So what's your next step?"

"I hope I get that Fighter Weapons School assignment. That would put me close to Denver. I could fly from Nellis up to Buckley Field on weekends. But Kate was underwhelmed, in spite of my excitement about it."

"Maybe she was underwhelmed because of she thinks airplanes come first with you." Vic moved his queen.

"Probably. That's intuitively obvious to the most casual observer, isn't it? I worry about all those rich doctors back at Denver General. Don't think I can compete with them."

"Kate doesn't strike me as a gold digger. Besides, she's madly in love with you, John."

"Think so?"

"I know so. I wish you could see the way she looks at you when you're not looking at her."

"Really? I'm glad to know that. Thanks. Now let me run another idea by you, my friend. I've been giving serious thought to going up to Phu Cat to be a Misty FAC. You and everyone else know I have never given up hope of finding Colonel English. I thought if I did a three-month tour up there I'd be able to spend more time over the Trail and look for him. Vic, I don't know where life goes from here. I am so torn between wanting to spend the rest of my life with Kate and flying fighters. I don't believe I'm going to be able to have both and I can't imagine living without either. But there is one thing I am sure of: I can't leave Vietnam until I'm convinced that I have done all I can to find Colonel English. Vic, I love him like my father. I owe him my career. It's just something I have to do."

"A man's got to do what a man's got to do." ·

"Yeah, well, Kate's going to have a fit...cause I'll have to extend my Vietnam tour to do it."

"Oh, boy, don't ask me to deliver that news."

"Well, I haven't decided for sure yet, but I'm really tormented by it, Vic. You know those nightmares of mine that keep you awake? I see Colonel English in them. He's very much alive and he's out there in the jungle...."

"Check."

"A-H-H-H. You always get me talking and I lose my concentration."

"You're just going to have to learn to walk and chew gum at the same time, John. I don't understand how the world's greatest fighter pilot can be such a bad chess player."

"Maybe if I pretended those rooks and pawns were shooting at me it would focus my attention."

"Maybe you got something there, John. By the way, you feeling okay? You look like death warmed over."

"Yeah, I'm all right. Just a little tired."

"Want my advice?"

"About what?"

"Kate."

"Yeah."

"Don't let her get away."

"Okay, so we agree on the strategy. It's the tactics I need help on."

"You remember that great philosopher, Pogo?"

"In the funny papers?"

"Yeah."

"Sure."

"He said 'We have met the enemy and he is us.' I'm gonna take a nap." Vic headed for the bunkroom.

John sat there thinking it over. It reminded him of a lesson he had learned in fighter pilot school. A curmudgeonly old instructor pilot, Major Charles Kock–they called him "Horse"–was leading John and two other students in a flight to the gunnery range early in their training. John was number two and they were all rejoining on lead's wing after their last strafing pass. Major Kock was in a gentle left-hand turn and John had cut inside his turn and was closing on him at an uncontrollably fast rate. Before neophyte John could see that he was going to overshoot lead badly, Major Kock called out over the radio in a gravely, grouchy voice, "Ellsworth, can't you see you're fuckin' yourself?" It was the same lesson, but good old Vic was far more subtle.

Sleep was getting harder to come by these days—but it was impossible for John to sleep on alert. The first time he'd gotten scrambled out of a dead sleep, he was passing ten thousand feet and couldn't remember how he got there—his seat belt and shoulder harness weren't fastened. If he'd had to punch out, odds were nine out of ten the ejection would have killed him. Then if he beat those odds he would have had to open the parachute manually—another long shot at low altitude at night. The thought of that scared him so badly he didn't even yawn when he was on night alert. That was not a war story he ever passed around at Dusty's Pub, but it did get added to the "if-only/just-happened" list.

At 0415, fifteen minutes after the alert shack phone rang, Vic and John were airborne. John preferred flying at night, except when it involved dropping bombs very close to the good guy grunts. All the old heads were convinced that if God had wanted man to fly at night he would have created him with a rotating red beacon mounted at the base of his tailbone. There were indeed some unique challenges at night, but John thought the action was always better. The ground fire was easier to see and thus avoid, and as long as the gunners had no radar he was a very elusive target in the dark. He liked the warm glow of the red lights and indirect, soft yellow lighting of the instrument panel at night. The dials and gauges seemed to talk to him in the dark, rather than just let him read their faces like they did in the daytime. And his aluminum clad lover, while not cuddly as Colonel English reminded him, did seem more affectionate at night.

The command post had said it was troops-in-contact, II Corps, when the phone rang. On climb-out John checked in with them on the radio and got the details. NVA coming over the perimeter fence at Duc Co Special Forces Camp. It was 230/29 off Channel 107. That would make it 29 miles southwest of the Pleiku TACAN, which was in the central highlands 110 miles northwest of Tuy Hoa. Vic's plane was snuggled in so close to John's wing tip light that he could have spit on it, were it not for a half inch of Plexiglas canopy and a 400 knot airflow. The Big Dipper over John's left shoulder pointed at the North Star at 2 o'clock high and an awesome Milky

Way split the heavens, but it was not a time to contemplate the beauty of the cosmos. Close air support at night with troops-in-contact with the enemy was the scariest kind of graveyard shift work.

Duc Co, situated near the top of a ridge at the northwest corner of the Ia Drang Valley, was only nine miles east of the Cambodian border on Highway Nine, again. John didn't know who assigned those road numbers. They were just dirt roads, maybe gravel sometimes, but he couldn't tell from the air.

Duc Co was always a hot spot. Since U.S. forces weren't allowed to bomb in Cambodia, it was a safe haven for the North Vietnamese. They'd sneak across the border at night and take a shot and sneak back to their safe haven, and the good old U.S.A. would just unilaterally keep playing by the rules. It was a unbelievably stupid way to fight a war, in John's view. North Vietnam would ignore neutrality agreements with non-warring adjacent countries and the U.S. would obey them. To John the U.S. was fighting like Smokin' Joe Frazier in an alley fight, wearing sixteen-ounce gloves and following the Marquis of Queensbury Rules.

A C-130 was overhead Duc Co when they arrived, dropping flares with parachutes overhead to light up the area. Decoy Two One, the FAC, was also there in an O-1, directing the air strikes and the flare ship. The dome of yellow illumination over the embattled camp lent an eerie, otherworld atmosphere to the scene.

The camp was an irregular circle about 200 yards across, made up of sandbagged structures, bunkers and concertina wire. John could see a couple of machine gun emplacements sparkling away and mortar rounds exploding, both incoming and outgoing.

"Dusty, the gooks are coming over the wire on the east side of the camp. They occupy that first line of trenches just inside the wire. The friendlies have pulled back into the center of the encampment, but they are no more than fifty meters away, hunkered down in foxholes and bunkers. Expect small arms fire. The C-130 is orbiting five thousand feet over the target and the wind is out of the east."

That meant that the flares would be floating east to west under their parachutes. While they did illuminate the target, they were another obstacle in the sky to avoid. That was relatively easy enough to do until the flares burned out and became just cans and nylon floating around in the darkness. It would be more than enough to give an F-100 indigestion, should they meet by accident.

"Set 'em up hot, Dusty. Bomb single."

"Two."

They ran parallel to the friendlies' position in the camp. It was much easier to be accurate left-to-right than it was long or short. An F-100 moving at 450 knots would toss a bomb five hundred feet long or short for every one second the pilot was late or early hitting the pickle button. So the rule was, when dropping within fifty meters of friendlies, run parallel to them, not at them or over them. The visibility and the terrain did not allow a level delivery at fifty feet—that would just be too close to suicide.

It was going to be like William Tell trying to hit the apple with a flamethrower at night. Give me a gun on the Trail any day rather than a target like this, John thought. After all these months he was still positively paranoid about killing a American soldier, and his first bomb pass proved it.

He rolled in on a 10-degree dive angle and threw the first can of napalm wide right by about twenty meters-away from the friendlies. The napalm probably took the temper out of the concertina wire, but it didn't incinerate any North Vietnamese inside the perimeter.

"Two, if you'd move your bomb not more than twenty meters left of where lead's hit."

"Two, copy. I'm in."

John watched the rolling fireball from Vic's napalm bomb envelope the trench line, lighting up the whole encampment. He closed his eyes and counted to three to hasten the return of his night vision. The floating flares were now between him and the target area. The harsh light of the burning phosphorus made white spots in his vision.

"Good work, Two. Lead, just walk the napalm on around the perimeter at twelve o'clock to Two's last bomb," Decoy called.

"Lead, roger. I'm in."

"You're cleared."

John had the air conditioner turned way up but he was still sweating profusely. Somehow he managed to get his second can of napalm right where he wanted it. There were a lot of fireflies down there but he couldn't be sure those muzzle flashes represented rounds coming his way.

Vic and John made two more passes apiece, and pretty well fried the eastern perimeter of Duc Co. Judging from the decrease in small arms fire on the ground, they must have done some good.

"Dusty, this is Decoy again. Things have quieted down there. If you can hold high and dry for a bit I may have a place for your twenty mike mike."

John glanced at the fuel gauges and said, "Roger, Decoy. We're good for another fifteen minutes." Since home was only 140 miles away, they could spend more time over the target than usual.

Vic and John stayed on opposite sides of a big circle at seven thousand feet, above all the air traffic, but still low enough to keep an eye on things on the ground.

Suddenly, from out of the inky sea to the west, the North Vietnamese began to fire rockets at the beleaguered camp. John watched their trajectory as they arced right into the center of Duc Co. It looked like a massacre—like they knew the F-100's were out of bombs and they could fire away without fear of reprisal. They were probably so well camouflaged that, even with flares right over them, no one would be able to see them.

The FAC called, "Dusty, there's an assault on the western perimeter now. I've called in for more air support, but I'd sure appreciate your hosing down just outside the wire on the west side now. Things are pretty grim down there. Repeat, stay outside the wire. Our grunts are still in the perimeter trenches."

"Dusty One One, copy. I'm in from the south." John kept the dive angle shallow again so he could get down among them and see something. He saw nothing. A black-clad figure, lying perfectly still on a hillside in the dim light of the flares, looked like all the other rocks. He held the trigger down for two seconds-a long burst-as he hosed the hillside down just below the rolls of concertina wire. The high explosive incendiary bullets exploded on impact like hundreds of flash bulbs in the night. Coming off the target John's pucker reflex told him he had pressed it too close.

The rockets were coming in again from a mile west. They just materialized out of the blackness like roman candles on a low trajectory. Once they stopped there was no frame of reference in the darkness to tell where they came from.

John had an idea. If he could get up high and steep and be in position just as they fired the next salvo, maybe he could get a shot at them. If something didn't suppress those rockets, Duc Co might cease to exist before more air support could arrive.

"Decoy Two One, this is Dusty One One. I'd like to take a shot at that rocket site. Those grunts aren't going to make it if we don't shut it down."

"I don't know how you're going to find it, Dusty, but you're welcome to try. The highest terrain in the area is fifteen hundred feet and it's all free-fire zone."

"Okay. If everyone will stay out of the airspace to the west I'm going to turn my external lights off and see if I can sneak up on them. Dusty One Two, make your runs north-south and pull off to the east."

"Two, copy. I'm in."

"You're cleared, Two," Decoy called.

The F-100 made a lot of noise, but with an O-1, a C-130, another F-100, and rocket explosions and machine gun fire in the air, with his lights out, John thought he might sneak up on the rocket site.

They appeared to be firing the rockets in salvos, one second apart for five seconds. Away from the light of the flares over Duc Co, the sky was the same shade of black as the ground.

There were no visual references outside the cockpit to aid in determining dive angle, airspeed and height above the ground. It was an instrument approach to gunnery.

Just as Vic came off his strafing pass the next salvo of rockets began. From seven thousand feet just north of the target, John rolled over and pulled the nose down to point where the rockets' flight began. He rolled wings level pointed nearly straight down and immediately mashed the trigger. By this time the salvo had ended and he was pointed into that ink bottle and shooting blind. He stepped lightly on the rudder pedals, first left, then right, so that his bullets would spray over a wider area. It was a long two or three-second burst, and it was the last one second that did it.

In the slow motion intensity of the moment, he came back hard on the stick, sucked on a solid six G's and grunted like a sumo wrestler. A series of enormous explosions lit up the night below him like lightening bolts. His eyes were glued to the altimeter as he strained to retain his vision against the G's, and watched it unwind—three thousand, twenty-five hundred, two thousand. At eighteen hundred feet the altimeter stopped unwinding, reversed direction, and began to wind back up as John rocketed back into the safety of the night sky.

"Bull's-eye. Bull's-eye," Decoy was shouting. Charlie obviously had quite a supply of rockets down there, and John had found them. Oh, the thrill of victory....

Decoy sounded so happy John thought he'd cry. If he was happy, how must the poor grunts at Duc Co—those that were still alive—feel? Old Smokin' Joe, sixteen-ounce gloves and all, had gotten in some good licks in this alley fight.

John flipped on his navigation lights again and held a gentle left turn as he watched the lights of Vic's plane close on him.

They flew into the dawn over the central highlands—two country boys going home winners. The sun was smiling, too.

*   *   *

Vic and John both accumulated some more broken steel cores and deformed copper jackets from 50 caliber slugs to add to their coffee cup collections of used NVA bullets.

"That ought to be worth an oak leaf cluster to your DFC, John. Maybe even the Silver Star. How do they decide?"

"I don't know and I don't care, Vic. I don't like that close air support under the flares. I was much more comfortable on the dive against the rocket site than any of those passes around Duc Co. I scared myself to death on that first strafing pass on the western perimeter."

"I won't tell. It's nice to know that you still have at least a nodding acquaintance with fear."

"Fear and I don't seem to get intimate till after midnight in my bunk."

"You don't have to remind me of that, John. But it does look like you've been doing better since you quit drinking."

"Looks can be deceiving, Vic. Let's go eat some breakfast." If you don't sleep you can't dream, John thought to himself. Going to bed was starting to feel like going out behind the woodshed with Dad for a spanking.

*   *   *

The girls were over for happy hour. Vic and John had just lounged the day away between the bunk and the sun deck over Dusty's Pub.

Their mission of the night before was on its third or fourth telling, and well into legendary proportions. But the boys in bibs had lost a plane and pilot in Steel Tiger, so things were subdued. The Grim Reaper was calling with more regularity these days.

Kate, was her usual, long-suffering, self. "So the Lone Ranger and Tonto came to the rescue of the Cavalry again?" Straight-faced. "I can think of only one thing, Kate, that gives me more satisfaction than rescuing the cavalry.... It was tough...but luck was with us."

"I don't think it was luck, John. You're just good. You do this with too much regularity to blame it on luck."

"Aw, shucks, ma'am."

"Oh, stuff it, John. You're just good. You know, when I flew with you, you were...so...alive. It was like that airplane was part of your body. I think the reason you're so good is you put one hundred percent of your heart and soul into it."

"That's a very nice thing to say, Kate."

"I just want so badly for this all to be over, for you and for me."

"Well, you're down to four weeks and I've got twelve. It doesn't seem possible."

"I heard from Denver General today. I got the job. Start work July fifteenth. Classes in cardiac care start in the fall."

"Congratulations. What will you do between the time you leave here the end of March and July fifteenth?"

"I plan to catch the tail-end of the ski season and then spend some time with Mother in Colorado Springs."

"You're really looking forward to being a civilian, aren't you?"

"Yes."

"I wish I had my future mapped out as well as you and Vic. As I told him, I'm really envious."

"John, you'll be able to think more clearly about your future when this insanity is behind you, don't you think?"

"Oh, yeah, I'm sure." John was getting tired of these 'don't you think' harangues.

"Lieutenant Ellsworth, would you step into my office, please?" It was Colonel Redman.

"Yes, sir." John followed the squadron commander from the scheduling counter down the center hall to the last door on the left.

"I have two pieces of good news for you. Your Fighter Weapons School assignment has come through. Report to Nellis AFB on June 15, 1969, and next time you're down around Saigon, stop in at Tan Son Nhut. General Abrams wants to pin a Silver Star on you. Let them know the day before if possible. Colonel English will be getting one, too. I'd like for you to receive it on his behalf while you're at it. I'll see that it gets passed on to his heirs."

"Thank you, sir. That is great news, and I'd be very honored to accept for Colonel English, sir. You and I both know how much I owe him, and I haven't given up hope of finding him and telling him in person, someday, sir." The only item on the Colonel Redman's desk was an 8x10 picture of him with his family. They looked like grown children and grandchildren. John knew he should be polite and comment about them, but that would get the colonel going and his family stories took ten or fifteen minutes.

"It's an incredible achievement, young man. I'm very proud you're on my team. I believe you and I are briefing for a Steel Tiger mission in fifteen minutes."

"That's correct, sir. Thanks again."

"You're welcome. Say, are you missing any meals? You're looking awful tired and a little bony."

"Sir, I...uh...quit drinking and...uh...the chow hall food doesn't taste as good as when it isn't chasing a cocktail or two."

"Well, get your mother to send you a care package, son. This business takes endurance and it's important that you eat right. How about sleep?"

John just shrugged his shoulders.

The Colonel rose, walked around his desk and put his arm around John's shoulders. "Let's go brief, son."

"Yes, sir."

The old man didn't fly much in Steel Tiger—just enough to stay familiar with the nature of the mission. He was far more valuable to the taxpayers for the leadership he provided as trail boss of that rowdy bunch of young, arrogant cowboys at the 629th TAC Fighter Squadron.

It was the Ides of March and it was Vic's last mission before R&R and marriage in Hawaii. He was flying number two. Ron Johnson was three, and John was number four. It had been months since John had flown "Tail End Charlie."

The squadron had a new weapon. It was called CBU-24—a cluster bomb unit. It was shaped like an ordinary bomb. Halfway down its trajectory it split open along its longitudinal axis and spewed out hundreds of bomblets, like hand grenades, that exploded on impact. It wouldn't do a lot of damage to the steel and concrete of a gun emplacement, but it would sure make hamburger out of the human part. It covered a large area and therefore required less than pin-point accuracy.

It was an anti-personnel bomb and it would give the pacifists something more to cry about on the front pages, John thought. They had worked napalm to death, so to speak, and needed some new buzz words. The lieutenants called it the "Hammer."

John thought it was an improvement for two reasons. With each passing day that Le Duc Tho did his two-step in Paris—and faked out Kissinger once again—the NVA got their AAA emplacements more dug in and more protected. It took a direct hit with an iron bomb to put them out of commission. A CBU-24 was like firing a twelve-gauge shotgun instead of a high-powered rifle. The Hammer covered a circular pattern about thirty meters in diameter.

Lately the North Vietnamese had taken to firing on diving airplanes until they saw the bombs come off the airplane. Then they'd dive into concrete bunkers next to the guns, and barring a direct hit, would be up and firing after the bombs hit. The hundreds of little bomblets in a CBU-24 would find their way into all the nooks and crannies of the gun emplacements and bunkers and take care of anything living.

As number four John had the Hammer-four Hammers to be exact. It was to be used for flak suppression—everyone else had seven hundred fifty pound iron bombs. It was the first time anyone in Dusty squadron had gotten to use the Hammer and John was excited about it. He was convinced they'd given these things to the right guy.

In the pre-flight briefing Colonel Redman said they'd play it by ear. If the Misty FAC's knew where the guns were, John would go first. If no guns were active, John would fly cap while everyone else dropped, then he'd find a target. No one brought bombs home, at least not since the first month after John had arrived at Tuy Hoa. His friend from F-100 school, Tom Lucas, had died at Bien Hoa. He went out on a rainy night mission and couldn't drop due to bad weather. Instead of going out over the South China Sea and jettisoning his bombs before landing, he decided to do the taxpayers a favor and bring the bombs home. He landed at night on a wet runway, loaded with fuel and with all those bombs on board couldn't get stopped. He dropped his tail hook but it bounced over the arresting cable at the far end of two miles of concrete. He ran off the end of the runway, flipped over and slid through the perimeter minefield upside down. There was no body bag. They just sent his belongings home to his wife.

John was hoping the target would be near Tchepone, because he had some gun sites still filed away in the gray matter from the four-ship lieutenant flight. If nothing else came up he could try out that new exploding buckshot on them. And it was Colonel English territory. He'd be on the lookout and he privately reminded the other lieutenants of that fact. They all thought he was really losing his grip over the whole issue, but he was far too serious about it for anyone to yank his chain.

They tapped the tanker over Pleiku at 1300 sharp, and twenty minutes later were in contact with Misty Three One.

"Good afternoon, Dusty Four One Flight. We've got a truck park for you this afternoon, a mile southwest of the river ford. I'm putting a smoke rocket on it now."

John hated truck parks. They always looked like just more trees from where he was. Those Russian two-and-a-half ton trucks were so tough that it took a very close hit to do any damage. John had seen them laying on their sides one day and gone the next. The North Vietnamese would just push them right side up somehow and drive them off. Dusty Flight was going to be dropping in the trees, hoping to hit something. It seemed like such waste.

"Anticipate triple A, but we haven't seen any in this area thus far today." John knew right where to look, and it was still there. It didn't have bomb craters near it yet, which meant no one else knew it was there.

"Dusty Flight, set 'em up hot, bomb pairs. We'll give them two passes apiece."

"Twoop."

"Threep."

John held high and dry, staring intently up and down the ridge. It was a crystal clear day, but the NVA were so good at camouflaging their trucks and guns they were tough to see even when they did get some of the trees blown away. The smoke from the FAC's rocket floated up through the trees.

"Dusty Four One, put your first two bombs twenty meters east of my smoke. Our ground sensors indicate heavy traffic there."

"Dusty Four One, roger. I'm in," the old man called. John wasn't worried about the colonel hitting the target and he was determined to stomp on any North Vietnamese who tried to take a shot at his old man.

The whole ridge opened up. There were orange tracers of 23mm and white of 37mm. There were three or four sites shooting. Colonel Redman had tracers all around him, going from left to right on all sides of his diving plane. John saw his two bombs come off and then flak enveloped his plane. He never even began a dive recovery. His bombs hit right where they were supposed to and Colonel Redman went in one hundred meters at twelve o'clock to his bombs-a huge fireball.

There was stunned silence on the radio.

Finally Misty called, "Hold high and dry Two and Three. Anybody see a chute?"

Silence.

"Dusty Four Four, did you locate the AAA site?"

"Affirmative."

"They're yours. Attack them any way you want."

It wasn't a time for sadness. It was a time for revenge. John lined up on the ridge and picked the middle gun site, so that if the Hammer hit long or short it would still hit one of them. It was all in his face, a lot more orange tracers than white. He was fast and steep and rolling. The first Hammer covered the ridge dead center in a circular field of sparkles. He pulled it up to fifteen thousand feet in a series of rolls, did the best approximation that an F-100 can make of a hammerhead stall—a maneuver Colonel English had taught him—and came back at them from the opposite direction. He hoped that they hadn't had time to crawl out of their bunkers and back onto the guns and reload before he gave them another dose. It worked. The air was seventy-five percent clear of hot lead, and his second Hammer landed on top of the next gun site south.

As he got back to fifteen thousand feet a second time, he realized he was hyper-ventilating like a panting dog. He held his breath for a second, took two deep breaths, and called to Misty. "I'd like to hold on to the last two till number Two and Three have dropped, Misty." "Roger, Four. Two and Three, put your bombs on the ridge, one pass apiece. To hell with the truck park. Four, that was some fine air show."

John didn't answer. He wasn't in the air show business and Colonel Redman was dead, and all he wanted to do was kill a lot more gooks. He stared at the ridge as the other two lieutenants went to work. Out of the corner of his eye, in a valley at the base of a line about a mile from the gun sites, John caught the reflection of something bright in a small clearing in the jungle. It lasted no more than five seconds and the trauma of the moment demanded his full attention. A signal mirror, perhaps…. He checked his TACAN range and bearing and scribbled it in grease pen on his kneeboard so he could find the spot again. He checked out the surrounding terrain for sight references. That was all he had time for. His brain was on overload. The old man had just died and he was in the middle of a horrific battle and he might die himself if he didn't start paying attention.

Vic and Ron both hit the ridge with their salvos, and John rolled in and pickled off the last two Hammers. Whatever was left of the gun sites chose not to fight anymore that day. He was unopposed.

"Good work, Dusty Flight. I'm awful sorry about Four One. We'll file a report from this end. So long."

It was a funeral procession home. As number Three in a four ship formation, Ron was second in command. They went straight home, no playing around, no thrill of victory. The Grim Reaper had a big prize this time. John was glad Ron was leading so he didn't have to talk or navigate...or think. Tears ran down his cheeks and under his oxygen mask and strained through his mustache, making his saliva salty.

All the big shots on base were waiting for them. The news had beaten them home. There were six blue Ford sedans parked at the fuel dump. John shut down but didn't feel like moving. He just sat slumped in his seat, head down. Sergeant Adams stood on the boarding ladder patting John's helmet like he was a friendly dog. He looked up and the sergeant was standing shirtless on the ladder, crying. John looked away quickly, his eyes stinging. He took several deep breaths before he was able to move.

*   *   *

After the intelligence debrief, which the wing commander also sat in on, they left with handshakes all around and a lot of sad faces. Colonel Redman was a prince of a human being. All the trucks and guns in Southeast Asia were not worth one Colonel Redman.

The girls came over out of a sense of duty, and there was another in a growing trend of wakes at Dusty's Pub. There were a lot of tears in the beer in the Pub. Vic came over and joined Kate and John as she quietly read aloud the 23rd Psalm from her Bible. When she was through she gently closed the book and said hello to Vic.

"It's a shame you're leaving in the morning for your wedding on such a sad note, Vic," John said.

"Colonel Redman was a good man, John. If he's where I think he is, his troubles are over. One day, if we follow him, we'll realize this should have been a time of celebration, not sadness."

"You're a rock, Vic. Nancy is a very lucky lady," Kate said.

"Thanks, Kate. John did a good job of making the bad guys pay dearly."

"I'm sure he did." Her tone was icy, but it couldn't have made John's mood any worse.

"They'll pay a lot more before I'm through," John said through clenched teeth.

Kate gave him a look of alarm. Vic was silent.

"Excuse me. If I don't go run this minute, I'm going to explode." John rose without waiting for an answer.

"Please come back when you're done, John."

He didn't answer.

He ran until his muscles were screaming. He sweat out a lot of venom, but it felt like the supply was endless. These little slant-eyed demons had killed a good friend, they might be torturing his mentor, they took his old man and were torturing his best friend. In the weeks remaining, I will make as many NVA die for their country as I can, John vowed to himself. Be calm, be cool, but kill the gooks. John played the "should've" game. Colonel Redman wasn't moving enough. He didn't fly Steel Tiger often enough. He should've been jinking more. He was probably more concerned with doing good in front of his boys.

John knew about one of those gun sites on the ridge, knew its exact location. He should've insisted to Misty FAC that he go first, wipe it out with a new weapon and convince the rest of the gooks to stay under cover. But that kind of thinking was a losing game, about as useless as the runway behind, or the altitude above.

John showered and returned to Dusty's Pub. He really didn't feel any better emotionally, but he felt in control of himself. Kate was sitting alone at the same table with a far away look in her eye.

"Kate, I'm sorry for my outburst."

She gave John a weak smile. "John, all the dead Vietnamese on earth won't bring back Colonel Redman."

John had his elbows on the table and his chin in his hands. "I'm sorry," was all he could say.

"John, being sorry means not wanting to do that again." Her voice was soothing, and her face had the look of a mother whose child had taken one step and fallen...again.

She talked on and John's eyes glazed over as he quit listening to her words. He thought he detected a minute change in her tone-a hint of weariness, and it wasn't physical. Ominous.

"Kate, you are so patient with me. I'll get over it. Don't worry about me. I want to make you happy, not sad. I want these last two weeks together to be so good that you couldn't possibly forget me when you're skiing with all those young tycoons in Colorado."

"I'm not into tycoons. They have monumental egos."

John chose not to respond to that. He was sure it was another subliminal message from Nurse Moffit.

He kissed her in Dusty's Pub, right in front of everybody. It was a sad evening—the saddest one yet—but he was afraid if he let himself cry he wouldn't be able to stop. Everyone, even the nurses, agreed that they would individually write a letter to Colonel Redman's widow and put them in a big box and mail it to her. Everyone loved him.

The girls left early. Nobody likes a wake. Kate mentioned on the way to the six-pack that she had a nice long talk with Vic. John told her that he had bought Vic and Nancy a little present for their wedding—the most expensive champagne on base—and signed their names to it. He gave her a hug. She crawled in the back seat of the six-pack, and he closed the door behind her.

John knew he would entertain his roommates that night, but he didn't have the nerve to ask for yet another pill. Kate needed to know, he needed to know, that his self-discipline was still intact. He stayed up late, letting Nina soothe the savage beast. None of the lieutenants on Colonel Redman's mission were scheduled to fly the next day. It was some kind of policy, like "No smoking within twenty-five feet of the airplane, no drinking within twelve hours of a flight—that was a joke—and no flying within 48 hours after watching a fighter pilot die."

He slept fitfully on the too-short sofa and talked to all his friends—Rock, Sam, Colonel English, and Colonel Redman. The little guy in Cholon and the faceless figure on the beach were there, too, while several hundred oriental shadows danced silently around the room.

Somewhere between midnight and daylight Vic passed through with his packed duffel bag in hand.

"Give my love to the bride and Captain Hyde, Vic."

"I'll do it, and listen, brother…don't do anything dumb while I'm gone."

"No sweat, but would it break your heart if I ended the war while you were gone?" John held out his hand to shake Vic's.

Vic just smiled and said, "Would that it were possible." He walked out the door and John couldn't go back to sleep. He wanted something alcoholic in the worst way. He thrashed for another hour, got up, put on his still-wet running gear and met the dawn while pounding the pavement. Only then did he remember the reflection of what could have been a signal mirror in the heat of battle yesterday. He would pass it on to the intelligence officer first thing when he got to the squadron building. It could have been Colonel English. It was something to hang on to, a reason for hope...and hope seemed about all John Ellsworth had left.

*   *   *

The notice on the bulletin board read, "Night missions to Steel Tiger: Sign-up Sheet." All notices had to be signed, or at least initialed, by everyone in the squadron, whether it was a sign-up sheet or just an acknowledgment that it had been read. Of course John initialed it. His was the second initial on the list, right after Lt. BFD. There was no Lieutenant with the initials BFD. It was just another prank by the junior officers. It stood for "Big Fuckin' Deal." When the old man had raised cane about it, it started showing up as Lt. Boris Finsterwall Dexterville, and then a month later it got shortened to Lt. BFD. The old man decided it was no longer worth the battle and let it ride. May he rest in peace, John thought.

The Ho Chi Minh Trail was bumper-to-bumper trucks nearly every night now, and those night sorties fit John's personal mission to a 'T'-go where the gooks are.

The latest addition to the war effort was a Starlight Scope mounted in a C-130 used as a FAC plane. It was so named because it magnified the light of the stars and focused it through a short, fat telescope so that the viewer could virtually see in the dark. It must have greatly increased the anxiety of the North Vietnamese truckers working the graveyard shift.

John decided they were asking for volunteers because they thought it was dangerous. To his way of thinking, unless the NVA moved their radar guidance onto the Trail, it was safer. Certainly it was tough to drop bombs accurately at night without all the usual visual references. The pilot had to spend more time checking the instruments and he needed to be very quick about it. John compared it roughly to shooting the ILS approach for landing at O'Hare Airport at a speed of Mach 1 instead of one hundred sixty knots.

He wanted to put Vic's name down, too, but decided that was too presumptuous. He might come back from Hawaii ultra-conservative – being a married man and all.

The first mission was scheduled for midnight that night, but John wasn't on it. He was up for a mission to IV Corps, the Mekong

Delta area south of Saigon. He called the command post to see if they would co-ordinate with MAC-V and see if General Abrams would be in his office around 1400—the time they would be passing over Saigon on their way home from the Delta. He gave the Duty Officer Colonel Moffit's name as the contact person.

Ron and John went ahead and briefed. John was leading and they were carrying Snakes and nape again. As they walked out the door, parachutes slung over their shoulders and helmet bags in hand, Major Gillespie stopped them.

"Lieutenant Ellsworth, it's all set for you to stop at Tan Son Nhut on your way home. Someone will meet you at the plane and drive you to MAC-V. Shouldn't be on the ground more than an hour. Hustle on back. We need that bird for a night mission. Johnson, you come on home alone." Major G. was basically the acting C.O. until someone else showed up, and he did not appear to be bearing up well under the added strain.

"Yes, sir," the two lieutenants replied.

Enroute to the planes in the squadron bread truck, John said, "Ron, you know, you can't be tentative in this business. You've got to be aggressive to survive."

"I agree," Ron replied. "The best defense is a good offense."

"I think maybe Colonel Redman was a little tentative. He wasn't moving enough. He was worrying more about hitting the target and not enough about protecting his own hide." John knew Kate would say he was whistling past the graveyard, again.

"Well, I think you're right. And I've been a little concerned about Mike Day. He's been tentative ever since he bailed out, and he's been boondocking more of his bombs."

"I noticed that, Ron, but what can we say?"

"I suppose we could tell him he's turning chicken on us and he's going to auger in if he doesn't change his ways."

"Not I, brother. He's going to have to fight his demons himself."

*   *   *

Tan Son Nhut Air Base had one of every kind of airplane known to man. John followed the blue pick-up truck with the yellow "Follow Me" sign on top of the cab to a remote part of the ramp. Transient Operations could not find a de-arm crew for the guns, so John parked with the nose pointed toward the boondocks, just in case a stray surge of voltage should set off one of them.

Billy Ray Fosbury met him at the plane. He seemed happy to see John. They drove down the ramp past an Air Cambodia Caravelle, a World Airways 707, and an ancient Air America DC-3. The old twin-engine tail-dragger was unloading Vietnamese families and livestock. They were all coming out the side door in a never-ending stream. It reminded John of all those clowns that get out of that tiny little car in the Ringling Brothers, Barnum and Bailey Circus. The Air America pilot, a giant of a man with broad, stooped shoulders and a ponderous girth was trying to keep the oriental mob under control.

Billy Ray drove over to MAC-V, picked up Colonel Moffit, and they all headed for General Abrams' office. The general's office was large, carpeted and austere. His responsibilities matched those of the presidents of any three of the largest U.S. corporations, but the pay and perks weren't even close. And surely the self-serving politicians telling him what to do were worse than any stockholder could be. Boy would John like to take any one of those pompous politicians with him on just one mission...show them what "compromise" was doing to American mothers' sons.

"I understand you bailed us out again, Lieutenant Ellsworth, up at Duc Co," General Abrams said as he shook John's hand.

"Sir, we got lucky again."

An aide walked in with some paper work, followed by a photographer. General Abrams, Colonel Moffit and Sergeant Fosbury stood in a line in front of John beside the general's desk, as the aide read from a large orange and white vinyl-covered folder:

Citation to accompany the Award of
Silver Star
to
John D. Ellsworth

First Lieutenant John D. Ellsworth distinguished himself by heroism beyond the call of duty as an F-100 pilot flying close air support, north of Tay Ninh, Republic of Vietnam on July 30, 1968. On that date Lieutenant Ellsworth led a flight of two F-100's against a heavily fortified enemy position that had ambushed a U.S. Army unit. The weather conditions were extremely poor for visual bombing and the enemy was only fifty meters from friendly troops. Although small arms fire hit his aircraft numerous times, Lieutenant Ellsworth attacked the enemy position with complete disregard for his own personal safety. As a result, two hundred thirty-five enemy soldiers were killed and a U.S. Army unit was saved from almost certain annihilation. The outstanding heroism and selfless devotion to duty displayed by Lieutenant Ellsworth reflect great credit upon himself and the United States Air Force.

General Abrams pinned the red, white and blue medal on John's still-wet flying suit as the photographer flashed away. He then shook John's hand and they both smiled at the photographer as he took another picture. Colonel Moffit joined in with his knuckle-buster handshake, and they all posed for one more picture. The aide handed John Colonel English's award folder.

John didn't feel happy or heroic. It was not at all like he thought it would be. He'd have traded this plus all his worldly possessions to have Rock and Sam and Colonel English and Colonel Redman back. He noticed the war wasn't wearing well on the general, either.

On the way back to Colonel Moffit's office, John said, "Sir, I really appreciate what you've done for me."

"John, I'd do it for anyone who's done what you have. Kate says you're the most intense person she's ever met. She said flying in an airplane with you was like sitting at the piano with Horowitz."

"Your daughter is a very special lady, sir." John wondered if he would ever see Ozzie again.

The night missions were the stuff that movies were made of, except it would be impossible to duplicate them on the screen. The emotions that accompanied them were off the Richter Scale. All the lieutenants except for Mike Day volunteered. Field grade officers, all family men, were glad to be off the hook.

They were all two-ship flights. Both pilots would turn their navigation lights out over the target and keep each other informed as to their positions. Triple A was more colorful and easier to see at night, and while it was not as accurate, there was at least twice as much of it.

Vic had come back from R&R with his ever-present smile even wider and a gold band on the fourth finger of his left hand. He signed up for night missions to Steel Tiger after John had briefed him on how it was going. They worked hard at getting scheduled to fly together. Vic was perfectly content to fly John's wing, even though he had just gotten flight leader qualified himself. John considered them a deadly duo.

But this night neither of them were flying, and it was the saddest day of the war—not sad because of another wake, but sad because Kate was going home. The squadron had a going away party for her at Dusty's Pub and gave her a plaque, as if she was one of the guys. Everyone, even the boys in the bibs, got a hug and a kiss from Kate. Then everyone gave Kate and John a break and they went for a walk in the moonless night. John had made his decision and he had rehearsed his presentation a dozen times in his mind. He had saved it for the last moment and he was nervous as a cat. He saved it till now because he figured if he did not win Kate over she would be out of his life forever, and if she was out of sight the agony would be somewhat lessened for him. But that option was so awful he couldn't think beyond that.

She would accept the deal. He was sure of it. It was fair, it was honorable, and in the end she would have what she wanted, what she had made clear from the beginning. She had been very open and honest about that, God bless her heart, and he loved her, more than machinery...more than anything. Captain Hyde had been right, Colonel English had been right, Kate had been right, and he had been wrong. Such a fool as he had been, with more second chances than any fool deserves. It was the toughest decision he had ever made, but Kate Moffit was worth it. He would have to live completely without her for a little while longer, and even that seemed like an eternity in this awful killing place.

"Kate, I love you. I have something I want to say and I want you to listen very carefully until I've said it all and then I want you to think it over very carefully and answer truthfully. Okay?" They stood under a streetlight so John could see her face. That was part of the plan. Kate looked up and focused those magnetic green eyes on his and nodded expectantly as he took both her hands in his.

"Kate, you have made it plain you do not approve of my vocation, but you have never given me an ultimatum in so many words, and I am very thankful for that and I respect you for that. I have tried to change your mind about that issue...I had hoped the plane ride might do it, but I was wrong." Kate's eyes were sparkling and she was wearing a half-smile. So far so good.

"You have a passion for life, all life, friend or enemy, and that makes you the closest thing to an angel I've ever met. You are the kind of woman I want to spend the rest of my life with, the kind of woman who could be the saintly mother of our children, the kind of lover who makes life worthwhile, no matter what." Her eyes were glistening now, and reflecting the love he felt.

"Would you, could you swap a lifetime for five more months apart?"

"But you only have two months left...."

John dropped his hold on her right hand and put two fingers on her lips to quiet her. "I cannot, I will not leave this place until I have done everything possible to find Colonel English or his remains. I have extended my twelve month tour by three more months for a Misty FAC assignment so I can spend all my flying time over the same area where Colonel English is missing." Kate was trying to talk now and John put his whole palm sideways over her mouth.

"Please let me finish. When my extension is over I will resign my commission and I promise I will happily never fly a fighter plane again, not even the Air National Guard. I'll go back to graduate school and get an MBA and be a stockbroker or something.

"M-M-M-M-M-M-P-H"

"I'm almost done...please. I love you, Kate. Will you marry me when I get home in five months? He dropped his hand from her mouth and his stomach had more butterflies in it than before all the combat missions he had flown...combined.

"JOHN, COLONEL ENGLISH IS DEAD. COLONEL REDMAN IS DEAD. AND YOU WILL BE DEAD FOR SURE IF YOU TAKE THAT JOB, IF NOT BEFORE. OH, MY GOD IN HEAVEN, JOHN...." Kate's face was crimson and she was trembling all over.

"Kate, Colonel English is missing. There is not a shred of proof he is dead."

"JOHN, THERE ARE 2,500 SOLDIERS MISSING AND 2,499 OF THEM ARE DEAD OR POW'S. YOU JUST WANT AN EXCUSE TO KILL MORE NORTH VIETNAMESE. PHILLIP HAD THE SAME KIND OF EXCUSE..."

"KATE, KATE... what if your dad were missing...?" It was a low blow, but it bought some time. She just stared back through tear-filled eyes as her lips moved but no words came out.

"Kate, I couldn't live with myself, you couldn't live with me if I don't do this...Kate, I have NOT sold my soul to the devil."

"Did...did you and my daddy...did he agree to...did you talk to him about this?"

John shook his head no.

"This...this was a unilateral decision? You didn't talk to me about it. You probably didn't talk to anybody about it because you are so...so...so DAMNED STUBBORN that you think you know more than anybody else...EVEN THE U.S. GOVERNMENT WHO QUIT LOOKING FOR COLONEL ENGLISH WEEKS AGO. WHAT CAN YOU POSSIBLY DO THAT ALL THE U.S. FORCES IN SOUTHEAST ASIA HAVE NOT ALREADY DONE?" Kate's voice was getting hoarse.

"What I can do is not give up, Kate."

"Oh, John, you are such a smart guy. Why don't you apply that warrior discipline to an analysis of yourself. Can't you see you're driving yourself to destruction? I just cannot get through to you." She took a deep breath and her tone changed abruptly to one of resignation. "John...I think your heart used to be filled with love for flying and love for these Vietnamese people. Now it's filled with hate. That's a very self-destructive disease. Maybe you're not scared, but I'm terrified. Since Colonel Redman died you've looked demon possessed. I can't live like this."

She pushed him away and held him at arm's length. "I'm out of ideas. Phillip was filled with hate and hate made him sub-human, and then it killed him...."

"Am I like Phillip?"

"YES."

John was dumbstruck. The street in which they stood pointed right at the end of the runway a quarter mile away in the blackness. Two F-100's preparing for takeoff ran up to full power. The ground under their feet trembled in harmony with the timpani drum roll crescendo of two powerful jet engines. With a booming climax their afterburners kicked in and two huge blowtorches roared down the runway and into the night. Two intense lovers, facing defeat, stood in the cone of the dim streetlight waiting out the noise and staring in disbelief at one another as they prepared their final arguments. The noise faded to a distant rumble and the torches winked out in the starry sky, and Kate continued.

"Why can't you focus that cast-iron will of yours on something constructive, John?"

"Helping a country defend itself against communism is not constructive?"

"Don't hide behind the flag, John. You're here because you love destroying things and killing people, period. You guys all repeat that crap about 'it's a shitty war but it's the only one you've got,' and you all really, sincerely mean it. I'm so sick of hearing it I could scream. I promised myself I would go quietly.... I spend all day trying to patch up mutilated GI's and you're out there killing and loving it."

"That's not true, Kate. I'm here because I love my country and I love these people and I love my job, and I'm going to do it to the best of my ability. I have watched my friends die and I am going to honor them the best way I know how by doing my job the best way

I know how. And when I have done my best to find Colonel English I will be home for good and I will never fly again, as God is my witness. It didn't have to be this way if our government really cared about its own GI's and these poor farmers who never hurt a flea. MY GOD WE COULD HAVE ENDED THIS FIASCO IN THREE WEEKS IF WASHINGTON WOULD LET YOUR DAD AND COLONEL ENGLISH AND ME AND EVERY OTHER SOLDIER OVER HERE DO WHAT HE WAS TRAINED FOR—WIN WARS. IF THEY DIDN'T WANT TO WIN IT WHY THE HELL DID THEY SEND US OVER HERE TO DIE?" It was a shouting match to end all shouting matches, and John's outburst was the grand finale.

Her voice was distant and barely audible now. "John, I hope when you get back to the real world—if you get back to the real world...." Those sparkling green eyes, the windows on that selfless, loving soul, were now opaque, and that compassionate, infectious smile was wilted like a rose in the frost.

"On R&R I asked you to be patient with me while I duel my demons. Give me five more months and I will be yours alone till my dying breath," he pleaded.

Kate exploded again. She was shrieking now. "YOU CAN HAVE A LIFETIME, JOHN. LOVE IS SUPPOSED TO CONQUER ALL, BUT ON YOU IT HAS HAD NO IMPACT." Kate was barely coherent. "YOU CAN JUST TAKE YOUR F-100 SUPER LOVER AND...AND FLY IT TO HELL." She jerked away and wouldn't allow him to touch her.

John was devastated. He didn't know what to say. They stood in the street near the chow hall entrance, the same street he'd carried her across on their first date last summer, the same street he'd carried her across that apocalyptic night in November, when he didn't know if she was dead or alive. Was this the reward for all that patience, will power...and love?

"Kate..."

"Good-bye, John. May God have mercy on your soul."

He didn't answer. Those words sounded too final. He could not repeat them. Kate walked down the street and disappeared into the night as John watched in abject despair, in total disbelief at the carnage of his love affair. The booming cadence of the heavy guns atop Tuy Hoa Mountain to the north, on the darkest night yet, marked the carnage of his love affair. They tolled the end of time.

*   *   *

Things were getting so hot in Steel Tiger that Seventh Air Force issued a directive that AAA fire did not have to be returned. It would be left up to the discretion of the flight leader. Returning ground fire when that wasn't the primary target never was mandatory, but the regularity with which planes were getting shot down on the Trail led Seventh Air Force to re-issue the directive anyway. Good old Henry the K, John thought. Every time he made another "compromise" in Paris another 1000 American boys died.

On Vic's first night mission to Steel Tiger as a married man, John laid out his philosophy of night air combat against the big guns. It was the same old philosophy, but delivered with more fervor.

"Vic, I want you to know that if we get shot at tonight, and we probably will, I'm going to shoot back, whether its 50 caliber or 57-millimeter. You know that headquarters policy leaves the decision up to the flight leader. Our primary mission is to stop the trucks, but if everyone goes home when the shooting starts, who's going to stop the trucks? Somebody has to care. I think my country is no longer trying to win this war—in fact I am sure of it—but I am. Duty and honor still mean something to me, even if the leaders of my country have abandoned theirs."

"You're absolutely right, sir, "Vic replied with a smile. John knew Vic used that "sir" business only when he thought John's intensity was getting out of hand. John did outrank him by a few months but everyone knew that rank among lieutenants was like virtue among whores. This time John chose to ignore the signal.

"This is serious stuff, Vic. That's not confetti they're throwing up out there, and I'm going to fly right down the gun barrels if that's what it takes to destroy them. You can call it revenge if you want, or a death wish or whatever. You can watch me or you can follow me. It's your choice and I won't hold it against you either way and I am very serious. Kate told me she thought I had lost it...well, if I have I want to go alone. Copy?"

"Copy. I'll follow you anywhere, brother." This time Vic was serious.

"Then let's go kick some ass, Lieutenant! And keep an eye out for Colonel English. We'll be in the right neighborhood." John replied, and this time they both smiled as they shook hands.

The mission scheduled on the frag order from Seventh Air Force that night was the usual—truck patrol. Their call sign was Dusty Seven One Flight. The rendezvous with the FAC-in a C-130 with a Starlight Scope-was over Saravane. That was about 75 miles south and a little east of Tchepone. Northbound at twelve thousand feet, 50 miles south of the rendezvous, they switched to the C-130's radio frequency.

"Blind Bat One, this is Dusty Seven One. We're a flight of two Fox-100s carrying six seven hundred fifty pound bombs, two CBU-24's, sixteen hundred rounds of twenty mike mike."

"Roger, Dusty Seven One Flight, this is Blind Bat One. Copy your munitions. We've got a truck convoy moving south below us. The Scope is showing about a dozen trucks. In thirty seconds we'll be dropping two white phosphorous logs." He gave Dusty Flight the target weather and terrain information. It was a road on a steep mountainside. Blind Bat concluded with what was becoming the standard warning, "We've had heavy ground fire the last few nights."

"Roger, Blind Bat," John answered. "Dusty Flight, set 'em up hot. Bomb single. Arm nose tail."

"Twoop," replied Vic.

"Okay, Dusty Flight, the two white phosphorus logs are on the ground burning," Blind Bat called. "Let's call the line they form north-south and the distance between the logs one hundred meters. Put your first bomb fifty meters east of the south log. We'll be holding off to the west between eight and ten thousand feet."

John rolled in from the south at fourteen thousand feet, high and close to the target again for a nearly vertical dive angle.

"Dusty Seven One's in."

Vic answered with the click of his mike button.

The night was as black as the inside of a cow. A high overcast obliterated all stars. John could not tell where the earth ended and the heavens began. Aside from the burning white phosphorus flares on the ground, there was no reference outside the cockpit to tell up from down.

He pickled off the first bomb at his best guess of fifty meters east of the south log, and then hauled back hard on the control stick. As the attitude indicator on the instrument panel showed the nose of his aircraft coming up through the horizon, he eased off the back pressure on the control stick. He banked left, continued climbing, and looked back over his left shoulder to survey the damages. It wasn't a bull's-eye, but it was close enough. The shrapnel pattern from the seven-hundred-fifty-pound iron bomb penetrated the fuel tank of the lead truck and flames flared up like a freshly lit match. Within seconds the flames engulfed its load of mortar shells and the truck began to cook like a popcorn popper with the lid off. The light from the burning truck illuminated the mountainside, revealing a dozen trucks nearly bumper-to-bumper.

Vic rolled in on the last truck he could see. "Two's in from the north."

"Roger," John answered.

It was impossible for John to see Vic because he pulled out of his dive above the dome of illumination formed by the burning truck, but there was no mistaking where his bomb hit.

"That was a bull's-eye on the number ten truck, Dusty Seven Two. You Dusty guys are all right," called Blind Bat.

Once they had bottled up the convoy, it was a midnight massacre. There was no place on the steep mountainside for the trucks to pull off and find cover, and the bombs had effectively barricaded the road fore and aft.

John's second pass blew the third truck in line off the road. It cartwheeled down the mountainside in an avalanche of fire and explosions. Vic and John dropped a total of three bombs each in the cool, professional style of the executioner. Since they saw no ground fire, they decided to save the CBU-24 just in case somebody decided to shoot back.

"Blind Bat, Dusty Flight would like to make a few twenty mike mike passes and hold a hammer apiece in reserve," John announced.

"You're cleared for the strafing runs, Dusty Flight."

"Copy, Blind Bat. Lead is in from the north."

Vic and John strafed that convoy north-to-south and south-to-north. With minimal conversation, they ravaged those trucks like two starving jackals working over a bloated rhino carcass. John counted eight of them burning or obliterated.

A glance at the fuel gauges told John the party was about over. "We've got enough fuel for two more passes, Dusty Flight," he called.

Coming off the next strafing pass it finally happened. A geyser of red, orange and yellow tracers erupted about a half mile to the east, pointed in John's direction, and he was bracketed.

"Look out, John!"

It sounded like Vic's voice was coming from outer space, as if he needed any warning. The airspace on all sides of John was filled with multi-colored tracers. Suddenly five hundred knots felt like dirigible speed. He slammed the throttle full forward and outboard into afterburner. Certainly the resulting blowtorch of the afterburner in the night sky would tell them where he was, but dear God, they already knew. After an eternity of six-G turns and rolls the shooting stopped.

"Dusty Seven One, this is Blind Bat. You can pack it in if you want. You've done a night's work here."

John's first attempt to respond to Blind Bat produced thumb pressure on the mike button, but no simultaneous vibration of the vocal cords. It was so close—the closest he'd ever seen at night. The tracers looked a lot bigger up close in the dark. Two deep breaths later the cords came unstuck.

"If it's all right with you, Blind Bat, we've got just the Hammer for those gooks, and enough fuel for one more pass. I think I know where that triple A was coming from." It was time to invoke the Ellsworth policy again. Nobody shot at this Top Gun without receiving a dose of same in return.

"Well, it's your choice, Dusty Flight. What size jockstrap do you guys wear?" Blind Bat asked.

"Some of us still think this war is worth winning, Blind Bat." It was the first insubordinate comment John had ever made over the radio in his Air Force career.

The AAA had come from somewhere in the blackness to the east of the target, but John had only a rough idea. He figured if he rolled in and pointed the nose in that general direction they'd shoot again, and he might be able to see the muzzle flashes.

"Dusty Seven Two, that stuff was awfully accurate. Keep it fast and steep, and for God's sake, keep it turning. Did your RHAW gear indicate any radar tracking?" John called.

"Two, negative." If Vic was scared, nothing in his voice betrayed him. If married life had rearranged his priorities, John couldn't tell it.

Sure enough, as soon as John pointed the nose toward the

ground, he got a face-full of Christmas tree lights streaking by the canopy, but he no longer flinched at such distractions. At five hundred knots and a 60-degree dive angle he pulled it over into a modified barrel roll. It bought him a few milliseconds of freedom from that fire hose of death. While inverted he could see the circle of anti-aircraft artillery guns winking away in that sea of black. The bottom half of the roll brought the wings level and right side up just under the tracer fire, still pointed down in a forty-five degree dive. He aimed at the middle of that circle of muzzle flashes, pickled away The Hammer, and began the dive recovery.

The bomblets hit the ground in a slightly oval circle. The shooting stopped. There was nothing but black ink on the ground where before there was a circle of deadly fireflies.

"Checkmate Charlie," he called to Vic.

Vic responded with a double click on the mike button. That meant he was smiling, John thought.

The mind does strange things under stress. It occurred to John that only a sick mind could lead a guy to stick his head into the jaws of death and pull it out thinking about a chess game. Maybe Vic wasn't smiling now.

Vic and John had left a chess game in progress in Squadron Operations to brief for the night's mission. Vic had insisted that John might as well concede the match. John's novice foresight could not see a checkmate in the offing, so he insisted that they declare a recess until after the night's work. John still seldom whipped Vic-only when Vic let him, for morale purposes.

"Dusty Seven One, where to?" Vic's voice jolted John out of his self-analysis.

"Same place as mine, Two. Let's give them a double dose." John was sure there was nothing but raw hamburger left at that gun site. "Roger," Vic responded, in that perfect bored-to-death tone of voice, the one they all worked so hard to perfect.

John couldn't tell if it was the same site that he had hit, or another one, but the geyser erupted out of that ink bottle again, right in the vicinity of where Vic should have been. "Come on Vic, you can do it," he said aloud to himself.

Again Vic's bomb hit the bull's-eye. The circle of bomblets perfectly super-imposed the ring of muzzle flashes. A second after the bomb hit the ground there was an enormous mushroom shaped fireball right at the edge of the circle of death. It momentarily lit up the mountaintop as bright as day.

I've got the best wingman in all of Southeast Asia, John thought to himself. "Bull's-eye, Two," he crowed.

"Fantastic shooting, Dusty Seven Two. Looks like you got their ammo supply with that one," Blind Bat shouted. He couldn't hide his excitement either.

"Dusty Seven One Flight, let's head home…Dusty Seven Two, this is Seven One…" John called.

Silence!

"Dusty Seven One, this is Blind Bat. I'm afraid that fireball was your wing man."

"Roger…" The fighter pilot cool was completely drained from John's voice.

"Dusty Seven One, I know you're low on fuel. You'd best head home. You can be mighty proud. That's the finest piece of work I've ever seen, and this is my second war. We'll hang around as long as we can and see what we can see. We'll make a decision on whether to launch Search-and-Rescue tonight or in the morning. Thing is, we can't get a good look from where we are and I'm not inclined to get any closer. We're a much fatter, slower target than you are."

"Roger, Blind Bat. There's no way he could have ejected successfully," John answered.

"Good night, Dusty. We'll forward your bombing results and notify headquarters. Expect a crowd when you get home. We love ya."

"Thanks, Blind Bat. Dusty Seven One out." John's voice trailed off.

"Dusty Seven Two, this is Blind Bat…Dusty Seven Two, this is Blind Bat. How do you read…? Dusty Seven Two, this is Blind Bat on guard. Come in, please…" Blind Bat's repeated calls to Vic were met with silence, deathly silence.

One was a very lonely number three hundred miles from home at twenty thousand feet on the blackest night in all eternity. John had a vague recollection of fuel gauges reading alarmingly low and of fear that the fire in the engine would go out prior to touchdown. Pretty critical stuff, but tonight it didn't seem very important. Life didn't seem very important to John, because life had ceased for Vic. It had ceased because John's hate had overcome his common sense. His killer-instinct had grown out of control until it overwhelmed his survival-instinct, killing his last best friend. Kate had warned him. She could see it happening. He would far rather have died himself than cause Vic to die. He felt consumed with abject depression at the prospect of a lifetime of nightmares and regret and self-recrimination.

The reception party consisted of five blue Ford sedans, with "Property of USAF" stenciled on the side in yellow, parked at revetment three, aisle five. John's F-100 bobbed to a stop. Before he could bring the throttle around the horn to shut off the engine, the fire in the belly of that metallic beast died of fuel starvation. It was a small matter under the circumstances.

Adrenaline is a wonderful thing until the supply runs out. It had assured John's survival any number of times when stress shut down his conscious mind. His supply ran out between the bottom rung of the boarding ladder and the steel planking of the revetment. His knees were the first to go. Major Gillespie, still acting squadron commander, saw the wobble, grabbed John's left arm, swung it over his head and across his shoulders and clutched John's sweat-drenched waist with his free hand. Someone reeking of stale gin materialized on the other side of him.

"I'm sorry, son," said Major Gillespie.

Then the dam burst and John cried right there in front of all those colonels. Sure, it's a lousy war, but it's the only one we've got. Right? Wrong! It's just a lousy war, fought by a sick human race in a lousy God-forsaken place.

The debrief lasted the better part of an hour. There was not a hint of condemnation in the room outside of John's own devastated conscience. No flight of two fighters had ever destroyed eight trucks and one—probably two—anti-aircraft sites in one mission. No one questioned the decision to attack the guns.

The chess game was untouched near the briefing table in Squadron Operations. John tried not to look at it, but failed. Of course his checkmate was eminent. It was plain as day from Vic's side of the board. He swept his hand across the board and chess pieces flew everywhere.

John refused repeated offers by the colonels for a ride back to his hooch. He told them he needed to walk off a lot of sadness. It was still a few hours before daylight but John knew sleep was out of the question. He opened the door of his hooch and checked the shelves above the fridge. Ron's bottle of scotch rested there and John reached for it and unscrewed the top. A glass would not be necessary. The whiff of it caused the hangover in Hawaii to flash through his mind in vivid detail, but fought it off and downed a slug, then walked to the bathroom for a water chaser. He drew a glass and studied it in the harsh bathroom light, anything to get a tormented mind off horrible reality. He looked at the hand that held it and it still was not the steady, smooth Top Gun hand of one who danced with supersonic angels. It was a hand that had killed...how many thousand people in the most violent fashion? The longer he looked at it the more it shook. He put the glass down and looked at the mirror. There was a wear, emaciated old man looking back at a kid six months shy of his twenty-sixth birthday. And there was guilt and anger and defeat...and shame and self-loathing in the eyes that stared into his soul. John did not know the man in the mirro.

He stumbled back out the door and into the night with the scotch bottle in hand and no thought or idea where he was going. Tuy Hoa in the pre-dawn hours was as desolate as John's heart. He just wanted to hide from it all, especially himself, in some dark place and not think—not think about the ruined life of a Kansas bride named Mrs. Vic Wilson, not think about the shattered family of a kindly old man named Dan Redman, not think about the living hell of James Peterson and the daily agony of his wife and kids, and not think about Jack English spending every minute of his life just trying to stay alive like a wild animal in the jungle, and not think about how life might have been living with an ever-smiling angel in an old house in Aspen, Colorado.

And all for what? Someday soon America would desert these simple peasant farmers—it was plain as day to John and he thought it was plain as day to Ho Chi Minh, too—and leave them to the Red hoards and then the carnage would really begin. Anyone who had chosen to side with the Yanks would be killed or imprisoned, maybe even mama-san and her girls.

John suddenly realized he was no longer walking but sitting in the sand near the water's edge. The eastern horizon was a deep purple and the South China Sea was as placid as his heart was not. Seagulls flew overhead, crying in an especially mournful way. It was the same spot where he and Kate spent their first date and where they both nearly lost their lives a few months later. And he felt a yearning in his heart for her that was just unbearable. He heard an agonized old man sobbing and mumbling and realized it was his own voice.

A missing man formation of F-100's roared low over the beach and out to sea. The deafening roar of 4 J-57 engines drowned out John's sobs. The sight chilled him till his teeth chattered.

*   *   *

Search-and-Rescue aircraft had been airborne since before first light and over the target area at dawn. In spite of the enormous fireball the night before, the rough terrain and two-hundred-foot-high, triple canopy jungle had swallowed Vic and his F-100 without a trace. The offical verdict was "Missing in Action" just like Lieutenant Colonel English. In seven years, if no evidence had been found, it would be changed to "Missing in Action/Presumed Dead." The only thing good about that was Nancy would continue to get Vic's paycheck for seven years.

After a forty-eight hour alcohol binge and an equal hangover period, John flew again, but it wasn't the same. The fire in his belly had gone out, but the hatred in his heart remained.

He saw no reason for life, even thought about ending it all Kamikazi-style, and it even occurred to him that maybe that's what the dancing demons were encouraging him to do.

John gave up the game of chess and knew he'd never look at a chessboard again without thinking of Vic. For the first time he went to the base chapel for Vic's memorial service. It was a week after the crash and search and rescue operations were terminated without ever even finding the crash sight. A Presbyterian chaplain, Major Martin I. Edwards, delivered the eulogy:

"Greater love hath no man than he give his life for his friends and his country. To serve your country with honor when the cause is unpopular is the highest form of patriotism. Nothing demonstrates the fallen nature of man more graphically than war. It is never popular, and the Bible is filled with just such demonstrations of man's inhumanity to man. It is proof of the radical lostness of man that 2000 years after Jesus walked this earth and taught us how to live, we persist in trying to solve our problems by destroying one another in ever more creative and hideous ways. Beloved, our only hope...our ONLY hope...is to throw ourselves at the mercy of the sovereign God of the universe, to acknowledge that we are sinners, to beg His forgiveness, and henceforth walk humbly with Him. Dear Father, may the soul of Vic Wilson rest in your eternal peace. Amen."

John sat and wept quietly in the pew long after everyone else had left.

Life outside the cockpit had become one nearly unbearable void. Ron, Matt and Mike were good friends, but Vic and John had been soul brothers, and Kate and John soul mates. He had lost them both, and he felt responsible. The black box was so full of suppressed terror and guilt that the lid wouldn't close.

On missions over The Trail when John was leading he checked out every strange thing he saw on the ground, hoping it would be Colonel English...and wasting valuable time and fuel in the process. He was the talk—the worry—of Dusty's Pub when he wasn't present, which was most of the time.

John stayed close to the only angel he had left. He was sure Major Gillespie was sick of him begging and pleading for more flying time. John told him he wanted maximum combat time to aid his chances of staying on at Fighter Weapons School as an instructor. He even flew the test hops after routine maintenance was performed on the airplanes. It was a minor thrill—no bombs, no tanks or afterburner climb, screaming for heaven like a rocket. Flying was the only antidote to his depression—the only time he didn't feel on the absolute edge of total exhaustion and despair. He even tried to get his Misty FAC assignment early so he could get on with looking for Colonel English.

He had come to the conclusion that his life was going to end in this jungle somewhere. He could tell by the way the frenzied black shadows danced around his bunk at night. They were laughing insanely as they danced. It was a large crowd—Colonel English was no longer a part of the nightmare—and somehow he knew it matched the number of Vietnamese KBA that he had accumulated. It was to be his fate and he was resigned to it—even at peace with it.

He'd crammed a lifetime into twenty-five years, soared with the angels and been loved by one. In the meantime, he'd just keep killing North Vietnamese and wasting the big guns till it was time to go up to Phu Cat. He wrote a letter to his mother and sealed it and put it in his dresser drawer, to be read only after he was dead. He wanted to be buried in Arlington National Cemetery—if there was anything found to bury—and he borrowed a line from Major Edwards for his marker—"John D. Ellsworth, patriot and fighter pilot by the grace of God."

The nightly dream had taken on a strange ending. It would end with the dawn. On the eastern horizon there were two suns. One was a large, orange globe and the other, smaller and yellow, off to the right-a sundog at dawn. When they appeared the laughing shadows evaporated.

John called Colonel Moffit and got Kate's home address. He wrote a letter to Kate, but couldn't bring himself to mail it. She was so intuitive he knew she would see the depression he was in, probably think he was genuinely suicidal, call Daddy, and he'd be grounded. That's assuming she'd even read it. She'd recognize his handwriting on the envelope. Every scenario he could conjure up was depressing.

John climbed back on the wagon; the stuff wasn't doing any good anyway. He stayed away from Dusty's Pub entirely. Ron said one of the other nurses, Lieutenant Allen, had been asking about him. But Kate was going to have to be gone a long time before John was ready to think about another woman. He became the Dusty Squadron hermit. He ran through the streets of Tuy Hoa Airbase at night like a headless, heartbroken horseman.

His roommates thought he was a love sick pup, FIGMO—an obscene term for a guy who's tour was nearly over, one dull teetotaler, or most likely, all of the above.

John wanted to do something for Mama-san's daughters. He was convinced that his country was no longer trying to save these beautiful people but only trying to extricate itself from what they thought was a noble cause gone horribly awry. He knew that if the communists took over anyone who fraternized with American soldiers would be apt to be killed, and his heart bled for those two little oriental dolls. Any gifts that were not consumable would be evidence of their association with the enemy, so he bought two huge bags of groceries with emphasis on sweet things to eat. The next time they came with Mama-san to do the cleaning he gave the bags to the girls and a twenty-dollar bill to Mama-san—an illegal act that would feed the black market. And though not a word of verbal communication was understood between them, he knew that they were thrilled. He hugged them both and left the hooch for Mama-san to clean before he made a spectacle of himself. He wanted them all to remember him as a brave American man whose heart was in the right place in spite of his nasty occupation.

Finally, enough time had passed that John could write Vic's wife a letter. He'd gotten far more practice at that unpleasant task than he cared for. Nancy had written, saying she knew John was Vic's best friend and could he please fill her in. The Air Force major who had knocked on her door, had simply told her in a polite, apologetic way that Lieutenant Wilson was missing in action. He told her that all his pay and benefits would be sent to her until he was found dead, returned safely home or seven years had passed. In her heart she would always believe he was alive until somebody could prove otherwise. And, oh yes, she was expecting Vic's child around Christmas time.

It tore John's guts out. Should he tell her the truth and let her get on with her life? Or would it be easier for her to believe Vic was coming home until a long period had passed and the memory was dulled? John opted for the truth. He was sure it's what Vic would have done for him.

Dear Nancy,

I am very proud to tell you that your husband was the best friend I have ever had, and the best fighter pilot I ever knew. In this quagmire that is Vietnam he was a rock. I am so glad that you two were married on the Ni Sa Bula in Hawaii. He loved you very much.

Nancy, I was with Vic the night he died. I say "died" because I am positive he did, even though you will not have a body to give a proper burial. We were taking a lot of very heavy anti-aircraft fire on a very dark night. Vic told me funerals should be a time for celebration, not for sadness. I hope some day I can understand what he meant and believe it with the same conviction he did.

Nancy, consider Vic's pay check for the next seven

years a tribute, along with your child, from him—a token of his love. Vic will live forever in my heart, as I am sure he will live forever in your heart, and through your child.

I will be back in the USA in June and I would like to come visit you. I will write when I know a time. In the meantime, if there is anything I can do for you, please let me know.

Sincerely,

John D. Ellsworth

John's personal conviction was ninety-nine percent that Vic was dead. But he knew if he said it that way to Nancy, she would continue to hold out hope, and he didn't think that was right. Packing up Vic's belongings was the saddest, toughest thing John had ever done.

*   *   *

It was the fifth of May—only three weeks left to kill North Vietnamese. Kate should have been home with her mother for a week but John was still afraid to write her. He decided that he would rather just wait till he got home and go see her. If his paranoia was just that, and he survived, he would just knock on the door and surprise her.

He would tell her again how much he loved her—more than anything. He'd tell her that his killing days were over for good and that she was right about his hate and he was wrong—it had gotten his soul brother killed and he would carry the burden forever.

If she wasn't home, he'd just sit down and talk to Ethel until she came home. If Ethel was as nice as Ozzie, that wouldn't be difficult. If Kate walked in with someone else, then, well, it was just his destiny.

John had dreamed the same dream with the laughing shadows and the sundog at dawn for over two weeks now. But this night he was working, and that beat nightmares anytime.

Ron and John were scheduled for the Trail at night, again. Steel Tiger was becoming a steel trap. It was an air war of attrition and the U.S. was clearly not making a dent in the flow of guns and supplies down the Ho Chi Minh Trail. John still felt his odds were better in the dark, in spite of what had happened to Vic. The AAA gunners were still firing in the blind.

Ron and John walked through the door of Dusty Squadron Ops

at 0200. The duty officer behind the counter greeted them.

"You've got a mission change. There's a massive Search and Rescue operation near Saravane. An F-100 went in late yesterday and the Jolly Green went down just at sunset trying to recover the F-100 pilot. Then about midnight an AC-130 gun ship went down while firing on the target. We've got at least eight people on the ground and they think most of them are still alive. But the ground fire thus far has been brutal. You're carrying wall-to-wall CBU-24's. They need flak suppression in the worse way. Hit the tanker over Pleiku."

"Oh great, just what I need. Night air-to-air refueling," Ron said disgustedly. John thought it was an indication of the state of Ron's mind that he was more concerned about night refueling than the brutal flak of Steel Tiger. Moral in Dusty Squadron was rock bottom and everyone was a little flaky. Ron and John had not done a night refueling since fighter pilot school and it was not a piece of cake. Everything seemed next to impossible the first time they were exposed to it in training, but night refueling was by far the worst.

John was leading, so he conducted the briefing. Intelligence came down to give them a special briefing. It was one of the worst disasters yet for the USAF in Laos, and it wasn't over. It began when the F-100 flight late in the afternoon uncovered a huge truck park and storage area. There were numerous trucks and piles of weapons and ammunition. Apparently every AAA battery down there opened up in an effort to prevent its destruction.

The AC-130 gunship was a rare loss. Its awesome firepower consisted of four to six 20-millimeter cannons pointed sideways out the left side of the fuselage of the plane. It would make a circle over the target at night, pouring lead into the center of the circle at a ferocious rate. Its tracers looked like a huge orange minute hand moving around a giant, black faced clock. What it lacked in accuracy it made up for in sheer volume of lead, and it was extremely effective against truck parks. But it was a big, fat, slow moving target.

Captain Raines, the weather man, was optimistic, but that was neither here nor there. It seemed there was never a correlation, not even a good negative correlation, between what he forecast and what they usually found. John decided he wrote his own script without ever looking at the charts—all style and no substance.

Ron and John walked out the door of Dusty Squadron Ops, parachutes over one shoulder and helmet bags in the opposite hand.

"It's a beautiful night for killing gooks, Ron."

"I'd rather be at Dusty's Pub," Ron replied. John's gallows humor was wearing pretty thin on his roommate.

"Somebody's gotta do it, Ron. It might as well be the world's two greatest fighter pilots."

"Yeah. Yeah...."

"What we have, here, Lieutenant Johnson, is a failure of leadership. If I were in charge we'd be headed for Hanoi and Haiphong Harbor tonight, along with every other plane that can drop a bomb. I'd have Ho Chi Minh suing for peace in three weeks...."

"You can change it all when you make general, John."

"Right, let's crank."

Box Seven One was on station over Pleiku and gave them an RDF steer to intercept him. He looked twice as big to John up close in the dark.

There was no way for the tanker to light up the refueling drogue in a way that would not blind the pilot trying to hit it. The lighting had to be supplied by the F-100. The base of the six-foot long refueling probe on the F-100's right wing had a small light that focused on the end of the probe. There was also a light on the right nose of the F-100 that focused on the end of the probe. Together they had an illumination range of a pitiful ten feet forward of the probe.

John lined up on the colored lights on the belly of the tanker, and moved forward at half the daytime rate. He stared intently into the darkness dead ahead. When he finally saw the drogue, it was perfectly lined up with the oval intake duct on his nose. It startled him. An inhaled drogue would snuff the fire out in an F-100 in a hurry. It was supposed to be about five feet to his right in line with his probe. He came back too much on the throttle, fell back and started forward again. This time he connected.

After topping off, John backed away and up onto the left wing of Box Seven One as Ron slid into position. Every muscle in his arms and legs were hard as pine knots. He practiced some deep breathing, talked out loud to himself and slowly his body regained some approximation of a relaxed state. He didn't understand why he felt this way, and the very fact that he did, after all these months, was ominous.

Ron had no trouble hitting the refueling drogue, and they were on their way. "You win the beer, Two. Box Seven One, we may need your services again. How long are you good for?"

"Dusty Five One Flight, we'll be on station for three more hours. We've been monitoring the rescue operation. Good luck."

"Thank you, Box."

Saravane was the final resting-place of Vic, and the old man was just north up the road seventy miles at Tchepone. And somewhere in that stretch of tropical jungle was the most likely place to find Colonel English—John was anxious to get up there in the daytime as a Misty FAC. The colonel would want to stay near the road so he would be within signaling distance of friendly planes. He would also know that friendly long-range patrols were on the ground in the same area—the incredibly gutsy Army Rangers, Navy Seals, and Marines who monitored troop and truck movement. John had spent dozens of lonesome hours trying to put himself in the position of a downed pilot and thinking about what he would do in that situation. But nighttime was an impossible time to find anything, especially this night when survival would require 100% concentration.

Twenty-five minutes after they left the tanker, Dusty Flight was over Saravane, talking to the FAC, who was in a C-130 with a Starlight Scope.

"Good morning, Dusty, this is Blind Bat Zero One. We've got a tough one here. We've been talking with Spad Two One and with the folks on the ground. There's a Jolly Green crew, an AC-130 crew and an F-100 driver on the ground below us. And a Misty FAC who's been missing for months has walked out of the jungle and joined the downed AC-130 crew. They're telling us the gooks are closing in. If we don't get them out at first light we probably won't get them out at all."

Chills enveloped John's body. "What's the Misty FAC's name Blind Bat?"

"We can't say it over the air but you Dusty guys know him."

"Oh my God…. Dusty, copy." John couldn't believe his ears-the only guy in the squadron who never quit believing Colonel English was alive and now he couldn't believe it. Alone in the dark cockpit, lit only by the dim red glow of the instrument panel, John shouted, "KATE, I FOUND HIM…I FOUND HIM! COLONEL ENGLISH IS ALIVE…HE'S ALIVE!" Tears welled up in his eyes and he was having trouble reading his instruments. He took some deep breaths as he trembled all over.

"There's heavy flak in all quadrants. We've seen flak bursts above twelve thousand feet. Must be some 85-millimeter down there, maybe bigger. There are two fires on the ground. The fire to the east is the burning AC-130 gun ship. The fire one thousand meters west of it is the truck park we uncovered yesterday. It's a doozy. The AC-130 was working it over when it got hit." Blind Bat sounded tired, like he'd been there for days.

"Where's the triple A, Blind Bat?" John asked. His mind was racing at Mach I and he was anxious to get on with the fight.

"Well, you know how it is in the dark. They don't want to shoot when they hear you fast movers overhead. They are so well camouflaged that my Starlight Scope isn't picking them up. But what I saw hit the AC-130 came from about a klick north of the truck park."

"Dusty, I'd like you to drop your first CBU one thousand meters north of the burning AC-130..."

Great, John thought. We've got Colonel English and eight other pilot's lives at stake and the guy wants us to probe all over eastern Laos looking for the guns. The odds against that working must be a thousand to one.

"Blind Bat, this is Dusty. We'd like to leave your frequency for one minute and talk over some strategy."

"Copy, Dusty. Blind Bat standing by."

"Dusty Five One, let's go Winchester freq." John hadn't played this game since his flight leader check-ride with Colonel English himself.

He dialed in 303.0, hesitated five seconds and checked in with Ron.

"Ron, we'll never get those guns this way. It's time to go trolling. I'll be the bait."

"With all those guns? Are you crazy?"

"Listen, pal. I'm not going home without Colonel English and I'm in charge here. Now I'm going to get down low and light the afterburner, and I'll be a target they can't resist. They'll go for me like a bass on a Junebug."

"Maybe I should be the bait. You're the best gunfighter in Southeast Asia." His tone of voice told John he didn't want to, and John wouldn't ask him.

"Negative. Negative. You're a married man. One widow on my conscience is enough. You set up to roll in on the area one thousand meters north of the C-130, where we think they are. I'm going to come across the C-130 fire at about one thousand feet and light the burner. They won't be able to resist shooting at my blowtorch in this night sky. You stomp on them. Come in from the north. Aim just short of where you see the tracers beginning. Copy?" John knew he was talking so fast he was nearly incoherent.

"Copy," Ron replied. His tone of voice sounded like "No way, Jose."

"One more thing. When I say 'Amos Moses' I'm going to count to three and light the afterburner. So be ready. Copy?"

"Copy. Who the hell is Amos Moses?"

"Alligator bait…and Ron…this is no time to miss. We need bulls eyes, baby."

"Twoop."

"Blind Bat, Dusty Five One Flight back on freq."

"Roger, Dusty."

"Blind Bat, I'm going to get down low and light the burner and give them something to shoot at so my wing man can see where they are and drop the Hammer on them. If you all will hold out to the west we'll stay out of that part of the sky."

"Well, okay, Dusty, but be advised I can't direct you to do that. You're on your own. The terrain around the two fires is one thousand feet MSL. The highest elevation within three miles is two thousand feet."

"Dusty, copy. Are we cleared?" John asked.

"You're cleared."

"Dusty Flight, bomb single, arm nose tail, external lights out." John called.

"Twoop."

John rolled inverted, and split-essed for the deck. It was acrobats on instruments—time to pull out all the stops. At twenty five hundred feet he leveled, headed due west toward the burning AC-130. Two miles short of the fire and indicating 500 knots, he called, "Amos Moses." He counted out loud to himself, "ONE THOUSAND, TWO THOUSAND, THREE THOUSAND," and slammed the throttle outboard.

There was the half-second hesitation when the exhaust eyelids opened, and then "whoomp" as the afterburner kicked in with a jolt. It took about two seconds of that ten-foot-long blowtorch in the sky and every gun within miles jumped on him. There were multi-colored tracers from left, right, and straight ahead.

He jinked left, right, up, down, zero G's, positive G's. It was as rough a ride as he could make it and still control the airplane. He made his angel as elusive as he could. After counting to ten thousand, he came out of afterburner and climbed back to 15,000 feet. If he hadn't heard his own voice counting in his ears, he'd have sworn time had stood still.

Blind Bat was calling, "Bull's-eye. Bull's-eye."

"Good work, Two. Holler when you're set up for the next round." John's voice was shaky.

"Two's ready."

Amos Moses." And they played the game again. This time the gunners were really mad. They didn't let up. Well after John doused the torch of his afterburner there were still tracers following him. Now we can get down to business, he thought.

He bent her around to see the source of the tracers. There were a half dozen choices, both north and south of the target. He had seen Ron's CBU-24 hit in a circle of sparkling death. There was a large secondary explosion and fire that gave them another reference point. There wasn't any need to troll anymore. They had the guns located.

Thank, God. He didn't think he could have handled another run through that gauntlet. John was panting and exhausted. His eyes were stinging from two sockets full of sweat. Even his socks were drenched. His shoes felt like flooded waders as his feet worked the rudder pedals.

"Dusty Flight, that was another great hit. All those gun sites to the north are well away from the downed crews. You're cleared all passes on them."

"Roger, Blind Bat. This is Dusty Five One, in from the east." John decided they were shooting in the direction of the sound. Whatever their tactics, they were good. The stuff was in his face and angling up from the left from the southern gun sites. With no bait to divert their attention he got it all.

He pickled away his first bomb, banked forty-five degrees, and then began a six-G dive recovery. With all the air traffic out west of the target he wanted to be sure to stay out of that airspace. While still grunting his way through the pull out, he heard Ron call in from the north. Almost immediately all the guns that were still shooting were pointed north. Maybe the gooks had a radio and found their frequency and were listening to their conversation. Maybe he was just paranoid, or maybe they were telegraphing their punches somehow. John couldn't figure it out and if Kate asked, yes he was more terrified than he'd ever been in his life. But lives were at stake, especially the life of a man he loved like a father, a man he owed more than he owed his own father, a man he had already forfeited his future to help after everyone else had given up hope. He would not give up until he'd drawn his last breath.

The eastern sky was beginning to turn orange and Ron and John were about to lose the cover of darkness. That was bad. The night had kept them invisible to the gunners without radar guidance. They could dance in and out of the darkness with their jabs and counter-punches while the gunners flailed away in the blind. In the daylight they and the gunners would be two heavyweights standing toe-to-toe in a slugfest.

This time John circled on around to the north and came in from the same direction Ron had. Fighters never follow one another down the chute. Hopefully they wouldn't be expecting this.

"Dusty Five One is in from Minneapolis." Ron would know that meant north, and if the North Vietnamese were listening maybe that would fool them. It didn't cost anything to try.

The tracers were fewer and further between, and not as close this time. John zeroed in on the only gun site that was still shooting north of the downed AC-130. There were four guns winking at him. He pickled his second bomb away and they winked no more. John was so scared and exhausted he was trembling, but this marathon run was not over. They needed to silence some of those guns to the south or a lot more people were going to die in the daylight in such a massive rescue attempt, and Colonel English would have survived all these months only to die anyway.

Two Jolly Greens and four Spads checked in. The airspace was filling up.

John had two Hammers left and Ron had one. They were going to have to get maximum mileage out of them if the Jolly Greens were to have a chance. Even one ZPU-23 would make short work of those big whirling monsters hovering motionless over the treetops. A glance at the fuel gauges told John he was going to have to hit that tanker again, just to get home. Those two ten second bursts of afterburner had depleted his fuel supply at three times the normal rate. One more pass would have to be it.

"Blind Bat, this is Dusty Five One. I've got enough fuel for one more pass and we'd like to have a crack at those guns south of the target." Actually he was lying. John had barely enough fuel to get back to the tanker, and if he had not known Colonel English was down there they would have been halfway home by now after following the FAC's worthless directions to probe the darkness.

"Roger, Dusty. You've got the downed crews somewhere in that area. But the way you guys have been shooting I think it's worth the chance, as long as you know exactly where the guns are."

"We know exactly," John responded.

"You're cleared. You guys are sierra hotel. A whole lot of folks are going to be mighty grateful." The equivalent of "cool" in fighter pilot language was "shit hot," but swearing was not allowed over the radio so the phonetic alphabet was used, and everyone knew what "sierra hotel" meant—it was cool to the max. But this was hardly the time to be basking in glory.

"Roger. Thanks. Lead's in from New Orleans."

They apparently knew John was coming and threw everything they had at him. The sky was probably just light enough in the pre-dawn for them to see him, because they had him bracketed. He was almost vertical, headed straight down as fast as he could make that beauty go and whirling like a dervish. He flipped the gun switch on and fired short bursts on the way down. It would never hit them but seeing his muzzle flashes might keep their heads down. From the looks of the tracers it didn't do any good.

He gave them both Hammers, honked back hard on the pole and turned toward the east. The nose was just coming up through the horizon when the first slug slammed into his angel somewhere behind him. It staggered them but they were still flying. Then another body blow, and another.

"I'm hit...." The radio went dead. The right wing dropped and John fed in left aileron. No good. It continued to drop. Fed in left rudder. Couldn't stop it. With full left stick and rudder he was doing slow rolls into the dawn.

Getting out of his epileptic angel in a whole piece was going to take divine intervention. The engine was compressor stalling in a series of violent explosions as it ingested broken airplane parts, but it refused to die and so did John.

The fire warning light was on. The flight system fail light was on. The A.C. and D.C. generator-off-lights were on. The cockpit was a Christmas tree of colored warning lights. The RPM gauge was winding down erratically and the exhaust temperature gauge was pegged well beyond the red line. The airspeed indicator and altimeter were frozen. They must have shot off the pitot boom. He could hear the emergency ram-air turbine still spinning behind his head, giving him the only hydraulic control available. John estimated he was about six or seven thousand feet above the ground...and headed lower.

The whole instrument panel went dark, as if he'd turned off the master switch. He was still flying-barely-and rolling. The sun was an orange half-circle on the horizon. There was no way he'd get to friendly territory and he knew it. She was a gritty, gutsy old gal and she was giving it her best, but that wasn't going to be good enough. John could smell burning hydraulic fluid and JP-4 and he knew the fire back there was getting worse. One more roll and he was going to have to go.

He caught a glimpse of Ron off to his right. Ron was frantically pumping his fist up and down with his thumb pointed straight up. John knew what he meant.

Come on, baby. One more roll. And when you're wings level I'm going to have to desert you. He had the very sad feeling that he and his swept-wing lover were parting company for all eternity. And he knew...this was the moment the dancing shadows had been laughing about.

He got straight in the seat and hooked his heels in the footrests. With his foot off the left rudder pedal the roll accelerated, the nose came around and the plane began to skid sideways. In the same instant another violent explosion filled the cockpit with smoke and fire.

In a single motion John raised both ejection handles and squeezed the triggers. He heard somebody screaming.

John ejected with the plane upside down. It was a slow-motion scene that couldn't have lasted more than a second. He had a fire inside his helmet. One hundred percent oxygen, fed into the face mask under high pressure by the small, green bottle in the parachute pack, had ignited. He was vaguely aware of being yanked to a stop with his chin on his chest, his feet over his head, and the leg straps cutting into his crotch, and then dangling under the parachute in deathly silence. He knew he was dying. It hurt so bad he wanted it to be quick.

John tried to get his mask and helmet off but his hands weren't working very well. Finally he managed to tear it off his head. It felt like most of his cheeks and scalp went with it. He could only see out of one eye. He was looking right into the orange globe of the morning sun on the horizon. Just to the right of it his dying angel was in her death dance.

She exploded in a brilliant flash—a sundog at dawn—and an earth quaking clap of thunder.

The night returned.

* * *

"Good morning, Doctor."

"Good morning, Karen. How's our boy today?"

"He's still with us."

"Good. How long has that young lady been here now?"

"Over a week, Doctor. She insists on staying here twenty-four hours a day. Sleeps in that chair. Some scruffy-looking old English sailor brings her something to eat. Calls himself Captain Hyde."

"Mom?"

"Doctor, listen. He's trying to say something."

"Mom?"

"Mom's not here, John. This is Dr. Wyatt. You've been a very sick boy."

"Can...you take my...blindfold off, sir?"

"I'm afraid we need to leave those bandages on for a few more weeks."

"I...don't...feel anything. Am I...all here?"

"More or less, but some parts of you are burned and some are broken and we're not sure yet how well all of them are going to work. But you're still among the living and that's a major accomplishment. You're a tough nut. Listen, John, there's someone here who wants to talk to you."

"John?"

"K-Kate?"

"Yes."

It took him a while before he could talk again. "Would you... touch...my face?"

"Yes."

It was Kate, all right. The electricity came right through the bandages. There was a body attached to his head. He could feel it trembling.

"Where...are we?"

"Tripler Army Hospital in Honolulu." Kate's voice was quavering.

"What...day is it?"

"May 31st, 1969. You've been here two weeks."

"I don't remember.... Kate...will I...see?"

"John, they say you might be short one eye, but no one knows for sure."

"Will I...walk?"

"I think you will, John. I don't know what the doctors think."

"My flying days...are over, aren't they?"

"Yes, I'm afraid they are, John."

"Oh Kate...I'm sorry...for what I put...you through." He felt Kate's hands on both sides of his face. "I...love you...Kate...more than any...thing."

"I'm sorry, too, for not standing by you when you needed me the most. I love you, John. I never quit loving you, and I never will. You had the courage to risk everything, you never quit believing and you were right."

John thought she was crying. 'It's okay...it's all over now...and I'm so glad you're here."

"I am too. Listen, John, could I read you a letter?"

"Yes."

> To: John Ellsworth
> From: Dusty Squadron
> Re: Stockholder's Meeting
>
> Patrons of Dusty's Pub, by unanimous vote, have elected you Chairman of the Board of the Sierra Hotel Corporation. Sorry you missed the rescue operation. They'll make a movie of it someday. Of course the operation was a winner. Colonel English is among the living well. You made it all possible, Ace.

"It's signed by all the gang at Dusty's, including the nurses from

Phu Hep."

"Great...guys."

"I'll send them a thank-you note for you."

There was another period of silence, broken only by shaky breathing, and then someone was whispering in his ear.

"Ask me again, John...please ask me again...please give me another chance."

John did not hesitate. "Kate...if I get well...will you marry me...?"

"Yes! Yes! No if's."

"Oh, thank God. You are...a gift from heaven. Just like...my second chance...at life. How about...on Captain Hyde's boat?"

"That would be wonderful, John. Oh, I love you so much." There was another long pause, then she said, "You have another letter here and now I have the courage to read it to you. It's from Colonel English. Would you like to hear it?"

"Please."

> To John Ellsworth, the world's greatest fighter pilot. I gratefully pass the title to you, John. Watching your last dance with a Super Sabre from my precarious position on the ground was a heart-stopping experience—almost worth those months in the jungle. That story will be retold as long as fighter pilots have breath. I was so proud when I found out it was you. The Good Book says, 'A man reaps what he sows.' I taught you well and in return you gave me life. Thank you, my friend.
>
> Don't ever quit dancing with that green-eyed goddess. One day you'll wonder why you ever thought cold steel and the wild blue could compete with her. Learn this lesson well, too, son. It comes from the sad, lonesome voice of experience.
>
> Cheers,
> Jack English

"Kate...tell Colonel English...I'd do it all again...for him. And tell him...I'm gonna dance...with Katherine...forever."

"John, honey, don't you think it's time to come to bed? You've got that board meeting in the morning."

John punched the transmit button on the intercom and replied in a weary voice, "Be right there, Hon. They're showing some really good gun—camera film here."

It was January, 1991, Desert Storm was one week old and the apocalypse of Iraq was underway. John's mind was mesmerized in a time warp. The air war on the wide screen TV had erased twenty-two years off the calendar and he was overwhelmed by an intense reawakening of long-stifled emotions—grief and guilt and anger.

Sitting in his opulent den in a leather recliner in bathrobe and slippers with his favorite pipe, John's mind was half a world away, in the snug womb of his swept-wing angel, dancing the wild blue of an Asian sky. On TV he watched the gunsight move across the bridge and saw the "luckiest trucker in Iraq" drive right up the vertical crosshair. John's right hand reflexively came up out of his lap as if it were holding a control stick.

"Smooth hands, smooth hands," he said aloud and stopped breathing for two heartbeats. Then his thumb mashed an imaginary pickle button at just the right time. He felt the deep metallic thump of the bomb leaving the airplane and heard himself grunting against the g-forces of his dive recovery. He winced at the sight of tracers coming up in the night sky. John reached for the remote control and hit the mute button, silencing the inane commentary of the news reporter-the same pompous one, now bald, who had badmouthed American GI's in the Vietnam War two decades before. From deep in the belly of that beloved beast he could hear the muffled whine of spinning turbine blades. Above the aroma of his burning pipe tobacco he smelled hot hydraulic fluid, and he shivered as he felt the air conditioning port blowing flakes of frost in his face.

He was exhausted in that same bone weary way he had been at the end of a year in Vietnam—he hadn't slept through the night since Desert Storm began. Every time he got horizontal and closed his eyes, the VCR between his ears went off. The dancing demons were back, after a two-decade hiatus, and it was like they had never been gone. John had left Vietnam as an unconscious passenger on a medivac plane-a passenger who had paid 9/10 of the pro rata purchase price of a massive black granite slab. He would have shared it with 58,200 of his fellow Vietnam vets, but for the grace of God.

In the intervening years the demons had stayed bound in John's black box with the lid tightly secured. There had been occasional midnight movies, minus the dancing demons, but the theme was different. It was all rage and vengefulness.

The timing was unpredictable and seemed to have no pattern that he or Kate could figure out, but they had always been one of two dreams: he was watching Vic die or Colonel Redman die, as it actually happened in lucid Technicolor. The dream always induced an emotional volcanic eruption that brought him bolt upright in bed, knowing, just as he knew the moment it had actually happened, that it had been within his power to prevent it. But the most depressing thought was the one he felt powerless to affect: His friends had suffered and died for absolutely naught—his country had walked away and allowed a massive bloodbath of the sweetest, gentlest people John had ever known. The fearless old Top Gun whimpered and shuddered and wrung his hands in the night until Kate awoke and calmed him down with soothing words and caresses.

The family in the big house on Regent Street appeared to live well. The highlight of his life, which John never ceased to remind Kate, was a singular marriage made in heaven—a rare thing in modern America. Kate was all John ever dreamed she would be as a wife, lover, confidant, mother and sea anchor in the storm-tossed ocean of a devolving, alienating culture. The obituary would no doubt tout his accomplishments—Medal of Honor winner, highly successful businessman, church elder, community spirited, gracious, loving wife, two bright, successful children, both adopted Vietnamese girls with college degrees.

Then there was the 5000 square feet of five-bedroom, slate-roofed opulence complete with maid and gardener to mow two acres of what passed for grass in Florida. The same competitiveness and bullheaded determination that served John so well in the cockpit worked equally well in the corporate executive suite. The rose garden out back was a joint project with Kate—a hundred different hybrid teas surrounding an octagonal cedar gazebo—and it had been therapeutic for John until recently.

But there were a couple of really irritating thorns in his flesh. He had decided to give up flying fighters for Kate before his battle damage eliminated the choice. He had never regretted that, but corporate America was excruciatingly boring after combat flying—adrenaline withdrawal pains were apparently a lifelong malady. No size bank account matched the fulfillment of rescuing the good guys from the clutches of the infidels. Money had replaced KBA as the measure of success, but there was no thrill of victory in it. John had framed his hero, Martin Luther's quote and hung it in his den: "Wealth is the smallest thing on earth, the least gift that God has bestowed on mankind." But the most irritating thorn, the one that just festered till it threatened to infect his heart and soul, was the never-ending drumbeat of negative commentary in the newspapers, on TV, and on most any social occasion, about the defeat of the United States by a tenth-rate third world communist country in its effort to free the South Vietnamese people from tyranny. Most appalling of all to John was the breaking of the covenant with the South Vietnamese people that led to Asian genocide by their northern brothers. Thousands of America's former allies in South Vietnam were imprisoned, tortured and massacred after the U.S. soldiers were forced to go home losers.

People, whose only enlightenment on the war came from TV news or best sellers by writers with an agenda, yammered on about the "atrocities" by a handful of frustrated American soldiers. The most outrageous atrocity, the one perpetrated by the North Vietnamese on their southern brethren after the Americans left, was completely ignored. John could not look at their two beautiful adopted daughters without a gut-wrenching ache for all their friends and relatives who did not have American benefactors like the Ellsworth family.

The "heroes" were the elite draft dodgers who were now in positions of power in government and the press, and they were quick to justify their own cowardly actions by discrediting the war and the warriors who patriotically responded to their country's call. It was, in fact, high fashion to do so. Why, even a dodger from Arkansas, who hid out in England through his draft age years, had the unmitigated gall to make a run for President of the United States—Commander in Chief of all the nation's military men and women. John could not believe such a thing was happening...or even legal. Surely it was an aberration that would evaporate by Election Day.

One nationally syndicated column John had read classified the men who fought in Vietnam as either "suckers or psychos, victims or monsters," and this was over twenty years after the war ended. One highbrow opinion maker, himself an expatriate during the Vietnam War, arrogantly declared "that over 58,000 mostly redneck young Americans weren't smart enough to evade the draft" and thus got themselves killed. John seethed when he heard and read such heresy. John's facial scars, which Kate called his "ragged red badges of courage," were a constant reminder to him every morning when he shaved. Children gaped at him like he was a freak. In business, church, or social settings his scars drew questions from strangers and reminded his friends of who he was and invariably led to Vietnam stories, most of which John found offensive. Finally, after years of trying to defend himself and the noble cause, and arguing until he had angered everyone listening, including himself, he just gave up. These days, if John said anything, he just repeated the words he had seen on a bumper sticker: "We were winning when I left," and walked away. But internalizing his anger and loathing just increased John's depression. The devil was getting the upper hand.

A month before Desert Storm began, John had finally gotten up the nerve, with the encouragement of Kate, to visit the traveling Vietnam Memorial wall when it came to town. "Closure" was the 'in' word in pop psychology and John was ready to try anything. Kate offered to come along but John told her it would be better if he went alone. The truth was he was afraid he might make a scene and he didn't want to do so in front of her.

There was not much of a crowd of grateful citizenry there—most were vets like John who came to pay respects to friends. A dozen small tents containing memorabilia sellers, designed to appeal to vets, located a hundred yards from the wall, were proof that mostly only vets visited the memorial wherever it went in America. There was a contingent of panhandlers scattered about begging for "spare cash to get a vet home." John doubted they were really vets. He fought off an urge to tell one offensive, unkempt "vet" to get a job. With the aid of a computer he found the four names he was looking for—Sam, Rock, Vic and Colonel Redman. Sam Peterson never returned from the Hanoi Hilton when the war was over—he died of natural causes, according to an inscrutable oriental diplomat. Yeah, right. John never believed that, nor did any other POW who returned. Sam and John's pact to end it all quickly now did not seem nearly so radical as the day Kate had condemned the idea, but it was a mute point never discussed by them again. John had given Vic's widow financial and moral support—she never remarried—calling her regularly throughout a sad, lonely life.

In John's view, Colonel English's name should have been on that wall. He had organized a letter writing campaign to the memorial committee from Vietnam fighter pilots, but alas it was futile. Vietnam was the colonel's last tour of duty. He had acquired some kind of microbe while surviving in the jungle like an animal. His early retirement on a full disability pension kept him supplied with good classical music and finely fermented scotch whiskey, but left too much time for him to drink it. His liver had given out ten years ago and taken his lonely, fever-ravaged body with it to an early grave. John was an honorary pall bearer when they buried his urn in a small hole at Arlington National Cemetery, complete with bugler, seven gun salute, and a missing man formation of F-16's.

After the war, a few pieces of bone no bigger than a dime were found where Colonel Redman crashed, but soul brother Vic's crash site was never found. The body of the Kansas son of the soil was transplanted in Asian earth, awaiting the end of time.

John rubbed his fingers across the engraved names of his friends as if to communicate with them in some kind of spiritual Braille. He wanted them to know that, no matter what others in the darkening wilderness of America thought, God, duty, honor, and country would always remain the noblest calling. Revisionist historians trying to justify their own cowardly conduct would never change that. With tears running down his ragged face, he told Vic how sorry he was for leading him to his death. He backed away from the wall about 25 yards and sat down on the grass under a clear blue sky and midday Florida sun. It reminded him of a Sunday morning a long time ago when, with Colonel English, he received his baptism by fire.

The wall, with all 58,200 names, consumed his field of vision. He tried to wrap his mind around the megatonnage of violence, carnage and ruined lives that it represented. And that did not count an even larger number who, like himself, would pay the deferred cost of the war till their dying breath. When he considered that Vietnam was only one small war in human history, he was overwhelmed with a sense of mankind's wickedness.

He felt himself getting sick. Staggering to his feet, he headed for a wooded area to the side of the memorial, but he didn't make it. His legs buckled and he dropped to his hands and knees and vomited on the manicured meadow. He stared at the bile-drenched grass through glassy eyes as his stomach tried to turn itself inside out. Above the ringing in his ears, he heard a little boy talking.

"Mommy, whatsa matter with that man? Lookit his face!"

"Come along, honey. He's probably one of those homeless Vietnam vets."

Bitter thoughts toward that little kid and his mother ran through his mind. John struggled to his feet and walked like a drunk toward his Mercedes. He climbed in, ran down all four windows on the sedan and just sat there until he had composed himself enough to drive home.

Now the dancing demons were doing their thing again as John dozed in his easy chair with the TV still on. He was alone and looking up at them from the bottom of a grave as they were silhouetted against a stormy sky filled with ragged lightning and the rumble of rolling thunder. The memory of what they foretold 22 years ago filled him with the same fear. He arose from his easy chair and walked unsteadily out onto the patio, around the pool and into the rose garden, headed for the gazebo where he spent sleepless nights.

The night air smelled of jasmine and there were a billion stars in the moonless sky. It reminded him of that dark night of the soul he had spent alone on the beach of the South China Sea, crying his eyes out over Vic. Watching him die in that mushroom-shaped fireball was his biggest load of baggage. He had thought about it every single day of his life since that night. Now his legs felt wobbly, like they did after a hairy mission when the adrenaline wore off.

In the darkness, he stepped into the gazebo and tripped over a five-gallon gasoline can left there by the gardener. He fell hard, slamming headfirst into the wooden bench. Stunned, he struggled to roll over and sat moaning on the floor of the gazebo with knees drawn up, arms wrapped around his legs and head on his knees. His ears were ringing and his head felt like it was laid open like a dropped melon. He looked up and saw a split vision image of the shadows now dancing in pairs around the gazebo like children around a maypole. Alarmed, he blinked hard, but his eyes were open and the shadows were still there. Then, with a start, he realized he was sitting in a puddle of gasoline. He saw the outline of the can on its side to his right, and reached over and righted the can. Then he remembered having a pipe in his mouth when he fell and he had a vision of that blazing Buddhist monk, Quang Duc, sitting unflinchingly in the street in Hue, South Vietnam, as he incinerated himself in courageous protest against repression.

Frozen in his upright fetal position, he looked around for the glowing embers of the pipe, but saw nothing. He checked the pocket of his robe and withdrew the only thing there: the old Zippo lighter with the 629th Tactical Fighter Squadron emblem nearly rubbed out on the side, a gift from Vic. It was the only memento he had kept from the war. He squeezed it hard in his right fist and felt his eyes flooding. The dancing tormentors were pointing at him—their insane laughter taunting him, penetrating his throbbing skull like a thousand AK-47 slugs.

There is a limit to the pain a mind and body can bear, both in time and intensity, and, like that Sunday morning over A Shau so long ago, John was outside the envelope. His stomach was about to toss its contents and he was too dizzy to stand up. An exhausted, overstressed brain short-circuited and sent the command for John Ellsworth to protest....

He took a deep, quavering breath and exhaled with resignation. With a quick, one-handed motion he lit the Zippo and dropped it into the open gas can.

*   *   *

Kate awoke with a bed-jarring jolt at the smell of smoke. She bounded out of bed in her oversized T-shirt and ran into the adjacent den. There, in his easy chair, sound asleep, was John with his pipe upside down on his chest and his bathrobe lapels on fire. She cut loose with a blood curdling, "JOHN!," and grabbed a cushion off the sofa to smother the flames. She met him coming out of the chair like a jack-in-the-box.

He hugged the cushion to his chest as he went through the sliding screen door, took two giant steps across the patio and dove headfirst into the pool. When he bobbed to the surface, Kate was at the pool's edge.

"Oh my God, John, are you okay?" There was hysteria in her voice as she knelt and reached out to him.

With three easy strokes John reached the pool's edge at her feet and rested with his arms on the lip of the pool. Kate put her hands on both sides of his wet head.

"Oh, Kate...I think so. Just a headache and maybe a little singed chest hair. Guess it's time to give up another nasty habit...I...uh... think I learned something tonight."

"What do you mean, dear?" John could feel her still trembling.

He handed Kate the blackened, water soaked pillow and his charred, soggy bathrobe and came out of the pool in his wet pajamas. He twisted around and sat with his feet in the water. Kate sat down beside him with her feet in the water. She put an arm around his waist and rested her head on his shoulder and the warmth of her love wrapped him like a blanket.

"Honey, I...uh...dreamed I tried to torch myself like that Buddhist monk in Vietnam...and as soon as I lit the fire I was sorry. Oh, what an awful feeling. I can't describe.... When you woke me up I felt such an overpowering sense of relief, even though I knew I was on fire as I ran toward the pool. It was just like that day in the hospital in Hawaii when I regained consciousness and you were there and I knew it was going to be okay. You have this heaven-sent sixth sense that just knows when I need you, whether you're half a world away or sleeping soundly in the next room. What did I ever do to deserve you?" John shivered as he told the story.

"John." Kate turned and put her free hand on John's scarred cheek and looked into his eye in the dim green glow of the underwater pool light. "Please don't give up. Please keep fighting. I love you. I need you. It's supposed to be a good sign if you dream about a failed suicide attempt."

"Well, I can promise you it won't happen in real life. And I have an idea. Kate, let's sell the business and provision the sailboat for an extended trip. I...would really like to sail to Vietnam and drop the hook in the mouth of the Tuy Hoa River and see if we can't do some good work for our old friends there…and make some amends for the way our country deserted them. Perhaps we could find some of our girls' relatives and maybe even Mama-san's girls. From what I read the government is so eager for tourism dollars they're now welcoming all us former Yankee Air Pirates and anyone else with money to spend."

"John, I think that is a wonderful idea. You may even be able to bury some demons in the process."

"I think I washed them all away tonight, honey."

Kate just smiled adoringly.

John leaned down and kissed the love of his life. "You can never know how thankful I am that you came up to that scared young fighter pilot in Dusty's Pub—the kid who was trying so hard to be so cool—a long time ago on the other side of the world…and changed his life. You are more beautiful today than the first day I saw you and I love you more."

"Oh John, you were my hero then and you will always be my hero."

"Well, it still warms my heart to hear you say that, hon. Love is the greatest of all God's gifts…the only hope for this depraved old human race…and all we need. And I have received it…in abundance …from you."

They sat in silent, loving embrace in the balmy night, basking in the sunshine of heaven reflecting off a half-moon and listening to a sub-tropical choir—tree frogs and cicadas and a whippoorwill searching for love in the night. Sometime later, in the big stucco house on Regent Street, two spent lovers fell asleep in each other's arms.